The

SAVING

Addictions Of The Eternal: Book Two

By
J.C. Stockli

First Edition: October 2015

BlueFae Publishing – Dartmouth, MA

Cover Design by J. Coulombe

ISBN 978-0-9862688-2-3 (paperback)
ISBN 978-0-9862688-3-0 (e-book)

TABLE OF CONTENTS

DEDICATION

To my selfless husband, none of this could have been
accomplished without you.

PROLOGUE

September 16, 1692

"You understand why I've done this, yes?" he asked me.

Instinct told me to snap from my seat and smash my fist into his face until bone, cartilage, and his damned lupine teeth underneath ceased to protest. My heart beat furiously to do so, but I clenched my jaw and held my tongue.

"Yes, sir." I leered back, stifling a growl.

In truth, my anguish had nothing to do with him, though I wished it did. I knew better than to test my boundaries.

And for my sins, she's died once more.

"Don't think it does not pain me to see you this way," he said. "We are blood after all."

"Yes, sir."

My brow furrowed at the persistent needling into my skin. The figure beside me inflicting this seemingly non-existent pain could have no idea what he was doing. I frowned at the poor *pintado*. He wouldn't see the light of the next day.

A whispering breeze called my attention to a grey sky swollen, primed to unleash a torrent of heavenly anger upon the world. Somewhere beyond the storm the sun set in the western sky, and I knew the hours of darkness were

1

approaching. I could feel the telltale tingling in my bones. The lush vegetation flailed in the rising winds. The palm trees danced wildly, while waves crashed against the shore. My nostrils itched from the pungent aroma of dried seaweed and salt-lined sands.

"This is torture," I said.

"Come now, you're being dramatic. It's just a passing storm. This is paradise, after all." He shook his head, arms spread out wide to embrace our exotic surroundings and his eyes settled on the small man by my side, a look which made my stomach roil.

"Not this." I nodded my head from the islander working on me to the pattern he etched in my once unblemished skin, and then out to the tumult overhead. "Why me?"

"You know why. You have proven quite capable. Such impressive strength. I'll admit I'm almost proud to call you family."

I glared silently. Almost proud. That's when the truth behind my question settled in his arrogant mind. A glimmer of enchantment danced across his pearlescent smile. It mirrored my features so closely, I hated myself for it.

"A bold question. As I've said, you know why. Whether you choose to believe in it or not, by now, you should see the truth."

"I don't give a damn for your fantastical truths or what you think you've bestowed upon me. Why keep me bound to this life? Can you not simply track me the same as you do her? I don't want these memories of perpetual failure. Let me die with her. Let my memory fade."

Belying his arrogant nature, I saw he was genuinely saddened by my request. Conflict etched his face. He had no more control over my fate than I did.

"Fantastical as they may be, they are the truth. And because of them, he is amused by your discomfort. I cannot deny him. None of us can. You know this."

"He denies you, does he not?"

"Yes, he does. That does not change the fact that we all do as we are told. You must learn to do the same." His head nodded, stern and affirmative, hardened by the reminder that he was no longer favored by that which he coveted so deeply.

"Then your discomfort also amuses him. We're all pawns—as is she. Why do we bend to him?"

The comparison angered him. Each time I ever mentioned her, a twitch pulled at the corner of his mouth. What did he expect? If we were all destined to suffer our certain fates, how did he suppose he could bend his heart's desire—any of us for that matter—away from her sin?

Her sin. Wondrous and burning regret washed over me. I'd warned myself more than once to resist, strained to learn my own lesson the hard way. But each time she was near, I fell. She was my hubris. Perhaps, in time, eternity could cure me of her. I turned up to the sky in silent and only half-hearted prayer.

The storm had lurched directly over our hut. When I looked back up at him, we exchanged a solemn stare. We were fools. We could never change, never escape the storm.

"You know the answers to these questions already." His annoyance was clear. "This conversation is an exercise in futility."

He muttered something in the local tongue of the *Cordilleran* at my side. I didn't understand him. I took no care to attempt such barbaric languages. We never lingered in these small island cultures for very long. They were too remote, too easily scared by all manner of voodoo and witchcraft outside their own superstitions. We'd never been safe here. So I stared and awaited him to repeat what he'd told me time and time again, from one mortal life to the next.

"He knows she cannot be without you, at least in part. You've thwarted his attempts from one past life to the next. And it was far too great a temptation to witness the pain from your memories. You are controlled amongst the Sempiternal. It's ironic, is it not, to be damned to the very existence you fight to keep her from?"

"Fuck you." I dropped my gaze to the sand under my toes. There would be no paradise for me. My own supposed wretched bliss, forever denied. Out of my periphery, I saw his brow raised and his lips pursed to hold in his delight.

Knowing what would become of her made it all the worse. A monster. Like me. Knowing she'd forever be bound to—I couldn't bear the thought.

The islander completed his work. My skin instantly healed, sealing in the ink. The sudden dread dilated his pupils as he beheld my resiliency. He recoiled subtly. No, he would not see tomorrow. The bastard, on the other hand, did not notice the *pintado's* fear. He beamed at the mark, which covered my scar. The faint pink line forever embedded into my flesh was far preferable to what he'd done to me.

"I quite enjoy the concept. I may have to mark all those I choose," he said.

"You'll never mark Khan, so what should it matter?"

The self-satisfaction from my sniping was bittersweet, mostly because deep down I knew my duty to him was for all eternity. The price of my insubordination would be paid many times over. The smile stretched across his face flipped upside down. The rage in his eyes was unmistakable.

The Heavens crashed above, thundering down in a wild rainstorm lined with white hot lightning. The fresh rains purified the seaweed-laced air.

I would never escape her tempest.

"Let this be a reminder of the role you play now. Each time you are tempted to question your duty, each time you feel so bold as to oppose him, this shall remind you that he has claimed her."

"And what if it is forever my natural compulsion to oppose him?"

"I suspect that is inevitable, and you are my burden to bear for that. You must understand it is his delight to see others writhe."

"Then oppose him with me."

"Oppose him? And in turn, oppose Khan? You truly are mad."

"Only for her."

ONE

Present Day

Rain. Rain feels good.

Evie lounged across a warped plastic chair out on her balcony, basking in the late summer shower. A silent prayer answered, the unpredicted downpour drenched her outstretched frame and soaked her white top and undies, now translucent against her saturated skin. Droplets unionized into beads then streams that trickled off the ends of her untrimmed locks. Crisp morning air nipped, encouraging a tiny wake of goose bumps across her flesh. Eyes closed, she propped her feet up against the balcony's wrought iron railing. She breathed in deeply and wished for the small globules of rain filtering in through her nostrils to drown her.

Please bring the nothingness. Pull us down into the depths.

The sun streaked golden rays through the clouds. As it peaked across the eastern horizon, so the blackness enveloping Evie's closed vision bled out in warm hues of citrine, garnet, and ruby. The showers tapered and ceased. If she were to bother to open her eyes, she'd see the ethereal steam lifting off the warm asphalt streets and calm harbor. If Evie were to bother opening her eyes, she'd see the same steam rising off her body like her spirit taking leave from her body. She squeezed her eyes tighter in a feeble attempt to push the warming sunrise from her body.

She gulped in a final deep breath, seeking to fill as many of her alveoli as possible. Pesky self-preservation broke her resolve and convinced her to exorcise the now-toxic air from her lungs.

The alarm on her phone sounded inside the apartment, signaling the official start of her day. She ignored it. Evie hadn't had cause to wake up at any particular time in months and forgot just how annoying it was. The incessant tone grew louder, pecked at her tranquility like vultures on carrion. Still, she lay back and hoped for just one more burst of rain to come along and top off her lungs.

It was the geisha who forced her eyes open. The morbid woman scratched into Rob's back, glowering and deformed amidst a pool of blood, shocked Evie into coherence.

With a stifled shriek, she nearly fell backwards as the wobbly plastic legs of the chair threatened to buckle under her weight. Grasping for the side railing, she planted her feet firmly against the splintery balcony floorboards. Her pulse raced. The sliver in her heel was unpleasant, but the sensation of falling terrified her more than any physical ailment.

Typical stupid girl.

Evie groaned, stood and looked over the harbor. A car horn blared. A jogger in the middle of the westbound lane couldn't seem to take his eyes off the sopping wet, good-as-naked spectacle above. Evie scowled, offering a theatrical and sarcastic curtsy to conclude the impromptu peep show.

***

Back in her tiny studio apartment, she silenced the electronic pest calling her attention. The cell read just past six in the morning. No matter. She'd been awake since three.

While sleep came more easily since her move to Boston, last night she couldn't ignore the demons surfacing from the fathoms of her subconscious.

The geisha chased her across dreamscapes, taunting her, accusing and scolding her. Unable to tolerate the courtesan's harrowing, the cold sweats, or the tossing and turning, she made her escape. Evie took refuge on her balcony to watch the sunrise, just as she did back in Fallhaven. It was then, in the early morning hours, the unforcasted rain refused the release she sought.

She placed the phone back down on the desk and glanced toward the sheets tousled across her bed. She wanted to be awake before him. If he slept, that was. Even after the past few months, his existence remained enigmatic. Regardless, Evie knew she wanted to be up before Evan.

She flicked on her laptop, pulling up her music library to fill her new home with the dulcet sounds of an acoustic guitar, a piano, and the soft whisperings of a singer grieving his lost love.

She peeled the soaked and see-through garments off her dampened skin, strode to the bath room, and immersed herself under a scalding shower stream. When Evie closed her eyes, there were no ghouls waiting to greet her. She was mercifully left alone to a veil of black.

While her body begged for sleep, her mind relished in its escape. Shunning the geisha also meant evading a more horrific vision. Without the mangled tattoo, there'd be no dead body crumpled behind the bar at Sirens. Such a sight haunted and corrupted the memory of Rob's smile until being snuffed out by the devil who'd creep from the darkened corners of her subconscious.

Each night in her dreams, Lucca came purring from beyond the gloom with deep, glowing eyes dusted over with glittering starlight and ill intentions. His voice dripped over her like warm honey. Her olfactory senses swelled with his scent of orange blossoms and mint laced with just a hint of metallic sweetness.

"Fall from your graces, Evie." His coo caressed her like a long-lost lover. "Come down into the depths. Join in my disease."

Each time, she was a moth to his flame. She ached for his touch and burned for his bite. That was usually when her dreams warped and the geisha returned with her sorrowful glare through a horrible flurry of sakura petals. Unlike the tattoo etched into Rob's back, however, it wouldn't be a samurai's head she held in her hand, but rather Rob's. The mouth Evie yearned to kiss hung agape as a serpent weaved through his hollowed ocular cavities. That serpent stared hypnotically at her, but it was Lucca's voice wrapping around her and squeezing. "I can show you the pleasure in your pain." It's viperous hiss stung.

Each night, in every tantalizing dream, Evie was trapped. Unable to wake. Powerless to fight off the cackling piercing the dark. Helpless to reconcile the constant conflicting emotions toward the demon who sent her running from Fallhaven.

***

Emerging from the shower, pink skin swelled over the towel hugging her curves. Evie stood in front of the mirror. The ghostly reflection watched as her fingertips ran multiple paths through her tangled tresses, caught here and snagged there. Her hair had been let to grow out over her months in isolation. The vivid red dyed streaks had faded, leaving her with a more natural variation of yellow, gold, and caramel waves skimmed with dark auburn layers underneath. Fingers free from the jungle of locks, she shifted her eyes to her complexion. It wore just a hint of sunshine from spending most of her days on the balcony staring out over Carson Beach and wondering when. Thanks to those moments of fresh air and wallowing in self-pity, her skin had acquired a faint sun-kissed appeal, though still pale in comparison to others.

Her eyes met an identical crystal blue pair in the mirror, but not those of the Evie from Fallhaven. The reflection had morphed into a deceitful specter of her inner voice. That bitch glared back at her, scolded her for running from Lucca, for thinking she could possibly hide from something she craved more than a shot of whiskey.

You cannot deny us forever.

Even the reflective menace couldn't refute she'd changed—physically—but inside, the thirst persisted. Being down by the water in South Boston felt too much like being home. It was difficult to convince the reflection that change was possible.

We shouldn't have run away.

"I was afraid," she said.

And this is so much better? We've been forced into hiding by Evan. Lucca didn't want to kill us.

"But Evelyn still died didn't she?" She dismissed her contemptuous reflection before its glare could burn through her.

Yes, she had changed—given up her family's home, room after room filled with familiar creaks and scents, for a tiny space just big enough for her and her inner voice to fester in her xenophobia.

Out in the studio, Evie sunk onto the foot of the bed. She pulled the towel taut around her body and took in her new, cramped life. It was a tiny studio, barely four hundred square feet in all, with a galley kitchen tripping the occupant as soon as they walked through the front door, spilling out to a small living area off to the left. She had just enough room to fit a tiny desk near the balcony. Beyond the living room was a small alcove large enough to fit a full-sized bed and nightstand. Finally, just off the tiny recess, was the bathroom adorned in gaudy shades of cracked blue tile and a stand-up shower stall. She conceded to let Evan buy her an oversized thrift store dresser for all her clothes, a small futon and a few overturned milk crates that she covered with a soft swatch of tie-dyed fabric to create a makeshift coffee table.

This place is barely bigger than a coffin.

Her chest tightened. The towel constricted her air flow. She loosened it to fight the building anxiety attack.

"Shut up... It's been months. Why are you judging me now?" Her whispers were forced as she focused to regulate her breaths. The spinning room settled.

Acoustic guitar filled the apartment, accompanied by gruff vocals lamenting over the pangs of sobriety. At one time the lyrics may have drifted in one ear and out the other, but more recently they resonated on an intimate level. Evie closed her eyes, feeling the singer's voice wash over her. She was parched. Phantom traces of her withdrawals—the vomiting— twisted her stomach in knots.

Was it really worth it?

Looking down to her lap now, a small tear streaked down her cheek.

"I had to." She sucked in a deep breath, fighting self-hatred and whimpering.

Music faded from one song to the next, but fell on her deaf ears. It wasn't until the soft scuffling of metal against metal drew her attention to the front door. Her cheeks flushed and a small grin traced across her lips before she made a slow path to the various locks lining the front door.

*****

"Are you sure you're ready for this?" Evan asked with a quirky smile across his face and a lidded cup of coffee in one hand, a bag dangling from the other.

"No, but I'm not sure I was ready for everything else you've put me through." She accepted her liquid breakfast with a melodramatic roll of her eyes and turned back into the apartment, leaving him behind in the hallway. The rare sound of his laughter trailed her into the room, followed by the click of a latch as he locked the door behind them.

Evan cleared his throat. "You knew the deal. I wasn't bringing you to Boston until you sobered up... and to be fair, you asked to tag along, remember?"

You asked for this.

A moment of self-doubt gave her pause. Evie rested her bottom lip against the rim of her cup and blew into it to cool the steamy contents. A twinge of regret had settled into her bones over the past few months as she was held captive in her three-story tenement tower.

"I asked you to help me sort out what Lucca was." When she turned to face him, Evan stood by the door with his eyes averted to the floor, a look she'd come to recognize as his own flavor of remorse.

"Evie, how many times are we going to get into this? You need a clear head to find answers. You couldn't keep hiding inside a bottle."

She glowered at him. "I wasn't hiding."

He matched her glare. "Well you weren't helping anything either, were you?"

The tension building in the air was electric, tingling down her body concealed by nothing more than worn out terrycloth. They could keep arguing, but to what end? Bickering with Evan was a circular process. She tired just considering it.

As she held his gaze, self-loathing stabbed at her chest for the hell she must have put him through. "Let's just drop it. I know you're only trying to help."

"Fine," he said.

She sipped her coffee and let the hot brew scorch her desire to wage a fruitless war over who did what to whom. Evie placed her drink atop the dresser and waded through its contents; T-shirts, leggings, tiny tank tops, the last holdovers from her previous employment back in Fallhaven that she would actually wear in public. She spun around to face him with a pout, frustrated and defeated.

"I have nothing to wear to a real job. Maybe I'm not ready for this after all."

He flashed a hopeful smile that made her stomach somersault. The plastic bag in his hand jiggled, and he tossed it across the room onto her bed.

"I thought you'd be worried about that, so I bought you something. I know it's probably not your style, but it's work-appropriate at least."

Evie couldn't fight the coy smirk that teased her lips. "So this is how it works? I dish out all the 'fuck yous' and 'go to hells' for you forcing sobriety on me, and you in turn placate me with material possessions?"

Evan reciprocated a lopsided grin, producing a smaller plastic bag from his suit pocket. "You never complain when I show up with this." He dangled the bag in the air, and her heart fluttered at the site of the fluffy green bud inside.

"I still think it's a little hypocritical that you admonish me for drinking, but you have no problem smoking me up when you check in on me."

He snickered. "One vice at a time, Evie. Otherwise you'd really hate me wouldn't you?"

She narrowed her eyes and puckered her lips impishly before plucking the shopping bag off the bed. Rummaging through, she found a light grey sheath, pink cardigan, and matching polka-dotted flats from within. Evie looked up at him with a crooked brow.

"Pink?"

He chuckled. "It looked nice on the mannequin at the store." The skepticism that appeared across her face felt much more comfortable than the cotton candy-hued fabric in her hands. "I'm a guy, Evie. I don't have a flair for fashion."

"Said the man with the triple-peaked pocket square in his suit. You're enjoying this way too much." She snatched some undergarments from the dresser and vanished into the tiny bathroom to change into her new work-appropriate ensemble.

Concealed from his view, she watched Evan's reflection through a mirror hanging on the bathroom door. "So who is it that got me this job?"

"Just a friend," he said, caught in the motions of his own habits. Evan was perched on the edge of her futon packing a tiny bowl, a pretty little piece of blue-and-orange swirled glass, which after so many rounds of smoking had tinted a pearlescent violet shade. The glass bowl was one of the few ghosts from Evie's past which she refused to leave behind in Fallhaven; that, and a few other relics she hoped Evan would never find interred under her bed.

"A friend, or a 'friend'?" She poked her head out of the bathroom to capture his eyes. Evan looked down at his work and smiled sheepishly.

One of the few tidbits which Evie had been made privy to regarding the Sempiternal was that they relied on the essence of humans for their immortality. Sometimes at night, she'd replay Evan's musings in her mind to help her fall asleep. She found a certain amount of comfort in learning more about his world—and Lucca's.

The immortals found sustenance most easily acquired via the blood stream, he'd once told her. Add in tens of thousands of years of history, secrecy, and occasional predation, and the romanticization of the "vampire" evolved. Evan had also once explained that many of the Sempiternal resented the term. However, the plus side of being a walking, talking pop-culture phenomenon was that there were plenty of humans out there willing to offer up their necks for even the smallest lapse into their eternal fantasy. He called them "Friends of the Sempiternal." Jealousy ripped through her chest when she considered how many friends Lucca and Evan may have made through the years.

"So what kind of friend, Evan?"

"Does it matter? You wanted a job to get out of this apartment. So I got you one," he said. "But, I do have some regular human friends, actually."

"Somehow, I feel like that's questionable." She stepped out of the bathroom, topping off her outfit with the cardigan pulled over her shoulders. "Okay, so what do you think? I feel a little weird."

Evie lifted her arms out to her sides and twirled around slowly, twisting her neck to regard herself in the full-length mirror hanging from the door. The sheath hugged her body perfectly.

When she looked over to Evan, he was staring at her with the same mystifying expression she'd come to expect from him. His warm chocolate eyes appeared on the verge of tears, his brow furrowed and lips slightly parted, like he wanted to say something but couldn't quite find the words. While Evie enjoyed the beauty of his mien, she felt guilty for evoking it so frequently and so easily.

"Evan? Does it look that bad?" She waited, anticipated his response, any response, but was left wanting. "Okay, maybe you were right all along. This was a bad idea."

She shed the cardigan from her shoulders like it was on fire and yanked at the dress's zipper.

"No, don't!" Evan jumped up with an outstretched hand. "I'm sorry. I've never seen you dressed like—you look beautiful."

He took hold of her hand. As he did, an undercurrent of thrill threatened to pull her to her knees. He stepped closer, holding her in his trance. Her cheeks burned as he came nearer still.

We should be "friends" with this Sempiternal. You can tell that he wants it.

"No," she said under her breath. Evan tilted his head, and she shook her internal discord aside. "I feel silly dressed up like this."

His quizzical expression melted into a smile. "Don't. You look beautiful, really. You're like a chameleon, Evie. You can wear anything and look gorgeous."

She took the moment to soak in his charms. A promise she'd made months ago to her best friend, one to stay away from her ex, had hollowed out and faded in her memory. Evie thirsted for whatever affections she could wring out of Evan. Being holed up in her apartment, he was the only man she'd had contact with in months. Her libido was screaming, and her hormones were starting to guide her toward his proximity.

Miss Prissy would kill you for enjoying this.

The moment lingered longer than she should have allowed. With a fair degree of hesitation, she pulled her hand from his, freeing her throat from the invisible, choking grip around it.

"Don't think I didn't notice the price tags on these clothes, Evan. You know I can't afford to pay you back for any of this."

He turned back to the glass bowl on the makeshift coffee table and took the first hit before handing it to her. Evie graciously accepted and licked her lips as she sucked the fragrant smoke into her lungs. The familiar act of passing the weed back and forth quashed her digressive thoughts.

"Consider it a good luck present for your first day of work," he said plainly. "Now come on, go finish getting ready. I'll walk you to work."

TWO

She choked on the humidity thickening the air as they made their way to L Street. Set free from her third floor studio, Evie rolled her tongue across a bitter aftertaste coating the inside of her mouth, one part zeal and two parts trepidation.

"You're acting like you've never been in a city before." Evan patted her hand and smiled reassuringly, but his underlying tease pinched all the same.

"Nothing this big."

"Do you want to go back to the apartment?" He slowed his pace, allowing her a moment to consider the proposal.

"No." She nudged him on. "And excuse me, but don't you think a few months of forced isolation and sobriety might amplify the introvert in a girl?"

Evan exhaled hard through his nose and pressed on toward the waterfront. "For the last time, Evie, it wasn't forced. You asked for my help, and I offered what I could."

"I know. I'm sorry," she said and silently cursed herself for arguing in circles with him yet again.

"It's okay, but be realistic here. Lucca's finally found you after more than one hundred years of searching. You can't expect to maintain the status quo like nothing's changed, or pretend he's not sniffing you out from one day to the next."

Reminiscences of her tenebrous stranger hovering mere inches above her body and breathing her in with every luscious inhale sizzled down to her sacrum. She licked at her dry lips and forced the delicious memory away.

She peered up to Evan who was monitoring her with a fair degree of caution darkening his gaze.

"He's killed you in another life when you were Evelyn. He'll do it again. Is that what you want?"

"No." She topped off her grousing with a scowl and looked down to the sidewalk. "You don't need to keep reminding me."

He huffed. "Apparently, I do."

"All right. Enough." Evie waved her white flag with a shoulder jab. Evan chuckled back, and they continued on their path.

The burning between her legs dissipated.

Street chatter and commerce buzzed in her ears as the congested air filtered through her lungs. Her lingering agoraphobia kept her clinging to Evan's arm for fear she may get lost in the hustle. Not that he seemed to mind her reliance on him. As they approached the waterfront a loud roar from overhead caused her to practically jump into his arms with a screech.

Evan's laughter lifted over the city's commotion. "It's just an airplane, Evie." He squeezed her hand cradled snuggly under his elbow while she trembled beside him.

"Those fuckers creep up on me. I'm still not used to living so close to an airport." She hesitated a step as the full, panoramic breath of downtown Boston was laid out before them. "I feel so out of place. I'm not ready for this."

"Yes, you are," he said. "You were too big for Fallhaven. It'll take time for you to grow into the city, but I have every confidence that you can do this." Evan coaxed her forward and across a bridge as morning commuters and joggers passed by.

She felt the knot in her stomach melt away, only to be replaced by throbbing in her chest. In the back of her mind, she hoped this new job would help her gain some distance from him. She began thinking of Evan in ways she shouldn't. She looked at him in ways she shouldn't. Though all guilt aside, the thought of letting him go was heartbreaking.

"So why didn't we drive? I know you have a car," she asked to deflect her internal lamenting before it chased her back up to her studio prison.

"Finding parking in Boston is a pain in the ass. I only use my car when I have to head out of the city. And public transportation would take too long because the bus and Silver Line routes are so crazy around here. Besides, I thought you'd like the walk."

"Sure. Whatever. I thought maybe it reminded you of the days before the advent of cars or something."

He smirked back, a docile variation of a sneer that Lucca wore often. It smoldered her insides. "That too, I guess."

"So where will you be while I'm at work?"

"Same as you, I'll be working."

"You actually work?"

Evan's head knocked back with laughter. She caught a glimpse of slightly elongated canines and her pulse kicked up a notch.

"Of course I work," he said. "I help my uncle maintain the family business, as it were."

"So where is your office?"

"Not far from yours."

Evie's eyes widened. "You have me close by so you can keep an eye on me while you're at work, is that it?"

Evan cast a shy glance to the ground. "Can you blame me?"

A rush of heat prickled across in her cheeks. "Do you live around here too?"

"I do."

"How come you never told me how close you are?"

"You never asked."

"Well, I—" Dammit, Evan was right. All that Evie cared about was that he showed up at her doorstep each day. She never bothered to inquire on the details of Evan's life away from her. "Will I ever see where you live?"

His smile was replaced again by his lovely furrowed brow. "No."

"Why not?"

Such a simple question twisted Evan's features further. "I couldn't bring you into my house. My uncle wouldn't—it's not—I couldn't risk you surrounded by so many Sempiternal like that."

"How many of them live in your house?"

"Hundreds," he answered plainly.

"Damn, how big is your house?"

Evan huffed. A smile formed at the corner of his mouth, breaking past the rose-colored lining of his lips. He squeezed her arm once more, but declined to answer. Evie decided it was better to avoid a third argument if possible. It was only the morning after all. She'd have plenty of time to replant her foot in her mouth after work.

Even after all they'd been through together, Evan remained distant from her. His house was just another item on the ticker list of truths he refused to divulge. The distress he wore so frequently on his face was a constant warning to Evie that he was more than she could imagine, a predator with her own body type being a preferred category of prey. And so, she walked slowly at his side, rejected, soaking in the summer for what it was worth.

Across the bridge, Evie and Evan veered to the right, away from the intimidating skyline of downtown, and into a cement sea of commercialism at its roughest. Each warehouse and building resembled the next. Through it all, something wonderful and familiar tickled her senses. The pungent funk of low tide and the sight of fishing vessels evoked a homesick feeling that she clung to with all her might. She hummed and grinned wide, her reaction echoed by an equally pleased expression from Evan.

"I thought you might like it down here," he said as he stopped in front of an undistinguished grey building. Evie paused, looked around at their non-descript surroundings, and realized they had reached their destination. Her body deflated and sunk a little lower into herself.

"Will you be here when I get out?" she asked.

"Do you want me here?"

Flutters started up in her belly again. She found the answer too easy to blurt out. Yes, she wanted him there. Yes, she wanted him. No, it wasn't appropriate at all.

"I'm scared," she said.

Evan cupped her jaw in his hand and lifted her face to meet his, leaning in closer to her. She'd been in this spot with him before, trapped in awkward silence, too close for good behavior, too nervous to guess his motives, too afraid to test her limits. Panic rumbled in her core.

"You can do this, Evie. I'll be right here waiting for you at the end of the day."

***

After introducing herself at the main lobby's reception desk, a security guard directed Evie to the top floor. Self-consciousness abounded with each echoing clack of her flats against the shiny marble floor. On her way to the elevator, she glanced over to the ultra-modern black leather chairs in the waiting area, wondering if the towering palm trees surrounding them were supposed to make anyone sitting in the rather impersonal space any more or less comfortable. Based on the businessman hunched over his newspaper, she guessed the latter and resisted the urge to rub her tailbone.

At the push of a button, a ping rang out through the lobby. The metal doors to the elevator scraped open. Evie stepped inside and stared at the numbers lining the wall. Cycling through a deep inhale and exhale, she mustered her courage and pressed the number five.

***

"May I help you?"

Evie was greeted by an administrative assistant who, according to her name plate, was appropriately named Ginger with red hair, wiry glasses, and a petite frame.

"Evie Westvale. This is my first day at work here."

Ginger tapped a few times on her mouse and nodded. "Okay Evie. It looks like Leda's expecting you. Follow me."

She led Evie through a maze of cubicles and introduced her to various faces along the way, all of which she'd never remember. Everyone looked the same. The women wore pencil skirts and blouses of various summery hues. The men wore khakis and ties. Evie's heart ached for the musty sweat and cheap body oil-filled atmosphere of the strip club where she used to work for Rob. The office was devoid of bass and hip hop music, replaced by the persistent staccato of fingers against keyboards. She was out of her element, and the landscape of the office melded into a corporate grey blur.

After whisking her door to door throughout the office, Ginger showed Evie the break room lined with vending machines and kitchen appliances. Next were the restrooms where Evie would be sure to run and hide when her swelling panic attack kicked in full force. The perspiration pooling under her arms heightened her self-awareness and the fact that she hated her new pink cardigan soaking in her sweat.

Finally, Evie was guided into a vacant corner cube near the windows.

"Leda from HR will be by shortly to go over your orientation packet. In the meantime, make yourself at home and welcome aboard." Ginger left Evie alone.

From her seat, Evie turned to marvel at an unobstructed view of the commercial waterfront.

It could be worse. At least we have a tomb with a view.

She sat mute, dazed by the cityscape outside her window. Helplessness ached in her bones.

"I asked for this." She spoke quietly to her shadowy refection in the tinted window. "Evan wouldn't put me in danger. This is good for me. This is the next step." She clung to the notion of his safety as tightly as her white-knuckled fists clenched the damned cardigan against her chest. And, he promised. Evan said he'd be standing outside just where she left him when the day was done. "X" marked the spot outside her window on the sidewalk.

She looked out past the waterfront to the heart of the city and wondered where he lived in a house with so many blood-hungry Sempiternal that he couldn't risk taking her there. An invisible force pushed against her chest. Evie backed away from the window and sunk into her chair by the uncomfortable notion he could be spying on her.

Then an alternative thought nearly left her breathless.

Lucca could be out there too, looking for us right now.

Her body throbbed as she sat in her grey dress, in her grey cubicle of her grey office doing God only knows what kind of monotonous clerical work to maintain some semblance of normality.

What do you think he'll do when he finds us?

She closed her eyes, summoned the memory of his perfect body mounting her, threatening to possess her. His deep dark eyes lined with golden rims twinkled in her mind's eye. She felt a pulsing in the dark, wet center of her being as she licked her lips.

Absolutely delicious.

"Hi there! Welcome to DC International." A voice chimed out from behind her. Evie jumped out of her chair, collected her composure and her balance, and hoped like hell that her complexion didn't betray her by turning a color to match her sweater. A dark skinned girl with a head overflowing with thick black curls laughed back at her. "I didn't mean to scare you." She extended a hand. "Leda Veiga from Human Resources."

Evie's chest thumped from the pressure of her heartbeat pounding within. She accepted the girl's soft handshake. "I'm so sorry, I wasn't day—I mean, I was just looking—"

"It's fine, Evie. We're allowed to space out every now and then. Just don't let the boss catch you." Leda winked and nodded out over the sea of cubicles. "C'mon, let's get this orientation business over with."

Evie trailed Leda across the building to a conference room located next to what Ginger previously identified as the executive suite belonging to the CEO. Evie peered over at the sturdy-looking lacquered doors sealed shut.

"Ginger mentioned the CEO works out of a different location," she said as they passed by.

Leda checked over her shoulder with half-hearted interest.

"No, he's usually here. But he's been setting up another office overseas, so he's been kind of out of pocket for a while. That's probably what she meant."

"Oh."

Evie gnawed on her bottom lip, feeling foolish for attempting small talk in the first place, and followed Leda onward to the board room. It was, like the rest of the office space, a large grey room surrounded by glass, whereby anyone passing through to the executive suite could see inside, and vice versa.

They sat at a large mahogany conference table while Leda sorted through paperwork, requested Evie to sign off on this form and that form, discussed policies, procedures, and benefits.

"So do you have an account set up for your direct deposit?" Leda asked. Evie met her honest features with a blank stare.

"I... umm... I don't know. I had a passbook account with my credit union back home, but I cleaned that out when I moved to Boston."

"So you're still settling in to life in the big city, then?"

Evie fidgeted in her seat and picked at her nail beds. "I've been in the city for a few months actually, but I haven't completely adjusted, I guess."

Genuine sympathy relayed through Leda's warm smile. It may have just been her job to help the new kid get acclimated, but Evie was grateful for Leda's silent show of kindness.

She looked to be about Evie's age, young, pretty and quite voluptuous. Her exotic complexion and curves reminded her of the Amazonian goddess, Natalia, who'd stripped at Sirens while Evie waited tables there.

As Leda continued flipping through paperwork with her canned spiel about employee conduct and dress code, Evie's mind wandered to thoughts of Lucca. The horror of him having killed Natalia merely flickered across her memory. The pulses beating against the thin veil of her lace panties, however, made their presence well known as Evie's heartbeat quickened. Leda's voice fell to a dull murmur. Her surroundings faded into an obscure cloud, and she continued to daydream about Lucca and his perfect skin. Her eyes dropped down to the mahogany table, inspecting the detail of the wood grain. She wondered if it would sustain their weight, or their movement.

Where is he?

Lost in her erotic fantasy, Evie missed the sound of a man's voice mingled with Leda's muttering.

"Let me introduce you." Leda's voice called out of the grey. "Evie, this is the President and CEO of DC International."

Evie's cheeks flushed for finding herself lost in reverie yet again and fumbled to her feet. Leda cleared her throat, stifling a giggle.

The man was tall, thin, and somewhat familiar. Hints of grey hair streaked through his slicked-back coif suggested he may have been well into his forties, but his androgynously attractive facial features made her question that. He was exquisitely dressed in a single-breasted navy suit with a light crosshatch offering the fabric a subtle textural appeal. The tangerine checked, silk tie and coordinating pocket square instantly reminded her of Evan.

A long set of fingers reached out and squeezed tight around her hand.

"My apologies for startling you, Miss Westvale," he said in a crisp tone that sent shivers down her spine—the bad kind. Evie gaped up at him, tongue-tied. He held back a smirk behind pursed lips and studied her up and down, allowing her to stew in her awkwardness. "Leda, I believe Ginger is looking for you. Would you please tend to her needs immediately before she has the entire office in an uproar over nothing?"

The CEO kept Evie's hand and eyes locked with his own. She was petrified under his stare.

"Of course," Leda said. "Evie, you can find your way back to your desk, right?" Evie nodded, but wished she'd been able to ask Leda to show her the exit.

"So, you are the young Miss Evelyn Westvale for whom Evan's called in a favor," the CEO said. The icy chill from his handshake spread up her arm and through the rest of her body, but he did not let go. It only intensified, constricting as he held her firmly in his grip.

This is Evan's "friend?"

He released her hand and circled her like a shark. Evie's adrenaline struggled to help her tread water in his whirlpool. He appraised her with judging eyes, not wanting but rather competitive. It was a peculiar stare that made her want to crawl up inside her skin and hide.

"I'm sorry. Evan never said he knew..." Embarrassment cracked her voice.

"The boss?" He sniggered. "Yes, I know Evan. You must know him quite well for him to call in a favor like this."

Her mouth ran dry while she searched for a response. "He's done a lot for me," she said.

"Yes, I expect he would." Confusion flickered across her face. "Well, welcome aboard Miss Westvale." He turned on the heels of his designer dress shoes and marched off to his executive suite, slamming the door behind him.

Bewildered, Evie looked down at her trembling hands.

"God, when the fuck is this day going to end?"

THREE

Back at her cubicle, another new face waited for her. This one with chubby cheeks, looked perturbed, like she had somehow already screwed up.

"The name's Dave." A large stack of papers dropped on her desk with a *thud* serving as punctuation. "Enter the dollar amounts on each invoice into the spreadsheet and save them in AP folder on the shared drive when you're done." Evie opened her mouth. A question worked its way to the tip of her tongue, but was abruptly halted by Dave's back turned to her. "I emailed you the spreadsheet already," he said over his shoulder and walked away.

She was careful to note where he sat, so she could avoid him whenever possible. Evie turned back to stare at the computer screen and mound of papers. Her fingers fidgeted nervously on the folds of her dress in her lap. Every part of her wished she were back in fishnets and booty shorts, taking drink orders from drunks instead of data sets from Dave. A buzzing from her bag extricated her from the avalanche atop her desk.

She looked around. Confident she was sufficiently camouflaged in her grey wilderness, Evie recovered her cell phone from her bag to read a text message.

Hey Babe. Saw a girl who looked like u 2day in Boston. Miss u. Wish u were here

Nate.

Evie scanned the office to see if anyone was watching her and was glad to remain invisible. Her pulse thundered in her eardrums. Faces flashed through her mind. She searched her scrambled memory for a trace of Nate's familiar ursine self while walking to work. His beastly size would be difficult to miss, even in the busy streets of Boston. No, she hadn't seen him. But with the fishing boats right outside her office, it was still plausible that he saw her... with Evan.

She couldn't recall Nate ever making port in Boston. If it wasn't about weed, booze, or when he was going to stick his dick in her next, she was quite adept at tuning him out.

Dammit! Why didn't you ever pay attention to him?

Sweat pooled under her arms and across her brow. Feeling the anxiety swelling inside of her, Evie walked as casually as she could manage to the restrooms. Turning down the main aisle of cubes, eyes to the floor, she bumped into a large doughy mass.

"Is something the matter, Evie?" Dave asked, one scrutinizing eyebrow lifted.

She held out her hands. "Where are the bathrooms again?"

He thumbed over his shoulder. "Second door on the left, past Accounts Payable."

"Thanks." She replied timorously and dashed past him.

Once safely inside the ladies' room, Evie made for the handicapped stall. Therein, she paced back and forth. Her chest heaved as she pulled at her blonde-streaked highlights. She looked back at the text message.

"In Boston... Wish you were here... Shit! Evan's going to kill me." She stopped pacing and closed her eyes. The lingering sanitizer in the air tickled the back of her throat as she drew deep breaths. "That's okay. Nate has no idea where I am. The likelihood of him actually spotting me in a city as big as Boston is slim to none. Right?" She nodded to herself. "Right."

Her fingers passed over her phone in a flurry.

I told u I need space.

Stupid stupid girl.
Her eyes flared at the cellphone screen when the implication of what she'd typed crystallized.

Ur in Boston? Where? Let's meet up :)

"Shit! Shit shit shit." She stamped her foot against the white tile floor. Her heel's sharp clack echoed through the cold space. It didn't take Nate long to respond.

Will b n Btown 4 a while. Wanna c u.

"No no no, this is bad."

I told u I NEED SPACE.

She repeated her reply hoping it'd take on some additional meaning, a sharper edge perhaps, this time around in caps lock.

Soon Babe. Need 2 c u SOON.

Evie held in a deep breath and let his final text go unanswered. When she opened the stall door, Leda was standing on the other side.

"Hi Evie, I wanted to make sure you were all right. Dave said you've been gone from your cube for quite a while."

That nosey bastard can go to hell.

"No, I'm okay. I had to respond to an urgent text and didn't want to do that at my desk. You mentioned it was against policy during orientation."

Leda batted at her with a playful hand. "Everyone does it, Evie. Just don't make it obvious or a habit," she said. "But truly, is everything all right?"

Persistent little bitch, aren't you?

Evie stifled a groan directed to her inner voice.

"It's fine. Just my ex-boyfriend. His lobster boat must be in town, not exactly a pleasant surprise. I was trying to turn over a new leaf in Boston." Evie glanced down and rubbed her thumb over the smooth surface of her cell.

"Is he a physical threat?" Leda asked, to which Evie cracked a tiny smile.

"No, not Nate. It's my fault, really. I may have answered his text messages once or twice since we broke up." She looked up to meet Leda's confused and concerned expression. Evie pushed her smile wider across her face. "I know. I know. I was just leading him on. I didn't mean to, but leaving home wasn't easy. I left everything behind. I never told him where I was, though."

"Are you sure everything's okay? I mean, how did this guy find you if you didn't tell him? I'm not trying to pry, just wearing my HR hat right now."

Maybe Miss Prissy told him?

Evie glared at her reflection in the bathroom mirror. "This is just dumb luck."

Now was not the time to defend her decision to reach out to Blythe—again—even if she never returned her messages. Evie still held hope that someday her best friend would forgive her for ruining her relationship with Evan and accept her invitation to visit in Boston.

Leda reached out a hand. Evie blinked at the mirror's reflection and awkwardly pulled away.

"Hey Evie, I know it's scary starting off someplace new, making new friends... Listen, I'm having a little get-together next weekend at my place, if you want to come by. Nothing big, just a few friends and drinks. It'll be fun. I'll email you all the details."

Before Evie could protest, Leda was gone, leaving her alone in the bathroom. She held up her hand in one last silent call to object. Such a protest was futile. Evie turned and matched her reflection's stare.

"Don't say it." She pointed to the mirror. "Evan can't begrudge me making friends. He wants me to have a normal life, right?"

***

She walked back over to her cubicle and stared, bemused by the mound of invoices on her desk. She struggled to navigate the company's intranet or even a damned, basic spreadsheet.

"Dave should've just told me to post these files on social media." She moved the mouse across the pad and mumbled to herself. "I could do that shit. Where the hell is this shared drive?" Her lack of general office competencies did nothing more than beat Evie into her own self-induced submission of idiocy.

Nate continued to text her throughout the afternoon, but she ignored her phone vibrating atop her desk, setting it to silent mode instead. Still, every time it glowed with a faint blue light indicating she had a new message, her eyes traveled toward it like a beacon.

Five o'clock couldn't have come quick enough, and Evie's pounding heart may have burst if she had to wait a moment longer. Not even bothering to log off of her computer, she grabbed her purse and made a quick left before reaching the elevator, thumping down the stairs like the building was on fire and bursting through the door to the lobby.

True to his word, Evan greeted her in the glow of the sunny summer evening as she came storming through the front doors of the building.

"How was your first day?" he asked, and then staggered backwards as Evie clung her arms around his waist and cowered into his frame.

"Just take me home."

FOUR

Safe in the seclusion of her apartment, Evie stared out over Carson Beach and the Old Harbor with a blank expression, the urban dissonance of South Boston thickening the already humid air. Both mental and physical exhaustion leaked from her pores.

Her run-in with the CEO made her skin crawl. With his sophisticated, grey-haired allure and viperous beam, dapper Mr. Slithery Silver was terrifying with a cold and calculating air surrounding him. How poor sweet Evan could be owed a favor from such a snake was a mystery. Her new co-worker, Leda was nosy, but nice enough. Hospitality aside, her new job made Evie feel completely inadequate in her own skin.

To top it all off, her ex-boyfriend was much closer than she could have imagined. She scrubbed the stupidity from her face and blinked up at the setting sun. She led Nate on. She knew it each time he reached out to her. Evan had made it clear his one stipulation for bringing her to Boston, other than the whole detox bit, was cutting all ties with Fallhaven. The fear of inciting his Sempiternal predilections ran a cold path down her spine in conflict with the summer heat.

"Stupid," she said, vocalizing the chide screaming from her inner voice.

From her third-story perch, Evie studied the bodies lining the beach, searching for anyone that resembled Nate's burly build. Nobody fit the bill. She felt lost. All at once, the idea of hiding from Lucca seemed an impossible and ridiculous task. She stood there on her balcony, staring while beads of sweat pooled between her cleavage and trickled down the inside of her thighs.

At her back, Evan sat inside her apartment installing software to give Evie a tutorial on spreadsheets and the various database products to which she was so atrociously ignorant. He played his own acoustic playlist off of Evie's laptop.

"This is bullshit." She burst back into the apartment, unzipping her dress along the way. Evan turned his head away from the computer as she sent him spinning around on the tiny desk chair.

"What are you doing?" He averted his eyes from her pealing the cotton off her bare flesh.

"This is me, Evan. I'm more comfortable prancing around in my underwear than in fucking business casual. I can't do this."

She tossed the dress in the laundry hamper like the dishonest piece of shit it was and flopped down at the foot of the bed.

"Evie, put some clothes on."

"Why? Does this make you uncomfortable?"

"Evie, get dressed." He marched past her to the dresser. Eyes at the floor and with one hand, he fumbled through a drawer and tossed a shirt at her. She stood defiant with her arms crossed, wearing little more than a rueful frown.

"Bite me, Evan."

"Excuse me?" His sharp eyes raised up over the landscape of her skin to land on her demanding glare.

"Do it. Just fucking bite me. Let's just get it over with. If Lucca's going to get to me eventually, why not just beat him to it?"

Anger was replaced by fear, sadness, a mixture of emotions she found too easily in Evan's big brown eyes and furrowed brow. Trepidation warning her of the potentially terminal outcome of her boldness. It increased exponentially when Evan stepped toward her and clamped his hands to her waist. His thumbs pressed into her hipbones. A rush of excitement scalded her from his contact, like lava washing over her in searing waves.

"You don't know what you're asking," he said.

She looked back up at him, wild-eyed. "Don't I? It's all I've dreamt about since moving here. Maybe I'm not made for a normal life."

His grasp hurt, but it felt too good to be connected to him. She relished his thumbs' pressure against her hips. The conflict in his eyes increased. His lips, as always, parted like he wanted to say something, but couldn't find the words. Evie marveled at his slightly elongated canines hidden behind his pout.

Just a tiny bite.

Her body leaned into his, pushing his hands harder into her sides with her own. She could sense the building tension of his muscles holding her at bay.

"Please don't... I can't." He nudged her away. Exasperated, Evie grabbed the t-shirt and slipped it over her head, the lines of her form disappearing underneath the oversized raglan. She plunked back down on the edge of the bed.

"I didn't mean to offend you or anything."

Sighing a mix of regret and frustration, Evan lifted his gaze back to her and sat by her side, his hands folded between his knees.

"Evie, I've been spending a fair amount of time with you." She scoffed and rolled her eyes at him. "Don't give me that shit. I've been spending a lot of time with you, and less time taking care of my own needs. I can't have you parading around naked. It's not safe for either one of us."

The notion that she was in danger in his company evoked something primal inside, a carnal need for flesh. Her inner voice danced excitedly through her mind, seductively twirling through the dark corners in warm swirls of crimson.

Blood pumping, the muscles between her legs throbbed as she remembered the moment Lucca sliced into her tongue with his fang. Her chest heaved as she sat on the bed next to Evan, so close she could feel his angst beating against her skin. She could see the shadow of the daggers hidden behind his parted lips. All she'd need to do was remove her shirt, exaggerate her breaths just a little more, and tempt his hunger. No doubt registering her internal plot, Evan cleared his throat and made his way back toward the computer desk.

"I downloaded some training modules. Do you want me to show you how to use them or not?"

Show us how to use you.

Only half-revolted by her inner being' prowess, Evie quivered in her seat and stared at him. She watched him pass his fingers across the keyboard of her laptop, wishing them to pass over her instead. A fresh hunger washed over her, one she'd hadn't felt with such ferocity in months.

"Evan, how long has it been?"

"How long has what been, since I've used a spreadsheet? A few hours." He was dismissive and focused on the glowing screen.

She stood tall to call his attention through his periphery. "No. How long has it been since you fed?"

He grimaced as though the mere word had sliced through his chest like a freshly sharpened blade. The Sempiternal didn't particularly care for the term of "feeding" on a human. They sustained themselves. They consumed—or so Evan said.

"A little over a month." His sights locked on the computer screen. Evie's blood pumped a little faster by his hushed confession.

"You once told me that you need to consume every couple of weeks?"

"That's been difficult since I've been spending so much time with you."

The booming tempo building in her chest emboldened her like a war drum marching her forward into battle.

"So you've been starving yourself to come and see me?" When he didn't answer she stalked toward him. "When was the last time you...?"

She let her inquiry trail off and imagined that if she were human, starved for sexual attention, then surely one of the Sempiternal would be starved for both a human's touch and their essence. Evan had spent months with her, and prior to that he'd been dating Blythe, who told Evie they never slept together. She detected such truth as Evan's eyes flickered toward the scooped hemline of the shirt draped over her hips. He sat transfixed, gaping at the feminine curvature of her exposed hourglass' lower half.

"When was the last time I what?"

"You know what I mean." She took another step toward the immortal monster. Evan sucked in a heavy breath. His normally solid demeanor dissolved slightly.

"Why does my sex life suddenly interest you?"

Because the Sempiternal interest me.

"I'm just curious," she said.

Her small hesitation was enough for Evan to regain a hint of composure. He stood to counter her predatory approach. Her throbbing picked up pace again as he met her in the middle of her tiny studio. The sweet aroma of weed lingered on his lips. Her inner voice goaded her on, calling out from the depths of her mind to reach up and bite at them with her teeth, draw out his own everlasting blood and suck hard. His sullen stare held her still. Evie wanted him just as much as she wanted a drink, a hit, or the Lucca from her dreams.

"It's been a long time Evie. Why?" There was a hint of begging veiled behind his stern demeanor. She gazed back, her body unwilling to give into his unspoken pleas or those of her subconscious. Blood raged through her veins. Evie saw that fire reflect off of Evan's normally masked eyes. "I…" Evan paused and blinked. "We'll pick up our computer lesson tomorrow. I'll come by in the morning and just walk you through the program enough so you know how to use spreadsheets."

Don't let him leave us.

Her mouth cracked open, her tongue poised to utter something, anything that would keep Evan there, but guilt gripped at Evie for her provocative behavior. She let him go and stewed in her own conflict. Subdued desire had escaped the dark crevices of her body and unleashed their want wrongfully onto Evan. His lingering scent coiled around her as he whisked by, but Evie found comfort in the hard slamming of the front door.

***

She locked the door behind him, stripped off her t-shirt and marched to the bathroom. Inside, she glared at her reflection in mirror.

"What are you doing?"

I want Evan.

"No, he's just a friend."

He's Sempiternal.

"He doesn't deserve to be dicked around like this."

Then give me flesh, any flesh. I am starved for a warm body.

"What is wrong with you? What the fuck do you think I am?"

We are inevitable, stupid girl. Evan can't hide us forever.

"Not him. He's a good friend."

He has what we need. He knows how to give us the release.

"I don't want to hurt him. Not like Rob."

You can't silence me forever, stupid girl.

Her stomach knotted. Her fight evaporated into the damp summer air.

Ashamed, she turned back into the studio. Evie grabbed hold of her trusty glass pipe and smoked herself stupid, muzzling her inner voice with a hefty dose of THC in lieu of a warm body. The primal hunger lingered in her warm center.

***

Later into the night, after climbing under her crisp bed linens, Evie used her own hands to relieve her tensions. Under normal circumstances, she would envision Lucca on top of her, forcing her fingers deep inside. However, following her unresolved conversation with Evan, one hand squeezed against her hip bone where his thumb left its impression. The other caressed her from the inside out in his absence. Not the normal finger-fucking she passed off as Lucca, Evie took her time, reveling in her interpretation of Evan's soft touch.

Inevitably, her own hands left her wanting and she could smell his weed-laced scent everywhere in her apartment.

FIVE

"I'm so sorry, Rob."

"For what, Evie?" His soothing rasp wrapped around her in the dark.

"For forgetting you. For running away from you."

Rob's warm, familiar hands ran across her core, guarding her, possessing her as only Rob knew how, his phantom lips whisking across her brow. She was safe in his arms, content and whole. "Evie, what would make you think I'll ever forgive you?"

The threatening boom of her heartbeat drummed in between her ears. Pain contorted her facial features as her chest cracked in half. When she tilted her head up to search Rob's sweet face for understanding, she found herself in the arms of her new boss. His slicked-back hair and shit-eating grin shone down on her. The instinct to wriggle from his hold nearly sucked her lungs through her throat as she shrieked. His cackle broke out of the surrounding black void.

"You looked frightened. Are you frightened, Evie?"

She blinked and stared up at Lucca. His devilish side smirk gleamed in the pitch black of her nightmare. She couldn't feel herself, but guessed her eyes widened with fear; pupils fully dilated to absorb as much light as possible in the darkness. The thrumming of her heartbeat increased. The golden rim around Lucca's irises gleamed in the dark.

"It's calling you, Evie. I know you can feel it. You cannot deny us. Our disease, it calls to you. He wants to stop us."

"Rob's dead." Her panic reverberated through her mind.

"Not Rob."

She fell into Lucca's hold. His perfect body arced over hers, enveloping her. "He wants to deny us, Evie."

"Who?"

Her head lulled back and forth, her body enraptured by his touch. How easily she found comfort in Lucca's nothingness.

"Fall with me." His whisper caressed her ear and along the length of her neck.

"What about Rob?"

"It's not Rob who wants you, Evie. He wants you for himself."

Her labored breathing increased. Her mind fought to steady itself, vertigo shaking her. The dark cold slipped in and out as she gasped for air in Lucca's arms. A razor's edge scraped against her skin, and the vibration from Lucca's purr pulsated through her ethereal body, launching thrilling shoots of pain. His purring turned to sinister, ravenous growling, but his touch remained tender. Her eyes roamed through the darkness, and through the gloom she found the source of distress. Evan was perched, collared and chained across a wide expanse of obsidian dust sparkling under a dim spotlight.

She pushed against Lucca. He jeered and leaned back from her. As he pulled away, Evie felt a series of stabbings run around her neck, pushing in and piercing her vocal cords. Each breath burned through her. She wore the same collar as Evan, a choke collar lined with dozens of needle-sharp spikes. The harder Lucca pulled away, the tighter the chain constricted around her neck.

"Will you deny me?" he asked in his low melodic tone. "You were born for me. You will bleed for me. He wants to

43

keep you for himself, Evie, but I've claimed you as my own. We are the same."

She tried to speak, to cry out, but all that surfaced from within was bloody gurgling. Her own sweet coppery essence bombarded her senses. She collapsed and choked on her own screams as thousands of sand grains carved their way into her palms and knees. The sparkling nothingness pulled her down, sucked her down into its black hole. Through the corner of her vision, she saw Evan fighting to break free from his chains, only to be choked and bled the same as her.

"You want to know what it feels like." Lucca said. "You want to feel the release. I can show you. You and I are destined, Evie."

She squeezed ruby tears from her eyes and her body was soon gore. Evan was crazed by the sight of her blood, her essence, growling and struggling against his restraint like a rabid dog. She tried to reach out to Lucca. With each slight movement the collar choked, and she bled more. Her voice ripped through her. A hematic torrent spewed from her mouth. Still she needed to reach Lucca.

An uproar cracked the darkness, and she was able to move more freely. She looked over to Evan struggling to break free and gorge on her lifeblood.

"You must know Evan quite well." The sharp hiss of dapper Slithery Silver carried through the murk.

She turned up to him. He held both chains in his hands. His androgynous features morphed, eyes slit, luminous yellow. His body contorted into a serpentine image she knew well, one she'd hoped to have left behind in Fallhaven.

"I can show you." The chime of Lucca's voice called Evie to her right.

She jerked. Pain ripped through her body, and she hemorrhaged some more. She combed the dark, but Lucca was nowhere to be found.

Calling out her attention, Slithery bellowed sick laughter. The sound ricocheted through her mind and nearly shredded her eardrums to a grainy pulp.

***

Evie awoke just after two in the morning in cold sweats and body tremors. She lay in the fetal position, sobbing quietly into her knees. Chattering teeth allowing pathetic whimpers to break through the wall of her pursed lips. Rob's sweet voice echoed in her memory, *what would make you think I'll ever forgive you?* Lucca's soft touch lingered in her skin. Evan's voracious snarling terrified her.

"I'm so sorry." She repeated her apology like a chant, hoping if she said it enough times someone, something, might listen and offer her mercy from her perversions.

He is you and you are him.

"Fuck you."

She sobbed. Her heart silently begged the treacherous inner voice to relent. Too long it had repeated the words of Hope, the psychic who had read Evie's fate months ago when the Devil tarot card flew from the deck, calling out to her. She thought she'd purged it from her body with the alcohol detox, but tonight's nightmare proved her wrong.

Evie watched the sun rise from her bed, curled up into a tiny ball. Too petrified to move. Too horrified to fall back asleep.

Six

The next morning, Evie didn't mark Evan's arrival with the same ceremony as the day prior. In fact, she didn't even bother to get out of bed as he let himself in.

"Good morning Sunshine." His voice carried across the apartment, and she retreated under her comforter. His soft chuckle soon followed. "Rough night?"

"I didn't sleep well."

Her answer was muffled under the duvet. The thought of another workday was impossible. Contempt wrinkled her forehead from the crisp sound of the deadbolt and creaking of floor boards under Evan's dress shoes. The bed pitched to the left under his weight by her side, and his palm running over her back made his close proximity known.

"Let's try this again," he said. "What's the matter, Evie?"

Huffing out her frustration, she ripped the covers down toward her waist. But making eye contact with Evan only evoked a harsh wave of repentance. The pain she witnessed, the hunger tearing him apart in her dream crept from the back of her mind's eye as his benign trust beamed down on her. Coupled with guilt for objectifying him last night with her own hand and self-induced orgasm, she bit down on her tongue.

"I'm sorry, Evan."

His nose crinkled. "For what?"

Eyes raking him up and down, she chose her words with care.

"I can't go back to that office."

46

"Is that why you couldn't sleep? You're stressed about work? Evie, it's been one day. You'll be fine." His hand moved from the comforter to the hair wrapped around her face. Such care only fueled her inner conflict more.

"Why didn't you tell me you know the guy who runs the fucking company?"

The rigidity of his spine and eyes widening gave away his unease. "What are you talking about? You mean the CEO?"

She held in her resentment, bridled by her pursed lips. "Is that who gave me the job?"

"Don—he wasn't supposed to be in town for another month. Are you saying you actually met him?" A twinge of trepidation lifted his brow.

She sat up in bed, the haunting cackle from her dream echoed in her mind. "Do you remember the tarot reading I had back home? The one I told you about? Where that crazy psychic predicted Lucca entering my life."

"Of course, I remember. But I thought you didn't believe in psychics?"

"Well, I don't really, but she was dead on with Lucca. She said the devil was coming after me. I saw the fucking card jump right out of the deck. It's even haunted my dreams."

"Okay, but that's Lucca. What does that have to do with Don or you going back to work today?"

Embarrassment cast her eyes down to the bed's comforter. She gnawed harder on her top lip and mustered the gumption to say it. "Last night, he appeared as the image of the devil in my dream."

Turning back up to lock gazes with Evan, she waited for his response. He was stoic. The silence and stagnant air of another humid morning nearly did her in until he finally burst into a fit of laughter.

47

She scowled. "Are you laughing at me, Evan?"

"That depends." His face was red as he struggled to rein in his amusement. "Are you really serious? I've put my neck on the line for this job, and you want to quit after one day, all because you had a bad dream comparing your new boss to some bogus tarot card image?"

The acidic burn of shame in her mouth turned her stomach. "Go to Hell, Evan." She pushed against his chest and sent him stumbling off the side of the bed to storm off to the bathroom.

"Evie, come back." He called after her, but she'd already slammed the door shut and had no intentions humoring him further. "I'm sorry. Come out here and let's talk."

As she stared into the mirror's reflection, her pulse raced. Her bones ached for the simplicity of Fallhaven; get high, get drunk, fuck and go to work.

You wanted change, stupid girl.

"Do you think I'm being ridiculous?"

You already know what I think.

Her introspective dialogue was moot. The rustle of Evan moving around the apartment was the only sound which resonated at the moment. Hands clawing the rim of the pedestal sink, she gazed back at her reflection.

"Fine. Evan stuck his neck out for me. He's done more for me than I deserve. I can do this. I'm just being paranoid."

When she returned to the living room, he was at her computer. He didn't even raise an eyebrow at her when she resurfaced from the bathroom.

"I assumed you'd used a computer before," he said. "Did you even do anything with the tutorials I downloaded for you?"

She thought to apologize for freaking out on him just now, or for being so dramatic about her dreams. Instead, she decided to leave well-enough alone as it appeared Evan had as well.

She rested at the foot of the bed, arms hugging her waist, and watched him work. "Nope. I wasn't in the mood to do homework after you left yesterday." She found her eyes moving down the length of his body again and squeezed tighter around her waist when she fixated on the way his grey dress pants bunched up in his lap. "I mean, I know where to buy vinyl underwear online. I should be able to figure out a goddamned intranet, right?"

Evan chuckled under his breath. "Vinyl huh? I'd like to see that."

He flashed a quick smile and stood from the tiny desk and made his way to the glass pipe nestled on the makeshift coffee table.

As she admired the way his tailored pants hugged his ass when he strode across the room, her tongue played against the inner wall of her teeth. "I brought some with me in the move. I can go throw them on if you'd like."

Evan watched her through a cloud of smoke as he drew a deep inhale and licked his lips. A warm wave rushed over her and pooled below her waist.

"Maybe later," he said. Guilt quickly rose up and sucker punched her in the gut for enjoying his visual stimulation. "Go get ready for work." His wheeze preceded a deep exhale and a hacking cough.

Evie was both relieved and bemused by his rejection, a jumble of emotions she found curious. The guilt waned.

"Fine, hold on." She disappeared back into the bathroom. This time, however, she emerged freshly showered and wearing a black miniskirt topped with a short-sleeved cherry print blouse. Her tousled hair framed her face in bleach blonde-streaked ringlets.

"Is that acceptable office attire?" Evan asked, passing her a freshly packed glass bowl and scrupulous brow.

"Well, it's all I have that's remotely close," she said looking herself up and down in the mirror before accepting the hydroponic heaven.

"Okay, so shopping this weekend it is." He tossed her purse at her and lifted a guiding hand toward the door.

***

Evan walked her to and from work every day that week, each day a re-run of the last. She found ways to circumvent Dave's cubicle. Each night she'd torture Evan with the choke collar. During their walks, he kept quiet company, and Evie was left to her own guilty thoughts. She'd been left alone for months, and it was beginning to show. Her inner voice grew restless, feening hard for a hit.

I want more.

It would chide her, sickening her with want.

"More what?"

I want out. I want the Sempiternal.

Shivers wracked her body each night as her internal dialogue continued to puzzle her.

By the end of the week, she had mastered her spreadsheets at work, but certainly not her emotions. Afraid to further objectify him or goad her subconscious on with fantasies of his eternal body, Evie withdrew herself further and further away from Evan with each step by heartbreaking step to and from the office.

The weekend came. Her body ached from the inadequacies of her own fingers, and her mind throbbed from the twisting torture of wrestling her inner voice into submission. Evan took notice, and his rare smile had all but vanished completely by the end of the week, replaced by gorgeous melancholy that Evie committed to memory.

Come Saturday, shopping demanded she offer Evan her undivided attention. The excursion with him both thrilled and worried her.

Outside the subway station, Washington Street was a sclerotic artery, thin streams of locals squeezing through clumps of slow-moving, gape-mouthed tourists. The stench of asphalt and sweat continued to permeate the air.

"If we can't find work clothes for you in Downtown Crossing then we can't find anything at all," he said. "Whatever you need, Evie. Don't pay attention to the price tags. I'm not." Evan escorted her off the congested sidewalk into the crisp air conditioning of a store advertising a huge blow out sale on summer clothing.

Evie raised a crooked eyebrow. "There's no way in hell you're spending seventy-nine dollars on this shirt for me. It doesn't even have sleeves," she scoffed, crumpling a polka-dotted shirt back into a clearance bin.

Evan just chuckled back. "I will if it's work-appropriate."

Evie picked out black skirts and sheer blouses of various whites and creams, shopping off of the clearance racks as the listed entries in her mental ledger extended.

They made their way into a boutique that had the Boston-market cornered on business casual. Each mannequin donned a pin-striped pencil skirt and freshly pressed blouse. Evie scanned the sales floor for any sign of familiar faces; her co-workers, or God-forbid Dave and the pudgy girl in Operations he was rumored to be banging in the parking garage after hours.

"What's wrong?" Evan asked.

A pretty blonde in a floral top and khaki capris squeezed between them and the closely packed racks. Evie glanced down to her vintage Lynyrd Skynyrd t-shirt and cropped, barely-held-on-by-a-thread jeans. "Nothing. I don't think we're going to find anything in here for me."

Evan came up close and lifted her chin up to command her line of sight to meet his. "You're a chameleon, remember?" He lifted a blue blouse with a ruffled collar from a nearby rack. "What about this one? It matches your eyes?"

Mesmerized by his immortal stare, Evie didn't bother to consider the shirt. Her eyes were set on something much more immediate than clothing, running up and down Evan's storefront instead.

"Not my style." She forced her hungry eyes away, failed to convince her more primal needs burning in her core that she didn't prefer him to the stupid blouse, and thumbed through a display of black dress pants.

Evan cleared his throat and followed her lead to the sales racks. "Well, can we at least buy you a new pair of jeans to go with your morbid wardrobe?"

"I can't wear jeans at work. So no. Besides, my jeans are called 'distressed.' And they're in style." Their playful banter helped a tiny bit to lighten the gloom hanging over her head as the sales girl cast Evie the stink eye from across a table of cardigans and camisoles.

Evan shook his head with a smile. "I'll give you distressed." He tossed a pair of black leggings in her face. She giggled back at him.

The two walked side by side through Downtown Crossing in the silence that became all too commonplace between them. Evie focused on her phone as text message after text message chimed in, a welcome distraction. Evan, however, was not so amused.

He watched her curiously before questioning. "Who are you texting?"

She held her phone away, blocking his view by holding the phone against her chest. If he knew she'd been in contact with Nate, he'd spirit her away even deeper into hiding.

"A friend from work." She nudged him with her elbow and moved on, scooting around something that may at one point have been an ice cream treat, but had melted into a globulous form of froth and spongy waffle cone on the sidewalk.

"Well that's good, right? You're making friends."

She nodded back at his encouraging grin. The lie drifted across her lips easily but the lingering remorse burned in her chest. It had, however, opened the door of opportunity to discuss a topic she'd been avoiding with him.

"Would you be upset if I went to a party?" she asked hesitantly through a nervous cringe. Evan's furrowed brow spoke for him before he turned his head down to the sidewalk in front of his feet.

"I'm not your keeper, Evie. Do whatever you want."
Bullshit!

"No, that's fine. I won't go." She shrugged. A moment later, Evan echoed her mannerisms.

"What kind of party?" His feigned curiosity was not so convincing that she couldn't tell it was forced. A tiny smile tugged at the corners of her lips nonetheless.

"This girl Leda, from the office, she invited me to her place on my first day of work. I don't really know many details. I think she just felt bad for me because I don't know anyone in the city besides you." Evie paused. "Not that she even knows I have you."

Her hushed tone did nothing to hide an honest sadness. Evan stopped in the middle of the sidewalk and stared at her.

It took Evie a few steps before she realized his quiet company was no longer at her side, and she turned.

"You're unhappy," he said.

"Evan, that's not what I meant."

"But you are." He reiterated with sad eyes.

Evie let out a frustrated breath at herself for allowing her emotions to reveal themselves so plainly.

"Look, maybe I'm just lonely, Evan. I've been in hiding for months. It's wearing on me." She moved back to him. "I suppose it explains my behavior toward you lately. I'm sorry. I know you're only trying to help."

"Toward me?" Brow knitted, Evan strolled onward.

***

They finished off their shopping spree at a local burger joint, Evie with a rare-cooked cheeseburger and sweet potato french fries.

A glob of ketchup squished its way out the side of her burger. She used the tip of a fry to wipe it off before devouring the fry whole. Every now and then, she thought she noticed Evan indicate the tiniest hint of amusement at her eating habits. She took his subtle happiness as a good sign, and her remorse began to wash away.

"How come you never slept with Blythe?" She ceased toying with her food. Her eyes flared, realizing her inner voice had emerged to drive the conversation.

Evan's trace of a smile vanished. "This again? Why are you so fixated on my sex life?"

Evie fidgeted in her seat, but submitted to the internal nagging prodding her on. "Blythe said you guys never actually had sex. I know you didn't date for that long, but still, how come you never slept with her? She wanted to."

"I don't see how this is a relevant conversation." His annoyance was emphasized with a low groan and arms folded across his chest.

"Are you asexual?" Evie asked. "Blythe thought you were because you wouldn't sleep with her. I mean, she's so cute and all. I'm pretty sure even I'd fuck her." Evan raised an eyebrow. "If I was a guy, that is."

He jutted his chin in the air, slow and controlled, before leaning toward her. His approach stirred an electrifying fear inside. Her inner voice thrummed with excitement in the pit of her core, ready to die for that predator's stare.

"You don't stop until you get your way, do you?" Evan said with a side-smirk that she archived for her dreams. "Evie, this isn't a topic of conversation I'm particularly comfortable discussing with you, but as I've said to you before, I did actually care about Blythe. I didn't want to hurt her."

Evie returned his intense stare, narrowing her eyes and only half-concealing her inner musing's smirk peeking through. "I think denying a girl sex when she wants it is cruel and unusual punishment." She presumed her little joke would evoke a tiny grin from him, but Evan's seriousness held strong.

"Evie, listen, I enjoy sex." The fierceness harnessed behind his russet eyes intensified as he ran the course of her body from across the café table. "Believe me, I do. But over the years I've transitioned my yearnings to... other things. When I do... you know... it makes me want more."

The severity of his insinuation was sobering. Evie shoved the swooning high priestess back to the dark confines of her subconscious. She shifted, uncomfortable in her seat. "Oh!" She gasped. "You mean it makes you want to..." She choked on the word. "Consume?"

"Exactly." Evan sat back, arms folded across his chest once more, this time to prove his point. "Do you get it now?"

Evie shook her head. Evan cared for Blythe enough not to want to suck her dry. A chill ran down Evie's spine, and a resentful pinch in her chest caught her off guard.

"Do you sleep with every person you feed off of?" Her jaw fell slack.

"Would you keep your voice down?" He growled and lunged for her. His hand clasped over her mouth. His outburst called the attention of two girls at a nearby table, who giggled and whispered to each other. Evan rolled his eyes at them and settled back in his seat, freeing Evie. "And no, to answer your question, I don't. I also don't expect you to understand what it feels like to need... It's different."

We know exactly how it feels.

The look that crossed his face made Evie remorseful, fearful, and embarrassed she allowed her inner voice to unleash itself.

The somber mood created by Evie's gaffed efforts at conversation over her late lunch hung over them like a black cloud. Opting for a bus line that would take them just two blocks away from her apartment, they made it home just as the sun settled over the harbor.

Acoustic guitar filled the studio apartment, and the two settled side by side on the futon. Evan sat playing with an unwound paper clip as he poked at a resin-lined glass bowl. Evie watched him take his time packing it with a bright, crystallized bud.

"What is that?" She yelped out over the guitar's strumming and whispery vocals.

"What? What's wrong?"

"What, are you contemplating the vastness of the universe? Pack the fucking bowl already." Her order relayed with a healthy dose of sarcasm. Evan cracked a smile, and the two passed the bowl back and forth, suffocating in the mix of smoke and stuffy summer air.

"This one's yummy." She inspected the burning embers in the bowl. "What do you call it?"

"It's called Blueberry Kush. Do you like it?"

The pot, like Evan, was sweet, fragrant, and slightly piney. She hummed contently. "It's delicious. I think I love it. More than the pineapple stuff you had last month." She nuzzled against his shoulder.

"I'll have to remember that. Kush is real easy to come by." After a long pause, he sighed with a combination of contentment and unpreventable regret. "I have some business to take care of. I have to head back up to Fallhaven for a couple of weeks."

Evie tilted her head to submit a cockeyed glance. "Is everything okay?"

He took a hit and, through a cloud full of smoke, nodded.

"Hope so. I have to meet some contractors at my family's estate… and someone is interested in buying Sirens." Evan paused. She felt his eyes on her, but could not bring herself to link with them anymore, didn't want him to see her pain. "I'll let you know how it all works out," he said quietly and exhaled a large puff of smoke before passing the bowl back to her. She accepted it and stared at its tip, lost in the purple swirls and captured fractions of light.

The memory of the strip club where she worked summoned painful mental images of the man she'd left behind in Fallhaven Cemetery. A tear escaped down her cheek.

"Evie, are you okay?"

"I still don't understand why he left me the club in his will. Neither one of us was very comfortable there."

It was the only place you felt at peace… with Rob.

"The two of you were close. The only family you said you really had in Fallhaven, right?"

She caught a second tear before it escaped her lid, and then sniffled. "Yeah." Her voice broke on the pent-up emotion, the culpability of Rob's death still tormenting her. "Thanks for helping me get rid of the place, Evan."

"Of course."

He reached over to push aside a rogue curl of hair from her face, but she pushed him away with a vehement shake of her head. He nodded and stood to leave, but not before placing a small kiss against her forehead. The sensation of his lips against her skin burned, causing a new wave of tears to flow down her face.

"I'll be back as soon as I can," he said. "Go to work and come home... And please, Evie, be careful. I'm not very comfortable leaving you alone. I know it's just a matter of time before Lucca figures out where to look for you."

Her wetted eyes shifted up to meet his, but stopped just shy of begging Evan not to leave her. Evie craved a drink more than anything.

She waited until he had locked the door behind him before breaking down into hysterics.

SEVEN

Evie awoke cramped and curled up in a ball against the back of the lumpy futon cushion.

With only the sound of Evan's acoustic playlist queued up on her computer, she remained on the futon for the duration of that summery Sunday. Her cell phone and glass bowl competed for her attention like sibling rivals. In between tokes, her phone was aglow with incoming messages, though none from the one person she hoped for. Each time she checked her phone, her chest heaved with anticipation and quickly deflated with disappointment.

"Not now, Nate." She left the phone on the table and pulled a rip from her bowl.

The afternoon passed, and he began calling.

"Fuck off, Nate."

She left the phone on the coffee table, letting it go to voice mail. In no time, it chimed again with a new message. The vibrating lingered, itching along the skin at the nape of her neck like nails on a chalkboard. She tried to ignore it, thought to turn off her phone completely, but was too afraid to miss a call or message from Evan.

The vibrating continued, creeping under the toss pillow she'd held over her head to muffle the thrumming tone.

What are you hiding from?

"Evan will kill me if I keep talking to Nate."

He's not here, is he? He's not fulfilling our needs now, is he?

"What the hell is that supposed to mean?" Confusion was beating her brain to the rhythmic buzzing of a new incoming message on her phone. Her eyes hyper-focused on the flashing like of her phone.

How many times do I need to remind you? I want more.

"Nate?"

He's a start.

She cycled through a few deep breaths and reached out for her phone.

Please Babe. Meet me 4 lunch.

She read his message over and over. Each syllable synced with her pulse. Her mind reminded her she'd recovered from her addictions in Fallhaven—most of them, and didn't need to reopen old wounds. But her subconscious and solitude picked at the scabs, itching, twisting, and gnawing at her insides. She could hear Evan, see him pleading her to remain strong, but her body ached for some relief.

More.

"Goddammit." She groaned passed her fingers over the phone's touch screen.

Fine. Lunch and that's it.

She arranged to meet him during her lunch break, downtown at a park just a few blocks away from South Station. Evie's High Priestess giggled with delight in the back of her subconscious.

Evan will never need to know.

***

Evie only had one hour for lunch, and it took her nearly twenty-five minutes just to make it to South Station. Another five minutes and threat of shin splints, and she finally made it to the park. The sun shined bright, car exhaust fumes choked; summer in the city showed no signs of relenting to September. Evie stood in the midst of it all; it was time to search for Nate. Her thumbs passed over her cell phone.

I'm near a coffee stand. Where r u?

She texted and raised her eyes from her phone to survey the crowd. A new message came through the phone vibrating in the palm of her hand almost instantly.

Look 2 your right.

Her eyes lifted to an ivy-covered canopy and settled on the figure underneath. What first caught her off guard about Nate was his glow. Never in a million years would she have recognized him. In fact, she didn't recognize him—he materialized out of the shimmering summer air like a walking mirage. Nate smiled, a hint of his familiar stoner grin peeking through his shine as he identified her with ease through the crowded grassy plain.

Closing the gap between them with a brilliant toothy grin, he scooped her up in a bear hug and spun her around in a circle, holding her in close and breathing her in deeply. His customary odor of alcohol, smoke, and sea salt was nowhere to be found. He smelled clean, soapy, and powder fresh.

"I've missed you so much, Babe." He spoke in a low melodic voice she'd not heard from him in years.

"Nate." She gawked up at him. "You look amazing."

He did. The dark circles that had come to accompany his strung-out appearance were gone. He looked invigorated, anew. His soft and squishy physique had been whittled down to like it was in his younger days, before he'd fallen into the drug-laden fisherman's life back in Fallhaven. His eyes gleamed a brilliant shade of hazel in the summer light, his ginger beard and auburn hair like a flame around his wide grin. Evie hung in his arms, limp and dazed.

"Babe, what's wrong?" The boyish smile he gave melted her heart, and she reciprocated that smile with a slacked jaw and wide eyes.

"I've just—You look amazing." She repeated in a breath. He was sober, handsome, put-together—hell, Nate was sexy.

He laughed heartily and hugged her close again. "You look pretty damn good, yourself."

He leaned in to land a kiss against her lips. Even through his mesmerizing charm, and to Evie's own shock, her body instinctively pulled away.

"I'm sorry. I'm just a little in... umm... I'm... things are different."

Nate frowned, but his disappointment lingered only for a moment before flashing his dashing smile again. It was brilliant. Evie hadn't seen that smile in years. It set off a long-dead flourish of butterflies in her stomach.

He settled her down on the grass, holding her hands in his.

"It's okay. I get it, Babe. I do. C'mon, let's get lunch."

He dragged her over to an outdoor café and paid for her green tea and scone, but insisted he'd already eaten. The two settled onto the grass while she enjoyed her meal in awe of him, slightly uneasy at the sight of his miraculous transformation.

Pulse thumping between her ears, Evie stared, stuffing the scone in her mouth to avoid having to ask the obvious question.

"I know. You don't have to say it. Losing you hit me hard, I'm not gonna lie, but I'm different now Evie. You've got to believe me, I've changed."

Even in their cleaner days, she'd never seen Nate like this. It was awkward and inspiring at the same time. She took a quick glance at her phone.

"Shit, I have to get back to work. I'm going to be late." Her reluctance to leave was a shock, but she pushed up to her feet nonetheless.

"Can I ride with you back to your office?" Genuine excitement twinkled in his eyes. Through such a gleam, flashes of Evan's saddened features bombarded her mind and a pinching sensation in her chest indicated a notion of remorse, like she'd cuckolded him.

"No, it's okay. I really need to run." Evie fumbled over one bogus excuse after another in her mind. Excuses were moot. Guiltiness consumed her. Though such culpability, however, would not keep her from meeting Nate again while Evan was away in Fallhaven. Loneliness was loneliness, after all.

"How about later in the week?"

Her chest was cracking for the thumping of her heartbeat. This new Nate—this ghost of a Nate from another lifetime ago, was too much to deny. "Sure. I'll text you," she said with a closed-mouth smile, running off before Nate could try and pull her into a kiss again.

***

Evie twitched nervously riding the Silver Line back to the office. The damned subway took so long, what with all the ridiculous stops and circumvention of the waterfront. She kept close eye on her cell phone and the time. Twenty minutes late and counting. She wasn't quite sure how that would go over back at the office, considering she'd never actually taken a lunch break before. What could twenty little minutes hurt? It took another eight minutes to make it back into her building's main lobby. She hammered the up arrow and paced back and forth waiting for the elevator.

"C'mon c'mon c'mon," she said under breath. She looked down at her cell phone. She was almost a full half hour late. "Dammit!"

As the doors parted, Evie hopped into the cabin and shaky fingers selected her floor. She made nervous little popping sounds with her mouth as she recalled her lunch date with Nate. She couldn't fight a tiny smile, bowing her head, embarrassed that the non-existent co-passengers around her might see her blush. Nate was so charming, so much like the jock he'd been when they first met, before they over-indulged in each other and their various poisons of choice. She licked her bottom lip and a tiny giggle escaped her mouth as the elevator doors opened. The familiar voice on the other side of the doors grew louder and clearer as they opened.

"Evan?"

Shit!

She quickly dismissed her paranoia. There was no way Evan could have known she was out meeting Nate for lunch. No way. Right? His equally stunned reaction settled her nerves, as indication that he hadn't expected to run into her either.

"Evie?" Shock, a hint of pain and embarrassment colored his cheeks.

"What are you doing here?"

She looked over to see the Mr. Slithery Silver, himself, standing by Evan's side. Both men were distinguishably dressed in tailored suits. All thoughts of Nate's improved appearance vanished from her mind's eye, as she took in a deep breath full of Evan, his spiced aroma and immaculate appearance. The glower lining Slithery's face by his side pinned her in place, repentant for her tardiness or some other sin she hadn't realized she'd committed against him.

"I... uh... I had a meeting." Evan dropped his eyes away from her and to the floor.

"Miss Westvale... had a bite to eat, did you?" Slithery's crooked smirk that made her cringe. She forced down the knot in her throat.

"Yes sir."

"And where did you go?" he asked.

None of your fucking business.

"Just exploring the local area." Evan looked up at her curiously, but didn't push the issue. She mirrored his bemusement. "Evan, I thought you were heading back to Fallhaven?"

"I told you, I had some business to wrap up before I left."

Maybe he's checking in on us?

Slithery chortled, calling Evan's attention, who quickly straightened in posture.

"I'm sure we'll be in touch when I return," Evan said with a foreign formality.

"Miss Westvale, I'm sure you're needed back at your desk." At Mr. Silver's derisive remark, Evie stepped aside to make way for their passage onto the elevator. "Now Evan, as I said. These projections you've compiled look great. I only have a few..." His voice trailed off as the elevator closed. Evie and Evan exchanged an awkward glance before the doors sealed shut.

Evie took another moment to compose herself before returning to her desk—the difference between thirty-five minutes late and thirty-seven minutes late seemed negligible. A few deep breaths and a steadied pulse later, she glanced at Ginger as she passed the reception desk. The administrative assistant was preening herself in a compact mirror, fidgeting with the bubblegum-pink scarf wrapped around her neck.

"That's a really pretty scarf, Ginger. It goes great with that lip gloss."

Ginger jumped in her seat. "Evie, I didn't see you there."

"Sorry, I didn't mean to frighten you." Evie walked out into the great grey expanse of cubicles. She could feel Ginger's eyes following her into the labyrinth of partitions. A sense of judgment she'd been saved from since leaving Fallhaven, since Evan had her safely hidden in her tiny studio, pricked her between the eyes. Now, open in the office, the cold echo of the insecurities she tried her best to leave back home crept from the back of her mind, emerging from the graves she'd buried them in like the living dead.

Judging—all judging.

She shuddered into her corner cube. When Evie sat down at her desk, she checked the time. Close to forty-five minutes late. Surely someone would have noticed. Peering out into the cubes, Dave was watching her suspiciously. She pulled back out of his view, as though that could free her from his scrutiny.

Checking her email, one lonely unread notice waited for her; it was from Leda. The full details for her party were laid out inside: date, time, address, and all of her contact information just in case. Evie sighed and scrunched her brow, remembering the hurt in Evan's eyes when she mentioned it over the past weekend.

Evan did say it was good to make friends, didn't he?

"Sounds... good," she said aloud to herself, typing out the same message in her email response. With a click of her mouse the email traveled through the ether.

One of the girls next to her, who Evie vaguely recalled introducing herself as Beth on her first day, a non-descript employee with short brown hair and pencil skirt like so many others flitting around the office, popped her head around the cubes' partition.

"Did I see you talking with Mr. Carver?"

Evie responded with a crooked-brow. "Yes, why?"

Beth swooned. "I love when he comes into the office. Yummy."

Evie frowned and glanced back out toward the lobby. "Does Evan come by frequently?"

"Evan?" Beth giggled, bouncing her short brown bob against her shoulders with an amused wag of her head. "Mr. Carver comes by for a quarterly meeting with the boss. Sometimes he's around more often, I guess. I wasn't aware you were on a first name basis with him. Do you know Mr. Carver?"

Evie chuckled at the decorum with which Beth addressed him. Evan was an authority figure around the office? She pictured him packing a bowl on her futon with a pair of jeans and a t-shirt on. Her body warmed as she recalled nuzzling up against him night after night over the past few months as he supported her through recovery and discussed the severity of immortality. Picturing him meeting over spreadsheets, projections, and bottom lines was laughable. She wondered if anyone actually knew what he was; her Evan.

Your Evan?

"Ha!" Evie released a loud outburst that drew the attention of several co-workers close by. She threw her hand over her mouth. The notion conceived by her inner voice was ridiculous; her Evan. Her laughter lingered longer than it should have, awkward, sinking in, crystallizing; her Evan. "We're good friends, I guess you could say."

"Good friends, huh?" A second girl who sat three cubes down from her, Valerie, if Evie remembered correctly, scowled from around her partition. "I think I've heard that before."

Evie's smile vanished, jaw snapped shut, taken aback by the stranger's hostile tone. She looked at Valerie, and then over to Beth for an explanation.

"Oh, don't worry about Val," Beth said with a flighty hand gesture. "She claims to have had 'a thing' with Mr. Carver last year." Beth covered the side of her mouth to block Val's view. "She thinks taking meeting minutes a few times last year was a marriage proposal. She also claims the boss has a thing for her too, but I always thought he was a little feminine, if you know what I mean."

Evie raised a skeptical brow in Val's direction. The two girls glowered at each other for a moment, then the very plain-looking girl skulked back into the cubicle from whence she came. Evie couldn't picture Evan with someone so ordinary. Not beautiful, not cute or chic. Not...

You?

Evie frowned. "Not special enough," she said under her breath and disregarded the cross-eyed stare from Beth before turning back to her work.

***

Evie spent the remainder of her afternoon reveling in fanciful thoughts of Evan walking around the office, popping his head around her cube instead of Beth. Such daydreaming also left a trail of remorse in its wake for objectifying him.

Adding insult to her self-inflicted injury, Nate continued texting her. She smiled each time his caller ID popped up on her phone, grateful for his distraction, but still repentant for the sense of infidelity it triggered.

But between texting and typing, Evie was fairly pre-occupied at her desk and her worries about Evan were not allowed priority. She only had a few more sheets to print and deliver to Dave, and then she'd be alone for the evening. Then she'd really have to worry about objectifying Evan with her own hand in his place.

She walked over to the print area and heard a set of voices around the corner. One she knew well.

"I haven't seen him since." Val said.

"Mr. Carver must have been around here since then, right?"

Whose voice is that with Val? Evie stood still as stone, ears perked up.

"He's been out of town for a while. I haven't been called into any of his meetings. Have you?" Val asked.

"No, come to think of it, I haven't. I miss those big brown eyes."

Who the fuck is that? Evie struggled to identify the second girl's voice.

"I hear you. God, I miss his..."

What? You miss his what?

"It's not fair. Now who's this new chick he has working here?" Val continued.

"I have no idea. Flavor of the month?"

Flavor?

69

A hot wave flushed her cheeks and burned in Evie's center.

"Whatever. I just wished he'd start coming back around for meetings more often. I miss that eye-candy," Val huffed.

"Me too," the second girl sighed.

Enough of this bullshit.

Evie grabbed her printouts and, with a nasty sneer, turned around to reveal herself. She nearly walked right into Val, who stood leaning up against the corner of the wall. Instead, she tripped over Val's foot and tossed her prints into the air. She was saved from falling by the second girl, whom she now recognized as Dawn from the accounting department. Both girls fumbled on impact, but held each other upright.

"Evie, I didn't see you there." Whether or not Val's indifference to her sudden appearance was forced or not, she quickly turned from Evie and walked away.

"Do you girls know Evan?" Evie asked Dawn as she knelt down to collect her scattered reports.

Dawn grinned and bent down to assist her. "You heard us? Yeah, some of us know Mr. Carver pretty well. How do you know him?"

Evie took in a deep breath. Curious to know if they knew what Evan was. "Umm... He's a close friend from back home. How do you know him?"

Dawn shook her head. "I don't, really. He's just so fun to look at when he comes in for meetings. We all have a running pool to see who can bag him first."

"I see," Evie replied slowly.

"Oh, if you're friends with him, please don't say anything. It's kind of an inside office joke amongst us, girls. I mean, come on; he is hot, isn't he?"

Isn't he?

Evie's eyes widened with insult and a protectiveness she found totally justified.

"No, I won't say anything." She agreed, but not out of some unspoken sense of camaraderie or sisterhood. If for no other reason, she didn't want Evan to feel awkward when he came in for his meetings. No, she'd keep their little office bet a secret, but a very strong part of her felt in the wrong for doing so.

These girls are worse than at the strip club.

EIGHT

After work, Evie walked home alone. Before ascending the three flights of stairs, she crossed the street over to Carson Beach, unwilling to sit in her once-craved solitude. She removed her shoes and let her toes sink into the gritty sand. The sun hadn't quite settled for the evening. It glittered gold and silver streaks across the water. Its orange glow was warm and soothing. The salty air tugged at her memories. She felt like she was home, even if only in spirit.

Life in Boston continued to prove so much more complex than it had been in Fallhaven. As much as she hated herself and her inner voice for antagonizing her, she couldn't stop dreaming about Lucca. She hated him for what he did to Rob. She wanted nothing to do with him, but when night came and she curled up under the sheets, she couldn't keep herself from dreaming about his silky skin against hers, his warm breath lingering on her body, pulling her down deeper and deeper into his darkness. Pulses of agonizing pleasure rushed through her bones. Evie knew that no matter where Evan hid her, she'd never escape her own desires for Lucca.

She sighed, as visions of Evan flashed through her mind, the Evan from her dreams, the Evan she'd been wrongfully objectifying—her Evan. Better than her mind's image of him, his body standing in front of her at work constricted her chest. Tall, slender, tousled hair, and pin-straight tie tucked behind his tailored suit, those big brown eyes locking with hers, aghast. She remembered what Dawn said about the bet the girls had running around the office.

Evie hugged her body tight while caramel ribbons of hair flailed around her face in the warm summer breeze. She scowled at the sand between her toes washed over by the surf as the tide rolled in. She lifted her foot, twirling her pointed toes around in circles through the foam.

"Those skanks don't deserve you, Evan."

Do you?

***

"I'm leaving now. Do you need anything before I go?"

Evie's eyes opened. Senses alerted, heart thumping, she looked over at Evan now standing by her side, his trousers rolled up and bare feet firmly planted in the sand next to her. His suit jacket and tie were gone. He had his shirt sleeves up past his elbows, hands tucked into his pockets. He met her gaze with a cautious stare through his periphery.

"I thought you already left," she said.

"I told you, I had some business to wrap up. I didn't think I'd run into you at the office. I hope that didn't embarrass you."

She huffed and turned to stare back out into the harbor, transfixed by its golden beauty, its gorgeous warm light. "It shocked me a little. I didn't realize you went by there so often."

"I told you I did business with the company." He joined her gaze cast out over the water." And what do you mean, so often?"

"Nothing. Some of the girls there enjoy when you grace the office with your presence, that's all." She snickered and continued twirling her toes through the wet sand.

Evan cracked his sweet crooked grin, maintaining his sideways glance. "Is that so?"

"Mm-hmm. I'm pretty sure they're all trying to get in your pants. It's safe to say I'm the only girl there who doesn't want to fuck you."

Who said we don't want to?

Evan's amusement waned, eyes shifting down to the movement of Evie's toes in the sand. "So you're all set then? I'm going to leave tonight." His tone saddened her, such poignancy made all too prevalent in her eyes. She kept them hidden from his view. No, she wasn't ready to be alone. She wasn't ready to be without him.

"I'm sorry, I told the girls I wouldn't say anything. I didn't want you to feel embarrassed next time you went into the office," she said. "If it makes you feel any better, I was tempted to bitch-slap one of them. I can't stand her anyway, and I know how you feel about sex and all. It's not right that they—"

"It's fine, Evie." His tone was curt. "I have to hit the road. Do you need anything or not?"

She straightened her posture from his terse response. "Geez, Evan. I was only joking about the whole sex comment. Do you even know how to goof around?" She batted him playfully across the chest, searching for a bit of levity in their otherwise awkward accord, beaten to death on multiple accounts. She looked back up to the harbor.

There was a long pause between the two, and Evie watched Evan through the corner of her eye. His jaw flexed as though mulling over a thought in his head. She'd seen that contemplative stare before—on her—on Lucca.

Before Evie could decode his thoughts, Evan nodded, decisive. He cleared his throat and pulled his hands from his pockets.

"Goof around, huh?" he said with a crooked brow. He bent down, tossed Evie over his shoulder, and then marched in a determined line into the surf.

"Whoa! Evan, what the fu—" She yelped out in protest before being submerged under the waves. Evan dropped both their bodies below the surface and clung to her, preventing her escape as she floundered.

Evie closed her eyes and sucked in a deep breath. Her hands searched through the waters to find his body while he adeptly handled her, raising her back up above the surface. Her legs whirled through the surf and found themselves anchored to his waist. She coughed thick salty water from her lungs as she clawed at his shoulders for stability.

"What the fuck was that?"

Evan smiled. "You said I didn't know how to goof around."

"Yeah, but that's not what I meant." She wiped her face, licking at her salt-lined lips.

They remained submerged for a few more moments before Evie looked down at her drenched white blouse, now transparent, revealing the black brassiere underneath. Self-consciousness had always been an emotion reserved for the unwarranted glares of strangers, but floating so close to Evan, those insecurities seeped into her pores. Her short skirt floated under the water's surface like seaweed, doing little to prevent his hands from reaching up to cup her rear, preventing her from washing away with the tide.

He was equally soaked. His white shirt, equally translucent, clung to his body. She ran her fingertips across the wet linen, inspecting a black mark showing through along his shoulder.

"What's that?"

Evan's smile faded as he looked down to her fingertips. "It's nothing." He hesitated. "Now let's get you home before you float away."

He carried her over his shoulder back up onto the beach. Evie mocked protest, but enjoyed every second of playful Evan, carrying her from the sea like a prize. Her savior—her Evan. She slid down him, safe and secure to the sand, unwilling to tear her arms away from his neck. Her body trembled, a faint quake deep within her core. She recognized it—the nearness, too close to be decent. Her inner voice purred, craving the flesh.

Feels good, doesn't it?

***

They walked hand-in-hand and smile-to-smile back up to her apartment. Once inside, Evie disappeared into the bathroom for some towels. Tossing a few in Evan's direction, he placed one or two along the floor to prevent the pooling water from damaging the floors. She disappeared back behind the door to shower and change.

When Evie stepped out from the tiny bathroom fully clothed, she was taken aback by Evan standing in the middle of her living room wearing nothing but a soft pink towel around his waist. She gasped out loud, her hand held up to conceal her startled outburst. He turned to face her with apology before her inner voice crept up from the confines of her core.

"Sorry, I don't have any extra clothes to change into. I'm just using your washer and dryer, and then I really need to hit the road," he said.

It took Evie a minute or two to roll her tongue up from the floor and snap her jaw shut. Her inner voice chided her to remember to breathe, but the sight of Evan's body reminded her how long it had been since she'd seen a man naked, and the last was not just any man—it was Lucca. Their bodies were so similar. Long, lean, and expertly carved. They were almost identical—almost. Evie noticed the black mark she saw under his shirt on the beach was a tattoo, a broken wing across his left shoulder, a very crude rendering, but artful and detailed nonetheless.

"When did you get that?" She waved a hand toward the ink. Evan looked down to his shoulder and scowled.

"A long time ago."

He turned his back to her. She studied his ink-capped shoulder, cut over to the muscular formation of his shoulder blades, and lowered her eyes, drifting down to the base of his spine.

"Must be rough regretting a tattoo when you'll see it forever… literally." She laughed, nervousness set off small tremors in her vocals, and her smile soured when Evan didn't respond to her humor. She shook her head and dismissed her jest. Gnawing at her lower lip instead, she used the self-inflicted pain to divert her attention from his flesh, a task that proved difficult. She forced her sights away before she assaulted her friend with her eyes or her mind any further. Her legs proved weak as she attempted to walk toward the futon.

"Are you hungry?" Evan asked.

Evie shot him a look of complete astonishment. "Am I what?" She flushed from the innuendo.

"Are you hungry? I'm guessing you didn't have dinner yet. I can make something for you in the kitchen while I wait for my clothes."

Evie hated her hormones.

"Oh… No, thanks."

She grabbed for her glass bowl without hesitation. Evan sat beside her in his towel. Evie's hands fumbled over each other as they fought their compulsions to rip at Evan rather than break up the marijuana bud therein. Head held down to the drug in hand, her eyes wandered to their corners, aching for a glimpse at the pink towel and what lay hidden beneath it.

Stop that, unless you plan on doing something about it.

Evie jumped up off the futon, disturbed by the proximity of his near-naked body. She marched over to the computer desk and plopped down in front of the laptop, allowing her licentious fingers to take out their angst against the touch pad instead of Evan. Damn the first track that played on their playlist—one of Evan's, tender musings, piano and acoustic guitar. Sweet, painfully beautiful music, just like Evan.

He made no comment. Instead, his eyes revealed all the sorrow her recoil may have caused. He resumed her efforts at packing the bowl and took a hit before extending the piece in her direction.

"Want some?"

Evie looked at him with wide and wanting eyes, incredulous.

Yes!

"What? No. I mean, yes but... no." She growled with frustration. "Give me that." She ripped the glass piece from his hand to take a long hard toke. She hoped the effects of the weed would numb her senses, calm her hormones, and silence her inner voice. She put all of her wants and needs into that hit, closing her eyes and holding the smoke in. Her head dizzied in an instant.

"I'll go wait out on the balcony, so this isn't so awkward," Evan said and motioned by her.

Evie shot up from her chair in protest. "No, you can't!" He turned to her, shocked, perplexed no doubt by her outburst. "You can't go stand outside in a towel where everyone can see you. That's got to be considered indecent exposure or something." She cursed her bumbling. "No, I'll go wait outside. You stay here where I can see yo—where no one can see you." She stormed past him onto the balcony.

Evan stood frozen and confused. She didn't bother to explain her behavior further. Let him think what he wants, she thought. Hell, maybe he could shed some light on the whole conflict of emotions raging through her body, because Evie was lost in her own darkness.

***

Neither one acknowledged each other through what felt like the longest hour of her life. Through it all, she stood with her back to her apartment, eyes closed and summoning visions of Lucca in her mind. At the moment, her murderous conquest seemed the lesser of two evils. Her efforts proved dismal as she evaluated their perfect bodies together. Her mind's eye arranged the apples-to-apples comparison, and melted her. They were so much alike.

Where are you, Lucca?

She dared to peek through a cracked eyelid at the darkening streets. He was out there somewhere. And for the first time since she went running from Fallhaven, Evie knew she'd run into his open arms willingly to escape the torture of hurting another friend.

***

79

Evan dressed and left without as much as a word to her. She was grateful for that. She stood on the balcony, listening to his sad music waft through the open French doors. Lovesick lyrics nipped at the nape of her neck. A single tear escaped and rolled over the crest of her cheekbone. Too afraid to turn around and miss his sticky sweet aroma, she stared out at the moon now hanging high above the harbor.

Why won't you let me have him?

"No. He's a good friend. Too good for me."

You can't hide forever.

"What is wrong with me?"

They're so very similar—and yet not.

"What are you talking about?"

Lucca and Evan—the Sempiternal.

"Hope said you were supposed to guide me. What are you saying? Who's the monster and who's my destiny?"

Do we really need to choose?

"There has to be a choice. It wouldn't be fair to Evan."

What about what's fair to Lucca?

"What if he decides he doesn't want me once he finds me?"

So you're choosing Evan then?

"No, I'm not. Even if I wanted to, I'll never shake Lucca."

He is perfect.

"They both are. What do I do? What do you want?"

I want out of this human existence. I want to rule the Sempiternal. He can help us.

A burst of crazed laughter came thundering past her lips. "Rule the Sempiternal?" She snorted. "I'm fucking crazy." Evie planted her forehead into the palms of her hands. "What am I going to do?"

You'll know. You'll feel me.

Evie released a heavy breath, unsure of even her own obscure reasoning. "I'll feel you." She repeated the whisper. "I'll feel you."

***

At about half past midnight, Evie told herself to go to bed. Evan was gone. Before long, Evie was alone in her bed and dreaming of Lucca. She dreamt of his perfect body stalking across the room sopping wet and naked. His ever-present sideways smirk teased as he loomed overhead, just as he did in her dreams each night. He purred. He clawed. Her body tingled as he ravaged her throughout the night. His adept fingertips traced nonsensical shapes along the contours of her body. She accepted whatever demeaning punishment he saw fit to administer.

"Fall from your graces," his melodic voice called out. "I know it calls you," he said. "I can show you the pleasure in your pain."

Her body quivered in his dark nothingness, wanting nothing more than to embrace his disease. His elongated canines scraped along her flesh, scratching, but never breaking the surface. Even in her dreams, she pined for his bite.

Thankfully, Rob's geisha remained in the shadows, unable to work her way into Evie's frustrated psyche. Just before Evie awoke the next morning, she peered up at his beautiful face. She gazed at large warm chocolate orbs floating overhead, framed with soft pale skin and pink pouty lips.

His name rolled off her tongue. "Evan."

NINE

The week endured. Summer temperatures during the day relinquished control of the nights to the uprising autumn.

Though they'd exchanged the occasional text message back and forth, Evie missed Evan's physical presence. Meeting Nate for lunch in his absence did little to tear him from her thoughts. Evan had replaced Lucca in her dreams. He catered to her every demented whim, and then left her moaning aloud and alone. She was grateful for the end of the week, when she wouldn't be by herself to fantasize over him, hoping for a short reprieve, even if only for one night.

As she stood outside the brownstone, she rolled back and forth on the balls of her feet, pulling at the thin scarf around her neck and jiggling the metal clasp on her bag. She'd not made new friends, aside from Evan, in nearly a decade.

"This is stupid," she said under her breath, but without any opportunity to second-guess herself and walk away, the door opened. She was committed.

"Evie! I'm so glad to you decided to make it." Leda welcomed her with a cordial grin and outstretched hand.

They ascended two flights of stairs to Leda's apartment, which Evie surmised was at least four times the size of her own little studio. A bit dazed at the sight of all the guests, she cringed as the memory clicked into place like a jigsaw piece—the party at Evan's family estate outside Fallhaven; the way Lucca's friend Mae threatened her, the college boys that slipped something in her drink and subsequently died for their misdeeds. The chilling memories ran down her back and shot down her legs to her feet, pinning her to the floor like nails.

"Are you okay, Evie?" Leda asked, closing the door behind her.

She blinked, refocused, and scanned the living room. It was populated by about a dozen people, but still offered a foreboding atmosphere that made her want to run and hide in a dark corner.

"There's no need to be shy. These are some of my closest family and friends." Leda nudged her forward. "Everyone, this is Evie, one of my co-workers. She's new to the city."

Some waved. Others lifted their cups at her.

Evie pried her feet free from their invisible anchors and was introduced to variations of Leda's warm and welcoming smile. The family members helped to account for the thick and springy curls crowning Leda's ebony complexion. Evie wasn't used to such diversity back in Fallhaven and felt completely inadequate and out of place immediately upon introduction.

"Come on, Evie. The wine is in the kitchen," Leda led Evie toward the back of the apartment into a large modern kitchen. The island was lined with several bottles of red, white and blush wines, opened and unopened bottles alike. "So what's your poison?" Leda selected a glass from the cupboard.

Fucking wine.

"I'll take water if you have it," Evie answered heavy with apology, still evaluating her surroundings and settling onto a kitchen stool in front of the wine. Leda looked back at her curiously, but offered her a chilled bottle of water. Evie coaxed a smile that didn't quite reach her eyes. "I kind of gave up drinking when I moved down here."

"See, Leda. We're not all boozehounds like you." A deep and inviting voice called out from behind Evie. She turned to find, a mouthwatering mocha-skinned man pass by her with a tinfoil-covered tray in hand. The aroma of the tray's spicy contents tickled her nostrils. He set it on the island near the wine, and then retrieved his own bottled water from the countertop behind Leda. Evie found it difficult to peel her eyes away as he placed a ceremonious kiss against Leda's cheek.

"Ha ha, very funny. You make me sound like an alcoholic." Leda giggled. "Evie, this is my brother, Claudio."

The man flashed a dazzling smile at Evie before nodding his bottled water in her direction and taking a swig. Her stomach flipped and her cheeks flushed before reciprocating with a shy grin and tipped her bottle likewise.

"Careful using that term, Leda. Those of us in recovery will string you up if you mock us for being strung out." Claudio winked at Evie as he dug under the tinfoil of hot food and popped a bite of whatever was in there past his lips. Evie followed his path, dazed as he sauntered to the living room.

"He's a bit blunt, but he's cute isn't he?" Leda smiled at her. "And he's single."

Evie pretended not to pay any attention to that last comment.

"He's a musician," she said.

"Does he play around here?"

"Yeah, he's got a few steady gigs at some pubs in Southie, but I don't think he markets himself right. He has the talent to play bigger venues."

Evie glanced over her shoulder toward the living room and made a mental note. Maybe one night she'd be brave enough to venture out on her own to see him play. An invisible noose of guilt tightened around her neck. She turned back to see Leda studying her with a coy smile hidden behind the rim of her wine glass.

Evie thought about asking for just one little sip to help ease the awkward tension gluing her to her perch at the kitchen island. Her mouth watered, but damn the wine. She'd only find Evan's disappointment in her at the bottom of the glass. So, Evie clung to the water bottle in her hand, her thumbnail picking at the label.

"So where is your family from?" Evie asked, staving off the awkward silence that threatened to settle between them. The peppery aroma of spiced meats and dishes were indicative of some exotic culture she'd been oblivious to, and was a welcome distraction from the topics of both men and liquor.

"Our family emigrated from Cape Verde when I was a little over one year old. Claudio was about four, I think. We grew up kind of southwest of where you live. Do you know the Upham's Corner area?" Ignorance remained plain on Evie's face, to which Leda waved her hand. "It doesn't matter. What about you, Evie? What brought you to Boston?"

Evie surveyed the food laid out around the kitchen and salivated. As fantastic as everything smelled, her stomach was still an anxious ball of self-doubt. She focused again on her bottle's label, but then looked up from violating her water's packaging to find Leda staring expectantly. Having done little to reciprocate in their conversation thus far, Evie didn't feel like starting now. Leda waited for her to answer by filling her glass with the remains of the moscato.

Evie's sights honed in on the lees sliding down the now empty bottle.

"I moved down earlier in the summer after someone very close to me was killed. I guess you could say it was a sobering experience." Blinking the pain away, she met Leda's wide-eye expression. "Anyway, I moved down here from Fallhaven and haven't done much since."

"Evie that's horrible." Sympathy and a bit of awkwardness carried in Leda's tone; Evie shrugged it off. For a split second, she feared she'd piqued a morbid interest in Leda. The threat of discussing Rob's death, or the person responsible, wrenched her belly like a knife. Such tense worrying didn't last long though. Leda's gaze softened as she drank from her glass. "I'm sorry to hear that... Where are you from, again? I've never heard of Fallhaven."

Evie chuckled and continued playing with her water bottle. "I'm sure not many people have. It's a small fishing town about four and a half, maybe five, hours north of here." She was hoping the interrogation was coming to close, her pulse only slightly reduced by Leda's presence.

Just ask her if she's anteed up to fuck Evan.

Evie bowed her head down to stifle the rumbling of possessiveness surging in her core. She doused her subconscious' curiosities with a gulp of water. Though eyeballing the selection of wines across the countertop, she considered silencing her inner voice with something more potent. Quickly dismissing the notion, she straightened in her seat. Evan's efforts aside, past experience dictated drinking again would only surrender control over to the bitch. Evie decided against it.

When she peered up, Leda was countering her glare with quiet innocence over the rim of her wine glass before looking up over Evie's shoulder. A flicker in her eyes, a silent nod, and Leda sipped her wine once more. "Let's go in the living room and join the party," she said.

The anchor of anxiety that usually kept her in place was curiously absent. Evie followed, glad to be amongst fellow humans. After months of solitude cooped up with Evan, she thought Leda, and possibly even Claudio if she were lucky enough, could offer her some semblance of a normal life again.

***

As Evie settled into a seat between two large Cape Verdean women, she noticed the whole group sat in a circle with one woman standing in the middle. She was dark, darker than most, petite and naturally beautiful with curves and long sun-kissed hair.

Evie took in all the faces around her, settling on Claudio's warm and inviting smile. He stood at the edge of the room leaning against a doorjamb. Her cheeks flushed with a warm tingle, likely turning a shade not easily concealed by her pale complexion. She distracted her thoughts with her water bottle.

Leda moved to join the young beauty at the center of attention.

"Okay, everyone, I want to thank you all for coming this evening. This is my dear friend, Sister Lima visiting from Cape Verde. She's graciously offered to present us all with our own past-life readings tonight. Remember everyone, this is all in fun, so please don't be jealous when she tells you that I was the Queen of Sheba in a past life and you were all my adoring subjects." Everyone laughed—except for Evie. She sat up in her seat cautiously masking her compulsion to jump out of her skin.

This ought to get interesting. Normal people don't have Sempiternal monsters hunting them—not like us.

Her inner voice purred deep within her subconscious, delighted by the prospect of being summoned forth. When she checked, the exotic priestess was smiling back at Evie. The young woman had a calmness about her much like the old sage named Hope who'd read Evie's fortune a few months back.

Though docile grin aside, Sister Lima's presence killed Evie's comfort.

Evie listened as the psychic went around the room, telling of past lives of peasant women and exotic locales, each story as jovial and heartwarming as the last. The room of friends and family buzzed with laughter, and it all translated to chaos in Evie's head. As soon as her time came, the laughter would cease.

There's no happy ending for us. Is there, stupid girl?

Evie's last tarot card reading replayed in the static channels of her memory. She'd been given a cryptic message about the Devil and her inevitable love for him. There was mention of a past life, but it was so tragic Hope struggled to continue the reading. It was soon after that she met Lucca and Evan and learned of her destiny intertwined within the secret realm of the Sempiternal.

All the memories of the reading gripped at her heart. She'd never placed much stock in the likes of psychics and fortune tellers, all theatrical kooks and fraudsters. But Hope was terrified by what she saw in Evie. No amount of Broadway theatrics could account for the accuracy of what she saw in Evie, her past, and her future. Nor could she deny the truth behind who and what Lucca was. Evie doubted things would be any different with the young priestess and cringed from the thought.

Once Sister Lima made her way to Evie, she paused. Her Cheshire grin widened and her hazel eyes danced with excitement as she moved toward Evie. Her skittishness again being taken out on the thin scarf around her neck. The more Evie fidgeted, the more Sister Lima appeared amused by her.

"You're nervous, Evie. There's no need to be. You're in safe company." The priestess' thick Creole accent carried sweetly through the air. She extended a delicate hand out toward Evie. "I am truly honored to be in your company, and I am awed that you've won his favor."

A cold threat stiffened Evie's spine. All eyes honed in on her. From across the room, she heard Claudio harrumph before marching out to the kitchen. Her skin crawled as she continued scanning the room.

"I don't know what you're talking about," Evie said on heavy guard.

"You're amongst friends, Evie. There's no need to worry. You are truly special. His gift is beautiful, isn't it?"

Leda stepped over, gesturing her hands through the air.

"Whoa, whoa, whoa. I'm the Queen of Sheba, remember? I should be getting the gifts, not this commoner."

The room erupted in boisterous laughter. Evie forced a smile and was immensely grateful for the diversion so she could excuse herself.

"Leda, where is your bathroom?" Evie asked.

"It's just through the kitchen."

As Evie excused herself from the party with a nod, the priestess reached out and grabbed her wrist with a firm grip. The woman's touch sizzled up Evie's arm and rushed through her body.

"You're being selfish, Evie." She hissed under her breath. "You can't keep them all to yourself."

Evie shuddered at the young priestess' touch and did her best to inconspicuously yank her arm away. The dark-skinned woman glared at her through sparkling green eyes, her tongue danced across her lips. Evie recognized the mannerism, though she was used to it being accompanied by depthless pools for eyes glittered with golden flecks. Evie's entire body screamed in terror from the correlation.

Escaping into the kitchen, she stopped short of the bathroom, merely a diversion to hide from the voodoo woman's scrutiny. Evie slouched down on a stool with a huff, her hands supported her heavy head. She fought a tremor that chased her from head to toe.

"What the fuck just happened?" Feeling drained, weak, and violated, Evie was careful to keep her thoughts to a low whisper.

The young priestess had sensed something in her; that much she knew for sure. She had no idea what she meant by being special or selfish.

"To be honest, I don't believe in that voodoo bullshit either."

Evie raised her eyes up, dazed and unaware she wasn't alone. Claudio flashed an arresting beam and extended a freshly opened bottle of water across the counter to her.

She sat up straight and accepted his offering.

"Well, it gives me the creeps," Evie said, raising the water to her lips. "Thanks."

Claudio turned his eyes down to his own bottle and smiled. Evie enjoyed his boyish charm rimmed with sarcastic wit, all wrapped up in a creamy mocha package with hazel eye trim. And his presence calmed her in a way she needed. She looked down at his arms, tattoos of various Bible passages and religious symbols interwoven with tribal and abstract designs covered his skin.

"You have a lot of ink," she said. It had been some time since she had made small talk with anyone. Her inability to confidently flirt with a man was frustrating.

"Yeah, some were planned… some weren't. I've made some pretty dumb decisions in my day. Hence the bottle of water." He waved his bottle in the air between them. His low chortle that prickled along her skin in a delightful way. "Anyway, I find I make fewer stupid decisions when I'm not wasted."

"I know what you mean." Her eyebrows hiked up her forehead.

After a short pause for Claudio to finish off his water, he sucked at his teeth and asked, "Are they real?"

Evie nearly spit a mouthful of water in his face. She gaped back at him in wide-eyed amazement. "What?"

Her jaw fell slack. Claudio laughed while she searched around her body for any indication of what he may have been referring, clutching at her chest.

The Sempiternal?

"Your eyes, Evie." He continued in his fit of laughter. "I've known some girls who wore contacts to make their eyes that blue... But since you appear so concerned, may I say everything looks perfectly proportioned to me."

Her cheeks tingled, and she accepted his compliment. Her crystal blue eyes were one of her best features, after all. Even Lucca found pleasure in them. But her reaction to Claudio clinched it; she really was out of practice interacting with men.

"Are you having fun tonight?" he asked.

The frissons running through her body were a mix of emotions she found difficult to qualify. "I guess I'm not very good at socializing."

"Yeah, I always found it easier with a drink in my hand, too."

Evie's shoulders dropped by an inch or so. "Something like that."

"Don't worry, Evie, I'm not trying to pry. I can tell this is new for you."

"Am I that obvious?"

Claudio bent down to rest his elbows against the island top between them, leaning in and wetting his lips. "A little." He hitched his shoulders. "For those of us who've been there, it's just easier to pick up on the signs. I hope I'm not making you uncomfortable. We don't have to talk about booze and recovery."

She wanted to melt into his smile, hold up in his charm and rest peacefully is his charismatic company.

"Do you have any tattoos?" His eyes rolled along her. Unlike when Lucca surveyed her bodyscape, Evie wasn't nervous under Claudio's gaze. Her high priestess was churning in the dark crevices of her core, igniting with excitement.

More...

"I have wings on my back. That's it."

"A pretty little angel," Claudio beamed. "Do they work? Are you going to fly away on me?"

She giggled and shook her head. No, she didn't want to run and hide from Claudio at all.

***

Evie caught a cab back to her apartment and chalked up her evening as a win.

Overall success aside, a restless, throbbing ache refused to allow her body peace over Sister Lima's "selfish" remark. The excitement of being called out, the prospect of encountering someone who sensed she was more than she appeared, stirred her inner voice. It also left Evie queasy.

Well past midnight, but barely over the Summer St Bridge, Evie struggled to admit the implication lacing the priestess' comment.

"Impossible."

Is it? She knew.

She shook her head. "No."

"You say something sweetheart?" Muffled by the Plexiglas partition, the cabby's voice reminded Evie that she wasn't alone. She glanced at the old man through her periphery. A weary set of eyes overlaid with bushy eyes brows scrutinized her through the rearview.

"Nope. I'm fine." Her voice croaked, and she treated it with a wad of saliva forced down her throat.

Rather than focus on the grimy film layering the partition and the eyes monitoring her from the other side, or the stench of the taxi's interior and the running meter, she watched the city whiz by in a blur of neon lights. Beyond the glow of the city, shadows shifted in the dark, unsettling her stomach. One such movement caught her eye, just past the red radiance of a traffic light. The hair at the back of her neck stood on end. Golden orbs floating through a thick black cloud consumed her mind's eye.

"Stop!" She called out to the driver and immediately fished through her purse for some cash.

"Here? We're still a ways up L Street from your stop. Are you sure you want to get out?"

"Yes, please. That's fine." She tossed more than her fare at the cabby and slammed the car door behind her.

He's here.

A need to seek out the sinewy figure drifting behind the nearby convenience store called her body forward like an invisible cord pulling, encouraging her into the dark. Guided by her subconscious urges, unsure what she planned to accomplish, she stalked behind the storefront. A shiver ran down her from head to toe. Her core throbbed and melted below her hips.

"Lucca?" A faint quiver in her voice carried through to her lower lip. A light layer of tears beaded along the rim of her eyelids. Evie wrapped her arms, squeezing around her waist.

She stood at the mouth of the alley. Light poured over her shoulders, but did not illuminate the passage enough to reveal much more than an old dumpster and an overabundance of garbage bags surrounding it.

She waited, her heart pounding and pumping dread through her veins, her high priestess thrumming from the center of her body like a beacon. "Hello?"

Every nerve in her body crackled. Adrenaline surged, but the magnetic force waned. The bass of a passing car shook her from behind, ringing in her ears, but she hyper-focused on the few empty feet in front of her.

Relief gave oxygen to her lungs and fueled the scourge of her inner voice.

Nothing.

TEN

The trek back home taxed her muscles. Each footfall inspired a chain of seismic waves to scream up her body and resonate through her chest. Their ricochet settled in the soft crevice between her lungs, and was then snuffed out by the frantic rhythm of her heartbeat. Amidst her brewing anxiety attack and the streets of South Boston, the high priestess resisted their retreat.

Go back.

"Shut the fuck up." Her hiss carried through the cool midnight air. She slammed her hands against her ears to stifle the inner chaos. Though too compelling, her subconscious' goading nipped at the back of her neck. Its acidic pull, like an exposed nerve, held her in place. Evie glanced over her shoulder.

He's out there.

"Stop it. We had a good night. Let's leave it at that."

Resolve hardened. Sights set a foot ahead at the pavement, she pressed forward.

Along the edge of her periphery, golden lights drifted across the crest of her wake. With each glance over her shoulder, they'd vanish. Their phantasmal form never took shape. Lucca never materialized. Before long, Evie was scampering up three flights of stairs and huddled under her comforter.

Soon...

Her eyes itched, her lids heavy. Last she checked her phone, it was two in the morning, and clouds dominated the night sky, concealing what pale light the moon shed into her apartment.

***

A sound, like thunder, pulled her from the geisha's usual taunting, followed by the rustling of footsteps. Evie's pulse quickened. A mental check cued up in her mind. The feature highlight on the reel: when she slid the deadbolt into position. The grating of the metal on metal scored the inside of her skull.

"The door's locked. It's just a dream." Her mouth moved, but her voice remained prisoner to the terror holding it inside. She opened her eyes wide. Consumed by the black of night, she shut them. Her body stiffened, and Evie begged her treacherous heartbeat not to give away her position. Such silent prayers failed as hands found purchase under the covers. The only sound, the swooshing of the bed linens.

Tears seemed moot. Screaming, pointless and secondary to the fear. Resisting the urge to identify her intruder, Evie lay on her back, paralyzed and strategizing her defense. Each tick of her racing pulse counted down to the moment she could headbutt the figure, and then follow up with a knee to the groin, gut, or anything else that might afford her enough opportunity to wriggle out from underneath him.

A set of calloused fingertips caressed her ankles and moved their way upward. Tickling and teasing, they rounded over her knee caps, sliding around the tendons behind and spidering their way up the back of her thighs. A breath's silky coating followed in the path of those slithers, layered by a voice.

"Can you feel it calling? Let me show you." Upon registering the low baritone, the tension in her body thawed. Lucca's soft murmur rolled over her like the homesick tide.

"How did you find me?"

"I'll always find you, Evie."

She released a tremendous exhale, overwhelmed with relief. The weight of her body melted her into the mattress. His own mass had her pinned. The golden flare of primal urging rimming his deep pools—those eyes she fantasized about night after night—was vacant. The aching need in the center of her body throbbed, anticipating their starlight's glow.

No more waiting.

While her high priestess surged with provocation, a moment of reality called out from the back of Evie's conscience. The image of a smile, infrequent and mesmerizing, along with deep set russet eyes protested in the shrouded corners of her mind. Her body quivered. A pinch in her chest, a bit less willing than the building moisture at the base of her core.

"Wait…"

"Shh." Lucca traced the tip of his noise along her jawline, taking her in with a voracious inhale. His hand navigated down her belly to manipulate the agonizing node between her thighs. Evie curved her back, pushing her chest upward. Skin and nipples puckered, her body feening for a hit of his citrusy zest. Thirsting want intensified in her center, bleeding out to all extremities. Lucca purred. "It's time, Evie."

Yes, please now.

Her subconscious ignored the strident sirens blaring in her head. She willingly spread out beneath him, allowed him to settle between her legs. The bare minimum of her panties did little to hold him back, as Lucca crept underneath them.

She groaned, while his fingers massaged her from the inside out. Hands as familiar as a vibrant memory, as haunting as a ghost, handled her body with expert precision. His lips dragged across her collarbone.

I want more.

"Yes… more," She said in harmony with her inner voice. She angled her hips and directed him deeper into her erogenous epicenter.

His snickered rumbled over her before he ran the tip of his tongue across her lips. "Anything and everything you want. Just tell me…" His head dipped down, teeth dragged along the taut skin across her breasts. Every playful nip strained her muscles, challenged her reserve.

The significant pressure of his arousal pressed down on her. He pulled his working hand away, leaving Evie with a hollow, unfulfilled need, but only briefly. Lucca shifted over her. Slick with her own pleasures, that same hand came down against her hip bone, possessing her in his hold.

"Tell me." A sharp force laced his words.

His mere silhouette-form against the pitch black of her apartment set Evie's heart alive with warning. Unbearable and undeniable. His golden-flecked glare remained elusive.

"What about…?" Her brow knit. Her chest burned. A vision of warm, caring eyes flashed before her. The high priestess stirred in the caverns of her dark core. Despite her reluctance, Evie's hips moved, commanding Lucca into her.

Stop being selfish, stupid girl.

"He knows the rules." Lucca's growl, a bit more penetrating, reverberated against her as it was exorcised from his body.

"What…?"

She reached up. His angular features, recognizable to her fingertips, but the lack of his devilish stare continued to frighten her. She questioned her lucidity and recalled the wraithlike figure sitting across her bedroom back home, its amorphous form resting in her rocker recliner. She dizzied from the notion that the man on top of her was nothing more than a dream.

For a moment the fear penetrating her chest diminished as a spark lit, like a fire ignited in the blackness above her. She prayed to see his eyes, to know this was real. The heavy scent of his excitement permeated the stagnant air. His body, a clear contrast against the crisp linens encasing them. The joining of their bodies, every firm inch of him, had never been so tangible in all her dreams.

She moaned and writhed under his seemingly perfect reality.

"I've followed the covenant," he said, impatience thickening his tone. Lucca worked his groin against her, grinding into her. Her body reflexively acquiesced and mimicked his movements. "I've waited for you to tell me. Say it."

"God, just fuck me…" Her panting grew erratic, mind obsessed with the here and now.

Desire and alarm fused together in rhythm with their hips. The faint glow of his eyes intensified and smoldered. The glow she'd hoped to bask in never came, a crimson fire ignited in its place.

"You can have the world, Evie. Nothing will be impossible, but you need to tell me."

"I…" She tossed her head back into her pillow. Battling the panic attack and converging orgasm, her breath hitched. She pinched her eyes shut and bit down on her lip. Delicious pulses wracked her body and clouded her judgment. "Please…" Her whimper, though undeniably the result of penned up carnal aggression, carried an air of guilt and desperation.

As Evie looked up to him, the blood red of Lucca's stare deepened. She taloned his shoulders and pushed against him.

"He knows we are inevitable," Lucca said.

She cried out. Her voice cracked, working to an unbeatable climax, but continued to resist the pleasure it afforded.

More…

"Stop…" The conflict tore into her as Lucca held her in a firm grip. He continued thrusting, pulling against her skin, pressing deeper into her. Her excitement waned. "Stop!"

The forceful bucking of his hips ceased almost instantly. His fiery gaze disappeared into the night.

Evie awoke, belly down, dry humping the mattress. Her movements slowed, eyes strained to focus.

Regulating her breaths, she turned on her back in a cold sweat and huddled under the comforter. Across the black of her studio, she found no trace of his shadow, that grim phantom figure. The only evidence of her dream was the creamy dampness between her legs, the thundering beat of her heart, and the sweat lining her brow.

"Shit, I don't know how much more of this I can take." Evie licked the salt off her lips and rolled over.

***

It started off as a soft murmur, a delicate vibration creeping up from her murky subconscious. The subtle annoyance grew louder, clacking, and pulled Evie from her REM cycle. In whimpering protest, she rolled over, pillow wrapped around her head to muffle the disturbance. As the rattling persisted, her frustration increased. She growled and peeked one eye open. Stark white light blinded her, and she fumbled with one hand for her cell phone atop the nightstand.

Upon her first attempt to answer the call, her voice broke. She cleared the morning grogginess from her throat and took a second stab. "Hello?"

"Good morning, Sunshine."

"Evan?" Excitement sat her up at full attention. "You're home?"

Evie blinked, pupils adjusted to the sunlight, pulse quickened. His chuckling response tickled down her spine.

"No, I'm still in Fallhaven. Why do you sound so surprised it's me? Were you expecting someone else?"

For a split-second, she had considered Nate since he had a knack for pestering her lately, but shook the thought away. "No... When will you be back?"

She didn't mean to, but worry echoed in her tone. Her fingers twisted the pale blue bed sheet across her lap.

"Probably not for another week or so, but I should have something for you when all is said and done." If Evan wasn't returning from her hometown with an answer to her prayers; a body, a cold drink—a Sempiternal offering, then she wasn't biting. Brow furrowed, Evie dipped her head down and allowed silence to fill the pause in their conversation. "Evie...? What's wrong? Did something happen while I've been away?"

"No." Disappoint lay heavy on her chest and set her back down onto her pillow with her free hand across her forehead. "Everything's fine. I'm just... lonely, I guess."

The aching between her legs resurrected from just a few hours prior. She rolled onto her side and squeezed her thighs tight to savor the throbbing that synced up perfectly with Evan's next exhale.

"You're going to work and coming home, right?" he asked.

"Yes… Well, I went to my co-worker's little get-together last night."

"And?" His reproachful tone evoked a shrug, Evie tossed around in the bed until coming back to a seated position.

"And I drank water, then came home."

"You haven't run into anyone have you?"

She recalled the electric buzz in the midnight air, the shifting shadows along the edge of the street. Though mentioning such portents to Evan would likely only cause needless concern.

"No." Evie accentuated her answer with a roll of her eyes hidden from her tone, and such movement prompted her to survey the layout of her apartment. No, there was no indication that Lucca actually visited her outside of her dreams last night.

"Well that's good." Evan continued clearly oblivious to her digressive thoughts. "I'm sorry this is taking so long, but I promise I'll be home as soon as I can… And Evie…"

As she stood to make her way to the coffee table and collect her glass bowl and baggy of weed, Evie paused. The unspoken proposition in his tone left her hanging. Her tongue played along the edge of her lower lip.

"Yeah?"

She shivered as his raspy sigh transmitted through the phone's receiver. The thrill of his breathing, like an echo from her dream, left her waiting and wanting.

"I miss you too," he said.

"I didn't…" say she missed him, though to state such a claim was a lie. The heaviness of the truth she held in set her down on the futon. She toyed with the pipe in her hand, inspecting the colorful swirls trapped in the glass. "Please just get back here as soon as you can."

Evan harrumphed before answering, "I will." The force of his huff scraped against her ear pressed to the phone. "Just remember to be careful and call if you need me. Otherwise, I'll try to check in with you later."

"Okay, bye." Evie ended the call, stared at his number displayed on the screen before breaking apart a tiny bud and packing the bowl. Eyes closed, smoke rolling over her tongue, she concentrated on the ritualistic act of taking a long hard toke. "I can't live like this anymore."

We can have the world.

Eleven

Doing as Evan instructed was a simple task over the week to come. The habitual process of filtering in and out of the office, submitting spreadsheets and heading home, reduced her to a ghost-like state. Evie embraced the anonymity of it all, even as the affliction of her thirst deepened with each passing day.

Into the tail end of her work week, she stood at the ladies' room counter, lathering her hands with harsh antiseptic hand wash.

"Just a few more hours to go, and then we can head home," she said quietly and connected with her spectral image glowering through the mirror.

And do what, wait? I'm getting restless.

Her body ached under the pleating of her black skirt. The sensual hauntings from her dreams refused to relent, no matter how she fought to focus on the monotony of her work throughout the week. Only in these moments by herself did they demand her attention.

She stared back at her reflection, desperation jabbed at her chest

"Maybe we just need to get laid."

That's a start, but not enough, stupid girl. Listen to me!

She shook the chide away and failed to detect the whoosh of the door opening behind her.

"Hey girl, there you are." Leda's voice came pouring over her shoulder like an icy wind gust. "I feel like I haven't seen you all week."

Evie froze, considered for a moment that Leda caught her internal dialogue. Embarrassment tingled under the skin stretched along her cheekbones. Her fears dispelled, however, as Leda approached with an innocent and welcoming grin.

"Hey Leda, how's it going?" Evie dipped her head down and feigned interest in the hem of her skirt.

"I'm good. I'm good." Leda stood with her arms folded across her chest, the innocence of her smile yielding to something far more telling. "You know my brother hasn't stopped asking about you since last weekend. I was hoping I could've connected with you sometime in the office, but it looks like we've both been busy."

Evie huffed softly and turned to mask the smirk pulling at the corner of her mouth. Her interest piqued with the mention of Leda's charismatic musician-brother. He had occupied a tiny corner of her mind since the party, not entirely exclusive from her building carnal thirst or Sister Lima's hushed commentary about her selfishness.

Evie glanced at her reflection in the mirror.

Yeah, he'll do.

"Your brother seems like a real charmer." Evie cleared her throat and continued to play with her steel grey blouse, rubbing her contours and inspecting her curves in the mirror. The faint quiver of her body, barely concealed by the motions of her roaming hands.

"Uh huh… and he's a great guy. I'm not just saying that because he's my brother. He keeps asking me to give him your number, but as an upstanding member of the Human Resources community, it would be unethical of me to divulge such information without your consent."

Evie lifted a hand to her neck, brushing her palm along the phantom burn from the spiked collar in her dreams. She caught the dulling excitement reflecting off her mirror image.

"I don't know Leda. Timing is really bad for me to be meeting someone new."

"Is it because of your ex-boyfriend from back home?" Leda asked. "Because Claudio's not an aggressive guy like that. He likes to play it cool and sneak in on the friend tip." She extended her hand in a long swooping motion for emphasis, popping the last syllable between her lips.

Evie giggled. "Good to know... but no, that's not it." Then she paused to reflect on Leda's remark; Nate was the perfect scapegoat. "Well, maybe a little."

Leda eyed her and shook her head with a crooked smile. Evie felt as though she'd caught onto her vibe well enough. She set her shoulders back and motioned toward the door.

"Well, I guess I should get back to work. I have a ton of paperwork to wrap up before the weekend," Evie said and slipped past Leda.

"Oh yeah, no problem." Leda cleared her path. "So I'll just let Claudio down easy, but if you should happen to run into him on the streets..."

Evie turned back to her friend, knowing nothing good could come from a comment like that.

***

Evie pushed Leda's comment as far back in her mind as it would allow. She half-expected to find a follow up email when she logged back into her computer, some cheeky comment from Leda about how charming her brother was. Thankfully, her inbox was empty.

Her cell phone unfortunately was not so lonely. Nate had issued a relay of texts while she was in the ladies' room.

How's ur day going?
Miss u.
Dinner tonight?

Evie shook her head and allowed a half-hearted smile to line her mouth before declining. Meeting for lunch was one thing. It was the middle of the day, out in the open, and for a set duration. A date with Nate was an impossible prospect.

Sorry, not tonight.

She set her phone aside and began sorting through invoices again. Residual gnawing, an unsettling sensation in her gut kept her glancing back at her phone.

I want more, stupid girl.

"No. Not Nate... Not Claudio. Get it out of your head."

Whose head?

She groaned and forced her mind to the task—and papers—at hand. Dollars totaling in obscene amounts and destined to or from various worldly locales twisted her brain as she entered one digit after the next into her spreadsheets. One particular payable caught her eye. Carver Assurance International Co, Inc. was being paid over three million dollars for services rendered.

"Shit, that's a lot of money," she said under her breath.

Evie attempted to interpret the invoice, but the damned thing may well have been written in Cyrillic. One point of information leaped from the page; the business' address. If her bearings were correct, that meant Evan worked only one block from her office.

Phantom fingertips skittered down her spine. She peeked out of her cube and scanned the office. Content to be left alone with her curiosities, she turned and spied out her window.

A yellow cab whizzed by. With otherwise minimal traffic, the streets were quiet in her corner of the industrial park. However, roadway activity was far from her concerns; what lay beyond it called out to her attention. Evie analyzed the details differentiating surroundings that she'd not bothered to notice until now. Skewed just to her left, the nearest building sat diagonally across the way. Its minimalist design of concrete, mirrored-glass, and faintly-chipped exterior paint offered clear indication the structure was relatively new. Just past it, a taller, stronger-looking building with weathered art deco detail stood like an alabaster titan overshadowing its stout neighbor. An industrial warehouse, made of brick and grated window panels, flanked the elegant stone edifice. Evie took in a deep breath and strained to peer further down the street, all but pressing against the window pane for greater access to the outside. Most other buildings, while all commercial in nature, offered up their own uniqueness amongst the others. One building had a revolving door at its entrance; another, a small portico. Most warehouses looked similar, though one or two were blanketed by scaffolding and tarps, specifying construction efforts. Beyond their grey landscape, she made out the tips of the masts from the large draggers come to port at the nearby fishing docks.

An intangible pull drew her eyes back to the elegant building not much more than a block away. Its aged exterior did well to camouflage the structure amidst the utilitarian forms abounding within the industrial park. Evie squinted to make out the address etched into frieze above the entrance, but was unable to read the worn out numbers.

"He couldn't possibly be that close?"

The vibration of her phone answered her hushed musings. Evie jumped in her seat and turned to retrieve the cell off her desk.

2moro? Need u Babe.

Evie groused as her thumbs moved across the touch screen.

Sorry. Not a good weekend.

Quick to turn her phone off and stuff it in her bag, she only had a few more hours of work, and didn't need to engage in a back-and-forth texting marathon with Nate. Not with the stack of invoices she had waiting on her desk for processing. There were enough to keep her busy through the following week for Christ's sake. Evie picked up the Carver Assurance invoice again and entered the numbers she needed into her spreadsheet. Biting her lip while fighting a smile, the company's logo caught her eye; a set of wings not unlike those tattooed on her back.

Better judgment having succumbed to temptation, online search engines beckoned. Evie executed queries for "Carver Assurance" and "Evan Carver." Though with both yielding over four million search results, none quite fit the bill. Bitterness flooded her taste buds.

"There's got to be something out there."

She continued. Fingers pounded keyboard, their tempo precipitating the adrenaline swelling inside her. Evie entered terms such as "immortals," "vampires," and lastly "Sempiternal," but with thousands of websites, so many tailored toward popular convention, she found nothing definitive.

"Stupid pop culture. They've made it way too socially acceptable to be a blood-sucker these days." She spoke in whispers, scoffing at the computer screen and returning to her invoices.

***

At the end of the day, she stretched in her chair, rolling her head around to set off a crackling of joints down her neck. While she was in no rush to head back to an empty apartment, she didn't want to stare at paperwork anymore. Evie collected her belongings and sauntered slowly to the elevator.

Most of her co-workers had gone home already. Leda's office light was out and her door was locked. Val, thankfully, had left. Only a few faces lingered.

"Hey Evie." Beth chased after Evie while tossing her bag's strap across her chest. "A bunch of us are meeting up for some drinks downtown. Do you want to come?"

Evie's pulse quickened as dread pressed on her chest and forced beads of sweat across her forehead. A beer, maybe two, five, or even seven had a certain appeal. She salivated, recalling the sweet tang of a cold golden brew and thick foamy head. Her tongue played against the inside of her mouth.

"Umm... I'm really tired. It's been a long week," she forced herself to mumble.

"Are you sure?"

Evie took a second to seriously consider it, but with the address to Carver Assurance embedded in her brain, she had other plans before heading home. "Thanks anyway. I have a headache."

"That sucks." Beth shrugged. "Maybe next time?"

"Sure."

The girls boarded the elevator together. Beth stood by her side, humming and texting back and forth with friends, no doubt making plans to meet up.

Evie connected with her shadowy image reflecting off of the elevator doors and sunk into herself.

Who do you think she's talking to?

"Shut up," she said, careful to keep her utterance to a low growl.

"Hmm? Did you say something, Evie?" Beth turned up from her cell, a quizzical brow raised.

The guffaw of Evie's subconscious reverberated through her bones. Her jaw tightened, closing her teeth down into her tongue. The coppery bitterness of the self-inflicted damage pooled in her mouth. She nearly choked on it before clearing her throat. "Nope, just thinking out loud. Sorry."

As if to say "good enough," Beth dismissed her with a shoulder shrug and went back to texting before the elevator chimed and the doors opened. "Have a good weekend, Evie." She waved goodbye and split left off of the elevator.

Evie headed in the opposite direction, in pursuit of the alabaster titan and satisfying her curiosities. The prospect of Sempiternal in close proximity sent a welcome chill down her spine. Stepping out into the street, she was stopped short of her reconnaissance efforts.

Claudio waited, hands tucked into his jean pockets, tattoos displayed from under his rolled up shirt sleeves. He stood where "X" marked the spot she'd designated for Evan on her first day. His warm mocha complexion slightly rosy, and charismatic smile beaming at the sight of her.

The high priestess purred from inside her dark cave.

TWELVE

"I didn't think you were ever going to leave," Claudio said and strode forward.

Evie pulled the strap of her bag around her shoulder, reciprocating with a timid grin. "How long have you been standing here?"

"Leda got out of work about forty-five minutes ago, so…? Yeah, about that long."

"You've been out here waiting for almost an hour?"

"Some girls are worth waiting for." His beam spread ear-to-ear and coaxed a genuine smile free from her. "C'mon, let's get something to eat," he said.

Claudio offered his arm, but little choice in the matter. She paused before accepting his proposition and rolled her eyes over his tall, casually confident stature. The aching in the pit of her core made its presence known once more.

I want him, stupid girl.

Her inner voice's predatory coo knotted her stomach, and much against her better judgment, she accepted. She peered over in the direction of Carver Assurance, but was led away by much more corporeal urges.

***

Cutting the same path she was accustomed to walking with Evan, the two crossed over the bridge in the direction of her apartment. As was her natural inclination, Evie checked down side streets and scrutinized faces passing by.

"So how was your day at the office, dear?" Claudio raised with a playful brow and gleamed a brilliant white smile that was near impossible not to blush from.

"Just another day in paradise... And yours?"

"Not sure yet. It just started," he said. "I'm what you'd call a night owl."

"I get that." She nodded. "I used to stay up all night and sleep late when I lived back home."

"But now you're a slave to the nine to five."

She released a snorty chuckle. "Something like that, I guess."

Approaching Broadway and honing in on the familiar territory of her neighborhood, simulating normal life grew easier with each step by Claudio's side. Evie lost the compulsion to monitor the shadows.

"So what's for dinner?" she asked.

"You'll see."

He lured her along their path. Venturing dangerously close to her apartment, Evie's pulse raced under the assumption that Claudio may already know where she lived and had no plans of taking her out to eat. A mixture of dread and desire twisted in her belly.

Thankfully, he diverted her into a corner pub, which she'd passed by day in and day out, but never noticed. The hole-in-the-wall restaurant was lined with rich colored glass and dark mahogany wood. The familiar scent of booze and dust ignited painful nostalgia. Evie licked her parched lips. He guided her toward a table for two in the middle of the room. Tension eased as she scanned the room, confident she didn't recognize a single person in the place.

"I play here a lot," Claudio noted as he took his seat opposite her. "They set up an acoustic stage right over there in the corner."

"This must be the place Leda mentioned last week? She said you play in the area frequently." Evie stretched her neck out to see over Claudio's shoulder at a corner crowded by tiny wooden tables. "But how the hell do they fit a stage in here?"

He bowed his head slightly, and his smooth laughter carried through the pub's musty atmosphere. "They manage."

"I'd really like to come see you play sometime."

Claudio lifted an eyebrow. "Yeah? Well I'm here every weekend. Come check me out."

Already done. You look good enough to eat.

"Stop," Evie whispered under her breath.

"Stop what?"

She flushed. "No, not you, my phone. I thought I felt it vibrate."

"Texts from the ex?" Her brow knit, her head cocked sideways, and Claudio smiled back. "Leda told me about your ex-boyfriend. It's cool. There's no pressure here."

Before she could consider whether she was relieved by his pass on her, the bartender came over to take their order— or at least hers. He'd placed a sweating glass of water in front of Claudio.

"Seamus, this is my new friend Evie," Claudio said. "Evie, this is Seamus."

The tall brute of a man was covered in shamrock tattoos, and wore very little hair atop his head. Evie felt small in his presence. Seamus offered her a gentle grin though, and another edge of nerve melted away.

"Glad t'meet ya, love. What can I getcha?"

"I'll take a water too, thank you," she said shyly. With a nod, the barkeep handed menus to each of them and turned to fetch her drink.

"So you've never been here?" Claudio asked, sipping on his drink, more ice than water.

Evie shook her head and perused the night's specials. "No, I don't go out that much."

"That's a shame. This is a great city, if you ever get the chance to check it out."

A lump solidified in her stomach when she thought about exploring the industrial park for Evan's office. "I just haven't gotten around to it yet," she said.

"I'm a great guide." He raised both offering hands in the air.

"I bet you are."

Seamus returned, placing her iced water on the table. "So, d'ya know whatcha'd like?"

Evie looked to her left and eyed the beer taps. Her jaw gaped open slightly.

"I'll have my usual, Seamus." Claudio handed over his menu and jutted his chin at Evie. "Something caught your eye?"

She peeled her eyes away from the bar and back down to her menu. "I, uh... I'll have a Guinness pie."

Claudio grinned as Seamus left to place their orders. His tongue curled to cradle the tip of his glass as he eyed her.

"Looks like you want something other than pie." He took a swig of water. She replied with a coy grin and tucked a loose strand of hair back around her ear. Claudio took hold of her free hand. "Every day is different. It gets easier, I promise."

Instantly, Evie felt calmed by his touch. His features were striking; his voice, melodic and soothing. She looked down at her hand in his, and then wandered up his arm to the various tattoos lining his dark skin.

"So how long have you had those?"

Claudio shrugged off the question. "Each one varies," he said. "Every time I feel the urge to stick a needle in my arm I just go get some ink. It's healthier than the alternative, don't you think?"

What's our alternative?

Evie forced her introspective questioning to the back of her mind and focused on Claudio. He'd divulged a few details of his substance abuse last week, but if he indicated he was into needles and heroin, then she never picked up on it. She tried to read through the ink for signs of track marks along his beautiful brown skin, but found no such scarring.

"How long were you...?" She let her sentence hang, unsure how appropriate it would be to finish.

"It's okay, Evie," he said with his beaming smile. "I don't mind discussing it. It's actually kind of empowering. I've been clean for two years. I started off young with alcohol, pills, pot. Then a little coke here and there. Eventually none of that was enough. Dope was what broke me. A lot of people don't like needles, but I always have. I fell in love with the entire process of shooting up; that little pinch as the needle broke the skin, the overwhelming warmth, and then the chill contentedness that followed."

Evie cast her eyes down to the table, empathizing, though in a completely different manner. Getting drunk or high was one thing, a great escape. More precisely, she knew that yearning to get sucked into the void—to feel Lucca's nothingness. The fear of falling deeper was what held her back, but it was the longing for oblivion that kept her on the hook. As Claudio described his experiences, her desire intensified. The glaring difference between Claudio and herself was clear. He'd fallen into the abyss and found the courage to climb out. She still teetered on the edge, seduced by the euphoria.

She held her eyes away from him, but Claudio jostled at her hand, shaking away her reticence in the process.

"It's all right, Evie, really. I don't mind talking about it," he said with reassurance. "I also don't mean to romanticize it or anything because it also ruined my life. I betrayed my whole family's trust. I literally stole from Leda to get high. It was a one-sided love affair, I can see that now."

"I don't know that I've really talked about my... habits like this."

"And yet you're clean. That's amazing. How'd you do it on your own?" Pure caring and supportive interest relayed through his voice. Such earnest support was difficult for her to accept, but it warmed her heart nonetheless and prompter her to consider the question; how did she do it?

She searched around the room for the right words. From the exposed beam ceiling to the tread-beaten floor boards, nothing jumped out, save for a starting point; the veil of fog rolling across the harbor of her memories thinned. Greyed images of fishing boats, a lighthouse, and the neon signage of Sirens drifted from the gloom to the forefront of her mind.

"I drank a lot back home—too much according to my old best friend. My ex and I, we played around with pills and other hard shit a few years back. I made some stupid decisions and hurt a couple of people, so I gave it up before things got too bad, but he didn't. I couldn't let go of booze though, I loved getting wasted. Apathy was addictive, not alcohol." Evie paused and checked Claudio. He wasn't smiling or frowning. Instead, he squeezed her hand for comfort. "I used to drink my sorrows, I guess. But I quit that cold turkey when a close friend of mine was killed." Swallowing hard, she refrained from tearing up. "And then a new friend moved me down here and has been helping me stay sober. Although, to be honest I still smoke a lot of pot." She looked up, and Claudio snickered. "Don't hate me because of it."

"Never, Evie." He shook his head. "What you're trying to do is difficult. Since we're being honest, and if it makes you feel any better, my new dealer is a psychiatrist. Someday I hope to be reliant solely on tattoos, but right now I still need some help. It's all part of the process; replacing one dependency for another is common. Look at me; my new obsession is tattoos. Every time I feel the need for that little pinch, I run out and get something new. You should see me naked. I'm covered."

We could gorge ourselves on his body.

Carnal thrill flourished in her chest and rushed down, settling in her lap, and then withered out in cool waves down her legs. "Is it typical for new cravings to include a person, or even... sex?"

Evie lifted her eyes up and was met by Claudio's dazzling smile.

"Yes, even sex. Your body is waking up from years of chemical effluence, like it's recharged. Everything you're experiencing is normal. It's not uncommon to project our addictive inclinations onto a different substance, process... or person. It's not recommended by specialists on recovery, mind you. But I think it's human nature to redirect that need. You just have to manage it. And probably abstain from human contact throughout the first year."

What about the Sempiternal?

Evie shivered in her seat and held Claudio's eyes with hers.

"Recovery is a constant battle," he said. "But as long as you focus on the end goal, keep your eye on the prize, I think you'll be fine." The earnestness in his tone liberated the choke collar from around her neck. "I'm no expert though," he added. "Just repeating what I've been told."

Seamus returned with a monstrous burger and heaping side of curly fries for Claudio, and a steaming pot pie to place in front of Evie. Claudio's beam returned and he released her hand.

"Now c'mon. Enough commiserating. Let's eat."

Feeling lighter than prior to their impromptu dinner date, Evie grinned back at Claudio and spread her napkin over her lap. "Hey…" Intrigue arched his brow. "Thank you. I really needed this."

Pride flooded his features. "Healing begins from the inside out. Focus on you. The rest of us will still be here in the outside world ready to accept you when you're ready."

Listen to him, stupid girl. Feel me.

***

"Dinner was fantastic, Claudio. Thanks again," Evie said, rubbing her belly full with satisfaction and carbohydrates as they stepped out onto Broadway.

"It was my pleasure. So which way is your place?"

"Down that way, by the beach."

Claudio's brow lifted. "Wow, how'd you score that kind of real estate?"

"My friend." A flicker of culpability stabbed at her chest. As they neared her street, she found herself unwilling to let go. For the first time since moving to Boston, she was starting to feel normal. Acting against Evan's orders triggered remorse, but the need for human interaction was too great. "C'mon. Let's walk off that meal," she said.

"No arguments from me. Where do you want to go?" He smiled back.

Evie scanned her immediate surroundings. Though certainly not alone with Friday night city life on the rise, she found no trace of glowing orbs or trepidation. "Let's just walk."

Under a clear night sky, conquered by an intense full moon, she dragged him up and down nearby side streets. While the shadows followed at their heels, Evie didn't let them deter her from enjoying the simplicity of strolling side by side in comfortable silence with Claudio.

Before she was ready, they approached her front stoop. "This is me," she said.

Claudio looked around and approved. "Got yourself a nice little set up here."

Her accustomed crushing weight settled back down on her chest. "I really don't want to head up to an empty apartment," she said. "But I think I've occupied enough of your time tonight."

He laughed. "You are wearing me out with all these laps around your block, but it's all good." Evie pursed her lips, holding back a flirtatious grin while he laced his fingers with hers. "Do you want me to walk you in?" he asked, leaning in closer. To even Evie's own amazement, he placed the smallest of kisses against her hesitant lips.

Bring him upstairs. Let's have some fun.

"I don't know if that's a good idea."

Her whispered response, meant for both Claudio and herself, spoke hard truth. Though a wonderful time'd been had with Claudio, ruining it with sex—albeit some much-needed—seemed an injustice. If and when she slept with him she wanted it to mean something. She wanted to be free to enjoy him. And if anything he'd said over dinner resonated, it was that she was nowhere near ready for a meaningful relationship—not yet.

He hummed softly and straightened his posture. "You're right. I should follow my own advice." He chuckled. "Take your time, Evie, really. I can wait. Like I said, some girls are worth waiting for."

He raised her hand to place a small kiss atop it and walked her to the door. "Do you think you'd give a guy your number at least?"

Giggling back at Claudio was an easy task as she glided over the threshold. "I'm sure you can ask Leda."

"You can believe that." He tried to pull her into to one more embrace. She pushed him back him back out onto the front stoop.

"What happened to waiting?"

"It's been a couple of minutes." He licked his lips and shook his head. "No, sorry. You're right."

Every part of Evie's body knew this playful banter. As she recognized it, the night wrapped around Claudio's warm smile, revealing a familiar ghost. Boyish charm, dependable strength, and Rob's sweet smile bombarded her mind's eye. Her breath caught, the vision twisted. The darkness cleared, and the geisha stood with Rob's head dangling in her porcelain hand. A crimson shower came down, covering the vision in gore.

Evie shuffled back half a step and blinked. The nightmare faded.

Confusion clouded Claudio's face. "Evie? Are you okay?"

A frown replaced her light-hearted smile, and she pulled away from him.

"This was a bad idea," she said, and Claudio's expression mirrored hers.

"Right." He nodded and bowed his head down. "Have a good night, Evie."

Crestfallen but exuding resilience in his stance, Claudio descended the front steps and turned up the sidewalk, hands tucked in his pockets and murmuring a tune she recognized.

Stupid, stupid girl.

THIRTEEN

"I see you've made a new friend." A voice drifted through the shadows. Its low vibration rattled Evie to the bone.

She jumped and stifled a shrill "fuck" before flipping the light switch. Evan sat on the futon, staring straight across the room toward her bed. A sigh of relief softened the tension lining her shoulders, but her heart still raced despite seeing it was only him.

"Shit, why are you sitting here in the dark? Are you trying to give me a fucking heart attack?" She attempted a soft laugh, but when he didn't reciprocate, she continued. "Claudio is my co-worker's brother. I met him last week at her place. Why? How come you didn't you call me when you got back in the city? How long have you been here?"

"I've been trying to call you. Your phone goes straight to voicemail."

You turned your phone off to avoid Nate, remember?

Shit, Evie cursed herself. Being too preoccupied with Claudio, she'd forgotten to turn it back on. She gawped at Evan, wordless and blameworthy.

His deadpan stare broke and turned down to his feet. A small huff escaped between his lips. His stoic demeanor held her in place like a statue, apprehensive to move toward him.

Evan's silence was a double-edged sword. At times it was welcome and comforting, other times it worried her. She wondered when the beast would emerge. Because she knew that's exactly what he was. Just like with Lucca, Evie knew someday her time may come with Evan, when his more primal

123

needs would surface and she'd become his victim. Being that she'd never heard Evan use such a menacing tone with her in the past, she wondered if her time was tonight.

Through silent prayer, she begged the wild rhythm of her heartbeat to settle before she provoked the animal growling amidst the obsidian dust, starved and ravenous.

"He seems quite taken with you." Evan said, breaking his silence.

More frantic pulses ran through her body.

"I guess." Evie strained to focus on the conversation over the pounding of blood between her ears. "He's really sweet, and I think he has a thing for me—according to his sister any way."

"Aren't you a lucky girl?"

His sarcastic retort slapped her across the face. Evan had always seemed quite adamant at maintaining Evie's level of normalcy in her life. Wouldn't normal for a girl in her twenties mean dating, for fuck's sake? Her curiosity at his riposte turned into annoyance—her annoyance, to anger.

"Evan, why the hell do you even care?"

He glared at her. His soft, tortured expression morphed with vehemence and burned, invoking a strange repentance in her. With her relevance or commitment to him still unclear, conflict swirled, angst ripping through her core like a mad torrent as he stood and approached her.

"I keep telling myself I shouldn't," he said.

Still edgy, but accepting his indirect apology, Evie nodded, and then closed and locked the door. She set her keys on the entryway table and pushed the sickness aside for the moment. He came inches away from her, and she searched his face for some understanding. Only worry made itself evident—more so than usual.

"What's wrong, Evan? What happened while you were gone?"

Stop being so naïve. This isn't about Claudio.

"Khan's been confirmed to be hiding out in Boston."

Evie froze. If Lucca's cohort, the mysterious immortal with his exotic accent and molten fire in his eyes, was spotted nearby, then Lucca couldn't be far off. She knew the answer—had felt his magnetic energy following her for weeks, but still needed to ask, to utter his name aloud.

"Is Lucca—"

"Yes."

An explosion of uncultivated, fleshly want burst at the base of her spine. She savored the throbbing and held in a moan, recalling the intensity of her dream and the likelihood of making it a reality. Both thrill and fear rushed through her body as she reconciled her emotions.

Evan monitored her with watchful, worried eyes. "Evie?" She stared off straight through his chest, through the walls, beyond the night sky to some celestial horizon beyond her sight. "Evie?" His voice beckoned again and it pulled her mind back into her body.

"What?" she said, breathless.

"Yes, Lucca is here. Are you okay?"

"I don't know what I am." She brushed her shoulder against his as if in a trance passing by him. She maintained her blank stare, turning on some music and lighting the aromatherapy candles on her computer desk. She moved through the tiny apartment, turning off the overhead chandelier's bright light and wandering over to the bathroom as soft acoustics filtered through the space. Evan remained in the middle of the room, waiting for her. She resurfaced from the bathroom, changed out of her work clothes and into comfy cotton pajamas. Her catatonic expression held firm.

He's finally here.

"When?" The question, barely posed on the edge of her breath.

"I'm not sure. Recently."

"How close is he?"

"All I know so far is that he's at a safe house downtown. I can't imagine he'd been dumb enough to come into South Boston, so close to my uncle's house," Evan said with firm conviction. "But who knows how bold the bastard could be if he knows you're here."

Evie plunked down on the futon and looked up at him.

"What's a safe house?"

"Do you remember me telling you about the Sempiternal outside of the Houses?" Evan asked, and then rolled his eyes at her puzzled expression. "Some people get infected and don't even know we exist to help them, but then there are others who disregard our ways and oppose our laws. They take refuge in these squatter developments hidden all over the world."

"Infected? Don't make it sound so glamorous... But if you know these places harbor criminals, why don't you just stop them?"

Evan replied with a short, mirthless laugh. "I'm not trying to make it sound sexy, Evie. And it's really not that simple. These camps are nomadic, moving around frequently to evade authorities. Word has it there's one downtown, but that could change tonight if they know we've caught wind of it."

Her mind flooded with white noise. Through the static, Evie only absorbed bits and pieces of what Evan said. Golden orbs and sharp fangs pierced the veil clouding her mind's eye. She blinked and refocused. "I don't understand."

"There's a balance to be considered." Evan continued. "If we went and raided each safe house we'd be risking ourselves just as much as those criminals. Civil war would only risk exposure to the unknowing mortal world. That could lead to a new reign of persecution." He studied her, waited for a reaction, but she couldn't bring herself to connect with his stare. "I can't believe you don't remember discussing any of this."

Evie shook her head, the complexities and politics of the Sempiternal being well beyond her comprehension. "I'm sorry."

A small grumble escaped past Evan's lips. The beast settled next to her and produced a small joint from the pocket of his jacket draped over the arm of the futon. Evie pushed her eyes to gauge the severity of his angst. It radiated off of him until he took one long hard toke off of the joint and passed it over. She took the pinner in between her fingers, inspecting the saliva-soaked tip. She licked her lips, her inner voice anticipating Evan's taste.

"The Great Purge," he said, stretching across the back of the futon and watching her through squinted eyes and a screen of fragrant smoke. "Witches weren't the only creatures sought out by angry mobs hundreds of years ago. A flare-up of Sempiternal unrest ravaged Europe. That's when the personification of the 'vampire' you're familiar with today emerged. We were demonized—hunted. People feared we'd ruin whole villages with our hunger. Elders, like my uncle, used the Houses to form alliances with mortals. They developed the rules and regulations that govern us today."

"Okay, maybe I remember you mentioning that before," Evie said under her breath, exhaling a mouthful of the sticky sweet forgetfulness. As Evan's history lesson echoed through her mind, her pulse boomed against her temples. She displaced the pressure by squeezing her fingertips into the sides of her head. "Regardless, wherever he's staying, you don't actually think Lucca's here just for me, do you?"

"If he's in the city, then it's because of you. There's no other reason, barring cocky spite, that would bring him this close to Bendis," Evie tilted her head sideways, her face scrunched with confusion. "My uncle's house," Evan said plainly. "You really don't listen to me at all, do you?"

His snip set her shoulders straight. Her back stiffened with defense. "Sorry, but don't you think I've been through enough lately? Sobriety, vampires—and now houses, criminals, and safe havens. I mean, come on. Give me a fucking break."

His nostrils flared, but Evan softened the hard lines across his brow. "Fine. What this all means is that I want you to be more cautious about when and where you go out—and with whom."

Evie took in a deep breath. The high priestess purred, pacing in the dark caverns of her core. A deep heat emanated deep inside her body as music swallowed their silence. A female singer moaned about regretfully falling into the gravity of her lover. The woman's whispering lyrics pulled at Evie. She closed her eyes, searching through the dark, but found only more confusion festering in the shadows of her mind.

"I don't see what this has to do with Claudio," she said calmly and handed the joint back to Evan.

He sucked in a long drag before answering.

"I don't know who he is, Evie." Evan wheezed and exhaled. "He may be a 'friend' to the safe house where Khan and Lucca are staying. I've heard there are others with them. I don't know anything about who they may be."

Others?

Nervous shivers sizzled down her spine. "You think they might be Claudio?"

"I don't know, but I don't want to take any chances," he said as he extinguished the diminished joint, now nothing but a tiny roach in the ash tray. Evan patted the top of Evie's hands kneading the flesh atop her knees.

"So you found out about all this and tried calling me. When I didn't answer my phone, you came down here to tell me?" Her stomach soured at the thought of Evan sitting and agonizing over her.

His lips parted to answer, but he caught his words and retracted his hand. "Yeah well, now that I know you're home safe, I'll leave you alone. Please just lock up behind me and get some sleep."

He skulked toward the door. It took a moment to register, but when she realized he was leaving, she jumped.

"Evan?" Her voice cracked, and he turned around with his telltale wounded expression. With only slight hesitation, she asked, "Would you please stay a little longer?"

He sucked in a deep breath, his russet eyes revealing an unsettling darkness, the potential consequences of her proposal evident to both of them. It was wrong to put such requests on him, knowing he'd likely not deny her for anything, even his own hunger.

He moved closer. His constant bewildered stare and tightly pressed lips held back a wave of emotions. Evie's pulse quickened from fear or something else, she couldn't quite decide. His scent was familiar, sweet, spicy—all the aromatherapy she needed. Evan reached out to intertwine his fingers with hers.

"Why do you want me to stay, Evie?"

If she didn't know any better, she'd guess there was a hint of longing in his voice. Ears perked up, her subconscious stirred. The voracious claws of her high priestess scratched their way up the back of her throat, eager to lash out with her tongue. She swallowed the duplicitous seductress back down.

"Please? At least until I can fall asleep? I've missed you, Evan," she said as the voice growled deep inside.

His brow creased, rejecting her with a shake of his head. "That' not a good idea. I'm… hungry."

She forced her conviction, but Evie persisted. "You won't hurt me. I trust you."

"No. Don't—"

"Evan, throughout all the time we've spent together, you've done nothing but try to protect me." Her heart rate increased with his resistance. Her tone increased in desperation. "Evie, don't ask me." He deflected her hands attacking his response.

"No you don't." Relinquishing control of her vocals and emotions to her inner voice, she strained to hold back tears. "No, you dragged me down here. You made me sober up. You made me keep to myself."

The tears flowed now, wetting her cheeks and evoking a similarly distressed response from Evan. He clasped her hands, wringing her wrists and jolting her out of her building frenzy.

"Evie, stop." He growled. The strength in his grip warned her. She'd provoked the animal inside, but beast be damned, she wasn't giving in. The inherent anxiety of being alone overpowered the fear of his Sempiternal nature.

"You owe me."

"Evie, stop!" The anger in Evan's tone silenced her, but couldn't stop her tears from falling. He thrust her hands to her sides; his force, shaking her to the bone. "All right, you win."

She should have felt nervous around him. She should have felt remorse for twisting his emotions like that. It didn't matter. Her inner voice got what she wanted. When he needed to consume someone so badly, he stayed.

***

They settled onto her thrift store futon. Evan pulled out his trusty bag of pot. With precision, he rolled another joint and passed it Evie's way. Each of them reclined a foot upon the makeshift coffee table. Piney, aromatic smoke filled the air of the tiny apartment. As they sat in silence, singers intoned upon the miserable soundtrack of Evie and Evan's life.

Evan took the final hit off the joint before it singed his fingertips.

"Evie?" He exhaled the last puff. She nestled her head atop his shoulder, her eyes half closed, a combination of THC and sheer exhaustion overwhelming her body.

"Hmm?" She hummed contently with the music.

"Don't ever call me out like that again." She sighed, understanding he must have been just as alone as she was—or so she presumed. It was unfair for her to say he owed her anything. After all, hadn't it been Evan who had saved her from Lucca and his friends when they stayed at his house in Fallhaven? Hadn't it been Evan who tended to her the day after Lucca walked out of her life? In all actuality, Evie owed Evan more than she could ever possibly give him.

"I'm sorry," she said, and nuzzled further into the crook of his neck.

He rested his head against hers and brushed his lips against the crown of her head. She relished the sensation of him taking in a deep breath of her scent.

"I know, Evie. Me too." He kissed the top of her head. She closed her eyes, contented.

Coercing her emotions for Evan to remain at bay was becoming increasingly difficult. Blythe was convinced they had a thing back in Fallhaven. She always protested against that, but the truth she refused to acknowledge was screaming from her subconscious.

Open your eyes, stupid girl. Stop denying it. Let me have him.

She scowled at her inner voice. Not tonight—not now, she thought.

Evie's breathing grew heavy. Warm, cloudy sleep descended, sealing her eyelids tight. But as Evan climbed out from under her body propped against his side, she jerked. Eyes opening and falling off the ledge of her slumber, she grasped his arm.

"Where are you going?" she asked.

"It's okay." He covered her with an afghan plucked from the back of the futon. "Go to sleep, Evie. I'll check in with you in the morning."

"No, please, a little longer." Groggy and half asleep, she stood and coaxed him toward the bed. "Come lay down next to me… until I fall asleep."

He cleared his throat. "I really don't think I—"

"No more arguing, come here." She climbed under the covers, then patted the top of the comforter. "See? Innocent, I promise."

She smiled and rested her head atop her pillow, waiting for his arms to envelop her. Evan complied, resting his head cautiously behind hers. His body's tension lessened as he settled in. The sensation of his protection wrapped around her filled her chest with warmth. She felt safe, whole, and in no time Evie was fast asleep.

***

She didn't remember him leaving. Evie awoke the next morning well-rested. The candles were extinguished. The music was turned off. And Evan was gone. The trace of his spiced scent lingered on her pillow.

FOURTEEN

The acoustic track that came up first wasn't from Evie's playlist. It was one of Evan's songs, one of many he'd added to her library, and just as sad and lonely as hers. The delicate guitar plucks and whispering vocals escaped through the open door to the balcony. From her outdoor perch, she peered across the street toward the beach, mentally reenacting the moment Evan dragged her into the waves. Lack of fear, willingness to be swept away by those sparkling ripples of silver and gold as far as the current demanded, instilled a sense of blissful emptiness. While she enjoyed spending the Saturday afternoon with her eyes closed, her mind blank, and intoxicated by the comfort Evan afforded her, guilt remained an inevitable comedown.

A disturbance in the back of her mind commanded her attention. The ghoulish courtesan prowled forward. The silent judgement in her gaze burned. The bloody mass in her hand, vaguely familiar; soft and pained—but not Rob. Evie cried out, her eyes opened, pulse racing. The tender features dangling in the geisha's grip no longer resembled the man she left behind in Fallhaven, but the one who brought her to Boston.

"Shit." She scrubbed her face to remove the vision from her mind's eye, but the mute geisha held her glower. The nip of a cool breeze wrapped around her neck like a silky noose. "Leave me alone. I never wanted to hurt him. I never wanted to hurt anyone." The acidic prospect of Lucca repeating what he had done to Rob churned in her stomach.

134

You have no choice in the matter, stupid girl. He will get what he wants.

Unwilling to venture down the path of her converging internal discord, her mouth opened, but was snapped shut by the ringing of her cell phone.

Evie nearly hurdled over the thin wrought iron railing and stumbled to her feet to retrieve the call. Grateful for the interruption, her heart leaped, anticipating Evan's voice from the other end of the line. Her excitement deflated seeing Nate on her caller ID.

She groaned and reluctantly answered. "Hi, Nate."

"Hey Babe, I haven't been able to stop thinking about you. I'm really glad you picked up."

"What do you need?" She skulked back out to the warped plastic chair on the balcony.

"What are you doing tonight? Do you want to grab a bite?"

She gave herself a moment to consider the offer. Her stomach rumbled.

We can have more than dinner. Nate's a guaranteed great fuck.

Evie scowled to herself and shook her head. "I don't think so. Thanks anyway." She sighed, relying on her rejection to be sufficient.

"Hey, Babe, I got a question for you." Dammit, she thought. Evie didn't answer directly, but let her silence allow him to proceed. "Are you seeing someone else?"

"Nate, don't ask me that." Her stomach knotted.

"Who is it?" he asked sharply. She rolled her eyes, having little patience for his petty jealousy.

"Why does it have to be anyone, Nate? I just need to be alone right now."

"Bullshit!" His roar transmitted through the speaker. Evie held the cellphone from her ear, stared at it like it had jabbed her with a hidden needle. "I know you, Evie. There's always someone. Who is it?"

Shock aside, annoyance erupted in her gut and stirred with the torturous knot kneading her insides. "Nate, I barely have control over my own life at the moment. I don't need this shit right now."

"Just answer the fucking question." His growl penetrated her to the core. Nate had his drunken, obnoxious, or even pig-headed moments. He was quick to lash out when the cause was just, and he preferred his girl to be just that— his. Aside from one night of provoked anger when he'd caught Evie and Lucca one hip-thrust away from infidelitous ecstasy, he'd never lashed out at her. If this was the new, clean Nate, then she wanted him doped up with the quickness. His anger was disconcerting, to say the least. The sirens were screaming in her head.

"Goodbye, Nate." Evie said with finality and zero desire to barrel head first into an argument with no foreseeable conclusion.

"Don't you hang up on me!"

Her stomach plummeted to the floor. Adrenaline surged hard and fast through her body, trembling her extremities. His tone may have terrified her, but it only served to fuel the high priestess' spite. Heated with a resentful angst, her inner voice's hackles raised, teeth baring. "Look Nate, I told you things are different. I need this time for me, to get my shit together. I don't need you or any other guy. Not Lucca, not Evan, not any of you trying to confuse me right now. So, just back the fuck off."

He went mute for a moment, but his ire emanated through the speaker before snarling back, "Who the fuck is Evan?"

"Nate, I just asked you to cut the shit. Evan is a friend. He's trying to keep me clean."

"It's him, isn't it? Blythe's ex," He said as confirmation rather than posing it as a question. "I heard all about that asshole when you left town. He conveniently skipped town too, didn't he? Is he the reason you left?"

Yes.

"No. Shut up." She took in a deep breath to regulate her raging pulse. Instigating one battle with Nate was enough. She didn't need her inner voice waging war. "I told you," she said. The tremors found their way into her vocal cords. "I moved for me."

"Does Blythe know you're seeing him?"

"I'm not 'seeing him.'" She barked back more so to bolster her own courage than anything. Being a terrible liar, Evie grew desperate to find a way out of this argument. "Just drop it."

There was another long pause between the two.

"Meet me for lunch this week—no blow offs—just meet me at the park during your lunch break."

"Nate, I really don't—"

"No." He warned. "I said no blow offs—you'll meet me."

As the call went dead, Evie covered her mouth with her hand, failing miserably to control her quivering lower lip. Lost in the vacant space in front of her, she stared bemused and speechless. A minute later, her stomach turned, anxiety pulling its contents up her esophagus. She ran head first inside to the bathroom. Her head over the toilet, nerves spewed out and were flushed down the drain.

***

Nausea continued throughout the week. Back in the day, a promiscuous Evie would have run to the drug store for a pregnancy test, but the celibate one knew the queasiness stemmed from some place different entirely. She attempted to dull the anxiety with Evan's THC, but the weed's medicinal qualities could only treat her miseries so much, and he took notice.

"You've been edgy all week. Are you worried about Lucca? Because I've got my guys tracking down that safe house. We'll find him before he gets to you. In the meantime, you and I have been very careful all week to go to work and come home. I think we're as covered as we can be," he said as they shared one last hit off the glass bowl.

Yes, she was grateful to have Evan's heightened attention, but no, this wasn't about Lucca. Quite the opposite. Anticipation of the deliverance Lucca sought to administer was preferable to the apprehension she felt when considering meeting up with Nate, whose scorn resonated with each demanding text throughout the week.

You could only treat him like shit for so long.

Self-loathing averted her eyes from meeting Evan's. Evie snatched up her cell and keys. Checking the phone, she saw yet another text from Nate, one of dozens she'd been trying to ignore all week, but there was no use. He wasn't giving in.

It's Friday. STOP ignoring me. We R meeting TODAY.

"Evie?" Evan's voice glided through the air atop ribbons of weed-infused smoke. Its transmission distorted by the static weighing on her.

"It's been a long week. That's all." For a moment, she considered telling Evan about Nate, to ask for help with avoiding him, but decided against it. Bile worked up her throat. She was sickened by the idea of disappearing again—acclimating to a new life somewhere else. The dyspepsia of yet another former love in harm's way against any Sempiternal beast burned. "Let's just get going to work," she said and passed her fingertips over the screen.

OK. Lunch at the usual time.

She plopped the cell in her purse and looked up at Evan. His usual dark stare held her mute for a moment. "Let's go," he said his hand held out for her. "At least it's Friday, right?"

She forced a smile and headed for the door.

***

The paperwork piled up. In lieu of plugging numbers into spreadsheet cells, Evie deliberated over piss-poor breakroom coffee throughout the morning. The same probable verdict kept presenting itself; leading Nate on would only ruin him. Unwilling to fathom Lucca tearing him down the same as Rob, she'd rejected that conclusion early on. Casting her invoices aside, she decided pulling Evan into the loop would likely cause more issues. He'd be furious if he knew she was headed downtown, straight into the lion's den, possibly delivered right into Lucca's delicious arms, just to break up with an ex she purportedly left behind months ago. She decided it best for Evan to remain high off of ignorant bliss with all matters pertaining to Nate. No, she fucked herself into this mess, she'd find a way out on her own.

Inevitable loneliness roiled in her stomach along with the bitter coffee and her scheming. Halfway through the day, as her phone's alarm chimed, that stomach-turning combination converged and resulted in an outbreak of unpreventable guilt and regret. Evie groaned and pulled the cell from her purse.

Are you sure you want to do this?

"This needs to end." She was cautious to keep her dialogue to a low murmur as she packed up her bag.

Nate was always a good lay. Maybe just one more time…?

"No." The bitch had a point, which Evie lamented over all morning. Nate was a constant and familiar physical presence in her life—and his body was as much a part of "home" as was the sea salt air. The sex-deprived crevices of her body would miss his more pleasurable endowments, but giving Nate up was safer than the alternative.

"Let's just get this over with."

Evie logged off her computer and set off for the Silver Line.

FIFTEEN

Traversing the MBTA's system afforded her ample opportunity to reconsider cutting Nate loose. As she neared downtown and her eyes moved with extra caution, Evie knew this was best. She ascended to the street level outside of South Station and made her way over to Congress Street. The congested city air couldn't fill her lungs fast enough.

The crispness of autumn in New England was in full swing, but that didn't stop the throngs of young, urban professionals from assembling in the park. Evie was grateful for the crowd, trusting Nate wouldn't do anything too brazen with so many people around, and she felt certain if Lucca was out there looking for her, he'd have a difficult time finding her amongst the mass of her fellow Bostonians. Not until she was ready.

I'm ready.

"Not now." She whispered, though not soft enough. A woman standing next to her at the crosswalk gave her a funny look like she was talking to herself.

You are talking to yourself, stupid girl.

"Just shut up."

Evie let the woman, with her inconsequential and mortal opinion, stare. A brewing anxiety attack swirled in her chest, and her resolve faltered. Should've just argued with Nate and refused to meet him, she thought.

Then go. Does he even matter?

Cursing at herself, she turned around to suffer the consequences of rejecting Nate's demands. All it took was a moment's hesitation, though. The crowd surged forward with the stoplight's permission, dragging her along like a rogue undertow. When the swarm dispersed across the street she was instantly scooped up in Nate's arms.

"I knew you'd come. I knew it," he said and nestled his face into the crook of her neck.

She wriggled free from his hold. "Nate, please. Don't make this harder than it needs to be."

"Make what harder? I knew you'd come see me."

She sighed heavy with the same regret from back at her office, and continued to scan her surroundings. Searching each face for one in particular. At least Lucca was nowhere to be seen.

Turning back to Nate, the bilious mixture in her belly stirred. It would have been easier if she'd told Nate to go fuck himself before leaving Fallhaven. Maybe she should have been more of a bitch to him when he pursued her via text. As she looked into his warm and refreshingly sober smile, her anxiety only increased, amplified by culpability.

"Nate, let's talk."

***

The two sat in the grass. The sun high above the city, warming them in the cooling autumn air. Nate already had her green tea and scone waiting for her.

"Just tell me what I need to do, Babe. Blythe told me I was full of shit, but I knew you still loved me."

"Do you talk about me with Blythe often?" She surveyed their surroundings again, and then looked down at her scone. She found no appetite through her nausea.

"I don't have any other interest in talking to her, if that's what you're asking."

Evie couldn't have cared less if they were fucking, but refrained from blurting that out. Struggling to overcome the sickness, she sipped her green tea. All that did was result in phlegmy heartburn.

"It doesn't bother me. Just a little awkward, I guess. Not like you're huge fans of one another."

"No shit." Nate's soft chuckle and casual humor made this all the more difficult.

Each of her breaths was labored. Evie caught her lip curling when she stared too long at him. Given the choice of fight or flight, she was ready just to bolt and let him fit the puzzle pieces together on this one. Figuring, they'd shared at least a few good years in the past, she mustered the will to talk things out.

"Nate, listen, I—wait?" Her stomach plummeted. Her jaw fell slack, eyes bulged. "Did you mention anything to her about Evan?"

Apprehension carried on the edge of her voice, and registered on Nate's features. He didn't answer directly, but a definite possessiveness colored his face. The tension lining his bearded jawline was tangible, and she inched back from him.

This was a huge mistake—coming to meet him. She'd never felt such a sense of infidelity in her life. Never once when she flirted with Rob while Nate was out on the boats. Never when Lucca pressed his body up against hers. Never when Evan stared at her while Blythe sat right between them. Never had she felt as though she'd betrayed another's trust in her—before now.

"Nate…?"

"First it was that Lucca, asshole. Now this guy, Evan. What's next Evie? Who else have you been fucking behind my back?"

Her spine stiffened. Osmosis channeled the scolding temperatures of her tea throughout her body, or maybe that was just her body heating up with defensiveness. She glowered, teeth clenched as her entire being burned.

"First off, if you remember, I broke up with you when I moved. Second, I'm not sleeping with anyone." And most importantly, "How do you know about Lucca?"

Her heart was racing as she recognized a hint of amusement pull his bearded frown into a smile.

"You think I'm an idiot, don't you? Dumbass Nate, is that it?"

Blame crushed hard and present against her chest. "Stop it. You know that's not what I think… and don't change the subject."

"I know all about Lucca," he said and dropped his gaze down to his massive hands, white knuckles flexed in and out. Evie dug her fingers into the grass at her back, ready to jump up and bolt if he posed a real, physical threat, and dreading the notion their relationship had deteriorated to such a possibility.

You really are clueless, stupid girl. What did you expect?

"Fuck off." She whispered to her inner voice, but brought Nate's attention off his fists and back to her. She scrambled to cover up her verbal blunder. "Blythe has a big mouth, but no, this isn't about him."

He snorted with disdain. "Are you sure this has nothing to do with that piece of shit?"

Evie closed her eyes and took a long hard breath to clear her mind and focus on the right words. Antagonizing Nate wasn't going to get her anywhere, even as the high priestess paced in her dark cave, growling, brewing with abhorrence. Evie was fucking this up royally, and her inner voice's defensive demeanor was only making things worse.

"Look Nate, the problem is with me. I need to figure myself out first. You asked me about Lucca. I haven't seen him in months, and I have no idea if I'll ever see him again. The fucked up part is, I have no idea how I even feel about that... And then, you mentioned Evan. I don't know what to tell you. He's been the only constant in my life since I left Fallhaven. He's a good friend, and I have no idea what else."

She watched him as she rattled off one thought after the other about the emotion whirling through the tempest in her head. His facial features remained placid, but there was fire building behind his eyes. She could see it. The jealousy, something she'd never actually seen in him, even after years of leering looks and stray hands at Sirens. Maybe she should have tempered her response a bit, so as not to call out the ugly green monster inside, but the damage was done. She threw the monster a bone. "And then I see you again. You're clean. I don't know that I've ever seen you like this. You look absolutely amazing."

He smiled from ear to ear. "I knew you still loved me."

"I'm saying I'm fucked up in the head, Nate. I don't know what I want. You can't push me like this. I can't handle the pressure. And then there's—"

She almost did it. She almost blurted out the conflicting issue of immortality versus mortality. Would she even be alive in the next few months to love someone like Nate? Would she be alive long after his body had turned to dust?

He tilted his head at her. "There's what? Another guy?"

"No." She exhaled. "No, it's my... living arrangements. I don't know how long I'll be around."

She expected Nate to interrogate her. He just looked back at her with a silent understanding across his cooling eyes.

"I get it, Babe. You don't have to say any more. All I ask is that you don't write me off just yet. We've always worked well together. Let me help you through this."

Evie's face scrunched with confusion as his rage suddenly subsided. The jealousy vanished, and Nate accepted her open-ended statement without question. His docile smile felt out of place.

"I don't—" Just like with Claudio, a rain of crimson covered Nate's features. The shadow of the geisha lurked forward from the back of her mind. Evie blinked, banished the image, and jumped to her feet. "No, I'm not doing this. I told myself I was coming here to break up once and for all. That's it."

She turned to make her trek back toward the subway, but Nate chased after her. "Evie, get back here. We're not done." He caught her just before reaching the crosswalk and spun her around.

Disbelief and annoyance lowered her brow. "That's the problem, Nate. We are done."

His grip tightened around her bicep, dispelling her anger and invoking a wave of fear to flush her body. She squirmed, but was caught in his net.

"Stop saying that," he said. "We're not—" He paused, leaving the cacophony of mid-day traffic to compete with her pulse for her attention. Keeping her in his grasp, Nate pulled his cell from his back pocket with his free hand. A growl rumbled from his chest. "Fuck, not now."

Bewilderment softened the tension lining her face, but failed to settle her raging pulse.

Nate loosened his grip. "Look, I'm not accepting this as your final word, Evie, but… I need to go meet someone."

"Who…?"

146

"Don't worry about that," he said. "We will continue this conversation." His tone was firm, but his hold on her lessened. Evie thought to question his sudden shift in behavior, but decided to let him leave. Nate slammed a scratchy kiss against her cheek, and disappeared into the pedestrian traffic. She stood bemused on the corner, hands shaking, and mind reeling.

***

Nate took off west down Franklin Street. As tempting as it was to satiate her curiosity and follow him, Evie decided it best to let him leave.

"That was weird," she said quietly and turned back to toss her tea and scone in the rubbish. Her hands still shook from the adrenaline rushing through her system. In the midst of a crowded park, full of strangers, and completely out of her element, Evie paused and closed her eyes, centering herself before heading back to work.

A cold chill caused her to shudder under the warm sun's rays. She allowed the sensation to run its course, and then realized it wasn't the weather evoking such a reaction. Eyes, cold and hungry, bore into the back of her head. The feeling, like golden flecks in the shadows, held her transfixed in the middle of the grassy plain as metropolitan life buzzed all around.

"What happened to my fiery redhead? I was quite fond of the red."

SIXTEEN

She could've recognized his voice anywhere. It crept down her body and lingered at the base of her core in the most blissful manner. Having felt his presence for days, she expected he'd come by surprise, skulking from the shadows like he did each night in her dreams. Evie didn't expect it to happen in broad daylight, and certainly not in the middle of a crowded park.

Yes...

As she turned to look at him, her breath caught. Her memory betrayed his sharp features, the angle of his jaw line and his shadowy eyes beneath his brow. His dirty blond locks were radiant in the midday sun, like a golden halo framing his face down to his shoulders.

Perfect.

His long, lean figure stood straight and tall, a body she'd recounted in her dreams a myriad of times. Somehow she'd forgotten the detail of his veins bulging from his forearms tracing striking trails through his skin. She eyed his rough and firm hands, failing to recall their touch and hating herself for not being able muster their sensation.

Her memory hadn't failed her where it counted though. His wicked crooked grin was exactly as she'd remembered it. His lips, just as lusciously pink as she'd dreamed. He stalked her over the grass. Evan's warnings signaled in her mind. Every step Lucca took sent a conflict of emotions rushing through her body. Her pulse quickened as she silently prayed this wasn't just another hallucination. His natural magnetism reeled her in. She inched away from him little by little, but was unable to make up for the distance as his long strides consumed her.

"You've let it grow out." He cocked an eyebrow as he remarked on her hair, no longer the choppy inverted bob from when last he saw her, no more bright red tendrils teasing the lining of her face. "Not that I mind. It… softens your features. Very beautiful, actually, but there was something about the red." He lifted a hand out to her, calling her to him. She flinched. "Come now, Evie, what have I done to evoke such a repulsed reaction from you?"

Even as his voice wrapped around her like silk, his snickering at her made her blood boil. "I'm pretty sure killing a man I loved is deserving enough, don't you?"

"Tsk-tsk. Strong words, Evie." Lucca's grin widened with a reproachful head shake. His eyes sparkled under the afternoon sun's glow. A few passers-by looked in their direction with increased curiosity, but he disregarded them. "My lovely dear, why would you utter such silly and gross accusations?"

He grabbed hold of her elbow, yanking her toward him and covering her mouth with his. Her first reflex was to push him away, but his zest, his body heat, and his firm hold on her were far too evocative to deny. Her body moistened, and she melted into his arms. Allowing Evie to catch her breath, he pulled his lips away and dragged his fingertips along her jaw, staring deep into her eyes. His dark eyes, rimmed with golden flecks of light, locked with hers. Her inner voice swooned.

"There," he said in a low purr. "I truly do enjoy how I can affect you like that."

"Not one of my proudest traits." Her voice croaked, and she cleared the thrill from her vocal cords.

"Ah, but it is one of mine." He exuded self-satisfaction.

His very nearness stirred a burning deep below her core, searing the tender muscles between her thighs and weakening her knees. His voice, a sensual symphony to her senses. He was irresistible to her, and she hated him for it. Wrapping his arms around her, his hands anchored to the small of her back. He rocked her back and forth against his body, further exacerbating her compulsion to fall deep into his abyss.

"Are you still trying to fight us?" he asked in a mocking, pained tone, a playful frown smeared across his face.

Evie's heavy breathing intensified, fighting her urges. Months had passed since he walked away from her, but now those months felt like seconds as the pain of losing him resurfaced. She didn't want to let go again; she was parched for him—feening for one tiny hit.

"Do you still not believe we were meant to be together, Evie? You and I? That you were born for me?" His words swirled through her like smoke through her lungs.

"I…" She was lost in the depths of his eyes. "I don't know."

I know. He is you and you are him.

She dizzied. The halo around his head swirled into a rainbow haze, bleeding out from behind him.

"Surely you must know more about what I am by now?" he asked, licking his lips. Though her id was distracted by desire for that tongue against her skin, her ego and the rest of Evie were puzzled by his presumptuous statement. He smiled, as if reading her mind. "I know Evan's been watching over you. He must have revealed something about what we are."

Her heart pounded between their bodies. "He's told me about your—"

"Disease." Her nightmare came to life as his voice carried through the air on his hiss.

150

"What did you call it?"

He came closer. Caressing her cheek with his, Lucca whispered into her ear. "Our disease… infection… condition. Call it whatever you'd like, Evie. It's a plague, which alters our genetic makeup. Doesn't that sound simple enough? Natural even? And the side effects are wondrous. You'll see." His voice was gentle. The outside world lost its importance as he embraced her amidst the lunchtime traffic. She breathed him in with a ravenous hunger. "I remember the last time I cradled you in my arms," he said. "You still fit perfectly."

Contentment washed over her like the tide.

For too long she'd craved a warm body. Unlike all the times Evan restrained from giving it to her, Lucca offered his sensual touch willingly. She accepted it and cooed into his chest, taking in his familiar scent of orange blossoms and mint.

Alerted back to reality by a series of honking horns in the distance, Evie jerked.

"Shit, I have to get back to work." She tried to pry herself from his arms, but Lucca had her in a firm hold.

"It's time. Let's end this."

Go… Go!

"I can't," she said, trepidation running rampant through her body. "I'm not—"

Lucca clamped down on her waist and growled. "Titillating as it is, Evie, to anticipate the inevitable conclusion to our chase—knowing what we're are—I'm tired of playing their games."

"Who are they?"

His sneer revealed sharp, pearlescent daggers. Evie was mesmerized by the fear and thrill they evoked.

"Evan would never be so foolish to risk another scourge. Donovan would never betray Khan."

Her mind spun attempting to process his cryptic ramblings.

"Who is Donovan?"

Lucca leaned in and traced her lip with his tongue, bringing her dreams to life. His flavor, far more intoxicating in reality. "Oh God, not here." She begged and he lifted back from her.

Lucca stared into her eyes. His hypnotic glare froze her in fear. "He's kept so much from you, Evie. I want to give you the world. Let me show you."

Her body was on fire as he grazed her neck with the sharp tips of his canines. Quivering all over, Evie nearly said it. The high priestess was alive inside, begging to be released, but the echo from her dreams spiked her desire with a dread that held her tongue.

"Wait," she said. "Have you been tracking me?"

He jostled her in his arms. "Forever, Evie, I will hunt you down. Evan can try to free you of me, but I will follow you from one life to the next until we are together."

He leaned in again. This time, she noticed a few people nearby had taken notice of their discord, further intensifying her panic.

"Please don't do this in front of all these people. I can't—Evan will—"

Lucca cut her off, crushing their bodies together and clawing her jaw. "Haven't you been listening? He doesn't own you, Evie. You're mine. I've claimed you. He knows this. Evan can't keep you from me forever. Tell me where he's hiding you."

Her heart was ready to explode as Lucca transformed into the monster she feared. A tiny whimper escaped her before a chilling thought brought a smirk to her face, a thought that both liberated and terrified her.

"You'll find me," she said in a cocky whisper, realizing their game of cat and mouse would never truly be over until he'd consumed her fully. She'd die in his arms—willingly when the time came. She could run to the edges of the earth. Evan could elevate her to the top of the Haiku Stairs, bury her in the darkest depths of the Krubera Cave, Lucca would be there waiting with open arms and fangs unsheathed. There was nothing that would stop him, not even if she wanted him to. The gleam in his spellbinding glare held testament to that fact.

But not yet, she thought. Try as her inner voice might to give into his calling, the fear of submitting to his monstrosity, his murderous tendency, and his lack of humanity held her back.

"You'll always find me, won't you, Lucca?"

"Say my name again." His coarse grunt reverberated through her entire body as he jostled her in his grip.

"Lucca." Her whispered obedience tickled on its way out. The enunciation of his name clicked off the roof of her mouth, the act of forming each syllable parted her lips just so. A breathless moan barely escaped her as he kissed her hard, biting her lip and drawing the tiniest drop of blood.

Lucca pulled away sharply. "I love to hear you say my name. Try not to enjoy this play too much, Evie. It will be over soon. You can assure Evan of that. If he dares to repeat the past, then so shall I." He panted heavy with gratification, and then released her.

The menace lacing his last comment sliced through her chest like a knife. A fair warning, but one that she had no idea what to do with. The resulting shivers down her spine triggered a stream of tears down her cheeks, though she managed to hold back the panic attack until he was out of sight.

He strode away, never turning to bid her farewell or indicate when or where he'd see her again. She stood, licking the bloody ribbon tracing the edge of her mouth.

Lucca disappeared into the daylight and crowded streets of Boston's Financial District.

***

"Shit." Evie collapsed on a vacant park bench, dismissing how late she would be from her lunch break. Such normalcies were trivial in comparison to what Lucca had implied. He'd referred to himself as a disease, just as he had in her nightmares, and wanted to give her the world. And he made it sound so… simple.

His insinuation that Evan was manipulating her was infuriating.

"Evan's not trying to trick me. He doesn't even want me to be part of any of this."

Perhaps that's the problem?

The constant roiling of her stomach doubled her over in her seat. Evie stared down at her feet, taking in deep breaths to fight the queasiness. "He's going to kill me."

Which one?

"I can't do this. God, I don't want to hurt him."

Who's that, stupid girl? Stop being selfish.

"No, I just want to feel normal again," she said, wiping beads of sweat forming along her brow.

But what is "normal?" We are Sempiternal.

"Dammit." Evie lifted wide eyes and surveyed the park once more. She felt eyes crawling all over her, though no one nearby paid her any attention. Lucca may have disappeared from plain sight, but his essence lingered and suffocated her.

She jumped when her phone buzzed. Retrieving it from her bag, she cringed when she saw yet another text from Nate.

Luv you.

"Leave me alone." She yelled at the phone as two girls passed by. They exchanged curious expressions and giggles, but she didn't give a shit. "I need to end this."

The sickness spread from her belly up through her chest.

He is you and you are him. Stop fighting us and listen to me.

After one more lick at the fresh wound from Lucca's nibble, she checked the faces in the park for his. Lucca was nowhere to be seen, but she felt him everywhere.

She lifted herself onto wobbly legs and hailed a cab.

***

On the cab ride back to the office and for the remainder of her day at work, Evie was perplexed, not by the manner in which she both loved and hated Lucca, but by the way his words resonated in her mind. He knew Evan was hiding her, but didn't know where.

"He'd know by now if he was following me, right?" she said, fingers tapping along the edge of her desk.

Unless Evan had us guarded.

"This isn't about Lucca, is it?" She held a blank stare at a mound of invoices, wings of Carver Assurance screaming up at her from the top of the stack. "What are you doing to me, Evan?"

Unsure whether to interrogate him or evade him all together, Evie sent Evan a text message asking him to let her walk home alone. Of course, the answer she presumed he'd give, was one she found difficult to choke down.

Not sure that's a good idea.

Massaging her forehead with the palm of her hand, she stared down at her phone atop her desk. She responded back with a "please" that didn't sound as desperate in text form as it did passing her lips.

What's wrong?

She grumbled back at her phone and typed her response. "Nothing. Just need quiet time to unwind. Please, Evan?"

Her phone's buzzing ceased. She could tell by his lack of reply that he wasn't happy, but he acquiesced nonetheless.

Evan did not wait outside of her office.

When she stepped out onto the street, she glanced over toward the address for Carver Assurance. A cold breeze whipped around her. She shivered, but turned from the stone tower across the way and strolled out of the industrial park.

Constantly checking over her shoulder, the golden orbs didn't haunt her like they did a week ago. She had a vivid recollection of Lucca's features, and she saw him at every corner, on every face passing by, and from every window lining L Street. She wrapped her arms around her waist, as though that could ward off his specter.

"Maybe I should just run away… on my own?"

Her head pounded. She contemplated divulging everything that happened today with Evan.

If he's hiding something from us, then asking him directly won't help matters.

"Should I just wait it out?"

We could go find Lucca.

"If Evan can't find that safe house, then neither can we."

We won't need to. He'll find us.

That was the simple answer, she thought. But Evan never indicated he meant her any ill-will. Though adamant Lucca was a very real threat, the flip side of her truth couldn't deny Evan's intentions seemed pure.

"No. I need to know what Evan's hiding."

The brisk walk soothed her physical pains, but the paranoia and mental woes persisted as she climbed three flights of stairs.

SEVENTEEN

When she passed the threshold to her apartment, he was waiting for her. Evan sat on the futon in his office casual, twiddling his thumbs pensively. When he turned to look at her, his omnipresent worrisome expression faded, replaced by a genuine smile of relief, a sight so uncommon that it shrouded Evie in disgrace. The look on his face was positive affirmation that he remained unaware of her interactions with both Nate and Lucca earlier during her day, though she was sure if he looked into her eyes deep enough he'd see through to her truth.

Just ask him. Stop being selfish.

Casting her subconscious aside, she dropped her bag and keys near the door and skulked over to the futon to plop by his side. She flipped her shoes off, sending them flying across the short expanse of the tiny studio towards her bed, and nearly knocked over a votive on her nightstand. The two shared a tiny chuckle.

The minutes passed. Few words were actually exchanged. Evie realized just how well they had settled into their unspoken relationship. The culpability of questioning him twisted in her chest. The thought of losing his company was beyond upsetting. It was unthinkable.

And lose it, she surely would. Her mind replayed her reunion with Lucca over and over. Her lip was sore, she sucked at it to hide it from Evan's view. The memory of Lucca's bite sent a wonderful rush of blood between her legs.

"Long day?" Evan asked.

She lifted a shaky hand out for her glass pipe. "I guess." Evie sparked a flame across the top of the bowl.

"Is everything okay? I didn't exactly see that text coming earlier today. That was a pretty bold move."

"I'm sorry. I just needed some time to try and clear my head."

"You had me worried," he said.

She turned to him. His smile had vanished, replaced by a guarded expression. Not bothering to consider it until now, she wondered if it was possible Lucca could unlock the mystery behind Evan's tortured eyes?

Evie looked around the apartment, struggling for a diversion, anything to draw her mind's attention from Lucca. The more she thought about him, the more awkward her movements became. The more she feared giving herself away to Evan's perceptions.

"I've got a headache, that's all." She spun the tale and stood to fill the room with the low strumming of a guitar from her playlist.

"You have a headache, so music should help?"

Evie shrugged. "It was just an annoying day, Evan. Really, let's just drop it." At least until she could figure out who to trust, she thought. In that moment, she wished she had a drink in her hand, much like the laments of the singer in the background. Life was much simpler when all she needed to do was get drunk and fuck Nate.

The thought of her ex made her stomach turn. Much for his efforts to repair the damage inflicted upon their relationship, Nate's recent show of force was alarming. Evie squeezed the pressure points at her temples and found her place beside Evan again.

"I have this for you." Evan produced an envelope from his suit jacket pocket.

Evie opened it and read through it, the legalese overwhelmed her education. "What the hell is it?"

"It's your proceeds from the sale of Sirens."

Vomit rushed up her throat. The strip club was officially gone. Her last link to Rob had been severed. She shuddered, holding the paper in her hand.

"Who bought it?"

"A fisherman. He said he didn't want to see the club close down, so he took it on as an investment."

"I just hope he doesn't run it like a brothel and disgrace Rob's memory." Evie tucked the large bank check under the ashtray. Rob had worked so hard to protect each and every girl that worked for him from the drug-riddled streets of their small fishing town. Even though he was the sole proprietor of a "gentlemen's club," he was the most upstanding citizen Fallhaven had to offer, in Evie's eyes. Now, all that was gone, and he was just left to her nightmares with the geisha. The promise she'd made to him after his death chimed in the back of her head. No, she couldn't let herself fall to Lucca. If for no other reason than to respect Rob's memory.

Then we take our chances with Evan.

"What do you want me to do with the check?" Evan asked, but his voice barley registered over the static in her head.

She stared at the check long and hard, a small fortune printed on a thin piece of watermarked paper. It was enough money for her to run as far as she wanted to from Evan, from Lucca, from Nate and the whole Sempiternal mess she found herself trapped within. A flicker of excitement twitched at her eyebrow, but quickly vanished. There was no place in this world or the next that she could go to escape her monsters— or her loneliness.

"What do you think I should do with it?"

"I think you should meet with a financial advisor. Between this money and what I can get for your house, you'll have plenty of time to lay low and sort things out for yourself."

The house?

"What are you doing with my house?"

There was no way he could have been considering selling her family's house; a home built by her ancestors, by her own past life, passed down from one generation to the next. She was tied to it, heart and soul, and would surely die there again if given the opportunity. It never occurred to her that returning to her home—to Fallhaven—wasn't an option.

"Do you need to keep it?" he asked. "It's not like you're going back there any time soon."

"But I am going back, Evan." She glowered at him, arguing emphatically. "It's my home."

"Evie, I think we need to talk about this." He spoke in a calm, subdued voice and shifted his body to face her head on.

Defenses on high alert, she stood with her hands tightened into pointless fists. She had no intentions of attacking him, nor would she succeed if she wanted to. Still, her blood raged through her veins, and she needed to express those emotions somehow. Clenching her jaw and squeezing her hands into tiny handfuls were instinctual reactions.

"There's nothing to talk about, Evan. Did you think I was going to hide like this in Boston forever? This isn't a life. I'm not allowed to go out. I'm not allowed to have friends. I'm not allowed to drink."

Her pulse quickened as anxiety built up in her chest, clutching at her lungs. Her fists loosened. She felt the panic setting in as her vision blurred.

"Take it easy, Evie." He approached her with cautious hands held out in front of him. "Where is this coming from?

You asked me to help you hide, remember? If you go home, Lucca will find you. If he changes you before that, then what's the point of going back home? Either way, you won't be able to stay in that house forever. I've been where you're at, Evie. I know those emotions—the fear—better than anyone. Think reasonably."

She gawped at him. First Nate, and then Lucca. Now Evan was commanding her. Their unjustified possessiveness had boiled over. The room spun as rage pumped through her veins. Feeling the reins controlling her life slipping from her grasp, resentment surged. This wasn't happening. She'd keep her promises on her own.

"Fuck you, Evan!" She spat at him. "How's that for reasonable?"

Evie spun on her heels and reached for the door, slipping on a pair of flats and scooping up her belongings in the process.

"Where are you going?"

When she turned to face him, pure hate burned through her eyes. "You're not my fucking father, Evan. You're not my boyfriend—not my lover. I don't know what you are, but stop fucking trying so hard to control me. Maybe I don't want it. I don't want any of it." She hissed pure venom in her voice.

Evan rushed her, twisting her wrist in his hand. Evie winced from the pain and froze as she peered into the deep brown eyes of the eternal beast. The enraged glare he cast down on her was terrifying. She'd seen those eyes before; they were inherent to Lucca's dark charm, but on Evan they were foreign and grotesque, beyond threatening. His jaw flexed and his nostrils flared. The building percussions from the music buzzing in the background set a rushed, syncopated rhythm for her pulsating heartbeat.

"You have absolutely no idea what you want," he said. "Otherwise, you wouldn't want me here night after night, would you? You ungrateful little—" Evan bit his tongue. Evie heard a thunder building in him. Rather than fear the beast within, she choked down the terror wadded up in her throat and stared him down with hard glass eyes, cold and sharp.

"Say it. Ungrateful what, Evan? Bitch? Is that what you think I am? I'm an ungrateful little bitch because I want you around me? God-fucking-forbid I crave some physical contact." She squinted her eyes at him and pursed her lips into a thin line before continuing. "You're trying too hard to save someone that isn't worth saving, Evan. Have you ever thought about that?"

Her words lashed across his face. Evie watched the anger in his eyes diminish, overtaken by agony or guilt. A part of her wanted to soften her gaze in return, but her inner voice wouldn't relent. She stared, hateful and defiant, into his eyes. His lined brow softened as he loosened his grip on her wrist. Again, Evie's heart begged her to offer him the tiniest bit of sympathy, but the high priestess refused. She yanked her wrist away with a huff and marched toward the door.

"Evie, where are you going?" The desperation in his voice chased her the short distance across the room.

"To get a drink." She took off down the hallway, refusing to look back.

You knew you couldn't keep them all to yourself.

"Shut up!" Evie stormed down the front steps of her building.

She clasped her neck, the invisible spikes stabbing at her throat. Like she'd been run through with a harpoon, a tugging in her chest pulled back and reeled her in toward Evan. She gritted through the phantom pain, continued out the front door and up the sidewalk. He didn't follow her. She was glad for that.

***

Evie huffed her way up Broadway with no idea where she was going or what happened back in her apartment with Evan. In some irrational bout of stupidity, Evie managed to pick a fight with the one person she had left in her life. Somehow her inner voice wasn't chastising her for it.

He's too protective. He's hiding something. Lucca said it. He's holding you hostage.

"He's just trying to help. It doesn't matter anyway." She marched past the brightly lit nightlife of South Boston. Most people she walked by paid no attention to her psychotic ramblings. Only one or two stared, most likely presuming she was drunk or high.

He's keeping you from him.

"He's the same thing. What's the difference?"

He is you and you are him.

"Fuck you!" Her scream drew more attention than before.

She screeched to a halt in front of a group of guys smoking cigarettes outside of a bar. She stared, jaw slacked open, as they reciprocated equally bewildered expressions. She noticed a familiar name on the chalkboard sign at the bar's entrance.

"Did I miss him?"

"Miss who?" asked a young, attractive man with a cool grin and slicked-back hair. He appraised Evie through objectifying eyes, lighting a cigarette and exhaling the smoke up toward the bar's neon signage.

"Claudio. Did he play yet?" She pointed to the sign.

"No, I think he just started," said a shorter, stubbier man.

She nodded at him and entered the bar.

***

Once inside, her shoulders loosened. Her guard was still engaged, but her nerves relaxed a little. She scanned the crowd, relieved not to be shadowed by anyone.

The pub was dark, gritty, and alive with the dissonance of vivacious banter. She turned a few heads as she perched herself at one of the empty barstools. The bartender, the large bald Irishman named Seamus she'd met last week, greeted her with a placid expression.

"Hi Love, what can I getcha?"

"Guinness." She slapped a ten dollar bill on the counter and sunk into her seat. It had been months since she had a drink. Her stomach did somersaults as Seamus set the expertly poured pint in front of her. She drooled at the dark brew, froth tipping over the lip of the glass. Holding the glass in between her hands, staring blankly into its abyss, she hadn't the nerve to lift it to her mouth.

She heard the guitar first, beautiful acoustic strumming. When she turned to locate its source, she saw Claudio in the far left corner of the room, beaming over the crowd. She watched him. His handsome features pecked away her hardened and anxious exterior.

Like they were joined, and he could feel her through the crowd, he glanced over to the bar. Their eyes met. His smile widened. Evie blushed, the warmth in her no longer a result of anger. She removed her denim jacket and hung it on the back of her barstool, settling in.

"I've been working on some new material," Claudio said to the crowd through the microphone, fingers gingerly plucking at the guitar's strings. "This first song, though, is a cover that I've been practicing since I met a girl. She's real quiet and reserved, but I'm pretty sure there's something between us—kindred spirits." Her heart pounded as he looked up at her with a playful grin. "I hope so at least, if only she'd just open up a little. Anyway, this song reminds me of her."

Anxious to numb her converging emotions, Evie lifted the pint. The stout's frothy head lined the outside of her lips. She paused before taking the first sip. The song—it was one of the somber tunes she played frequently at home. His voice floated through the air, the melodic humming words of a man pleading to his lover for mercy, to bleed for him, to offer some sign that she was in fact real. Claudio handled his guitar like a lover, brushed up against the microphone as if he were running his lips down her body. Tears welled in Evie's eyes as each word twisted around her heart.

"I'm so sorry, Claudio. You deserve better." She set the glass back on the bar.

We're leaving?

"I'm not dragging him into my world of shit," she said with her head down to keep her comments to herself, and then turned to retrieve her jacket.

You're being selfish, stupid girl. I need more—something. Change is coming.

A knot twisted in her stomach. Tears continued to bead along her lids. Evie turned back to watch Claudio play. Her heart swooned from the emotion in his voice as he sang lyrics she knew intimately. She had whispered those same words so many nights sitting alone in her house, or in her apartment, in the bath tub, or out on her balcony.

"Can I buy you a drink?" She turned, bemused as Nate's jolly and amazingly fresh and clean face grinned at her. He was still sober, trim and fit, and he looked remarkable. His skin glowed. She hadn't seen Nate this vibrant and healthy ever in his adult life. She'd noticed he looked quite well in the daylight, but under dim bar lighting he was absolutely delicious. Shadows caught the ginger highlights of his beard and cast a shadow over his ebullient eyes. Charisma aside, his appearance was completely unexpected and startled her.

"Nate... what, are you following me?" Her guard increased and her nerves wrenched in her gut.

"That's a little paranoid, don't you think?" He sat on the stool next to her. "Do you live around here?"

Damn, he looks good enough to eat.

Evie silently cursed her inner voice. "Just answer the question."

Nate smiled a bright and beautiful smile she'd not seen for ages, one that not long ago would have set her whole body ablaze. Such emotions felt foreign now.

"I'm glad I ran into you, though. Small world, huh?" he said.

He's purposely ignoring our questions.

The high priestess grew perturbed by his redirection. Evie began scanning the room for an escape route. Such relief was not easily attained as Claudio was packing them in. A crowd had formed, encasing her and Nate.

The song ended. She clapped, more slowly than the rest of the audience, and cast a remorseful grin in Claudio's direction.

"Another friend?" Nate glowered in the singer's direction, his menace had intensified in his lowered brow. Evie looked over and saw Claudio beaming at her. She smiled back, and then rolled her eyes at Nate.

167

"For God's sake, Nate. He's just a friend."

"Right, like Blythe's ex?" His insinuation burned. She cast as much venom as she could manage through her squinted glare. Nate just fingered the braided pigtail hanging over her shoulder. "I still love you, Evie. I'm going to keep telling you that until you accept it."

She did accept it. She just didn't want it anymore

"Nate, I—" Evie attempted to drop off her barstool, but Nate's meaty palm nudged her back down.

"Stop right there," he said. Endorphins flared and she glanced over at Seamus, who was monitoring their conversation as Nate continued. "I know things are different. You are. I sure as shit am." He looked down and licked his lips before chuckling under his breath. "Trust me, I'm different. I get it. We don't need to have this conversation again."

She stared at him, confused by the sincerity in his voice. "No, that's not it."

"I've been losing my cool a lot with you lately," he said. "I'm sorry. You left me. I guess I refuse to accept that's it?" He scowled down to the floor. "You've always been my Babe. You're not easy to give up, Evie."

She gnawed on her lower lip and turned to her drink. Her goal for the evening was to get drunk. That failed. She glanced up at Claudio, who'd moved onto another acoustic rendition of a song she'd sung from time to time at home. Anxiety beat down on her from every angle, and she slowly lowered off the stool onto her feet.

"I think I should get going."

Nate rose to his feet and towered over her. "I'll walk you home."

Panic froze her in place. "No."

Whatever emotion Nate wrangled in made its presence known through a tightened jaw. "It's getting late. You don't know what kind of crazies are out there."

We've got a good idea.

"I'll be fine." She monitored him through her periphery, cautious to deflect another controlling swipe at her while she pulled her jacket over her shoulders.

"I'll walk you out."

Leave him, already.

"Nate, stop." Now it was Evie's turn to try and push him down in his seat. A big guy like Nate didn't go down easy though.

"Just shut up and move," he said and twirled her around to navigate through the congested bar.

Seamus moved out of the corner of her eye, but Evie waved him off. She was done trying to argue with Nate or provoke him. She was more concerned with how to slip out of his burly mitts once outside.

Evie glanced over and offered an apologetic smile to Claudio. She felt awful for the clear disappointment that creased his brow as he played on. Unable to hold his stare, she looked away and weaved through the audience.

Outside, a line of yellow cabs offered her the perfect escape she needed.

"I'm going to just take a taxi." She squirmed free from Nate's grip on her elbow.

"If you live around here, I can just walk you."

"I'm good." She waved to the nearest cabbie.

Nate grumbled something she couldn't quite make out and walked over to open her car door. "I mean it, Babe. Don't write me off. Not yet."

"Good bye, Nate."

She cast him a warning glare, but let him place a wet kiss against her right cheek before she dipped into the backseat.

You can't keep them all to yourself.

No, she didn't want to keep any of them at the moment.

***

"Where ya headed?" the driver asked.

"Columbia and H." She chanced a paranoid look up at Nate's body towering over the side of the cab. "But can we swing up by Summer and come down West Broadway?"

"Sweetheart, you're taking us in the opposite direction. We're only a few blocks away from your destination."

She connected with the cabbie's scrupulous expression in the rearview.

"That's okay. I'm in no rush."

"Suit yourself. It's your meter." The driver pulled a U-turn, and they headed off in a route that Evie hoped would lead Nate far away from her apartment.

She sighed and turned to see his shadow fade out behind her. "What the hell is going on?"

"Some creep, eh?" the driver said, and she sat forward, cocking her head sideways to his gaze in the rearview. "Lots of wackadoos out there. Don't worry sweetie, he won't be able to follow us."

"Thank you."

"You gotta be more careful who you talk to in this city."

"Yes, sir." she said quietly and focused on her hands folded in her lap.

EIGHTEEN

After making it back to her apartment, Evie looked around the studio, but found no trace of Evan. The relief she felt burned in her chest as she made her way to the tiny bathroom.

She was lost in the mirror's reflection. The ghostly image who normally chided her for her stupidity and ignorance had been replaced by a vibrant, though still slightly pale, young woman with beaming crystal blue eyes.

"Everyone is going insane. Why does this have to be so complicated?"

But didn't Lucca make it sound so simple, so natural?

Evie glowered at the reflection, unwilling to accept the wisdom it projected. "No, I made a promise, and I intend to keep it."

A promise to whom? A ghost. Stop being selfish. We are inevitable.

Her shoulders folded forward. Dammit, the bitch was right. She was cursed, addicted to an eternal horror with the most beautiful of demonic creatures she'd likely ever meet. And anyone between her and Lucca was also cursed or had gone mad in the process.

"Shit, now what?"

***

Silky—cool—alluring. Evie bit down on her bottom lip, salivating at the sight of him across the room. His smooth

171

skin beckoned for her fingers to run across his body. They kneeled in the middle of the empty room amongst the dirt and grime, crimson and chartreuse lights bouncing off the earthen walls. Grit ground into her knees as she settled onto the earthen floor. The air nipped at her exposed flesh, tiny little pin pricks flickering across her skin.

"Just a tiny pinch," he said as Evie twitched from his touch. Her stomach flipped upside down. A small whimper escaped her body. Her breath misted through the dark toward him.

Her chest heaved as waves of wondrous ecstasy pulsed throughout her entire body. Her temperature increased dramatically, and she felt a throbbing sensation below her core. Evie then noticed the lack of sensation in her legs, like she was floating.

Claudio leaned in and dove into her mouth. He jabbed at her with his tongue, like he belonged in her. Their bodily fluids mixed. Ink seeped from his skin and crawled over hers. Her body absorbed the black liquid with a thirst that yearned from every pore, head to toe. She panted and moaned as his hands roamed across her bare flesh. Groans circled all around—hers—Claudio's—a host of others. The muffled sounds of a singer chanting over and over could be heard in the background. The voice was coarse, malicious and menacing.

She winced from a tiny bite in her arm. Evie looked down to find a syringe implanted there. The thin steel shard reflected glistening hues of amber and emerald as small splashes of colored light bounced off its thin and shiny surface. She flicked it off her like a bug and lifted her gaze back up to Claudio who smiled wickedly at her, a familiar and foreboding mien foreign to his soft features. She looked down at his outstretched arms and the black ink of his tattoos continued to move in waves across his skin and onto hers. She reached out to touch him, but her fingers couldn't find the surface of his body.

"Just a pinch." His wild grin widened. Colors swirled around her body like an ocean mist. Her eyes fluttered, her eyes rolled to the back of her head. "This is what you want, isn't it, Evie?" His voice hissed in her ears, tingling her senses.

She forced her eyes to focus on his. Claudio's gleamed, deep dark orbs with golden rims. Drums stomping around them fell in sync with her heartbeat. Her breath pounded against the multi-colored mist, and Claudio grinned devilishly, licking his lips. Golden lights skating across his dark irises.

"Lucca...?" Her vision blurred again. She blinked, and when she opened her eyes, he was wrapped around her, licking at her neck. His body moved not through the mist, but as the mist. Evie's pores widened to allow his thick air to invade her completely. Her entire body breathed in deeply to capture him as Lucca encircled her, like the colored smoke, and then solidified behind her. Arms wrapped securely around her, holding her in place.

"Enough games, Evie." He hummed in her ear. "I've claimed you."

She arched her back, head tilted to brace against his lean build, taking in the sweet scent of orange blossoms. The citric taste tickled the tip of her tongue. Her throat dried instantly thirsting for his essence. Her body desiccated, shriveling from the inside out. She licked at her lips again and bit into the air, teeth crunching and clattering with the threat of shattering from the force of her bite. The hard crunch echoed through her head. The wailing of countless strangers around her continued.

A familiar set of hands pulled her hips forward. Colossal paws pulled her lower body away while her neck stretched backward in protest.

Evie cried out loud in defeat as she was lifted off the ground. She outstretched her hands and made contact with a fuzzy, muscular build. Her head lulled forward and Nate was nuzzling his head into her neck. He took in a deep breath, a guttural purr emanated from deep within his chest, reverberating through her own. She curled into his massive and recognizable embrace.

"I miss you, Babe." He groaned, coaxing her to slide onto him. She still couldn't find anything below her waist, but she knew he was inside her. He was too familiar not to be. She knew this dance, had done it a million times, and so she rolled her hips, elated in the experience. The air remained thick and vibrant. Evie moved up and down, back and forth, and there she was, back into a comfortable motion. She made out the sound of Nate's heavy panting, and she delighted in the sensation of sex. Her chest began to ache. She didn't need Nate, only his one appendage she'd come to love so dearly.

"Just a pinch." She looked up. Nate had vanished, replaced by Claudio's image. She sunk her nails into his sturdy shoulders. Her laughter traveled in wave lengths through the colorful smoke surrounding them. The sight of Claudio's jovial smile made her hips dig deeper, pushing him deeper and deeper inside. Her head dipped back and Lucca was whispering in her ear again.

"Be careful, Evie. You can't keep us all to yourself."

The drumming increased around them.

She flinched. Her building orgasm waned as her hips arrested in fear. She looked forward, expecting Claudio, but was met by Sister Lima. The priestess held Evie in her small, gentle arms. Her body numbed and the experience of both

Nate and Claudio were lost. Evie felt a pang of shame wash over her through the thickening gloom. The intimacy of being held in a woman's arms seemed wrong, but she didn't push away from the priestess. Their physical embrace, almost natural, pulled moans from Evie's core.

"And how lucky are you to have won his favor?" The priestess cooed. The sultriness and spice of her accent felt wonderful trailing along Evie's quasi-lucid body.

"Let me go." Evie said though a moan, unsure whether or not she should be allowed to enjoy the woman's soft touch.

The young priestess held onto her. "You're amongst friends, Evie."

The woman's diminutive stature tensed and her once soft hands morphed into appendages much more closely resembling talons. Sharp edges dug into Evie's hips as the priestess pulled her in closer. Her docile smile mutated into an equally foreboding sneer.

"No." Her pulse quickened as she protested. "Let me go."

"You're being selfish." The woman hissed in a low and familiar groan.

Evie pushed back against the young woman's frame. Sister Lima released a shrill cackle. Evie's body shivered from the sound of her larking. Delicious thrills jetted across her flesh, like millions of little lashes of wanted pain, and settled deep between her legs.

"You're being selfish." Lucca scolded her from behind, grabbing the back of her hair.

Evie tossed her hands back to grasp onto his long, wild locks with a tantalized whimper. She seethed through her teeth, and pulled him closer into the crook of her neck.

"Babe, I need you." Nate's low voice called out from the shadows.

"Just a pinch." She heard Claudio whisper.

Sister Lima pressed against her chest. Evie scrambled to find Lucca. The priestess' hands roamed her body indiscreetly, her soft feminine touch exploring her silky insides. It electrified and embarrassed Evie, violated and excited. She was compelled to reciprocate, enthralled by Sister Lima's curves at her fingertips. Her pulse pounded between her ears and echoed in loud booming rhythm through the dark room, in sync with the ominous chants and cries surrounding their bodies.

"Lucca, please." He wouldn't answer her pleas. His presence faded and his grip on her melted away. "Please, Lucca. Save me."

His eyes burned like laser beams slicing through her, but she couldn't find them through the crimson and chartreuse murk. Anxiety pushed out from inside her chest, threatening to crack her open. Bones creaked under the stress, her heart on the verge and ready to explode.

"I can't breathe." She cried out, her vocal cords shredded. "I can't breathe." The drums beat louder.

All hands released her. As her body slithered into the dark nothingness of the dirt floor, Evie awoke in her bed, panting.

***

Sweat poured from atop her head. She breathed heavily and gripped her chest, pressing against it to settle the ache from within. Her soft cries could barely break the cool autumn air. A set of hands reached out to her.

"Evie, it's all right," he said, gently rubbing her back. With a great heave, Evie dove into Evan's arms where he hushed her. "It's okay. It was just a dream. Just a bad dream. I won't let you fall. I promise."

His soft lips pressed against the cold and clammy skin of her forehead. Her body convulsed in his arms. Tears poured easily into his chest. His sticky sweet aroma filled her senses, and after a few minutes, her pulse regulated under his protection. She clawed into the skin around his mid-section and squeezed. The intensity of her tremors lessened the more she constricted around him. He was all that kept her grounded. When Evie finally lifted her head to gaze up to Evan, he was gone.

NINETEEN

Evie picked at the resin caked against the dirty glass bowl. She grabbed at a twisted paper clip off her desk and settled onto the foot of her bed. She lifted her head to gaze over at the vacant futon. The chaos from her dream lingered in her chest. Her dreams had augmented, no longer transmitting echoes of her past—no more geishas, no more blood. Change had come. Loneliness consumed her as Evie stared at her cell phone.

It blinked at her with wild blue flashes. Nate had been texting her since their encounter last night, but her thoughts didn't rest with Nate and their doomed romance. Evie didn't want to think about how he felt last night in her dream, either—or Claudio for that matter.

She missed Evan.

She ached for the security of his arms, those she'd dreamed of repeatedly until the sun wouldn't let her sleep anymore.

Her only friend, the one person left to believe there was anything in her worth saving, she rejected him. She projected her lust onto him, unleashed her frustrations and blamed him for her misfortunes. For all his efforts, she questioned him because Lucca said so. Evie hated herself.

She closed her eyes and his sorrowed manifestation made her cringe. Far too frequently her own selfishness evoked that expression. He was there for her last night to comfort her, to protect her. She betrayed him with vitriol and defiance.

She sat silently, and for the first time wished for her inner voice to offer its opinion. The silence was deafening.

Evie jumped to her feet and snatched up her phone. "Fuck this." She thumbed through her cell and selected his number. Cradled in the fetal position against the back of her futon, she hugged her knees, hoping and praying he wouldn't actually answer.

***

"Hello?" His voice drifted from the speaker, and the sound of pain in it made Evie physically cower. "What's wrong?" She sat silent, unsure of how to begin her apology. Instead, she listened to his breathing, faint and controlled through the phone. The knot in her throat choked her. "Evie, say something."

"I'm okay," she said, whispering. "I'm sorry, Evan."

He sighed. "Do you want to do this now? I'm working." The brashness in his tone made her tear up in an instant. She felt insecure and weak and couldn't decide exactly why it was she felt that way.

"I'm sorry I blew up at you yesterday," she said.

His sighs belied his frustration. "Okay, so we are actually going to do this... It's fine, Evie. Forget about it."

"No I said some things..."

"You said some things. I said some things. We needed space from each other last night. Forget about it."

She didn't reply. She couldn't find words to answer his insolent tone. It wasn't what she'd expected from him. She trusted Evan to be warm and accepting of her apology. She needed the reassurance from her dreams.

You've pushed him too.

"Now you say something...?"

"What was that?"

"Nothing." Evie cleared her throat. "I... uh..." She fumbled for a reasonable excuse to mask her internal dialogue inadvertently verbalized. "I don't know what I'm saying."

We don't need Evan.

"That's not true," she said to her inner voice, but let him hear her. "Evan, I do need you."

"I thought you said you were okay." Concern grew more prominent in his voice.

"I am. I'm fine... I mean, I still feel awful about yesterday. Can you please come over? I'd like to see you, so I can apologize to your face." After a long pause, he cleared his throat. The rustling of papers and tapping of fingers against a keyboard in the background overpowered his increased breaths. Still, Evan hadn't responded.

"Evan? Did you hear me? Can you come over so we can talk?"

"Evie, I told you I'm working."

"Okay, later then." She was insistent. "Please?"

"I don't think that's a very good idea."

"Why? Give me one good reason why."

"Evie, you know I hate discussing this. I don't want to be around you right now."

He doesn't want to be around us?

The rejection hit Evie square between the eyes. She held the phone out in front of her and stared at it as if Evan could feel the shock of her glare through the cellular signals.

"Are you really that mad at me?" she asked, incredulous.

"No, it's not that." The sincerity in his voice calmed only a few of the wings fluttering haphazardly in her stomach.

"Then please tell me what I did wrong? Why don't you want to see me?"

She picked at the hem of her tank top. Nervous energy sent her fidgeting across the futon and then standing to pace back and forth in her living room.

"No, I'm sorry, I didn't mean anything bad by that," he said.

She collapsed across the futon, rubbing the bare flesh of her thighs with her fingertips. Her sights honed in on the imperfections of her skin, a terrible nervous habit she'd developed since moving to Boston—or sobering up, one of the two.

This is beyond ridiculous. You know what this son of a bitch is trying to do. You know he's hiding something.

And then Evie asked a question she regretted as soon as she vocalized it. "Evan, what are you hiding? Why are you trying so hard to save me?"

"Save you?"

"Protect me... from you, I mean. I'm guessing you're going to say something about needing blood and that I'm not safe around you."

"Something like that, yes. I've been thinking that we spend too much time together. It's probably not a good thing. Fortunately, it seems you don't even want me there to help you."

"Is Lucca so bad? Is that what you're hiding?"

Her interjection elicited a low growl from the phone's speaker.

"Do you know anything about him and what he is?" Evan asked.

"He's like you."

He snorted. "He is nothing like me, Evie."

"Oh? And how are you so different?"

"Well for one, I have a fucking conscience. I follow a structured society. I obey the rules which have protected my kind for centuries."

"And he doesn't?"

"No, he doesn't. He doesn't give a shit for the sanctity of life."

"Sanctity? Evan, that makes no sense. You kill humans to survive."

"Not by choice," he said in protest. "Listen, Evie, this is bigger than you or me. The purge drove many of us here to America seeking refuge. The alliances we built strengthened the houses that govern our kind. Others like Khan and Lucca care nothing for what we've done to protect ourselves from discovery and future persecution. They're reckless, murderous, and evil. Lucca embodies every evil trait I detest. Don't ever compare me to him." The rage in his tone was an intense force. The heat of his anger seared through the phone.

"So you have some personal vendetta against him?"

Evan sighed, exasperated. Tension oozed thick in his silence before growling back. "No."

"Then why do you care about me? My life sounds very trivial in comparison."

"Evie, what do you know about the change?"

"You know I don't know anything about it. Why?"

His huff scratched her eardrum through the speaker. "It's not easy. It's not for everyone."

"I already guessed that. Otherwise wouldn't we all want to live forever?"

"No, Evie, that's not what I meant. It can be a deadly process."

"Obviously."

"No, just listen. You would need to ingest my essence, my blood. It's cold. It's bitter and not at all pleasant to choke down. You will morph. You will change. In all aspects of your being, you will die. There is nothing natural about the Sempiternal."

Listening to Evan describe it made her feel excited, thrilled even, envisioning ingesting his blood, his essence. And "his blood" could be Lucca's or Evan's—either way, she was aroused by the notion, and nibbled at her bottom lip. "So, what's your point? So far it doesn't sound that bad."

"My point, is that not everyone survives the change." His voice had grown thick with annoyance and aggression. "In fact, most don't live to see eternity. I don't want to see you go through it and lose you in the attempt. Lucca doesn't care otherwise. He'd rather try and face the odds that you will most likely die than preserve who you are now."

"You really don't think I can do it?" Evan sighed and mumbled something Evie couldn't quite understand. "What was that?"

"I said, you just love running off with a thought, don't you? No, as much as it kills me to admit it, I have no doubt you're strong enough. You make that abundantly clear with each passing day. But that's not the point."

"So then what is it? Why are you protecting me from him?"

"Because I—" He paused and groaned. She wanted so badly to reach through the phone and squeeze the truth out of him. She slid her hands up and down her body to divert their attention. Their glides only worsened her arousal in tune with the sound of his heavy breathing on the other end of the line before he continued. "I did not choose this life, Evie. It chose me. You can still have a choice."

"What choice do I have without Lucca? Or you?" She heard him sigh heavily again, pained. "You do that a lot, you know."

Evie traced the contours of her own body with her eyes closed and visualized Evan sitting on the opposite end of the phone with his perfectly shaped body stretched across an office desk chair. He was possibly stretching his firm grip over his knee or maybe even up his thigh as he held the phone with a brilliantly vexed look across his face. His soft pink lips parted and his weed-tinged breath beating hot against the phone's receiver.

"What do I do?" he asked.

"You have a hard time talking about us, and then you sigh. You usually end up changing subjects. So what now, Evan? What do you want to talk about ?"

"It seems to me like you're the one changing subjects now." The roughness of his voice pulled a crooked grin across her face, one she was glad he couldn't witness first hand. Her fingers played across the top of her cotton panties.

"I want to talk about what you're hiding." Longing surfaced from within her voice. As Evie breathed into the phone, something about their arguing was exciting her. A blissful burn ignited in her core.

"Evie, what are you doing?"

"What do you mean?"

"Evie, I won't be the one to see you die."

Die?

Arousal doused, Evie shot up straight in her seat. She was envisioning her and Lucca, her and Evan. What did her fantasies have to do with dying? Her yearning subsided as she was brought back to the morbid reality of their conversation with a definite unfulfilled aching between her legs.

"I thought you said—you really don't think I'll survive?" she asked, harkening back to the crux of their argument.

"I think you're fucking crazy—or paranoid—probably a little bit of both."

"And you're full of shit." She snapped back into their circular bickering.

"You're being ridiculous, Evie. I'm not arguing with you about this over the phone."

"Then come over here. That's all I wanted in the first place." Her strident tone bounced off the cramped wall-space of her studio.

"So we can argue in person? Haven't we done enough of that lately?"

"Dammit, Evan. Just get your ass over here so I can yell at you in person." Evie ended the call and tossed her phone across the room with a frustrated howl.

The audacity in his voice offended her. The way he chided her about his laws and his kind made her blood bubble over her sanity's edge. Maybe she wasn't strong enough. Maybe she would die, but shouldn't that be her choice?

***

She stood amidst the fading daylight bleeding orange hues through the windows. The rays tingled against her skin. With a frustrated groan, Evie made her way out of the sun's reach into the fluorescence of the bathroom. She stared at her mirror image with an indignant glare reflecting back at her

"What the fuck was that?"

Isn't his aggression maddeningly delicious?

"What is wrong with me?" She rubbed her face vigorously, snorting as she took in a deep breath and kneaded her eye sockets.

"Evan's a friend."

A good friend.

"Not that kind of friend."

Maybe he should be that kind of friend. Maybe you should test immortality with Evan. Then you could face Lucca with an open mind, instead of bogus fear or broken promises.

She stood, bewildered and shivering in front of her reflection. Pulling her promise to Rob into the mix was a low blow, even for her subconscious. "That's not fair."

Then stop teasing.

"I'm the one teasing? You're the one trying to seduce Evan half the time, or leading on Nate or Claudio. What the fuck?"

I know what I want. I want Evan—Lucca—I want immortality.

"And I want to be normal," she said desperately. "You and I are the same person. What is wrong with me?"

I told you to listen to me, to feel me.

Evie pulled at her hair and turned away. She flipped the light switch and walked away before the ghost in the mirror could scold her further.

Back when she lived in Fallhaven, Hope told her to listen to her high priestess, her inner voice. She was told to let it guide her. Now it was telling her to test immortality on Evan? How does one test immortality, she wondered. It's not like she could take Evan out for a test drive like a car. Actually the thought of riding him wasn't half bad, but she shook the notion away. Nate or Claudio would be easy to snare. Mortal men were so easily teased with the prospect of sex. In reality, she knew they were inconsequential. All that mattered to her were the Sempiternal, but Evan said he wasn't teased by sex. He was afflicted by a different hunger.

She grabbed her glass bowl and quickly packed it with fresh green bud. She sat back on the futon and watched the smoke waft through the air in front of her. More addictions, she thought. Her immortal addiction was proving much more caustic than any other drug she'd experimented with in the past. Now she considered experimenting with Evan.

"Crazy," she said, fingering the resin along the edge of the bowl.

TWENTY

Evie hoped a long, hot shower would help to purify her mind. She let the steaming spout spew scalding water down her back. The burning sensation was familiar and welcome. She examined the cracked tiles littering the stall, searching through the spidery lines hoping answers would ooze out, but found none.

Her stomach turned and her brain throbbed. She'd found herself so concerned with Evan lately, so particular of his opinions about her. Her lower lip quivered. The image of his saddened features stabbed at her chest.

The ache in her stomach increased, nausea overwhelmed, and she doubled over in agony. Panting heavily from a building constriction in her chest, Evie sat down in the shower, hugging her knees and allowing the shower's stream to suffocate her. She knew that even when Lucca came to liberate her from her torturous mortality, she'd forever be plagued by guilt for undermining everything Evan had done for her.

Then do something about him. Fix this.

After a considerable amount of time, the water cooled, and Evie shook from the its plummeting temperature rather than her own internal strife.

The spectral image glaring back at her from the mirror kept quiet as she dressed in a simple cotton camisole and skirt. She wrapped a thin scarf around her neck to keep warm from an unrelenting chill sourced from inside her chest. She checked her phone and was drenched in disappoint when she saw no flashing blue light.

"Just call me, already. This sucks." She skulked over to the pantry to address the rumbling in her belly.

***

It all started with a guitar and a solid drum beat. The studio filled with music, and Evie was warmed by the orange glow carrying the melodic sound waves along the glimmers of the fading sun. Visualizing the air swirling around her, Evie's hips swayed back and forth to the music. Her long skirt wrapped around her body, whipping against her ankles. Lips moving, her voice found its way out in a whispery tune. Her head listed side to side, eyelids lowered. She spun through the tiny kitchen, reheating leftovers from meals Evan had fixed for her. Her feet tiptoed across the floor while her body moved fluidly. Lyrics drifted through the air and resonated in her mind. She sang along with the singer's cries from the pain of living two lives, much like the moon with its light and dark sides, each loving too much, and suffering a guilt that consumed.

It wasn't until she turned to see Evan standing in the doorway that she froze in place. He didn't smile or indicate any amusement from her performance. He looked saddened, strikingly wounded by the sight of her.

A culpable tugging in her chest accompanied his pained expression.

"I'm sorry, I didn't realize I had an audience," she said with a blushing smile. Evan didn't answer, but offered an intense stare. Dark circles rimmed underneath his eyes, a weariness she'd never noticed on him before.

He turned toward the living room. She followed, observing his tired posture as he lowered onto the futon. Worn as he may have been, he continued to carry an air of elegance in his movements, a soft beauty. This was about more than just their on-going argument, Evie realized. If she did cause whatever pain threatened to distort his brilliance, she wanted to address it.

Give him what he needs.

She swallowed hard and moved forward.

Afraid to spook him, Evie questioned the appropriateness of what she was about to attempt, but the circles under his eyes and his pallid complexion were too much for her to bear. She extended a hand out to him, cautious and trembling in the air to touch him.

Evan watched her through a sideways glance. The candlelight flickered in his big brown eyes, dancing through the pools of tears he held back. He pursed his lips, biting down on his lower lip as she closed in on him. Her hand descended on his shoulder. He flinched, scorched by her light touch.

"Evie, what are you doing?" His voice was thin, tired.

"You need me."

"You said you wanted to talk."

"I want to help you, Evan."

She knelt down in front of him, gazing up at his eyes glazed over. She unwrapped the scarf around her neck, revealing a nearly bare chest and striking collarbone. Evan's eyes widened. A tear found its escape down his cheek. Evie wanted to lick it off of his pale skin. His eyes dropped down toward the bare flesh below her shoulders.

"Evie, what are you doing?" Urgency heaving in his voice, he shifted to off-center his body to her. She was quick to grab his arm and leg, steadying him in place.

"It's okay. I can do this for you. It's the least I can do. Only for a little bit, all right?" She forced the resolve in her tone. Deep down, she was just as terrified as Evan appeared on the outside. Her heart thrummed, washing her over in heated waves.

How did this work? How badly would it hurt? And would he be strong enough to resist the urge to bleed her dry? She felt more confident when she embarked on her first hallucinogenic trip. This was worth the risk though. In order to keep him by her side with all her faults and indecision, she could offer a small prize for his attention.

The tears streamed more freely from Evan's face than hers, though his demeanor never wavered. His eyes remained fixed on her flesh, his body like a statue. With a hesitant sigh, he raised a hand up to her bare shoulder and gasped from the feel of her soft skin. Evie tilted her head to the side, allowing him greater access to her virgin neckline. His hand caressed its pristine surface, up along her collarbone to the nape of her neck. The rush of lust flooding her senses was amazing.

Just do it.

He leaned in, wrapping his other hand around her waist and pulling her neck closer to him. Tiny quakes ran through Evie's body, tremors she fought to subdue, but failed. Labored breaths drove her chest into his over and over again. His own breath was hot against her skin.

Evie closed her eyes in anticipation of his teeth cutting into her. She thought back to when she was home in Fallhaven, to the night Lucca penetrated her sanctuary and sliced into the muscular tissue of her tongue, the metallic flavor of her own blood haunted her taste buds. Would this be the same, she wondered.

The moisture from Evan's licked lips against her skin seeped into her pores. He barely grazed the tiny crevice where her neck met her collarbone, but such minimal contact was enough to set off a relay of delicious shivers down her spine, pulsating down to the base of her body.

She repressed a moan. Evan froze, and then pushed her away.

"I can't do this." He jumped across the room, as far from her as space allowed.

She monitored him. His tall, thin frame was hunched over in the corner of the room. She knew that tormented pose; the feeling, thirsting for a drink, a hit, anything to curb the sickness from withdrawal. That same feeling scorched through her. She needed this just as badly as Evan did, to know what it felt like.

She took in the dimly lit room, the candles flickered a warm glow around them drenched in the last wisps of the day's amber glow. Her eyes caught the faint shimmer of a glass object on the makeshift coffee table. With a spark of ingenuity, Evie bent down, grabbed the glass pipe from the table and slammed it against the edge. The tiny piece shattered in her hand, leaving a long glass shard, which she lifted to her neck. Using the jagged edge, Evie dragged it across her clavicle, just enough to break the skin. She yelped from the self-inflicted pain, which at first burned then quickly cooled from her own essence beading up in a ruby bubble on her skin.

Evan turned and glared with large, longing eyes. She stared back, defiant. Crimson pooled up in the base of her neck. Her hand dropped the glass piece to the ground, and she silently challenged him to deny her.

"Evie!" He rushed over to her, practically soaring through the air, and buried his face into her.

Evan suckled at the wound.

She flinched. Her body's first reaction was that of self-preservation, to recoil from the assault. Then as he pulled the blood from the wound, her body seized. Warmth, chased by thousands of tiny pin pricks ravaged her body. The sensation ran its course starting from her core and fizzling out at her extremities. Her head became feather-light. A soft halo distorted her surroundings. Evie threw her head back, elated as his tongue ran over her slicked skin. His teeth gnashed into the laceration—hurting, burning at first, and then melting into wet bliss.

The room spun. Evie wrapped around Evan, anchored her limbs to him before all physical abilities escaped her. She was drunk from the sensation. She was high off his scent. And she reveled in his touch. Primal need screamed through her body, escaping from her vocal chords through the simplest selfless—and selfish act. She came alive, and yet died in the same instant. Her eyes flitted to the back of her head, her body limp. Her fingers torn into Evan to sustain the comedown.

She scrambled to catch her breath, but wanted more for him—from him. Evan's hands held her fast, forcing her to all but fuse with his body, morphing into one entity. His tongue continued to lap against the wound. Ravenous groans emanated from within him as he dug deeper into the base of her neck.

Evan pulled away from the gash as though suddenly repelled by an opposing force. His hold on her hadn't lessened though, his fingers still digging in. He lifted his head, and she was instantly enraptured by his eyes. They were radiant, perfectly beautiful brown orbs.

Both breathed in syncope—euphoric.

"Why?" Evan's voice coasted on the edge of his breath and called her attention to his mouth, lathered in red.

Rather than answering him directly, her gaped mouth closed over his. She dove into him. Instinctively, she imbibed upon his flavor, searching through his mouth for more—more sensation—more connection. He reciprocated her kiss, his fangs just grazing the inside of her mouth. She forced her tongue deeper, clanking teeth against those cuspid treasures. Evan groaned and drifted toward the bed, falling back with Evie held captive on top of him.

She entwined her fingers through his hair and pulled with all her might. Sucking his hairline against her teeth. She was drowning, and he was her oxygen. He massaged the source of the bleeding with his tongue and rolled on top of her. She squeezed her thighs against Evan's ribcage to brace against his mad undercurrent.

Before she was ready to fully succumb to the encroaching darkness, Evan was finished.

***

Savoring the aftermath of feeding, Evie rested her head on top of her pillow, her hands folded under her cheek. She stared at him. As her lens blurred, physical surroundings overcast by a fog, Evan remained a crisp contrast. His skin was like porcelain, pristine, no doubt fragile and cool to the touch. She reached out, astonished to find his cheek soft, supple, and warm against her palm. The dark circles had vanished from under his eyes. The cherry red of his lips deepened against his paleness. He didn't frown, but he wasn't smiling either.

His stoic expression puzzled her.

"Why?" he asked again.

"You needed me." She offered a gentle smile as reassurance she was completely at peace with her donation. Evan lifted a hand over to rub his thumb along her cheek.

"How did you know I would stop?"

Evie smiled wider. "I trust you."

"But why... I want to know why you trust me."

She shrugged her shoulders. "Should I not?"

"Evie, I could have killed you."

"But you didn't." She considered something worse than that. "You're not still mad at me, are you?"

He ran his hand over and across her forehead, running his fingers through her hair, intently watching his own movements. She rested on the cliff of his silence, arms dangling over the ledge, prepared to plummet head first.

"You're completely reckless." He continued watching his hand weave through the highlights of her hair. "How do you feel?"

Evie beamed pure joy back at him as she recalled the blissful feeling of bleeding into him. The act had introduced her to a whole new high she'd never imagined could exist. Her body was tingling from the blood loss.

"Incredible," she said. "How do you feel?"

"Perfect." Evan replied without hesitation. Evie raised an eyebrow at him and giggled.

Evan smiled back, a welcome sight. In fact, it was a marvel to behold. His subtle, accentuated incisors didn't alarm her. Actually, they complemented his innocent face. Evie found it a simple thing to lose herself in his joyful expression. For the first time ever, she felt as though Evan felt no pain. And it was all because of her.

There was no sorrow in the acoustic musings playing in the background. Soft piano and beautiful lyrics made all the sense in the world as the singer proclaimed his love. Her experiment had revealed a strange new twist to her immortal fate, one even her inner voice had yet to reconcile.

Their comfortable silence was broken by a low vibration coming from behind her. Both heads turned to peer over Evie's shoulder.

"What's that?" Evan asked.

She rolled over to pick up her cell phone from her nightstand.

Their moment had passed.

Twenty-One

Whats 4 lunch 2moro?

She read the text message, and a spasm of remorse tugged at her heart.

"Evie, what's wrong? Who is it?" Evan glimpsed over Evie's shoulder. She twisted her body to block his view.

Staring down at her phone, she tuned Evan out and chewed on the inside of cheek. She would have given anything to rewind to a moment ago, before her phone buzzed, before she lost her moment with Evan.

"What the hell, Nate?" She spoke softly as she responded with a firm "No" in her text, but it was enough to pique Evan's interest. He propped up on his knees to gain better access over her shoulder, going so far as to turn her back toward him.

"What do you mean, it's Nate? When did you start talking to him again?"

Shit, she thought, finding the concern in his knitted brow. Such disquiet was spiked with betrayal. The noxious brew turned Evie's stomach.

"He's been working in Boston for a while," she said, and his furrowed brow deepened into a definite glower. Already reality resurfaced, and with it the intimate high shared with Evan had vanished.

In an instant, the phone vibrated again, but not due to an incoming text.

"Is he calling you?" Evan waited for her to respond, but Evie could only turn away from him. "Evie, tell me you haven't been talking to him."

She pinched her eyes shut, begging the phone to stop vibrating in her lap. A tear spilling over her cheekbone. The damned thing took its time, but ultimately sent Nate to voicemail. Evan snatched it up from her limp grip and jumped to his feet.

"Goddammit Evie, have you been seeing him?"

He tossed the phone, and it landed by her side. By a mere shift of her eyes, she saw the message on the screen before it went black.

I TOLD U NO. MEET ME 2MORROW!!

Shredding more than just one more tear, she squeezed the bridge of her nose. The room was spinning. Her vision was blurry.

It's happening, stupid girl. You can't have them all.

"Stop it." Her murmured pleas elicited howling delight from her inner voice, but served to further fuel Evan's rage. With more force then previously, he yanked her to meet him face to face. It took a moment for the dust to settle around her vision before she could focus. She had to brace herself on top of the mattress when vertigo tipped her sideways.

"Evie, how long have you been in contact with Nate?"

"I don't know. A while now, I guess. Why?"

He gawped at her. "Have you seen him?" His firm grip around her bicep relayed his demand. Endorphins flared, her instinct for self-preservation engaged, but the effects of feeding cemented her physical being in its place.

"Yes," she said in a thin voice. Evan released her and backed away slowly, like he'd seen the impossible behind her deadened stare. He stalked back and forth at the foot of the bed. "What's wrong, Evan? It's just Nate. What difference can he make?"

Evan stopped pacing and whipped around to face her once more. "Just Nate? Evie, how did he find you? How did he conveniently end up in Boston? Is he on the boats right down the street from where you work? Where I—does he know where you live?"

Naïve, stupid girl.

Evie bit her tongue and pushed aside her subconscious snub. She mustered some resolve to respond to Evan. "What do you mean, how did he find me? He's always had my number."

Power surged inside of her at their encroaching argument. Evie willed herself to her feet and met Evan head on in the center of the room.

He clenched his jaw, fists balled at his sides when she neared. "How did he find you in Boston?"

"He didn't. It just happened." With each passing moment, oxygen flooded her system, revitalizing her body and her annoyance with Evan's anger. She steeled her nerves before reciprocating his stone glower. "It's not a big deal. I told him to fuck off."

"Evie, don't you see? If a dumb-ass junkie like Nate can find you, then anyone can—including Lucca."

"That's not fair to call him that. Nate's been calling me since the day I left Fallhaven, begging me to go back to him. I've tried to break it off with him. I wouldn't accept his calls, and he stopped trying. Then he texted me to no end, so I started responding. I never told him where I was though. I don't know how he found me in Boston, but he did. He's trying to get his life back on track or something, but I have no intentions of getting back together with him if that's what you're jealous about."

The world froze. Evie watched in slow motion, as Evan's breath caught. The harsh grating of his teeth thundered through her head. The immortal monster stirred again. He held the beast back, caged behind those big brown eyes. It had grown strong, rejuvenated by her mortal essence, combined with each argument between them and her defiance. It threatened to burst out. In turn, its antagonism provoked the high priestess, pacing in her dark cavern. Evie honed in on the sharp point of Evan's canine just peeking out of the corner of his closed lip scowl.

"Evan? Say something." Enthralled by his aggression, she stood her ground and awaited his response.

He exhaled, cycling through another deep breath and reining himself back in. Evan turned away from her and stared out the window into the harbor. "What do you want me to say? Everything I do is because I want to keep you safe. How can I do that when you're disobeying my wishes behind my back?"

"You keep dishing out that protection bullshit, but I don't understand it. Why do you feel the need to be my saving grace, Evan? You were so willing to help me hide from Lucca, but this is all getting a bit extreme. It's not what I wanted."

The aggression electrifying the stagnant air of her apartment fizzled out to a dull sense of remorse. Evie tried to reach out to Evan, to get the tiniest bit closer to the intimate high they'd shared moments earlier. That was gone now as he stepped back from her.

"Evie, I can protect you from him. I can help you beat him."

His words twisted her brow with puzzlement. "Who said I wanted that?"

"Don't you?"

"No Evan." She sunk back into her shoulders. The hurt in his eyes had beaten the beast into submission, but something about that cut to her core and burned. "Look… Everyone I love is dead, hates me, or is immortal. If this is all some predestined fate that I have no say in, then I need to at least understand it better. Why has Lucca been chasing me, and why did his last attempt end up in my death?"

"But Evie, you don't get it. I—"

"Stop… No buts. Obviously something's wrong about his obsession with me, and he knows it. He even finds amusement in it or something." Evan's features hardened. The muscles along his jaw flexed, warning her, but Evie wasn't about to stop. There was freedom in her words, so she continued, "That's what I need to know before I can face Lucca. I don't like feeling out of control when he's around. I like getting high—being numb to the outside world—because when that happens, I still feel like me. Lucca, on the other hand, he tears me apart from the inside out." Longing interwoven with exasperation laced every one of her words.

Evan returned her gaze with fangs retracted behind pursed lips. "What do you want me to do Evie? Let you stick your neck out there—literally?"

"Tell me why it matters to you so much."

Just say it.

Evan didn't answer her. Choking on a growl, he furrowed his brow and stormed past her. She thought to, but decided not to stop him. Arguing further seemed futile as well. The burst of adrenaline powering her antagonism depleted rapidly. She let him go and flinched as the door slammed shut behind him.

***

Her cell phone buzzed again. Ignoring it, Evie stood staring at the door a moment longer, anticipating Evan's return that never occurred. She turned to her phone and found more texts from Nate.

Dinner 2morrow
Babe?

Evie winced. The throbbing slice on her neck drew her attention from her cellphone. The pain was piercing, but as a bi-product of the feeding process, she languished the soreness. Based on the way Evan stormed off, she'd never feel that high again. And what did she have left? Nate's damned text messages. Evie grumbled to herself. Fingers swiped madly over the phone's screen as she typed her response. "Leave me alone, please."

Need u Babe.

Evie groused at her phone. "What the fuck Nate?" Her wild pulse only furthered the ache in her wound. Loneliness getting the better of her, her fingers passed over her phone.

Fine. Soon.

"This is a bad move," she said to herself and cringed as his response came through.

Luv u.

***

Hours into the night, Evie was anxious, sweaty. She'd stripped down to her black lace underwear and tangled herself up in sheets that still reeked of Evan. With aching legs, watery eyes, and restlessness, she bolted from her bed and paced around her apartment. The track she made around the pantry and through her living room nearly wore down the floorboards' finish, but she repeated her path until the room spun.

You know what to do about this, stupid girl.

"I can't call Evan back here."

Not Evan...

"I can't go look for Lucca. Evan would..."

But we know how to dull the pain. We were so good at it before.

"No."

Yes.

"No, Evan would..."

What? Deny us more feeding? Fuck us? What? It's time, stupid girl.

She halted in her circuit around the studio. Eyes glossed over and itchy, she glimpsed at her phone still blinking from Nate's last text message. "Oh God." Disparity thickened her whining. "What time is it?"

She grabbed for her cell, and finding it not even midnight, her stomach twisted. There was too much time to be alone and restless, too much time for the high priestess to judge her. She glanced over to her coffee table, the knot tightened at the sight of the glass shards still strewn over the swatch covering the crates. "Shit."

You know what to do.

Evie checked her phone one more time, and then teased by the foot of her bed out of the corner of her eyes, caught the shadow of her treasure hidden underneath.

"Dammit." She dropped to all fours and rummaged through the boxes under her bed. The relics weren't far behind the mess. She brushed aside the boots, but snatched up the ratty old black t-shirt. She held it in her hands, brought it to her lips and drew it into her breath. She wrapped herself in Lucca's faded t-shirt left behind at her house in Fallhaven. It lacked his zest, but it was soft to the touch, like his skin. She thought of wearing the boots he'd left behind as well, but left them hidden under her bed. "That's a bit much," she said and headed out the door.

TWENTY-TWO

Just a few short blocks from her apartment, Evie found herself in a familiar scenario. She perused aisles displaying glass bottles of various shapes, colors, and sizes. The sickening bind in her stomach persisted as her mouth dried, her taste buds recalling the zing of their liquid contents.

Which one?

The green and clear bottles of amber liquid made her homesick, so she moved on. Wincing at the prospect of the nasty hangover left after a cheap zinfandel, she moved on and stopped at an end cap. "Maybe this was a bad idea."

Just buy something, any of them will do the trick.

Somewhat disheartened, she grabbed a bottle of clear poison from the display and headed toward the register. The clerk behind the counter couldn't have been more than eighteen by his build, though the lines along his worn eyes indicated he should've been double that, at least. He eye-fucked her hard, running up and down her body with a voracious leer and stopping at the bottom hem of her shirt.

"Live around here?" The sound of his voice drew her eyes away from the glass bottle on the counter and up to meet his. She hated the direct contact.

"Why do you ask?"

He pitched a shoulder up. "Don't usually get girls in here in their underwear in the middle of the night."

She set her jaw. "Does it bother you? Maybe I have shorts underneath that you can't see."

He shrugged once more and finished the sale. "I get off in an hour if you need company."

The high priestess stirred with provocation.

Why not? Let's have some fun?

Evie scoffed. "Pass, thanks." She turned away, rolling her eyes, leaving the clerk to chuckle in her wake.

"Offer's open anytime," he said.

"Not tonight." With her back to him, she lifted her middle finger in the air and headed back out into the night, precious cargo in hand, not giving a shit about who might be waiting for her out there.

***

Across the way from her apartment, she tossed off her flip flops and plopped down on the cool sand with her bottle of cheap vodka. It stung sliding down her throat. She gagged with each swig, but relished the booze's bite. It followed with a warmth in her belly. She needed the light-headed sensation and the clumsiness of inebriation.

The moon hung over the water, and the ruckus of city life lingered behind her. The sea salt air was as familiar as the burn from the alcohol. She hummed contently.

Evie made it only halfway through the bottle before her head was swimming. She compared the vodka's effects to the weightlessness she felt in Evan's arms. Holding the bottle up into the moonlight, she glowered at the sensation.

"You filthy bitch. You can't compare." She dropped the bottle into the sand with a thud.

"Can't compare to what?"

Evie turned to find Claudio sitting in the sand next to her.

"Hey." Her head bobbed side-to-side. "Hey, you."

Taking in her drunken state, Claudio eyed her up and down.

"Hey, yourself. What are you doing out here?" He picked up the bottle of vodka from the sand and examined the label. "This shit is nasty. What are you doing, Evie?"

"Well, what...? What'er you doin'... out here?" She slurred each word and stared at him through slit eyelids. Her lips puckered to hold back a burst of senseless laughter.

He chuckled. "I just finished a gig at the pub down the street. You, on the other hand, are looking for trouble." He lifted a hand to tame the long strands of hair flailing across her face. "It's nearly three in the morning. A girl like you is going to find herself killed out here—or worse. Let me get you home."

Claudio stood and stretched, dusting the sand from his pants and hands before reaching down to lift her up. As he did so, the high priestess lurked from her cavern. Evie's eyes meandered up and down his body, tongue playing at the corner of her smile. He supported her weight with one arm, grabbing his guitar case with his free hand. The half-emptied bottle of vodka was left in the sand.

"Did you come looking for me?"

Evie stumbled through the unevenness of the sand.

"Nope, but you're lucky I was walking home by the beach," He said.

Her head fell backwards as she attempted to meet his grin. She huffed, delighted. "Do you like blood, Claudio?"

He laughed, but his amusement was overshadowed by a perplexed look. "Do I like what?"

"You heard me. Do you like blood? Would you like my blood?"

He shook his head, playfulness rising above the fading confusion along his brow. "What, do you think I'm a vampire or something?"

"Exactly!" She waved a drunken finger in his face.

They stopped at the front stoop of her apartment building. Claudio pulled her in front of him and held her up with both arms wrapped tightly around her waist. "I'm sorry to disappoint you," he said. "But I'm not a creature of the night... not anymore, at least." She hooked around his neck and hung there, casting a fool's grin up at his own brand of charisma. "If I was though, you can believe I'd be all over your neck."

Claudio lunged down, snorting as if gnawing into her like a rabid dog. At first she laughed, cackling in the moonlight, then yelped as his chin banged against the tender wound on her collar bone. Claudio pulled away and gasped as he saw the incision. His laughter ceased and his eyes widened.

"Evie, what happened to—"

"Evie." A voice called out from the top of the landing. She and Claudio looked up to find Evan glaring down at the two of them.

Claudio looked at her, then back at Evan. Even through her stupor, she scowled at Evan—at the beast growling down at her.

"What the fuck are you doing here?" Her strident tone carried the bite she intended, but her words still slurred.

"What do you think you're doing?" Evan stepped down to take her into his arms.

Claudio's grip on her went limp as he took a step back. "Hey man, I'm sorry. Evie never mentioned she was back with—"

"It's fine." Evan cut him off coldly.

"Is she going to be alright?"

"She'll be fine," Evan said. "Thank you for bringing her home."

Evie fumbled in Evan's hold as he pulled her up the stairs.

"Wait. Claudio was about to suck my blood." She laughed. "Let me go. I'm not done with him."

Her arms flailed, reaching for Claudio, who remained frozen in place.

Evan squeezed her tighter, his annoyance rumbling between their bodies. "Say good night, Evie."

"Good night, Evie." She giggled and wiggled her fingers to Claudio before the front door slammed shut.

***

Evan flung her over his shoulder and ascended the three flights to her apartment. His tattooed shoulder dug into her belly as she slammed down onto him with each one of his frustrated steps. Evie fought not to hurl over his backside. If the neighbors heard their commotion, none of them felt the need to come to her rescue. The stairwell remained black, doors shut.

Inside her apartment, Evan propped her against the wall by the front door. She landed with a thump and knocked her head against the call box as he secured the deadbolt.

"Ouch!" She giggled, sniffling a little, and then lifted a wavering hand toward his face, trying to connect with it. "Hey there, handsome, what's your name?"

He batted it away with disgust. "Evie, seriously, what the fuck are you doing?" If the aggravation in his voice was meant to sober her, it failed miserably. She laughed, spraying spittle in his face.

"What do you care?" She lurched forward and dragged one foot after the other before flopping face first onto her bed.

"Are you kidding me, Evie? I've been worried sick about you. I came back so we could talk rather than argue, but you were gone. I found your cell phone, but there was no trace of you. Are you trying to get back at me for earlier this evening or something?" She mumbled a response into the bedding. "Evie, I can't hear you with your face down like that."

Evan walked over and flipped her onto her back. Her incoherent rambling continued until her mouth was free from its linen gag.

"You're damn fucking right I am." She annunciated perfectly and jumped up to stand straight in front of him. The effects of the alcohol knocked her back down on the bed before Evan could. He kneeled by her side and brushed her hair away from her face. She stared down at him warily. "You hurt me," she said, whimpering with eyes sore and wet.

He engaged with her stare, and then looked down to her bruised collar bone. His brow knit, jaw clenched. "I know. I'm sorry. I shouldn't have let you—"

"No, that's it. You shouldn't let me anything. It's not your place to control me like that. Dammit Evan, I've been through enough, haven't I? I don't need you confusing me like this. Why are you doing this to me?"

"What am I doing, confusing—"

"You... you're doing you. I can't..." Evie rambled as Evan looked at her in panic. "I've been all alone..." Her eyes wandered the room, never once meeting his. "... you left...... the Sempiternal..." She mumbled gibberish, her crescendo of emotions amplifying. "... in my dreams, and then you bit me..." In a cataclysmic fit, Evie burst into tears. "And why don't you want to fuck me?"

She buried her face into her hands, salty tears spilling out from between her fingers. Evan's heavy sigh preceded him rubbing her back, his other hand to her knees steadying her.

"Is that what this is about, Evie? You're upset because I won't—is that why you got drunk? Because I won't have sex with you?"

"This is more than that, Evan, but it's still true. Isn't it? You won't." She snapped her mucus-filthied face up to connect with his through red, puffy eyes. Her cheeks were wet and swollen from her own blubbering. Evan watched her. Pain etched across his creased brow. "Lucca will though. He wants to. I know he does."

Evan flinched as the acidic coating of her words splashed across his face. A mix of fear and anger washed over his features. His hands knotted into fists against her body.

"What do you mean, Lucca wants to? Have you spoken with him?" His voice flat, teeth gritted. The conviction in his eyes warned her to temper her response. Evie paid no attention. She answered him with a defiant, know-it-all grin.

"Yup."

He took a deep breath in. "Recently?"

She nodded, and his eyes blazed. Even through her tears and drunkenness, Evie was certain she detected a growl roll up out of his core.

"Has Lucca been to this apartment?" He asked.

A wicked smile spread wider across her face. She let Evan's question hang in the air, saw the desperation in his eyes, and reveled in the flavor of it. It was good for once to see the pain and to know exactly where it came from.

"No."

211

The nervousness faded from his expression. Evan loosened his fists, relaxing his hands on her. "Where have you seen him?"

The effects of the vodka waned just enough to allow Evie the determination to address Evan's questions head-on. She hadn't anticipated him finding out about Lucca this way, but so be it.

"I saw him when I went downtown to meet Nate for lunch."

Putrid vodka threatened to resurface from her belly. She fought the vomitus urge back down.

Evan's fingers dug into her knee. "Where?"

"Some park near Congress Street."

"You went downtown?" His eyes bulged.

A sour expression crossed her face before answering, "I took the Silver Line to South Station and walked over to the park. I figured it was a public spot, what could happen there?"

"How many times have you seen Lucca?"

"Just once. After Nate—" Evie was cut short by her own reflexes as a frothy mix of bile and vodka spewed from her mouth. She doubled over, retching between her knees.

Evan stumbled backward in surprise, but quickly recovered to hold her up while she emptied the contents of her stomach at the foot of her bed. Tears streamed from her face again and she gasped for air.

***

The rest of her night was a blur.

"I'm sorry," she mumbled as Evan toweled her off just enough to walk her over to the bathroom.

"Please just kill me." She moaned, body aching and limp, while he stripped her down to her undergarments. He hoisted her into the shower, scrubbed her down, and had her tucked under the bed covers before her vision faded to darkness.

"Evan, please don't leave me." Her slurred speech had deteriorated to incoherent blubber, watching with foggy, drunken eyes as he cleaned up the mess she had left on the floor. The black veil closed over her.

"Everything's going to be just fine, Evie. Get some sleep." His hand against her back reassured her that he was still there.

Evan ran his palm across her body like a dream, up to her clammy forehead. Evie passed out cradled in his arms and cuddled up against his chest.

TWENTY-THREE

Cocooned in her comforter, Evie sat up in bed. The hangover pushed her back down. The room spun. Both hands slapped against her face, holding her head straight, as if that would stop the rollercoaster in her head. Not too long ago she cursed the aching, but suffered it on a regular basis. Why did this hangover feel like she'd been sucked dry and spit out? She cried softly, squeezing her eyes shut.

A soft set of hands pulled hers away. Through slit eyelids she found Evan standing over her. He propped her up in bed and fluffed up the pillows behind her for support. Taking a seat by her side, a large glass of orange juice in his offering hand. She peered over to the nightstand at an equally large glass of water and four aspirin waiting.

"You're out of practice," he said quietly.

"Shh." She hissed back, and the volume of their voices was thunderous. The sunlight, too bright.

"Who's the vampire?" Evan walked over to the windows and drew the blinds, shrouding the tiny studio in dim light.

"Stop talking. You're too loud."

"Better?" He dropped to a whisper. She shook her head in acknowledgement, which proved to be an even worse idea than speaking.

"Damn, I've never felt worse. I don't even remember drinking that much." Pressing her palms into her eye sockets, she whimpered. Evan claimed his seat back on the side of the bed next to her. Once she'd gulped down her juice, he raised the glass of water and handed her the aspirin.

"What did you drink?"

"I don't know, some cheap shit."

"That'll do it." Evan smirked, a response she really didn't appreciate at the moment.

"Cheap or not, I didn't drink enough to feel this much like death."

He huffed. "Evie, you lost a lot of blood yesterday. You had more alcohol in your system than anything. Of course you feel worse for it this morning. It's my fault for not warning you."

The sobering thought registered with her. She gaped up at his face with irritated eyes.

"Oh," was all she could muster before chugging the remains of her glass of water.

Evan monitored her. She gave no indication of passing out or puking again. He patted her leg, and then disappeared into the pantry kitchen. The fragrance of sizzling beef wafted toward her as he re-entered the living room with a plate placed on the coffee table.

"Come eat while it's still warm. You need to get some protein back in your system to build up that blood loss."

Her stomach roiled, but the hollow pit demanded sustenance, regardless. She moved to roll out of bed and froze. Hands clasped to the sheet covering her body, she looked up horrified at Evan. "I have no clothes on."

"I know that. I had to take your clothes off." A half-smile pulled at the corner of his mouth, but he held it in. His cheeks burned.

"What did you see?"

Evan looked over to her, no longer able to deny his smile. She gawked in return.

"Nothing, Evie," he said with a tiny chuckle. "You're the one always dancing around half-naked anyway, what do you care?"

"You're laughing. How much did you see?"

The idea of him handling her unconscious and naked body was slightly violating. Evan paused, as if delighting in the playful tension the conversation created.

"I had to strip you down to your bra and underwear in the shower, and then I removed the rest under the covers. I didn't actually see anything—I swear."

She wanted to believe him. The sincerity in his eyes told her she could do as much, but that didn't help the fact that she was still currently naked and he stood not ten feet from her. Yes, she'd pranced around in her underwear before, but this was different, and not on her terms. Blacking out was something she was glad to leave behind in Fallhaven. She forced a feeble smile back at his expectant brow, standing from the bed with the sheet wrapped around her midsection.

His open hand hung in the air.

"What?"

Evan shook his head and chuckled. "Give me your empty glass. I'll get you a refill while you get dressed. You need to hydrate."

"Oh." Evie hushed and handed him the glass. She waited until he disappeared back into the kitchen, and then quickly shimmied into a tank top and soft velour yoga pants. She vanished to the bathroom to brush her teeth and tie up her hair. Black lace teased the corner of her eye, still damp, hanging from the shower faucet's soap-scummed handle. Water and juice bubbled in her belly.

"Oh God." She cupped her hands over her face.

Get your shit together.

Evie peeked up at her reflection's mocking glare. She swallowed the phlegmy wad of saliva caught in her throat and turned back out the living room.

Trying her damnedest not to blush, she settled on the futon where she sat to a full plate of juicy steak tips and legumes. Evan was cleaning in the kitchen, utensils clanking and faucets running, spray bottles disinfecting and fridge doors closing. Halfway through her meal, he joined her on the futon, placing a refill of water in front of her along with a dinner roll.

"When'd you find the time to go grocery shopping?" she asked filling her bottomless pit with warm, rare-cooked satisfaction.

"When you were sleeping this morning. Do you want coffee too?"

"Please." She nodded.

He poured her coffee just as she liked it, and then refilled her glass of water when she emptied it. He even presented her with a fresh dinner roll after she scarfed down the first.

"Thank you." With her fork, she fiddled the morsels left on her plate.

"Are you feeling better?"

Leaning against the back of the futon, she rubbed her belly. "Yeah, I think my headache is gone."

"Good."

***

Once everything was back in order, Evan found his place at her side again, producing a new glass pipe adorned with bright red and white swirls and a bag of weed. His fingers pinched a crystallized bud, breaking it apart and packing the bowl. She watched his precision and focus as he performed the mundane action. His brow was relaxed, his eyes soft, lips slightly parted. She eyed him up and down. His thick brown hair fanned messily atop his head. The high priestess stirred.

She thought back on the thirst shared between the two of them. A warm feeling welled up inside her belly. With a heavy breath, Evie remained fixed on Evan's immortality. She hated the idea of aging while he watched, remaining his beautiful, youthful self. The same thought held true with Lucca. She didn't want either one of them to stand by as she aged and shriveled up. Her heart throbbed at the thought of them burying her six feet below their undying feet.

You're being selfish.

She honed in on Evan's lips covering the glass pipe, taking a long hit off the tip. He then passed it to her.

She looked down at the piece, rubbing the pad of her thumb where his lips were, searching for the wetness of his saliva lingering on the surface. It was gone. With the pipe to her lips, she closed her eyes and summoned the memory of their last kiss, which was heavily guarded in the depths of her mind by the murmurs of her inner voice.

Sweet tortured Evan... so sweet.

The piney taste of the weed tingled her taste buds. It rolled in fragrant waves. Only a small plume of fragrant smoke escaped the restraints of her curled tongue. She then licked her lips, connecting with Evan's gaze, and passed the bowl. Evie rubbed her belly again, which was now ablaze with a feeling she couldn't quite classify.

Evan lit the bowl and inhaled deeply. "Nice underwear by the way," he said with a wheeze, holding the smoke in his lungs before over-exaggerating a long exhale. Hardly any smoke resurfaced.

Evie giggled. "You like?"

"Very sexy. Do you own anything that isn't made of lace?" He passed the bowl over to her again, to which she declined. One hit was quite enough considering the state of her mind as it was. He placed the pipe on the table and rested against the back of the futon with her. Contentment blanketed her, perching her head atop his shoulder.

"I worked at a strip club, remember? It went with the uniform."

"Fair enough." He chuckled and pulled her hand into his, intertwining their fingers. "But it makes it a little difficult to stay mad at you when you're soaking wet and barely covered in black lace."

"I'll try to remember that the next time I get sloppy drunk with you."

Evie expected Evan to laugh at her dark joke, but he didn't. She shifted her eyes to try and gauge his reaction to her comment, but couldn't clearly make out his expression. His thumb rubbed along her knuckles.

"Do you want to talk about last night?" he asked.

She took a deep breath and sorted through the mess of last night littering her mind, vaguely remembering Evan tending to her while she was sick. The sandy beach and Claudio were in there somewhere as well. Evie remembered acting like a petulant child, and then she remembered telling Evan about Lucca.

Stupid, stupid girl.

"Evie? Can we talk about last night?"

"What do you want to talk about?" She stiffened, anticipating the first blow of his interrogation.

"Why don't we start with Lucca? And don't think I didn't notice that you keep his boots under your bed."

Shit, she thought. "Okay, what about Lucca?" Her treasure's discovery flushed her with a flurry of mixed emotions.

"Evie, I need to know… do you want me to stop him from coming after you?"

Her gut reaction was to say "hell no" but she knew that meant Evan might walk out of her life for good. Considering the way her heart broke when she watched Lucca walk away a few months back, she knew it would hurt her more to lose Evan now.

Selfish. Her inner voice growled at Evie's indecision.

Until she could determine what it was she wanted from either one of them she couldn't answer his question directly. "I don't know." That was as indirect and honest as she could possibly be.

"You don't know? How do you not know? What is it about him?"

"I can't say, really. I find myself completely drawn to him. I'm infatuated with him. I don't know how to explain it, but I've never felt that way about anyone else…" Her sentence trailed off, did she dare complete it? Something inside told her she had to. "Well, that was until I started spending more time with you."

"I see," Evan said softly, and his thumb pressed deeper along her skin.

The heat running through her body wasn't the product of awkwardness or passion, it was rage. She had revealed a desire for him twice now, and he'd yet to offer her a straight response. She sat up and turned to look at him, but his placid expression gave her nothing further to go on.

"Is that all you wanted to ask about?"

"I'd like to ask if you plan on seeing him again," he said.

She lifted a shoulder. "I don't know. It's not like I can go find him. I guess I'll see him when he wants to see me." The aggravation in her voice did little to hide her distress. Her throat itched. She gawked at him, waiting. "So?"

"So what?"

"So if we're going to talk about last night, then perhaps you wouldn't mind discussing the fact that I flat out asked you to fuck me and you didn't acknowledge me?"

"Evie, you were drunk."

"I was drunk, but I was honest. Just tell me, why don't you want me?"

"Who said I didn't want you?"

"Then you do?"

Evan hinted at a very hesitant grin and subtle head shake withdrew his hand. "I didn't say that either."

"Exactly. You're not saying anything."

He stretched his arms out and brought his hands back to cradle his head. Finding his focal point along the ceiling, he mumbled something under his breath. "Evie, what do you want me to say, that I'm attracted to you?" he said calmly. "Fine, yes, I am. When I watched you hanging all over that guy last night—"

"Claudio." The tempo of her pulse increased.

"Yes, Claudio... I was furious. I was jealous. I was all that and more from the sight of you two together. I sat back in Fallhaven and watched you with Rob. I bit my tongue, every second envious of the place he held in your heart. When you came home drunk with Claudio, it was like watching you with Rob all over again, and I was..." Evan's motives remained hidden behind his tell-tale furrowed brow.

"Claudio is nothing like Rob." she said, more to herself than to Evan, eyes closed to hold back her tears. The geisha glowered within the shadows, squaring up with Evie's inner voice. She opened her eyes and looked to Evan with wet, wide-eyed wonderment. "You were jealous of Rob? We had this conversation months ago, Evan. Why didn't y—"

"Tell you? How could I? I'm not allowed—" He pursed his lips, chin jutted out, eyes fixed to the ceiling.

The disparity of emotions boiled inside her. "Not allowed to what?"

"It doesn't matter. I'm torn. I'm always torn by you."

"Evan, what—"

"I was never concerned about Nate." He cut her off. "Anyone with half of a brain could see you never really loved him. But Rob..." He paused, shook his head, violently ejecting whatever thought from his mind. He then cycled through a heavy breath to regain his composure. "You told me you had been seeing Nate. I wasn't jealous. I was angry... I think he may have inadvertently led Lucca to you. I was scared for your safety, hated the thought of something happening to you, but I was never jealous of Nate—when you threw Lucca in my face last night," he said, his tone defeated. "You want to talk about possessiveness? How can I admit that I love you when I know his main goal is to take you away from me? And you'll go willingly because that's what happens."

Something in Evan's words stung Evie down to her bones, a sharp piercing sensation. She shifted in her seat, faced him head on. Her arms hugging her tight.

"What do you mean, you love me?"

Evan lifted his head off of the back of the futon and met her stare. Both slack-jawed by his revelation before he turned away from her.

"There, I said it." His brow creased. Discomfiture etched along his jaw as he clenched it shut.

Evie stared, disbelieving. He had said what she wanted to hear, but now that he had, what was she supposed to do with it? The geisha was pushed back into the shadows.

Not anymore, Rob's gone.

She raised her hand up to her collarbone, still bruised from Evan's bite, and rubbed the wound gently with the tips of her fingers. Recalling the feeling of his tongue pressing into her skin, his mouth sucking hungrily at the open wound, the searing pain was a pleasurable burn. The weightlessness was unlike anything she'd felt for anyone or anything in her short mortal life. Just anticipating experiencing that again sent a warm wave throughout her body from head to toe. Another image crept into the forefront of her mind, and that image which flashed in her mind jolted her; the Devil card.

He is you and you are him. This will bring the change you need. You must know it is inevitable. The words of the old psychic played back in her mind. Whatever magnetism drew her to Evan was similar to what she felt for Lucca. As Sempiternal, they were both monsters in their own right, both devils.

He can help us.

"Now who's the quiet one?" Evan asked, thick with sarcasm.

Evie blinked her eyes, chasing the image of the tarot card from her mind. Her sights drifted across the room, settling on Evan by her side with his familiar guarded expression. The high priestess hissed with anticipation. The leash pulling through her chest cut short, yanking the choke collar tighter around her neck.

Before allowing to think better of her actions, she leaned over. Taking Evan's sorrowful face in her hands, she kissed him, their lips uniformly puckered against each other. She pulled back, inches from his face. She waited, counted

Evan's breaths beating against her. When he didn't push her away, Evie leaned in again and parted his lips with her tongue. Restrained at first, he reciprocated her embrace while tremors racked his body. His shaky hands lifted to her face. His touched softened as he brushed across her forehead to the back of her head, pulling her in closer. The heat of Evan's breath warmed her body like the summer sun.

She straddled his lap, snagging her fingers in his thick, feathery hair. His fingertips raced up and down her spine, sending little sparks of excitement through her. She shivered. Tiny moans and liberated panting escaped between their breaths. Evie ran her fingers down his face, tracing his jaw, holding him to her. Evan's hands moved to the front of her body, running across her torso, up to her chest. She winced when he brushed up against her wound. The stabbing pain was like a hot poker to her flesh.

Excitement subdued, Evan paused. A flash of guilt stung his face.

"I'm okay." She lifted his chin back to her, but he pushed her back. His hands firmly grasped her waist and pushed her away.

Evan tilted his face to the side, deflecting her advances.

"You're not okay… that's my fault. I hurt you, Evie. You said it yourself last night."

Her hands stiffened to claws and she gripped his jaw. She tried to hold his head in place, to command his eyes to hers. "That's not what I meant and you know it. Don't do this, Evan."

He slowly traced the edges of the bruise, refusing to relinquish his gaze to hers.

"This doesn't change the facts, Evie," he said coldly.

"What facts? That we're attracted to each other? That we both have a need for each other? What facts, Evan? Tell me."

The way he finally turned to look at her, the intensity in his stare, it relayed more than what she'd expected—more than hurt—more than lust.

"A need?" he breathed. "Evie, it's so much more than that. My wants and needs are easily defined; you. They've always been you, and they will always be you. Nothing and no one can ever change that." The pools that welled within his deep set eyes increased, and with a solitary blink of his eyes trickled down. "But your wants and needs aren't so simple."

She could feel the tears lining his lids ready to drown her.

"You're right. I'm fucked up. I don't know my head from my ass, but I know a very strong part of me wants and needs you too. What's our alternative, Evan? To sit around getting high all the time, pretending we don't care about each other?"

Her lower lip trembled from the potent mix of adrenaline, nerve, fear, and desire. Evan lifted his hand to steady it. His touch evoked a sigh of relief from her, and she smiled.

"It's been a long time, Evie. It's not an easy thing to lose the one you love."

She gazed at him quizzically. "I'm not asking you to. I can't see into the future. I have no idea what tomorrow will bring. All I'm asking is that you take me one moment at a time."

She expected her plea to encourage a smile from his face, but it didn't. He frowned, a contemplative expression, followed by a tiny flicker—a spark.

"Then I need to ask something of you." Evan spoke in such a soft whisper that Evie questioned whether or not he was speaking to her or himself.

"Anything. What is it?"

"I need you to get a tattoo with me."

TWENTY-FOUR

The tattoo studio was still in South Boston, but not where Evie expected. They strolled up L Street. She presumed Evan was taking her somewhere in her neighborhood, someplace she'd likely passed by countless times without ever noticing. Her theory was debunked, however, as they crossed over to Summer Street.

Her arm snaked around his, they strolled along with their safety net of silence. Evan's hands tucked in his pockets. Evie's fingertips twiddled the fringed ends of her scarf. It was odd to be out in public like that—with him—with the implication that their relationship could be more than platonic. Setting a course in the same general direction as her office, she presumed this little excursion for ink would reveal his intentions in no time at all.

Fall was in full swing. The cool breeze tousled her dress, its cold creep caressing her thighs as it passed through poly-blend layers. She was glad the new boots she'd decided to break in with this trek were merciful on her feet.

Comforting as it was to walk side-by-side with Evan, finding no need to mask their adventure with nervous small talk, she hoped revealing their feelings for each other would trigger some climactic shift in their discourse. Maybe his wall would break down, but it hadn't—yet. Their familiar silence reinforced that notion. His stoic profile persisted as she chanced a peek up at him.

He caught her out of the corner of his eye. "Can I help you?"

The corners of her eyes pinched, lips pursed. "Just wondering what's going through your head right now." He smirked and tugged one of her braided pigtails, but didn't answer. "Will you at least tell me where we're going?"

"You'll see," he said, stifling a sniffle.

We'll see the world as Evan does soon enough... when Lucca decides.

The chill that ran through her had nothing to do with the weather. Her eyes moved along the streets. Paranoia driving her need to peer into each window of every car passing by, every alleyway or storefront for the shadow her body craved.

What do you think Evan will do then?

She turned down to the pavement at her feet and then to Evan.

"Have you ever gotten into a fight?"

He lifted a curious eyebrow. "A fight?" His fixed glare hinted toward foreboding, but quickly softened to dismay. "Where's this coming from?"

"I'm just wondering what it looks like when Sempiternal fight? You told me once that you can be killed through trauma or force. I saw what Lucca did to Mae on his last night in Fallhaven, but that wasn't really a fight. What he did to Nate on the other hand... I mean, Nate's a big guy. He's doesn't go down easy, and Lucca crushed him. Then again, Nate's not immortal, so that doesn't count either. Does it? Are you like—"

"No."

"No...? You've never gotten into a fight?"

"No, I'm not talking about this with you, Evie." The finality in his tone set her back. She squeezed his arm, forcing her curiosity and her fears of the Sempiternal back down to the pit of her stomach.

The grey figure of her office building came creeping around the next corner.

"Seriously, Evan, where are we going?"

"Relax. We're almost there," he said and walked her around the block, into a mass of unmarked cement-walled warehouses. The smell of low tide singed her nostrils and she thought of being back home when the fishing boats returned. She closed her eyes and sucked in a deep breath.

All it took was that one second savoring the nostalgia for Evie to lose her bearings. When she opened her eyes, they were around another corner, approaching a non-descript side entrance to one of the warehouses. Evan knocked twice on the industrial door. A tall, dark man with wide shoulders answered.

"Evan, what's going on, my man?" The large man embraced Evan with a half hug-half handshake.

"Hey, Roque. How are you?"

Evan socializing was a curious thing to behold. Evie had never seen him out in public with anyone other than her friends back in Fallhaven. Come to think of it, she never pictured Evan having friends. A curious resentment slumped her shoulders down. She adjusted her arm coiled around his, squeezing just a little tighter than before.

"Here to see the big boss man?" the large man named Roque asked.

"No, just Yeung Jae." Evan rested his free hand against the small of her back. "This is Evie."

"Well, well... My, my," Roque said, wiggling his brow. "Very nice to meet you, Miss Evie." He took her hand and shook it much more gently than she anticipated a man of his stature would. By her estimation, he was three times as wide as Nate and taller than him at that. She was certain she'd get sucked into his gravity.

Funny, Evie thought, as Roque shot a dubious look toward Evan. He was quiet, as usual, grinning back and rolling his eyes. Evan nudged her through the entrance with his palm pressed into her back. His long fingers extended over the curve of her backside, setting of an eruption of heat at the base of her spine.

Evie flashed Roque a coy smirk and took in one final deep inhale of salty air. She let Evan lead her inside.

***

The door closed behind them. They progressed down a long grey hallway, lit by the nauseating glow of florescent tube lighting. The great length of a passage was sparsely broken up by the occasional door that blended with the colorless walls. Her nostrils tingled from the musty atmosphere. Evie squinted as some of the bulbs flickered overhead. Evan had taken a few long strides in front of her, but paused in his step and turned back to her.

"Is everything okay?" His expression was still discomforted, but empathetic. His beautiful brown eyes melted her as he extended his hand.

"Where are we?" she asked.

"We're going to get a tattoo, remember?"

A halfhearted huff burst past her lips. "Where, in a dungeon?"

Evan chuckled and laced their fingers. "This is the only guy I trust."

"Well, I guess that says something."

Blindly obedient, she followed for what felt like eternity down the never-ending hallway. They must have made it all the way to the north end of the city by now if she could plot their course on a map. With each step forward she squeezed Evan's hand a little tighter and reminded her thundering heartbeat that she trusted him implicitly. Finally at an intersection, they turned right, and then like navigating the Minotaur's labyrinth, meandered through a succession of lefts and rights until Evie was thoroughly disoriented.

***

Evan stopped in front of a door and knocked against a smoky-glass inlay.

She rocked back and forth on her heels looking up at the fluorescent lighting. "So this Young Jay, is that like a gangster name or something, like Roque?"

Evan stifled a hearty laugh. "No, his name is Yeung Jae. He's Korean. Roque is actually French."

"Have you known them long?"

"Roque and I have worked together for years. Yeung Jae…? He's a good kid. He's been working here for a little over a year or so, I think."

She smiled, satisfied. The calming effect he had on her justified the fluttering of emotions rushing through her.

Eternity passed, but eventually Yeung Jae opened the door. He smiled at Evan, a warm, toothy grin. Long feathery locks hung low to one side of his face while the other side was buzzed down to the scalp. His lower lip was lined with metal rings. His ears were stretched with massive plugs set in their lobes. One eyebrow had three barbells pushed through it, while the other only had one. Evie also noticed he was head to toe in tattoos, the most striking a dragon that curved around his neck with its head resting just behind his left ear, the lizard's tongue curled up, hissing in it from behind. It reminded her of the serpent slithering through the samurai's head from Rob's tattoo.

231

The image of the geisha came creeping from the shadows of her mind. A sharp pain pinched at her chest where her heart was located. Images of Rob's blood-soaked body, crumpled like a rag doll on the floor of the club, made her shiver. It wasn't until she felt Evan's hand rubbing her back that she was able to shake the gory image. The geisha slinked back into obscurity.

"Yeung Jae, this is Evie. She's my... friend." The hesitation in his voice made her curious.

"All right." The tattoo artist beamed. "Hey, Evie. The name's Yeung Jae. Pleased to meet you." The young artist took Evie's hands in both of his and shook them. Her entire body jolted from the exuberance of his jerking motions.

"Hi." She surveyed their clinical surroundings. The room lacked the usual display of tattoo design options. The walls were as barren as the hallway, but the center of the room was decorated with a brightly patterned Moroccan rug and a parlor chair. The table next to it displayed all the tools of Yeung Jae's trade. Incense and patchouli bombarded her senses.

"So what are we doing today?" he asked and looked toward Evan for the answer. She wondered what it was she was going to get, and why she didn't seem to have a say in the matter.

"Evie and I are here for tattoos," Evan said, and though the obviousness and absurdity of his response made her laugh a little, both men looked at Evie stone-faced. Her eyes bowed to the floor, and she bit her lip.

"I've always wanted an anchor," she said, as though her opinion mattered. Yeung Jae smirked, an all-knowing grin pulling at the side of his mouth.

"Yeung Jae knows—" Evan was cut off by the chirping of his cell phone in his pocket. "It's my uncle. You can get started on Evie," he said and walked out of earshot toward a corner of the room. He whispered as he took the call.

Evie watched him, dubious. Why was he being so cryptic, she wondered as Yeung Jae stepped into her line of vision.

"Come on, Evie. I know what you're getting," he said with a smile that prevented her from arguing. He led her over to the sterilized station and sat alongside her. From his hard metal perch, Yeung Jae connected the nozzles and organized the containers of dye.

"How long have you been tattooing?" she asked, finding the small talk eased her tension a bit.

"Here?" He looked up to meet her gaze. "A little over a year, but I've been inking people up since I was sixteen."

"Where is here?"

Yeung Jae first answered her with a goofy grin and head shake. "You're in the House of Bendis." His tone implied she should've already known and turned back to his work on the table.

"Bendis?"

"The Sempiternal," Yeung Jae said plainly. "It's okay, you can say it out loud. No one around here will care. Is this your first time visiting?"

Evie wanted to jump out of her skin, but her body remained frozen as Yeung Jae continued his prep work. Her eyes raced around the room for something that should have tipped her off. The collar tightened on her throat and the throbbing wound on her clavicle ached. "Evan never..."

Wanted to bring us here.

"How long have you known Evan?" Yeung Jae asked, studying her.

"About five months, I think."

"Really?" His forehead wrinkled up to his scalp.

233

"Is it that a short amount of time?"

In hindsight, perhaps five months was a fraction of a second for immortals. Evie countered Yeung Jae's pensive glance with equal scrutiny. His shiny toothed grin lacked the telltale elongated canines.

"Well, yeah, it's kind of a short amount of time if you're already here getting inked."

Her head skewed to one side. "This isn't just a regular tattoo, is it?"

Yeung Jae chuckled. She peeked over at Evan, who was monitoring their conversation, cell phone still pressed to his ear. His brow furrowed as he turned his back to her.

"No, it's not," Yeung Jae said. "But it'll be perfect. You'll see." He stuck out a metal-adorned tongue and waggled his eyebrows.

"Here, tilt your head for me."

He positioned her so that her head dipped to the right, openly displaying the flesh of the left side of her neck. As he removed her scarf to allow better access to her skin, she was grateful Evan's mark remained hidden on the other side of her body. She brushed her hair back over the top of her head. Yeung Jae applied an alcohol prep to the area behind her left ear.

"This is what I do, Evie. Trust me," he said in a soothing, friendly tone. The wild buzz of the tattoo gun picked up and set the tiny hairs along her arms standing on edge. All too soon, it descended upon her.

Just a pinch.

Displacing the discomfort of the invisible choke collar from her dreams, the needle pierced her skin in a constant motion, each strike hitting a microsecond before the next, injecting the dye. At first, the scraping impression burned, but then dulled to a rhythmic abrasion. She closed her eyes and lost herself in the vibrations of the gun. The wings on her back took hours to complete and the repetitive sensation of the needle penetrating her body was masochistically therapeutic. The moment harkened back to a simpler time in her life when she didn't have to worry about who wanted to kill her, who wanted to suck her blood, who she should trust.

Evan concluded his call and headed toward them. Before he reached them though, his phone rang again. "Dammit." He turned back to the corner of the room as he lifted the phone to his ear. "Did you forget something, Uncle?"

Evie strained to find him in her state of limited mobility. She pushed her eyes as far back behind her head as they would go, but she couldn't quite see him, and had to blink hard to relieve their straining.

"He's a busy guy," Yeung Jae said. "Can't say I've heard of him bringing someone down here for a tattoo, though. You must mean a lot to him."

"Why would you say that?"

"The big boss man's nephew? He's all business. No, he doesn't take this shit lightly. Trust me, Evie, you don't get marked unless you really mean something to somebody like him."

A sense of thrill shot through her. Whatever was being tattooed onto her was one thing; what was being imprinted into her was another.

A silly notion flitted through her mind. "Wait. You're not putting his name on me are you? Because I am not cool with that."

Yeung Jae stopped his work to explode in boisterous laughter that set her back. His chuckle emanated from his belly, multiplying as it shook his little figure. Given the short-lived opportunity, Evie twisted back to check on Evan. He was looking over his shoulder again from the corner of the room and scowling at Yeung Jae.

"No." The young artist chuckled. "Not at all, Evie. I'm putting a small cluster of stars behind your ear, kind of like a constellation."

"Like my zodiac sign or something? I'm a Libra."

"Oh, so you have a birthday coming up soon?" Yeung Jae said. "Happy Birthday if I don't see you... but no, this isn't part of the zodiac. It's this." He stretched out his neck to reveal a tiny cluster of bluish-silver stars behind his own left ear, embedded within the scales of the hissing dragon.

Evie nodded her head just enough to acknowledge him, but was still unsure what it all meant. "Are you...?" She hesitated to ask and, deciding against it, let her question trail off.

"Immortal?" Yeung Jae said, positioning his sly smirk in her line of vision.

"Yes."

"No, I'm like you—a 'friend'. Someday hopefully that'll change." The way he said the word made Evie realize what Evan had meant when he'd introduced her.

"A friend of Evan's?"

Yeung Jae laughed a little again, making her feel like a fool for how easily she amused him. "No, not Evan," he said, "Like I mentioned before, he's all business."

Evie was lost. What was this alternate universe, and what exactly was Evan's place within it? Before she could bother to ponder the immensity of her question, the buzzing ceased and Yeung Jae began rubbing her down again with green soap.

"I'm all done, boss." Yeung Jae looked up at Evan. "You wanna take a look, see if you like it?"

As Evan approached, tucking his cell phone back into his pocket, Yeung Jae turned away to prep for Evan's tattoo.

Evie connected with Evan's gaze. Her pulse raced under his intensity. Her heart pounded, but she remained still while he leaned down. Tracing the tip of his tongue against her fresh tattoo, his lips brushing against her ear lobe. His breath lay heavy on her.

"You look beautiful." His whisper set of an electric current down her body. Evie fought a pleasurable moan. A soft purr emanated from Evan's mouth before he stood tall.

Yeung Jae sniffled, interjecting into their slight indiscretion.

"It's perfect, Yeung Jae." Evan praised his work, and Evie, under the light of his smile. "I guess it's my turn now?" He lifted his sleeve, exposing his right wrist.

Yeung Jae nodded. "You can get up now, Evie. There are a couple mirrors over there if you want to check it out." He pointed to a corner in the room with mirrors strategically mounted on the walls to offer a 360-degree view.

She felt like she was floating. Her head was still whirring from the phantom traces of the tattoo gun's vibrations. Evie walked over to see what Yeung Jae had described, a cluster of tiny stars behind her left ear. It wasn't exactly what she thought of when Evan suggested they go get tattoos, but it was subtle and delicate. She smirked at the mirror.

In what seemed like half the time, Evan's tattoo was done. Evie marveled as the skin absorbed the ink and instantly healed. His marking at the base of his right palm just above his wrist and below the thumb's knuckle, a mirror image of hers.

"Is this what you wanted?" she said to Evan as he stared, mystified by the silver stars in his skin. His wetted eyes lifted to meet hers. The severity and conflict in his stare perplexed her. "Evan?"

Several breaths passed her lips before he answered. "We should get you out of here."

TWENTY-FIVE

Before leaving, Yeung Jae affixed a gauze patch behind Evie's ear.

"It's bleeding a little. You'll want to keep this on at least until you get home." He shot Evan a glance drenched in innuendo. Evie blushed. "Evan, my man, it's always a pleasure."

"You're the best." Evan shared the same half hug-half handshake embrace with him as he had with Roque, and then turned to her. "It's getting late. We should get you out of here before the others wake."

Her heart skipped multiple beats.

This is where we belong.

"Take care, Evie." Yeung Jae called out and waved from behind them. She turned and smiled back. "Maybe I'll see you around." He gave her another wiggle of his brow.

"Bye, Yeung Jae. Thanks."

Evan kept a tight grip on her, pulling her through hallways at a pace quite conscientious of the time on his watch.

"What happens when the others wake up?"

"Then you learn how vampires earned their reputation," he said.

Her inner voice danced with anticipation.

***

Warm citrus hues bled over the western horizon as they made their way back home. Their arms intertwined again.

Evan's hands in his pockets. Evie's fingers toying with her scarf. The wind picked up, nipping between her legs. She waited until they were a block away from Broadway before deciding to ask, "So what was that all about back there?"

"What do you mean?"

She laughed, her eyes widened with exaggeration. "What do I mean? You're kidding me. Who were those guys? What was with all the phone calls, secret door knocks, and handshakes? What are you, like, the president or some shit?" She tugged playfully on his arm.

"No, not me," he said in a direct and serious tone. "My uncle would be like the president. I'm just his personal assistant, I guess you could say."

"Personal assistant? You're joking, right?"

"Do you think I'm joking?" he huffed.

"So that was the House of Bendis?" she asked. "That's where Yeung Jae said we were."

"Bendis?" he said, annoyed "I should've guessed he would be too chatty not to mention anything to you. Yeung Jae is a very friendly kid, isn't he?"

"The comment about the others kind of gave you away." Evan nodded, admitting as much. "So that was your uncle's building? The Sempi—"

"Yes."

Her chest scorched with excitement that melted down to her lower half. "So that's where you live? Evan, why didn't you just tell me?"

Evan stopped and wrapped his arms around her waist, pulling her in close. "I didn't want you to get nervous being surrounded by so many of us," he said in a soft voice.

"How many?"

"Hundreds, Evie. The House of Bendis stretches for miles under the south side of the city."

No, nervousness was a poor description for the feelings running through her body.

"Is that where you work? Is that where Carver Assurance is located?" The image of the alabaster tower across from her office flashed in her mind. It looked different from the other side of the block.

Evan smiled.

She nodded, eyes fixed to the appeal of his curved lips. "This isn't a regular tattoo is it?"

Evan didn't answer, but rather widened his smile with a soft chuckle. He squeezed his arm around her waist and coaxed her on down the street.

Keeping a steady pace, Evie rested her head on his shoulder. Evan dipped his head down to rest on the side of hers. The sea breeze filtered its way through her scarf and layers of blood-tinged gauze to cool the sear of her freshly inked neck.

A sigh of contentment escaped her before Evan stopped in his tracks less than a block from her building. He tugged back on her softly, holding her in place. His body tensed at her side, setting her own nerves suddenly on edge. She followed his line of sight to a figure in front of her building. The high priestess growled, tightening Evie's claws into Evan's arm.

"Blythe? Holy shit, you're here?" She pried her hands from Evan and ran toward her best friend. Her subconscious fumed on the inside, halting her momentum just steps away from the petite brunette on the verge of tears.

"What's wrong?" Evie said. "Why do you look so up—" She stopped. Blythe hadn't acknowledged Evie yet. She looked past her to Evan, mouth pressed into a thin line to dam the tears that welled in her eyelids.

Evie peered back over her shoulder to Evan, who was transfixed on Blythe. Repentance lining his face. "Blythe." He nodded. "How are you?"

Even with the few feet between them, Evie could see how badly Blythe fought to subdue the tremors wracking her body. She was bubbling over, her cheeks flushed a definite shade of anger. Her hands balled up at her side. When she didn't answer, Evan leaned down behind Evie to graze her ear with his lips. "Please tell me no one else knows where you live," he said out of Blythe's earshot. "You two should talk. I'll be upstairs if you need me." He straightened his posture and headed up the front stairs to her apartment.

Evie watched him leave then turned back to her friend. "I can't believe you're finally here."

"I was right." Blythe scoffed.

"Excuse me? You've been ignoring me for months, and now you show up on my doorstep to start this shit?"

Blythe snorted and looked away. "Whatever, Evie. I actually came to catch up, but I'm not going in there if Evan's there too. Is he living with you or something?"

The venom in her tone stung Evie to the core. "You two have been broken up for months," Evie said.

"Looks like you wasted no time moving in on him, did you? Even though you promised me you wouldn't."

Who gives a shit what fucking Miss Prissy thinks. Walk away, stupid girl.

Evie reciprocated Blythe's glower. "You've been ignor—you know what, fuck this. I'm not arguing with you. If you want to catch up, let's go up the street for some coffee." Evie motioned Blythe to follow, and was genuinely shocked when she did.

***

They entered the pub and sat down at the bar. Evie waved at the bartender. "Hi Seamus, lemme get the coffee stout." She tossed a few twenties on the bar before turning to Blythe for her order.

"This isn't what I thought you meant by 'grabbing a coffee,'" Blythe said, mocking quotation marks in the air with her fingers. "I'll have a port noir." she said to the bartender.

After Evie's mishap the night before, alcohol seemed a large risk. Due to the hostility emanating from Blythe's tiny frame, Evie couldn't have cared less. "Yeah well, I don't really care at the moment. You said you wanted to catch up, so let's do that."

In a minute each girl had a drink in hand.

"Typical Evie, hide it all in a bottle," Blythe brought her glass to her lips. "Why couldn't you just be honest about Evan in the first place?"

Evie took a tiny sip of the beer, her stomach lurching from its initial bite. "Blythe, you have to believe me, that's not what you thought you saw back there with Evan,"

Blythe scolded Evie with a sharp glare. "I think it's exactly what I saw." The virulence in her tone pushed Evie further down into her seat. "Just be honest, how long has this been going on?"

"We haven't—look, nothing ever happened between us while you two were dating—honest. He helped me move down here after Rob…"

"Nope." Blythe sucked the port through her teeth. "I know something happened between you two. Don't try to fake it, Evie."

"I'm not faking anything." Her voice raised, drawing the attention of Seamus and a few bar patrons within earshot. Evie sunk down in her seat and lowered her voice. "Evan has been a good friend, helping me clean up my act, sober up… whatever. I lost you—for no good reason I might add—I lost Rob. Then I had to leave Nate behind. Who else did I have, Blythe? No one. Evan has been there for me. Don't hate him for being a good friend." She felt it unnecessary to acknowledge what Evan had divulged earlier, that he loved her—always wanted her and always would. The curiosity piqued by his choice of words lingered, but she couldn't possibly try to talk it over with his ex-girlfriend.

Blythe stared back at Evie, sipping her wine, unable to deny her conviction. "Well he's not doing a very good job of helping you clean up your act if you're at a bar right now, is he?"

"Yeah, I guarantee I'll catch hell for this," Evie said. She took another tiny sip, not so harsh the second time.

"Have you slept with him?" Blythe asked, looking down at her glass, shooting the rest of its contents down her throat in one gulp.

A chill ran down Evie's body. Did she really want to have this conversation right now?

"No… I've slept next to him, but we've never had sex." Guilt slithered up her spine and latched it viperous jaw into her new tattoo and bruised collar bone.

"Well, at least that makes me feel a little better," Blythe answered, and then looked over at Evie. "I never got to sleep with him either. He must be asexual after all."

Evie eyed Blythe. Tension persisted, but then weakened by years of adolescent friendship and lifelong sisterhood. Both shared a silent expression before bursting out into girlish laughter. Ice broken, Evie felt her old friend coming back to her. Blythe waved to the bartender for another glass of wine while Evie continued to nurse her beer.

"So does Nate know?" Blythe asked.

"Yes and no." Before their conversation could digress off the subject, Evie fidgeted in her seat and cast an accusatory glare at Blythe. "By the way, did you tell him where I've been?"

Blythe's pursed-lipped grin answered for her, allowing Evie's accusation to hang in the air. "He's all you left me with, remember? I got sick of him asking me where to find you. He said he'd been talking to you via text for a while, anyway. What's the big deal?" Blythe relieved her second glass of its contents and requested a third. Evie threw a cautious finger up to Seamus before he filled the order. "Excuse me, I'm a big girl, Evie. I thought you'd be impressed that I've increased my tolerance."

"Blythe, can you try to comprehend how difficult it's been for me to do this? To abandon my home, crawl out of my little hole, and move to an unfamiliar city? A fucking city, Blythe—not some Nowheresville town with a population of fifty—a goddamned capital full of thousands of strangers who can stare and judge and who knows what else. This whole sobriety bit isn't just some hair-brained scheme. I'm trying to sort my life out." Her voice quivered.

"Again, fine job sobering up." Blythe gestured to Evie's now half-emptied pint. Evie stared back, jaw dropped and eyes fixed on a girl she barely recognized. Where was the feminine little brunette who couldn't old her liquor worth a damn?

"I had to leave Nate," said Evie. "He was a source of everything." She pointed toward the beer. "He enabled me, day in and day out. Can you please just try to appreciate how hard it was to leave him behind?" Tears welled up. One small droplet dribbled down her cheek.

Blythe brushed the tear from Evie's face with an exaggerated pout. "I'm sorry. I know you didn't want anyone to know where you were, but I've been so angry at you for stealing Evan away from me."

"For fuck's sake, I didn't steal him! There was nothing going on between us."

"'Was' being the operative word, Evie." Blythe snickered and took her third glass, which Seamus had placed in front of her. "Fine, it doesn't matter now anyway. Just keep your voice down." Blythe cast a squinty glare over the bar, and then settled back in her seat to enjoy her wine in peace.

Evie wrapped her hands around her glass, palms dampened by the condensation. She took a generous gulp, eager to displace emotions with booze. Evan had only two stipulations in order to assist with her Sempiternal woes: sober up and break all ties. Staring deep into her glass, remorse gurgled up her throat with the aftertaste of beer.

"Jesus, what a fucking mess." Evie chugged the remainder of her beer. Seamus didn't wait for her, but placed another glass of wine and a tall draft in front of the girls. "So, what prompted this sudden urge to catch up?" Evie asked in a solemn tone.

Blythe sat up straight, sucking her teeth. "I've met someone."

"Of course you have. I think I've heard this since we were sixteen years old." Evie rolled her eyes and tapped her fingers against the full pint.

Fucking Miss Prissy found herself another poor sap.

"Ha ha, very funny," Blythe said with a snip. "I met a guy from out of town. He was visiting an old friend in Fallhaven and now he's down in Boston. I figured while I was here with him I'd stop by to see you."

Evie chugged her beer again, and then motioned to the bartender to cut her off before the room spun out on her. If she kept drinking she'd just have another fight with Evan when she got home, and couldn't muster the mental or emotional fortitude for that. He placed a bottle water in front of her instead.

"Thanks Seamus." Evie twisted off the cap. "So is he tall, dark and handsome?" Evie asked Blythe with feigned interest.

"I don't know so much that he's tall." Blythe searched the display of liquor behind the bar for the right words to describe her new beau. "He's taller than me, but that's not saying much. He is dark and handsome though. And the things he does…" She smiled, lost in her own reverie. "Oh! He fucks like a jackhammer too, which is saying something considering Evan barely touched me. Seriously, it hurts to walk sometimes." Blythe tongued the lip of her wine glass and giggled before knocking back the pinot like a shot.

Evie gawked back at her, amazed.

Blythe smirked and continued, "So anyway, next month is Halloween and it's your birthday. I thought maybe I'd come back down to the city and you could meet him."

The thought of going out with Blythe—like they used to—pulled at Evie's heartstrings.

"Sounds like fun," she said, knowing full well she'd have to deal with Evan later about this one. "I like your scarf, by the way."

"You know," Blythe said, looking down at the purple wool hanging from around her neck. "It's already wicked cold in Fallhaven. 'Tis the season and all."

Both girls' voices had tired. They settled into the dim lighting and musty odor of the pub. Blythe polished off her third glass of wine, while Evie downed her water and picked the tiniest fleck of dirt from underneath her nails.

"You look good, Evie. I like what you've done with your hair."

247

She returned a forced smile. "Thanks. Nate said the same thing. Lucca said he misses the red." She set her eyes back on the task of digging under her nailbeds.

"Lucca?" Blythe perked up in her seat. "You're still seeing him?"

"Just once, but yeah, he's here too. Seems no matter where I go I can't get away from the men in my life. Not unless they die." Her unenthusiastic chuckle waned into a scowl. Her off-color joke at Rob's expense made her want to punch herself in her face.

Blythe paid no attention. "You were crazy about that guy, right?"

"Completely infatuated."

"So...?"

"So what?"

"Why haven't you seen him more?"

Evie sighed heavily. "It's complicated."

She looked around the bar. Only a few other poor souls had made their way into the pub this early in the evening. Some well-dressed customers and a few worn individuals sat alone with their drinks and tablets, phones, or thoughts. The pub was so very different from back home, and yet it wasn't. All it needed was some coked-up fishermen and near-naked dancers, and you could overlook the fancy mahogany and stained glass discrepancies.

"So this party, when is it?" she asked.

"Next month, right before Halloween."

"Do we have to wear costumes?"

"Of course."

Evie sighed. A round of silence passed before Blythe spoke again. "So Nate and Evan, huh?"

"More like Lucca and Evan." She frowned and peeled the label off the empty water bottle between her fingers.

"I guess that sucks to be Nate. What's a girl to do?"

Evie buried her face in her hands. "I have no idea. I've tried so many times to tell Nate to fuck off, but he just won't go away. Lucca and Evan though…" Evie paused. "That's just different."

Blythe gazed, apathetically swirling her wine in her glass.

"Why's that?"

Evie took a moment to think about it. It was different because they were immortal. It was different because they were two halves of a whole. It was different because she didn't have much control over her feelings for either one of them. Life would be so much simpler if she could just go back to Nate. It would be perfect if she could recover from her addictions with Claudio and fade into old age.

Unfortunately, when Evie thought about Lucca, she knew that would never happen. His dark and shadowy mystique, those fiery deep pools for eyes burned through her and pulled her toward him. His devilish side smirk made her knees weak and her body melt. She thought of the ferocity of his kiss and the thrill of his hands holding her into to him. Her entire being came undone in his presence.

She then thought about Evan, his soft, painfully handsome features, dark tender eyes and feathery brown hair. His smile transformed his tortured appeal into something so light and awing. She thought of the gentleness of his lips and the way he caressed her body. Even when not intending to, he sent warm shivers through her.

She wanted the experience of both of them—needed their juxtaposition. One could not exist without the other and she was stuck in the middle. As Blythe awaited clarification, her answer was more of a riddle than anything.

"Lucca and Evan are like night and day… I don't want to imagine a life with one and not the other."

TWENTY-SIX

By the time the girls had concluded their somewhat somber reunion, city lights were ablaze. The dissonance of South Boston rumbled, though Evie hardly noticed as they stood outside of the pub.

"I'm going to catch a cab." Blythe waved her hand through the air at the nearby taxi entourage lining the curb.

Evie was busy thumbing through her phone. "Yeah okay. Do you think if I walk home the smell of booze will wear off? Evan's going to kill me."

Blythe snorted. "Tell him to get over it. He doesn't own you."

Not entirely.

A sour film lined her mouth as Evie peered up from her phone to the petite brunette. "Stop it. He's just worried about me."

"Sure, if that's what you want to call it," Blythe said, hanging on the cab's open door. "I'll be in touch about next month."

"Sounds good." Evie nodded. "Oh! And Blythe… it was really good to see you."

"Sure." Blythe grinned back, but the sincerity of her smile missed her eyes.

***

Evie took a few moments to herself before heading home. The weight of their conversation held her in place. After

251

watching Blythe's cab disappear toward the heart of the city, she set off down the street on foot, her mind a bit more scattered than usual.

"What did you think of what just happened back there?"

I think Miss Prissy can go fuck herself. Who cares?

"No, what I said about Lucca and Evan?"

We are inevitable. We can have the world.

"What if I don't want that?"

Stop being selfish, stupid girl. This isn't just about you.

The echo of Sister Lima's chide rang out from her subconscious. "That priestess also said she was awed by me, that I had won his favor. What do you think that means?"

Go find her.

"How the hell do I do that?"

Consumed by her inner dialogue, the memory of Sister Lima's hands roamed her memory and her body, competing with the autumn nip in the air. The haunt of the woman's delicate touch tickled under her clothes. Wrapped in her musing, Evie failed to register the footsteps.

Less than a block away from her apartment, a cold set of hands snatched her up and sucked her into the void. Her first inclination was to scream, adrenaline rushed through her veins. The jolt backward snapped her neck, the hard crunch of vertebrae popped between her ears.

"Hel—" She tried to scream, but was cut short by a hand over her mouth. Her new tattoo throbbed, hidden under the gauze and scarf.

"Don't think for one second that he's not denying you what your heart desires for his own benefit?"

Absolute terror held her mute. The hand loosened off of her lips, but still she could produce no sound. Then she detected a hint of his sweet scent.

"Lucca?" The beating of her heart switched tempos, no longer drumming from fear—not exclusively. His shimmery dark orbs glinted off the moon light breaking into the black as he pulled her in between two tenements. He held her close against his body. His wicked grin stretched the full width of his jaw line. Menacing and cold, it contorted his perfect features. Evie saw the monster behind the beautiful curtain.

"Evan will never change you... it's not his place," he said.

Her breathing grew increasingly erratic with each heartbeat. No longer afraid of her attack, but more so of her attacker. She looked off to her periphery, to the well-lit streets of city nightlife. Cars sped by. The disharmony of nightlife could be heard over dogs barking in the distance. The neighborhood gave no indication anyone witnessed her abduction. She was trapped in Lucca's dark embrace.

"Evan wants to help me," she said with a weak breath.

"Come now, Evie. We both know better." He pinned her up against cold vinyl siding that groaned withstanding their pressure. "Evan wants to bleed you until you can no longer sustain him. You'll die, and then be born again. His selfish cycle will perpetuate itself. How many of your human lives do you think Evan has used you for his own perversions?"

"You're lying." Her chest rapped anxiously against his. Her desire waned, replaced by stout froth gurgling up her throat.

"Am I?" Lucca closed in on her, running the tip of his nose against hers, brushing their lips together, and adjusting the pitch of his voice to an intimate tone. "Has he told you he loves you? Convinced you that he prefers you above all others? It's your essence he wants, Evie. He's the same as me." She trembled in his hold, fighting tears as her collarbone bloomed with liquid fire. "I want to share immortality with you," he said, continuing. "Evan's like a crazed addict, hooked on your body and your blood."

"But he...?" Her voice broke down to a whimper.

A low rumble seethed past Lucca's wicked grin, his clenched canines leashed by a building rage she'd only witnessed in her dreams. Those hands that she remembered massaging her from the inside out tightened around her, digging into her flesh.

"Let us entertain the notion that Evan may love you. The question is why, Evie? More specifically, what does he love about you?"

She thrust her head side to side. "You're lying."

His widening grin mocked her. "I may not be able to reveal all of the truth to you, Evie, but I never lie. That's not my way."

Her neck throbbed. Her tattoo ached. While her lower half burned to feel him against her skin, she sank in the fear that Lucca might find her scars—the remnants of Evan's bite or the stars along her neck. She squirmed, desperate to be free, unwilling to give in to the curious mix of desire and dread that accompanied Lucca's presence.

A brilliant gleam of light shone off his eyetoothed sneer as he leaned in. Evie dodged his sharp fangs, but failed to find purchase from his hold, kicking over a nearby collection of empty trash barrels in the process. Still, no one came to her rescue.

She grunted, battling not only Lucca's physical strength, but also her own internal conflict to revel in his assault or break free. The high priestess whirred about in a frenzy.

Stay! Fall!

Lucca jarred her a bit and easily pulled her back to him. His arousal, as direct as it was in her dream split her resolve in two. "I am capable of many things, Evie," he said. "But lying—like love—is not one of them."

A torrent of doubt and confusion rained down on her. "It's not possible. Evan's not using me," she said, half of her actually willing to consider the possibility.

"How are your habits, Evie? Which poison do you prefer these days?"

"What?" Trepidation pumped the blood through her veins, pulsating against the fresh abrasions under her scarf.

"Have you given up drinking?" He took in a deep inhale of her. "No." He grinned. "Is Evan trying to cure you of that addiction? It sours the blood, alters your sweetness. He's not predisposed to such tastes. Tell me, how is he succeeding in purging those demons? What has he proposed to displace your thirst?"

"Pot," she said, hesitant to indicate Sempiternal feeding was the first answer to pop into her head. Lucca raked her over, ogling with his tongue pressed into the tip of his dagger-like fang. His leering suggested her unspoken answer had been smeared all over her body.

"Marijuana, yes. That is his personal favorite, isn't it? You haven't let him consume your spice-tinged essence, have you?" Dread pierced through her chest. Lucca continued with repugnance morphing his once delicious smirk, "He's always enjoyed the effects of the plant for some reason. It leaves its own zest in the blood. But you're mine, Evie, remember that. Evan knows his place. He knows the consequences."

It was a miracle she remained standing as Lucca's implications sucked the wind from her. Consuming her in his gaze, his mad grin widened. His arousal pressed up against her. The warmth of her daylight faded as Lucca's nothingness wrapped around her like the chill from the depths of the ocean, closing in and filling her—suffocating her.

"I can give you what you want, Evie. I can give you the release you crave."

"You're lying," she said through tears. She moved her head back and forth, but her fight was waning.

"Hey, who's out there?" A gruff voice called out from a nearby window.

She seized the opportunity. "Hel—" Lucca's covered her mouth with his. Evie moaned, savoring the ferocity of his kiss, even as her instincts continued to oppose him.

"Hey, what are ya doin'? Not on my property, ya don't," the voice said. "I called the cops."

Sirens sounded a few streets over. With their howling, a surge of adrenaline rushed through her. Lucca pinned her to the side of the house and dove deeper into her mouth. They'd have their moment, she knew that. His promises for immortality were too enticing—but not here, not with freshly inked doubt searing her flesh. Evie wriggled free, but Lucca snatched her up at the elbow.

"Ask him, Evie—I insist—but know it changes nothing. I intend to collect my due."

The man inside the apartment banged against the sill, thereby rattling what little nerve Evie had left in her body. Lucca didn't so much as flinch.

"Hey guy! Get your hands off that girl. Ya hear those sirens, asshole?"

Lucca growled, fangs exposed, hackles raised. "I could kill the fool and take you now," he said quietly to Evie.

Go! Go!

Her eyes widened. Her stomach flipped. "No."

The golden rims of Lucca's eyes glistened in the dark, exuberance spread across his face. "Soon Evie," he said and ebbed into the shadows as flashing lights approached.

***

Evie stumbled out to the sidewalk expecting to come face to face with Boston PD, but the flashing lights zoomed by. Instead she was met by the gruff voice from the window. A short man with a terrible comb-over, plaid pajama pants, and swollen beer belly stood on his front porch.

"Yo'kay, sweetheart?" The porch railing creaked under his upper body rested along the railing.

She took a moment to catch her breath and steady her pulse before nodding. "What happened to the cops?"

"I just said that to spook whoever was out here? Those sirens were just good timin' is all. Why, ya hurt? Do ya want me to call 'em?"

She shook her head and clutched her scarf close to her neck. "No."

"Ya sure?"

"No, I'm sorry. That was just my... friend... playing a bad prank on me. I live right over there." She pointed a shaky finger diagonally across the street to her well-lit front stoop. Her hand quickly retracted for fear of what eyes may spy her from the shadows.

The man grumbled something to himself. "Goddamned kids. Next time I catch ya fuckin' around on my property I'll call the cops for trespassin'."

"Yes, sir." She nodded once more and righted the tipped-over barrels. The stubby man hobbled back into his apartment.

She scurried across the street, double and triple checking the shadows. Evie trusted the hairs lying flat against the back of her neck as a sign she wasn't being followed, and then dashed up the front steps. The red and blue lights she presumed were for her aid lit up the neighborhood just one block away.

TWENTY-SEVEN

Her body was physically defeated. Evie clung to the stairwell banister with hands still trembling from adrenaline. After climbing the three flights of stairs, her heels burned from the blisters that had formed breaking in her new boots.

She coaxed one foot in front of the other. At the top of the third floor landing, she was ready to collapse. Supporting her weight with her hand against the wall, she reached the door to her apartment, and then stopped. Evie patted her pockets, the floor nearly came out from under her. Her key ring was gone. She searched her person—twisting, panicking. Her pulse boomed considering she'd have to brave the streets in search of her keys, afraid Lucca was off waiting for her. Beyond that, she was terrified she'd follow him this time.

She turned to make the dreaded descent back down the stairs when the door to her apartment creaked open. Evan greeted her with big and beautiful brown eyes that drew tears from her own.

A swell of relief, heartache, and hunger pulled her forward. She swooped in, grasping at his jaw with both hands. He was spicy, sweet, and piney, a flavor she'd come to associate solely with him. At first taken aback by her kiss, he froze, but then wrapped an arm around her waist and hauled her into the apartment.

Inside the apartment, he gently nudged her away. She stretched her neck to its capacity, unwilling to release his mouth from hers.

"Well, hello there." He laughed.

"Hi." She said, searching his guarded stare for any ill-intent, and came up null. Evan's eyes were brilliant and inviting.

"Did you have a good time working things out with Blythe?"

He led her over to the futon. Her heart pounded inside her chest, thundering over their light footsteps. Evan began the ritual of packing the glass bowl and offered her the first toke. She pried her boots from her sore feet and gladly accepted the pot. Her mind and body, however, craved something far more enticing. She ran the course of his body with her eyes twice before taking the pipe to her lips, and then filled her lungs with him. She exhaled a ribbon of smoke, savoring his flavor rolling over her tongue.

"No, not really," she said and decided it best to keep Lucca's attack to herself—at least until she had time to contemplate his accusation toward Evan. Instead, she focused on the triviality of her chat with Blythe. "She gave me some bullshit excuse about catching up while she was in town with her boyfriend. I'm pretty sure she's still bent about your break up though… either that or she's way more cynical than she used to be."

Evan sunk back into the futon and took her hand in his. He dragged the tip of his thumb along her skin. The soft friction instilled a calm over her, and only then did the wild rhythm of her pulse settle. As such, Evie shifted in her seat, using his shoulder as a pillow under her right cheek.

"So, how many drinks did you have?" he asked.

She cringed. "You could taste that?"

He placed a tiny peck atop her head. "How many, Evie?"

His tone was stern, but not angry. A part of her was grateful he'd only detected the beer and not someone else's residual lust lining the inside of her mouth. She chewed her lower lip, forcing her body not to react to the memory of Lucca's body pressed against hers.

Diverting her own discomfort with humor, she lifted their hands still joined together and offered up her wrist. "Do you want to check my blood alcohol content?"

He chuckled and dropped their hands back down to rest along his thigh. "Smartass."

She giggled back and nudged her elbow into his side, choosing to leverage the moment of flippancy. "So Blythe wants to take me to a Halloween party next month for my birthday."

Grateful for her THC-induced apathy, she anticipated his inquisition with a stilled pulse.

"Oh? How much do you know about the party?" he asked.

"Only that we need to wear costumes."

"You know what I'm going to say?" he said.

Evie stared blankly into her lap. Yes, she knew he'd say—that it was too risky. Considering that perceived risk, a more pressing issue hammered down on her chest.

What is he protecting?

"Not now." She released Evan's hand and vanished to the bathroom.

"Evie...?" He called out behind her, but she closed the door nonetheless to meet her instigating inner voice head on in the mirror.

"I don't want to question his motives right now. Just for once, leave me alone," she said to the mirror, wrapping her hands around the edge of the bathroom's pedestal sink. Her reflection offered a mocking grin. "Stop that! Evan just wants to love and protect me, like he said." Neither body nor soul could sustain the alternative.

You must stop being so selfish.

"And you need to stop fucking with my head." She glowered at the reflection before dropping her gaze to her neck. It ached. She removed the gauze and began the process of cleaning the tattoo according to Yeung Jae's instructions. The fresh abrasions were still red and puffy. The throbbing of the small vein behind her ear continued to encourage bubbles of blood to surface. She stared at the marking, still unsure what it truly meant.

"No, not now." she said to her inner voice reflecting back with a scowl in the mirror. "Just let me have this time with him."

Stepping back out into the studio, she stripped down to a tank top and hot pink briefs. Evan was rolling a joint to the tune a piano playing off her laptop. He took a long drag, and then released a hacking cough when his eyes found her.

"Coming?" she asked.

He choked on his exhale.

"Excuse me?"

"To bed, Evan." She giggled. "C'mon, pass that pinner and tuck me in. I'm exhausted."

She watched his guarded expression, pained eyes, a flicker of excitement hidden behind them, and soft pink lips pursed firmly together. Evan took another toke. Through a veil of smoke, he licked his lips and joined her on the bed.

Her mind was abuzz with conflicting thoughts, but using the joint imbued with Evan's zest, Evie silenced the voices. She settled next to him as her high priestess trembled, exhilarated by his touch.

***

Piano transitioned to acoustic guitar. From atop the covers, flesh to the air, she lay on her back and pulled what few final drags she could off the roach singeing her fingers. Evie stared at the waves of smoke wafting up toward the ceiling, in love with the contentment of their moment. Evan rested on his side, running the length of her body. He ran his fingertips across her neck and the tiny beads of blood blooming from the shiny stars therein. She relished the sensation of him looming over her and the tickle of his fingers lightly tracing her skin. The barely perceptible sound of him suckling at the tips of his blood-dipped fingertips like music to hear ears. She gnawed at her lip to fight the smirk breaking through. Eyes closed, she imagined him suckling something very different. In the pot-spiced air of her cozy studio apartment, she let Evan's essence overwhelm her.

"You are so... different." Evan said quietly, almost as though the statement wasn't meant to be vocalized at all.

"Who am I different from? Your other 'friends?'"

She opened her eyes to find his lips pursed, and was dazed under the shadow of his stoic expression. He ran his fingers ran through her hair, and then leaned over and pressed his lips to hers.

"Something like that," he said.

Completely intoxicated by his presence, Evie flipped over to her knees. She extinguished the roach in the ashtray resting on the nightstand and then straddled Evan, pinning him below her weight. He laughed, feigned protest, but inevitably submitted to her.

"Is that a good thing or a bad thing?" She leaned over and held him by his shoulders. Evie savored the heat building at her base as she pressed her hips down on him. Damn the layers of denim and cotton barring her access to his body, she thought.

He flashed a crooked grin. "I think you'll finally be the death of me."

Her playful demeanor soured. She sat up straight. "That's not funny. Why would you say that?"

"It's not meant to be funny. It's a genuine complement." He reached up to her. Evan's idea of a romantic gesture skewed in her mind. Such conflict must have been plainly displayed across her face, because he laughed from his belly and pulled her down on top of him. "Don't worry Evie. I've already committed to do anything in my power to save you. I don't plan on going down without a fight."

"Will you change me then? If that's what it takes to hold on to me?"

It was a bold question. His furrowed brow answered for him.

We know why he won't.

She scowled.

"Why do you want this life, Evie?" asked Evan. "It's evil, like an eternal purgatory. What do you think makes this all so appealing?"

"Because of you..." she said then hesitated. "... and Lucca."

He sighed and lifted her off of him. Evie cursed her honesty and inner voice's compulsions. Evan retrieved the glass bowl from the coffee table and proceeded to pack it—for himself. Both the weed and his discontent thickened the air when he took a hit.

"I'm sorry," she said, staring into the void of his white t-shirt. "I didn't mean—"

"I know you." Evan turned back and faced her. "I know the pull he has over you, Evie. It's just like the one you have over me."

"You make me sound like a bad influence on you."

"The worst," he said with a chuckle and flipped Evie over onto her back in a single fluid motion. He pinned her down under his hips. "What was it you said?" Evan raised a crooked brow. "Take you one moment at a time? Well, I'm trying. That's something I never thought I'd be able to do." Evan rolled his eyes over her body trembling beneath him. "Tell me, Miss Westvale, what do you want this very moment?"

The answer was as apparent as the tremors causing her body to shiver. "You." Her breath was thick with wanting, and Evan's answering smile welled her eyes with salty tears.

"And in this moment, that is all I need to hear."

He pressed his weight onto her, his lips to hers. A delicious rush of blood swelled between her legs to the point of aching. Evie moaned. She pawed all over him, grasping at him, tugging his hair, and scratching her way down his back. She then fumbled with the zipper on his pants.

Evan groaned and pulled away. "Good night, Evie."

Her body seized. Her mind reeled.

Where is he going?

"Wait. Are you kidding me? We're not going to have sex?" She jumped up and chased him to the door.

Evan chuckled when he faced her. "Always about sex," he said. "Tell me, Evie. Who do you want right now, me or Lucca?"

"You." She huffed, exasperated by whatever games Evan thought he was playing with her libido.

"Why?"

"I—" Her jaw snapped shut, brow knitted. Her twisted expression fixed on him, unable to answer. "You're just being fucking mean, Evan. No one likes a cock-tease. Maybe I should go find Lucca? At least I know I'll get laid."

Evan raised an eyebrow. His grin revealed just a hint of sharp, pearly canines. "Are you making threats, now?"

She was thrust up against the wall. He closed in, invading her with tongue in mouth and hands under her thin cotton layers. For the first time in months, something other than her own fingers found their way inside her body, and she moistened instantly. Evan felt better than any of her interpretations. His touch was such that he knew her inside and out, conscious of all her pleasure spots, when and how to engage them.

More...

She latched her arms and legs around him, intending to hold him hostage until he gave in to her cravings. Success seemed as imminent as the internal pressure building. He massaged the throbbing apex between her legs. She pulled him in as close as physics would allow until crying out. Evie projected her orgasm directly into his mouth when the pressure became too much to bear. A tear trickled down her cheek, doing its part to release her of the utter elation flooding her body.

Evan slowed his hand and lifted his head back to connect with her eyes. "Just a little taste is all you ever need, isn't it?" He grinned, teasing.

Her body slinked down his, and her feet found the floor again. She honed in on the target of his prominent fangs. The high priestess shifted.

Make him give me more.

Evie's gut twisted with a dull ache—a thirst she knew well, though never caused by anything other than recreational drugs.

"You wanted tattoos... I want you. Stay." Her demand weakened to a plea by the taut cord connecting her heart to the darkness between her thighs. Her eagerness was further agonized by Evan's moment of reluctance. His eyes danced across her flesh and settled on her swelling breasts. He licked his lips, and she mirrored the mannerism heavy with anticipation for more.

"Evie…" He shook his head and peered up at her fresh ink. "Trust me, I don't enjoy playing like this, but… Shit, you have some serious thrill issues, seducing immortals."

TWENTY-EIGHT

He's not refusing.

Before Evan could reconsider, Evie seized his jaw with her hands. A rush of blood shot through her and pulsed between her legs, overpowered only by the gaping hole in the pit of her stomach.

Evan coaxed her away from the door, pulling free from her embrace. "Games," he said softly. "You play some dirty games, Evie." He leaned in to kiss her and unfasten her bra.

"I'm not too proud, and I'm not the only guilty party here." She smiled against his mouth. She'd leverage his hatred for Lucca if it helped her cause. Hell, she'd cover her body in silver stars if it got behind Evan's walls. The means was negligible so long as she found her end on the tips of his fangs.

"You're so impatient," he said, intent on the path he carved along her body with both hands and eyes, slowing across her breasts. "But God, you're gorgeous." He settled along her neckline, leaving a rash of goose bumps in his wake.

Her body shivered with need to be pressed against him, but she held still with bated breath. "We're really going to do this?"

He smirked. "I don't think I really have a choice. You'll never quit, will you?"

She bit back her smile and shook her head as he pulled his shirt from over his head. Evie watched him, awed by his frame; lithe, pale, familiar.

You think you can take on the Sempiternal?

Her eyes molested him. Her mind envisioned what she could do to his body, her stomach in knots. She disregarded her subconscious' chide, being more content with the throbbing below her belly. Her fingertips tingled as they traced over his chest, up to his collarbone, and along his neck. She paused at the tattoo on his shoulder, a broken wing twisted in a downward spiral. Evie outlined it, like it could tell its own story through her fingertips. Looking up to Evan, pain etched his face.

"How long have you had this?" she asked. Desperation carried in her tone.

"A long time." He regarded the markings. "My uncle ordered it shortly after... It's supposed to represent Icarus falling from the sun."

"It's beautiful." She leaned in to kiss it, but he caught her, pulling her lips to his instead.

"It's a reminder," he said and guided her toward the bed.

Watching him study every inch of her was maddening. Evie wasted no time sliding out of her panties and inching her way onto the bed. Her eyes fixed on Evan's fingers unbuttoning his pants. Her tongue played along the edge of her teeth. Following the swift sound of a zipper and rustling of denim, Evan was free from his clothing and poised to strike.

He crawled on top of her. Her heart skipped a beat when his body grazed hers.

"We're taking this just one moment at a time, right?" His voice drifted hot across her neck.

"Not now, Evan." She didn't want to deliberate over the implications of crossing this line. Such considerations were secondary to her immediate needs.

She grabbed ahold of his hips and positioned him between her thighs. After months with only her fingers to comfort her, Evan's full erection hurt. She groaned. Her body protested, but as he stretched her with each plunge, a relay of explosions set off through her body. Heavy breaths pushed past her lips.

"Goddamn, Evie." Evan panted in her ear and dragged his lips across her neck. He snatched at her, greedily pulling her hips and guiding her movements to coordinate with his rhythm.

She lapped up the droplets of sweat beading along the expanse of his shoulders. Savoring the way his spine stiffened as she dragged her nails down his back. The sound of his breath quickening echoed through her mind. She committed the pitch of his vocals to memory along with his savoriness.

He drove into her with purpose, each thrust perfectly orchestrated between their bodies. The pulsing inside her bloomed in hot waves from her core.

She cried out and clamped down, gnawing into his shoulder, but without the necessary bite of a Sempiternal canine, she failed to inflict any damage. Still, his salty zest was thrilling.

He snickered in her ear and nibbled the lobe before nudging her away with his nose. With his forehead rested atop hers, he cradled the back of her head in his hands. She reveled in the tingling sensation behind her left ear as the tattoo etched into Evan's right palm connected with hers.

Eyes closed, he whispered something she couldn't quite discern amidst their moans, but the rasping of his breath against her skin warmed her from the inside out. She was safe and controlled under him, and she would have died in his arms without a second of hesitation. The high priestess thrived with verve at her center.

"What do you need from me, Evie?" Evan decreased his tempo, allowing recovery from her second orgasm.

More...

Anticipation churned in her stomach. Her mouth went dry.

"Bite me," she said in a sultry coo and felt every muscle in his body tense up.

"Evie, you haven't had enough time to build up your blood supply. I don't think—"

"I don't care... I want it." She moaned and arched her back, pushing her chest up toward him. The need to be washed away by his undertow strengthened to the point of aching. She needed to displace the pain.

"I need you to bleed me." He shook his head. Protest screaming from his eyes. "Please, Evan."

"Evie..." The tension freezing his body weakened. Baring pearlescent daggers, Evan ran his hand across her upper body and dipped his head down. His palm pressed against her ribcage as he latched onto the fold beneath her breast. With an alarming stab, he sank his teeth in.

"Fuck! Evan..." Squirming beneath him, Evie screamed from the force it took him to break the skin. She fisted the hair atop his head. Her heart beat furiously just inches from his fangs. The contrasting wetness between her legs and across her chest stirred a craziness in her that threatened to break her to pieces.

Consuming her, grunting, Evan engaged his hips into violent motion. Blood gushed into his mouth and spilled down her side to the sheets. She writhed beneath him in delicious agony. Evie threw a pillow over her face to muffle screams that shredded her vocal cords.

Evan snapped up, face filthy with a red film, eyes wild. His bucking came to a halt. "Are you okay?"

"Yes." She breathed heavily resurfacing from her downy gag, mesmerized by the amount of gore rimming his soft features. "Absolutely perfect."

She traced her fingertips across his face, smeared her blood over his look of dismay, and pulled him into a kiss. Lined with her own silken essence, Evan pressed his lips against hers.

The high she'd been craving for weeks continued for as long as Evan drove into her. She was beyond euphoric under his body. Her head swam from the rush of sudden blood loss converging with the afterglow of immortal intimacy. After Evan's body seized in pleasure, she lay in bed, stained crimson and wrapped in his arms.

***

When Lucca visited her dreams that night he was changed, his touch soft and considerate—like Evan's.

They lay side by side, blanketed in the black satin of their echoic breaths. He nuzzled into the crook of her neck and dragged his parted lips across her skin, teasing her with fanged tips never breaking the skin. His hands caressed her, pulling her into him, shifting her hips to meet his. Her breaths wilted, swirled like wafts of smoke through each sensual moan.

"We are the same, Evie, you and I. Do not let him tempt you." Lucca ran his hand along the base of her back, the other against her rear commanding her closer. "Fall with me."

A third hand traced the curvature of her hip. Fingertips played against her hip bone, pulling her away from his lap. A fourth hand crept up from under her arm and cupped her breast, pinching the nipple and persuading her backwards.

Then she felt his mouth—not Lucca's—Evan's, nipping at her shoulder from behind. His tongue rolled along the base of her neck, up to the back of her left ear where her newly applied tattoo lay. His breath, warm against her skin, evoked shivers from the nape of her neck down to her toes. The tiniest groan escaped Evan's lips and trickled into her ear. The tangy spice of his essence permeated her olfactories.

"Tell me what you need," he said.

Caught in the vise of their bodies, awash in lust, Evie reveled in their ménage.

Lucca's hands grew more demanding of her. He tugged on her waist, yanking her away from Evan. "He knows his place."

She connected with Lucca's eyes, those gold-rimmed black orbs burned, his smile wide and wicked. Such menace only excited her and called her toward him.

Evan creeped up from behind her and pulled her back. His touch hardened, possessive. "Let me help you."

She gave in to their limbo—to their mouths suckling at her curves, to their hands reaching up and around the sinful pressure points hidden in plain sight all over her body. Their sighs and grunts fell in harmony with each other.

Then the pain—a sharp pinch on her shoulder interrupted Evie's rapture. She wailed out loud in an unnatural octave, so loud it nearly pierced the veil of her dream.

Evan took the first bite, clamping down from behind and tore at her flesh. His jaw locked down, unrelenting and ravenous. Fire erupted within her. Lucca followed in suit, slicing into her collar bone with razor sharp teeth. Layers of her skin were ripped away in large chunks, exposing bits of muscular tissue and bone down to the marrow, searing hot and wet as it made contact with the crisp air.

Her moans turned to howls. Terror seized her body. A red mist descended onto her nightmare. She pushed and pulled against the two beasts snarling like wild dogs on fresh prey.

Their feral growls boomed between her ears. They held her captive. Their gorgeous skin soiled in her gore. Muscles and ligaments were pulled in opposing directions, stretching Evie beyond her limits. Her heartbeat slowed. Panic settled into acceptance.

Eclipsed by their overlapping presence, Evie fell into the purgatory of their night and day. Fear was held at bay. She found peace being torn to shreds by their ecstasy.

***

"Evie, wake up." She opened her eyes to find Evan propped up against her side, still naked. Her heart pounded, and she struggled a moment to catch her breath. The look of consternation across Evan's face did little to calm her. "Shit, are you okay? You were having a nightmare. Your whole body was convulsing, and you were crying."

She lifted a hand to his jawline. In the shadows, his features sharpened, closely resembling Lucca's. Such a comparison stabbed at her chest. She ran her thumb along his bottom lip, somewhat disappointed the red stains had been wiped away. She smiled nonetheless.

"I'm fine," she said and hoped he wouldn't push the issue. Her mind was fucked up, her body ached.

Most of the effects of feeding were lost with her dreams, though not all of them. Her ribs were on fire from Evan's bite. Already her stomach was turning. The stinging ache in her rib sank deeper toward the protective chamber around her heart.

She tugged at his shoulders, and rolled Evan on top of her. Cautious not to crush her under his weight, he chuckled and supported himself up by his elbows. Caged beneath him,

274

Evie focused on his benign grin, rejecting her previous comparisons.

"What did you say?" she asked. His smile waned and was replaced by a quizzical expression. "You mumbled something before, during sex. What was it?"

His smile returned, but it was unlike any she'd seen grace his features before. It was an expression mixed with sorrow, love, and nostalgia. She found the sun of her days setting in that look.

"I said: *je ne peux pas croire que j'ai failli oublier comment tu me fait sentir.*" His words flowed from his lips eloquently, too quickly for Evie to catch up.

"Sher-what?"

He laughed softly. "It's French. It means: *I can't believe I almost forgot how you feel.*"

Evie gazed at his newly discovered smile. She could almost see beyond his guard, but it remained vigilant. His cryptic statement only fueled her curiosity more.

"Did you know me?" she asked.

"How so?"

"In my past life," she said. "You were around when the Carver estate was built. Wasn't that around the time Lucca killed me? I'm wondering if you knew me."

Shadows cloaked his soft brown eyes. "Everyone in town knew who you were. Your father was a respected sea captain."

"Well then, did I know you? You just said you almost forgot what I felt like. What's that supposed to mean?"

His guarded expression was fortified by a furrowed brow and thin line in place of his lips. "From yesterday... that's what I meant," he said hesitantly. "As for your past life, everyone in town worked on the construction of the Carver estate in some way. Yes, our paths crossed."

Evan ended the conversation by rolling onto his back and pulling her into a tight embrace. Pressed to his chest, she listened for a heartbeat. The one she found was erratic and not like the constant drumming of her own. Still, his skin was soft and warm, and smelled a mixture of spice, sweat, and weed. Evan was intoxicating. She took in a deep, breath full of him.

"What does it feel like to consume someone?" She felt the rise and fall of his chest, a rhythmic motion that soothed her like the rolling tides.

"It's amazing." He stared up through the ceiling to the celestial bodies beyond.

"Does it vary from person to person?"

"Yes."

"Am I—"

"Breathtaking in every aspect—delicious, sweet, and enthralling—unlike any others."

"So what does it feel like?"

Evan looked down to meet her gaze. "What does what feel like?"

"Sex. Is it different for the Sempiternal?"

She rolled onto her belly, stretched out along the length of his body. The conflict of their beating hearts pounded between them. Her expectant brow emphasized her curiosity.

Evan laughed through a closed-lip grin and brushed stray hair strands from her face. "Why do you ask?"

She pitched a shoulder. "I'm wondering if it will be different."

He frowned. "Will be?" He placed heavy emphasis on her inference.

"I was just curious."

A guttural growl surfaced from within him.

I could bite Evan now. We could end all of this.

Evie flinched and fought to mask the distasteful scowl lining her face.

"Sex…" Evan paused. "If you remember, I've said it's not as important for us as it is for you." She dropped her eyes from his and landed on his tattoo. "It's human nature to reproduce. That's not an innate compulsion for an immortal because we can't. For all intents and purposes, sex is a means to an end—consumption. It's part of our makeup, but it's not our obsession or motivator."

"But how does it feel?"

He forced a smile. "I can't say I know how to answer that. It's been a long time since I've been mortal, and I remember very little about human sensations. It's still very much enjoyable, but I suppose it is different."

"How long has it been?"

"Evie, it's been a long time. I was practically born and bred into this life. Please don't ask me how long I've been this way. I don't like to think about it."

She registered the anguish in his expression and bit back her retort. Emotions raged through her body.

If Evan felt this good, how would Lucca feel? What would happen when he actually sank his teeth into her and consumed her essence? Lying across Evan, with their skin to skin, it was difficult to imagine anything better.

It is inevitable, stupid girl.

She squeezed Evan's torso tight and peered back up to him. Remorse prevented her from looking him in the eyes. Instead, her sights fell to his shoulder again. She studied his tattoo and thought of the wings on her back.

"If you're Icarus, did you fall trying to fly away?" She stretched her hand out to trace the feathery spiral around his shoulder. His skin was warm, smooth.

Evan's frown deepened. "I challenged what I shouldn't have... and I learned from it."

"Will you ever tell me about it?"

"No," he said coldly. Like other cryptic answers he'd offered in the past, Evie let Evan's secrets remain just that—secret.

Instead, she peeled her eyes from the marking and focused on the length of his nakedness. Her mouth watered.

Her future may have been damned as far as Evan was concerned, but her present moment showed very real promise. She smiled, a sly side smirk conjured from the fathoms of her subconscious and slithered down his body.

"Evie, what are doing?" He twitched and gasped with sudden thrill as she took him deep into the back of her throat.

She answered him with a hum and a giggle, pinning him with a firm hold on his hipbone. Engrossed with Evan's salt, infused with a generous coating of her essence rolling across her taste buds, she sucked.

His hand palmed the back of her head, entwining his fingers through her multicolored locks. Fingertips dug into her scalp as he seethed with excitement.

"*Lilitu,*" he said, taking in a deep breath.

With a *slurp* and a *pop*, Evie looked up. "What's that French for?"

His head lulled back. Evan jolted, clawed at her jaw, and ripped her off of him. He threw her down into the cloud of white linens. "*Ma belle Lilitu.*" He growled before wrapping his mouth over hers and pounding into her with a more primal urgency.

TWENTY-NINE

"Lucca's wrong... he has to be." The next morning, Evie deliberated with her reflection in the full-length mirror hanging on her bathroom door, obsessing over her scarf in the process.

Does he? He said he'd never lie to us.

"Evan's not using us for his own perversions." She scoffed at the notion.

Her reflection smirked.

Why not? Aren't we doing the same to him?

"I—"

Evie's breath caught. She fixated on the discoloration along her clavicle. A soreness stabbed inside her chest, an agony greater than her bruise's sibling concealed by the underwire of her bra.

"No," she said. "You're wrong."

These games are wicked and fun. Aren't they, stupid girl?

She bit back her argument behind pursed her lips. Her eyes rimmed with tears. The scraping of metal pulled her away from her internal strife.

"If you're not going to offer me answers, then just shut up." She pointed at her reflection, waited a moment for it to quip back. When that didn't to happen, she turned her back to it and found Evan letting himself into her apartment.

"How do you feel this morning?" he asked and handed her a cup of coffee from a nearby café.

279

"Fine. Thank you." She accepted his offering and brought the piping hot brew to her lips. "Where have you been?"

He grinned. "I had to go home and change. Why?"

She raked him up and down. While she decided nudity was his best look, Evan looked quite enticing in a grey twill suit and tie. Obsessing over his physical appearance just increased the aching in her chest.

She scowled at her coffee in hand. "It was just weird waking up, and you were gone. I felt… used… cheap."

Both glanced toward the bed, sheets crumpled and spotted with burgundy stains.

"It's wasn't my intention to make you feel that way," he said. "It never is. I'm sorry."

She forced the blistering coffee past the knot in her throat. Finding nothing but sincerity in his eyes, she hated that Lucca's accusations rang out through her mind.

"That's okay," she said. "It's not like you're the first guy to take off in the middle of the night on me."

Evan answered her levity with gritted teeth. "That's not something I want to picture in my head."

She lifted the corner of her mouth and turned away from him. Resting the coffee on her dresser, she stood in front of the mirror again. Evan followed behind, connecting with her reflection.

He rested his hands on her shoulders. She was sure he'd see the deceitful bitch glaring from beyond the mirror's surface. His gaze remained concerned though, not confrontational.

"Evie, are you sure you're okay? You're very pale."

"Blood loss, right?" she said dispassionately. "I am a little sore too. Thank God, it's not the middle of the summer. Otherwise, I don't know how I'd cover your bite marks."

Evan pulled on her shoulder to face him. He played with her scarf, pushing it aside to inspect the cleavage hidden beneath her periwinkle blouse.

"Keep those covered up at work." He adjusted her scarf and smiled at his handiwork. "You don't want people to think you're being abused."

Looking up at him, his complexion was a stark contrast to hers. His skin was luminescent, his eyes a thick, russet brown—enticing. "Do we have to go to work? Can't we just stay in bed?"

He placed a kiss against her forehead. "You've bled enough for me already."

Her cheeks tingled, and her stomach flipped. "What's one more drop?"

"And what if I can't limit myself to just one drop." The deathly consequence lacing his tone stirred the high priestess.

Yes...

The world—her apartment—disappeared around them. She was lost in his eyes and the promise of oblivion therein.

No more pain, no more questioning. Nothing.

She shifted her weight onto the tips of her toes, leaning toward him, welcoming the chance to fall deep into Sempiternal darkness.

"Let's go," Evan said and broke the trance. "You'll be happy. I actually brought my car today."

***

"So what's the special occasion?" Evie asked as Evan closed the passenger door behind her. She rested back into the plush Italian leather and waited for Evan to settle into the driver's seat.

281

"It's starting to cool off this time of year," he said. "And we're expecting rain later."

She fingered the stereo. "Well, I'm not complaining, but how the hell do I work the radio."

Evan chuckled and tapped against the touchscreen embedded within the dash. "Here. You should be able to pull up your playlist on your phone and connect with the sound system."

"Technology amazes me sometimes." She set the music to play at random when the car prompted her. "I was excited my little hatchback came with a CD player."

The engine purred, and Evan shifted into gear.

The first song queued up. Instantly the plucking of guitar sent shivers down through her body. The song Claudio dedicated to her filled the sedan's interior, not nearly as beautiful as his live rendition. Evie sunk into her seat and fumbled through her phone.

"I thought you liked that song."

She glanced up. "I've overplayed it. It's time to move on." The acidic burn of coffee and regret gurgled up her throat. The prospect of a relationship with another mortal seemed a lifetime ago.

Her phone pinged through the stereo and followed up with a flashing blue light. She grumbled under her breath.

"What's wrong?" asked Evan.

URGENT! Need 2 C U

She sighed. "Nate's texting me again. He wants to meet up."

Evan's frustrations released on the car's transmission, banging through each gear. "Do you want me to answer that text for you?"

"Why, what would you say?" She tucked the phone back in her bag and let Nate's text go unanswered. Ignoring him had to be better than Evan's response.

Through a slanted glance, he offered his opinion. "I'd tell him to learn his place."

Her pulse quickened as Lucca's words haunted Evan's lips.

"And where is that exactly?"

"In your fucking past," he said, jaw ticking.

They accelerated up L Street and made it to the industrial park within minutes in comparison to their standard trek on foot. All the while, she sat taciturn, unable to peel her eyes off the beast stirring by her side.

***

Evan parked in a garage across from her building and escorted her inside. They remained arm in arm, even onto the elevator.

"Don't you have to go to work?" she asked, though in no rush for him to leave her side.

"I have an ad hoc meeting with your boss this morning." He played with her scarf as they ascended to the top floor. Pushing the knitted wool and her hair aside, he dipped down to her tattoo. Her body pulsed when his lips brushed against the back of her ear. "It's healing nicely. Yeung Jae is good at what he does."

Stifling a moan, Evie's libido cried when Evan stepped off the elevator.

Inside the office, she paused to look down the line of cubicles. Faces peered back at her here and there, indifferent to her arrival. No sound could be heard, save for the cadence of fingers across keyboards.

"I guess I'll see you later," she said to Evan and set off for her desk. After one step, he yanked her back with a playful tug. Evie yelped and was spun around, landing against his chest. Embarrassment flooded her as her outburst called the attention of those close by.

"What are you doing?" she asked.

"Just letting everyone know that all bets are off."

Evan cupped behind her left ear with his palm, his fingers tangled in her hair at the nape of her neck. A wondrous current washed over her body as their tattoos connected, an energy pulsing through her very core and melted down her spine. She met his gaze with confusion and a heart rate that threatened the structural integrity of her legs.

When Evan kissed her, the office around them faded into obscurity. Evie didn't give a fuck who watched. When he released her lips, his hand remained cradling the back of her head.

"What was that?" she asked at the edge of her breath.

He replied with a closed-lip chuckle, and then raising one eyebrow, looked beyond her. "I'm going to catch a world of shit for that."

She followed his line of sight over her shoulder to find Slithery Silver, himself, scowling from the doorway of his executive suite.

"You're going to get me fired, aren't you?" she asked.

Evan landed a small peck against her lips. "Hardly. I'll meet you after work."

He left her standing dumbfounded at reception and nodded by the CEO. Choosing not to acknowledge Evan passing by with Ginger in tow, Slithery glowered in Evie's direction. His ageless grace shone disapproval. He scoffed at her and slammed the door shut behind him.

Evie found air back in her lungs. "Shit." She turned to the cubicles and began the uncomfortable walk to her desk.

Some of her co-workers giggled. Others paid her no attention. Val's cold glare, however, lanced through Evie's chest as she walked by.

Evie set her bag down at her desk and peered over to the crest of cubes at the far corner of the office. Leda's door was closed, her office dark. Unusual, Evie thought. Leda was normally one the first people in the office. Though given Evan's sudden public display of affection, maybe it was best that Claudio's sister was out today.

"How the hell would I explain that?" she said to herself and spun around in her chair to find the faint trace of her reflection in the window. She tilted her head to the side and lifted her hair back. The silver stars of her tattoo were little more than shadows in the pane. They brought a smile to her face. The tingling residue from connecting with Evan's tattoo skated along her skin.

"What happened?" A woman's voice asked from behind. Evie jumped around in her seat to Beth, who'd popped her head around the cubicle wall.

"Who happened, what?" She fidgeted with her hair, draping it across her left shoulder.

Beth gawped. "With Mr. Carver at the reception desk?"

Evie dropped her head down to mask the girlish embarrassment pulling at the edges of her lips.

"C'mon Evie, the entire office saw that. So…?" Evie lifted back up to meet Beth's expectant stare with a don't-you-wish-you-knew kind of grin that just goaded the girl on. "Lucky little bitch." Beth winked and disappeared behind the cube's wall.

Evie let out a huge sigh and cycled through a few deep breaths to settle her pulse. "Today's going to suck."

She adjusted her scarf and went back to work. Concentrating on work proved to be an impossible task with the Carver Assurance logo staring up at her from atop her stack of invoices. Her tattoo itched. She rubbed against the protective layer of her wool scarf, but her nails dug between the knitting and found skin. The more she obsessed over it, the more it prickled, so she ripped the scarf from her neck. Air brushed against her skin and cooled the irritated stars. She continued to scratch at them nonetheless. Her tattoo screamed for inspection, to make sure she hadn't marred it by rubbing incessantly.

Having had her fill of attention-grabbing spectacles already, she skulked toward the ladies room, avoiding eye contact with co-workers along the way. Still, Val's hateful glare attacked her as she passed by. She knew what Val was doing.

Judging. They're all judging—hating.

Her steps quickened.

Inside the ladies room, Evie stood in front of the counter. She twisted her head and pushed her eyes to her periphery for a thorough inspection. Tattooed metallic-blue stars shimmered amidst enflamed skin.

"Who does that belong to?" a voice called out from behind her. Evie flinched, like she'd been sucker-punched, and turned. Val stood by the doorway, glowering with her arms folded.

"Excuse me?"

"That's Evan Carver's mark, isn't it?" Val stepped closer. "How'd you do it? What makes you so special? Did Yeung Jae do it?"

Incredulous, Evie's pulse boomed between her ears. Her eyes widened. Her mind twisted considering immortality had penetrated her workplace.

"How do you know about Yeung Jae?"

Val responded by lifting her mousey brown hair from her neck, revealing a similar set of stars. "You're not the only Friend of Bendis in this office, bitch."

Evie gasped and couldn't make sense of what Val had just shown her in order to react otherwise.

Her reaction amused Val though, who judged her with a know-it-all smirk. "That's what I thought," she said and bid Evie adieu with a throaty scoff and spun around on her heels.

Evie was held in a stasis of bewilderment and rage. She stood trembling, and then deflated over the counter once alone. Taking a moment to regulate her pulse, she splashed water across her face, mocked by the sneer shining in the mirror.

"God, Evan, what have you gotten me into?"

***

As she exited the restrooms, figures congregating in the lobby piqued her interest. Evan stood with creepy old Slithery Silver, accompanied by a few of Boston PD's finest. His deadpan expression fixed on the officer speaking with him. His was guard up. She saw it in his mannerisms, back straight, arms across his chest, legs spread wide in an authoritative stance. The vision of him conferring with authorities brought back haunting memories of red and blue flashing lights—of Rob's murder—of Evan convincing the cops that she wasn't involved in his attack.

It didn't take long for Evan to detect her hovering like an apparition at the edge of the room. Their eyes met, and his shoulders collapsed at the sight of her. She questioned him with a silent plea and her head cocked sideways.

Damn Slithery, who was discussing matters with the police, he gestured for Evan's attention. Upon catching Evan pre-occupied, the creep glanced in her direction. His sneer chased shivers down her spine.

The men countered back and forth with words until Evan nodded and turned toward the elevators. He cast a gaze screaming apology at her. Evie watched him leave, wanting to chase after him and quash the dread bubbling up from her gut. Any such efforts would have been in vain of course, as Slithery called out to her.

"Miss Westvale, follow me."

Her pulse thundered between her ears. *What the hell did I do,* she wondered but didn't dare ask. She dropped her eyes to the floor and obeyed, slinking across the lobby to Slithery's office. She jumped in her skin as the door closed behind them—no Ginger—no witnesses.

"Have a seat, Miss Westvale."

He gestured toward his desk. Much like the rest of the office, the CEO's executive suite was sleek, modern, and grey. His contemporary mahogany desk perched in front of tinted bay windows overlooking the waterfront. Two leather club chairs rested in front of the desk—for his prey, no doubt. She settled there, at the edge of her seat, hands tucked between her knees. Perspiration built up across her forehead and around her to the back of her neck. She brushed her hair away from her ear.

Slithery paused when he walked by. "What's this?"

He reached out and grazed his fingertips across her tattoo. His touch was cold and revolting. Her skin crawled but she remained a compliant statue.

"Oh! I'm sorry. I should have covered—"

"How long have you had that tattoo, Miss Westvale?" He punctuated his questions with a hum, half intrigue-half brooding contempt.

What the fuck do you care?

288

"Shut up." Evie mumbled under her breath, to which he raised an eyebrow at her. "I... umm... I got it over the weekend. I'm sorry. I know visible tattoos aren't allowed in the office." Quickly, she pulled her hair back over her neck to conceal the tiny cluster of stars. She knew better, but clearly this meeting wasn't about breaching the Code of Conduct policy. Her toes curled in her shoes, her skin awash in goose bumps.

"This past weekend?" His interest unnerved her. "Well, you're right. I'd cover that up in the office if I were you."

He rested back in his oversized executive chair, hands held in prayer against his lips. Under his pensive gaze, Evie was fraught, completely exposed and naked under his guarded stare, a look so familiar she hated the comparison.

"I'm sorry, did I do something wrong, sir?" she asked, ready to jump out the window.

He snickered. "Did you?"

Confusion overwhelmed, made all too visible across her face. "I don't think so. I mean, I didn't know Evan was going to do that this morning in the lobby. I'm very sorry. That was inappro—"

"Miss Westvale, you're acquainted with Miss Veiga, are you not?"

"Leda? I guess you could say that, sure."

"And her brother?"

"Claudio? Yes, why?" She sunk back in her seat. The enormity of the room blurred, the grey closed in around her. "Has something happened?"

He nodded. "Yes, Miss Westvale. You could say something has happened. I'm sure you've noticed Miss Veiga's absence today."

"Is she okay?" Evie sat forward, pushing against her anxiety.

"Miss Veiga will be out on bereavement for a bit. It seems her brother was found murdered over the weekend."

"What?" Evie wanted to jump out of her seat and slam her hands against the edge of his desk. Instead, she sucked in her breath and reined in her explosive emotions. Slithery monitored her reaction with a smirk and shifty brow.

"Does that upset you, Miss Westvale?"

"I saw Claudio late Saturday night, that's impossible. How could he…? What happened?"

"You saw him?" The CEO's smile widened. His voice pitched an octave. "I wouldn't go screaming that from the rooftops, Miss Westvale, lest you be considered a suspect."

The room spun. Bile lurched up her throat.

"What happened to him?" Her voice quivered. Her body shuddered from the adrenaline coursing through it. Her hands folded back between her legs, elbows fixed into her abdomen to displace the stabbing nausea.

"I honestly don't know, Miss Westvale," he said. "Mugged? Gang related? This is Boston. These things happen." Slithery brushed the indifference off his shoulders. "I did hear it was quite gruesome, like he was attacked by a wild animal."

She fought doubling over in her seat and dry heaving. The man's callousness should have offended her, but she was too preoccupied with the shock running rampant through her bones.

"You look peakish, Miss Westvale. Mr. Carver has made me aware of your familiarity with the Veigas, but I hadn't realized you were so close," he said, inspecting his nailbeds. Evie shook her head. "Yes, well, clearly you're distressed. We can't have you causing a rash of whispering throughout the office. Collect your belongings and take the remainder of the day to reconcile your grief."

Still speechless, she nodded and headed for the exit as fast as her leaden legs would take her.

He called out when she reached the door. "Miss Westvale." She lifted a defeated gaze back. He was already moving on to new business, his office phone in hand. "Be discreet, won't you?"

THIRTY

Evie managed to hold in the shock until reaching the main lobby of the building. There, she found Evan wrapping up a phone call. He paced back and forth, playing with his tie until he looked up and saw her. As she barreled toward him, he tucked his cell into his jacket pocket, his arms spread out to receive her.

"He's dead." She dove into him, aching for what comfort he could afford.

"I know." He burrowed into her hair. "Let's just get you home."

He guided her to his car quietly and calmly. His palm rubbing against her back soothed her on the outside, but internally she was fraught with tension and conflict. Strapped into the passenger seat, she was ready to explode. Tears cascaded down her cheeks.

"Murder wasn't common back in Fallhaven—domestic violence, sure—overdoses, of course—but not random acts of violence." Evie rambled as Evan pulled out of the parking garage into the cold sprinkling of fresh rain.

"Everything's going to be all right," he said

"How can you say that?" She glared at Evan. His placid demeanor infuriated her. "First Rob, and now Claudio. Shit, why?"

"That's one hell of a stretch, Evie. Claudio's death had nothing to do with you." His cellphone rang. Evan grumbled and shifted into neutral as they approached a red light. "Hello…? Roque, talk to me."

While Evan shuffled between the phone to his ear and his hand on the shifter, Evie stared out the passenger window. Rain drops danced across the glass. She hated the distortion, the din of urban life going on around her. It wasn't Claudio's death as much as Rob's revenant image—the implication of Claudio's death—that frightened her.

"It's more than coincidence," she said, though Evan was too wrapped up in his call to hear her.

Her sobbing subsided by the time they reached her apartment, only to be replaced by beating pulses ripping her apart from the inside out. She looked over toward Evan, who wore more trouble along his brow than prior to his call.

***

Her legs may well have been shackled at the ankles. She barely managed her way up the stairs, and only accomplished as much due to Evan's arms supporting her. Inside her apartment, she collapsed on the futon.

"I don't understand why I can't escape this," she said while Evan fetched her a glass of water. "I mean, he was fine when we left him at the door step... right?"

She looked to Evan with desperation etched into the contours of her face. He sat by her side and wrapped his arms around her. Not even his normal, spiced scent could calm her.

"If Claudio didn't find me drunk on the beach. If he didn't stop to help me..." Evie choked on her words. "Why does everyone around me die?"

"Evie, stop," Evan said, whispering in her ear. "You're being too hard on yourself. This wasn't your fault."

"It must have happened right after he left the apartment. He'd still be alive if he just went home."

She sobbed into his shoulder until her body stopped shaking. Evie was left mute and numb—and not the kind of chemically-induced apathy she preferred.

She held in her breath, terrified to ask. Though her silence was indication enough. Evan cupped her jaw in his hands, his eyes searching hers eyes. "What is it, Evie?"

"Did Lucca do this?" Registering his pained expression, she saw the truth in Evan's reaction. "Was that the phone call you got in the car? Was that why were you talking to the police, Evan?" He wouldn't respond. "You knew didn't you? The same way you knew about Rob. Claudio was attacked by one of the Sempiternal, wasn't he? Was it Lucca?"

Evan knit his brow and exhaled a long sigh before confessing. "Yes, it was one of us, but I don't know for sure that it was him."

Shockwaves wracked her body. Her heart pounded, locked behind the fragile cage of her ribs.

Evie stared off into the void beyond Evan's shoulder, reminded once again of the devil tracking her. Anger bubbled up from her core. "Make him pay," she said in a soft tone, but one thick with resolve.

"What?"

"He keeps taking them from me, like it's his choice, and his alone." She moved her eyes to meet Evan's. "You can do it, can't you? Make that motherfucker pay for taking Rob and Claudio from me. He's a monster, Evan. Kill him. I want you to kill Lucca."

A flicker of excitement lit across Evan's eyes. "You think you're ready...?" The idea of destroying Lucca teased the beast. She could see it leashed behind Evan's guard.

The conviction in her voice relayed her demands, but her eyes gave away their reluctance. As such, the zeal vanished from his features. "No, you're just upset, Evie. You don't realize..." He fidgeted in his seat and turned away.

The crunch of plastic killed their silence as he toyed with a bag of pot on the coffee table. His fingers shook packing the bowl. The spicy tinge of hydroponic heaven hit Evie's nostrils. She watched him with intent and vengeful hunger gnawing in her gut.

She wanted to medicate too—dull the pain and escape the vortex sucking her deeper inside herself. Weed wouldn't be enough, though—not anymore—not with Evan in front of her with that wildness dancing in his eyes.

Her chest heaved. Manic, her eyes fixed on him taking the glass piece to his lips. She ripped the bowl from his hands and pushed him down on the futon. Before he could protest, she pinned him with her body. The discomfort of her pelvis grinding on top of his belt deemed a worthwhile masochism.

His tongue struggled to keep up with her lashings. His hands fumbled over her. Heart hammering, synapses bursting at every moan and pant, the high priestess was exhilarated as Evan struggled beneath her.

He pushed up on her shoulders, working to hold her at arms' length as she clawed the buttons of his shirt. "Evie... wait."

Their teeth clanked when he objected to her attack. A fire raged through her muscles.

"I don't want pot." She pushed down on him harder. "It's no good. I want more. I want you. Make the pain stop, Evan. Bite me. Make it all go away." She yanked her wool scarf away and flashed her neck line. Evan's eyes flared as she leaned in.

"Evie, stop!" He threw her aside and jumped up. "What has gotten into you?"

"I don't want to feel this pain anymore, Evan. I don't want to feel anything. Nothing is strong enough. You're everywhere. I need you to bite me. That's the only thing that will make me feel better."

Her eyes roamed the studio, searching for escape. The only promise in the room rested on the shadowy tips protruding from under his parted lips.

"Evie..." She focused on his fangs and the way his jaw clenched tight to hide them away from her. "Evie, no. Trust me, this isn't want you want."

"Yes, it is. It's exactly what I need. Evan, please." The ache in her gut wrenched. She wrapped her arms around her torso and pulled her knees into her chest.

"Evie, you're hurt." She tossed her head back and forth to argue, but he stopped her before she could get a word in. "You're not thinking with a clear mind. I'm not going to bite you—not like this."

She steeled her resolve. Her body's tremors ceased as she honed in on Evan.

"Then fuck me." She jumped to her feet, knocking the glass bowl off the table. It skittered across the floor and shattered to tiny pieces against the foot of her dresser.

He gawped back at her. "What? No, absolutely not. This isn't right."

"Evan, please. Look, I'm sorry. Just help me forget the pain, even if only for a little while."

Again, his eyes widened. "Evie, listen to yourself. You want me to have sex with you—to treat your grief—because weed isn't strong enough anymore." He looked away and scratched the back of his head. "Dammit! I knew this would happen. No, this is why you shouldn't bleed for me."

"You knew what would happen?"

He's hiding the truth from us.

She protested, throwing her head side to side, her eyes pinched tight. "No!"

He's using us.

"Stop it! God, Evan, help me!" Spilling tears into her lap, Evie folded over herself.

"It's going to be okay, Evie." He sat down and allowed her to curl into his arms. He brushed the rogue wisps of hair off of her tear-soaked face and wiped away the mucus caked under her nose. Seasickness turned her belly while Evan rocked her back and forth. "I'm sorry. You're emotional, and you have every right to be. Death is never easy, but we'll get through this. I promise."

***

The first few days following Claudio's death took a toll on her psyche. Evie caved into herself and refused to leave her apartment.

"Evie, you can't keep sending Dave text messages to call out sick. You haven't accrued enough time off. He's going to fire you," Evan said, setting her cell phone on the coffee table.

Apathy relayed through weary eyes, her apparition drifted through the apartment and settled on the futon. Her body may have been locked within physical confines of her apartment, but her mind had imploded. She was lost in herself, her high priestess imprisoned by Rob's geisha back from the bloody dead.

"Dammit Evie, if you won't talk to me, can you at least eat something?"

She looked down to the plate of food he'd prepared, but gave it little consideration. Her cold-shouldered rebuke sent him fuming into the kitchen. Porcelain crashed in the sink, and then he was back. She shook from his force as he dropped down on the futon beside her. Her eyes moved to the joint he quickly spun up.

"You can drop the suicide watch. I'm not going to hurt myself," she said, only to be answered by the flick of a lighter and the soft crackle of rolling paper taking to flame.

Evan's reaction was slow, his movements controlled. He exhaled a plume of smoke and faced her with a matte-brown stare.

"It's been days, Evie. That's the first thing you say to me? You're upset—I get it. I've apologized to you already, but shit, a man can only take so much." He scoffed when she looked away. "For the record, I'm not worried you'll try to kill yourself... I'm afraid someone else will try to take credit for that."

More than hydroponic vapor thickened the air. Evan's angst electrified, setting off a rash of goose bumps across Evie's body. Taking another hit, he held the joint out to her. She stared at its hot ember tip and followed the ribbon swirls reaching upward. She didn't accept the joint though, held submissive by the phantom courtesan haunting her mind.

Evan released a phlegmy huff and stomped over to the computer desk. The whirring of her laptop coming to life prefaced a chord, a musical note she knew well. The first song on the playlist sung by a man begging for his lover to bleed, to offer proof she was real. Nausea stirred in her hollow gut. Heartache lurched up and stopped, teasing at the back of her throat.

"I told you that song was overplayed."

He snorted and changed the song. "Dumb fucking me," he said. She glared at his back turned to her.

"Do you know when the funeral is?" she asked.

Evan faced her and reclined back in the small desk chair, stretching his lean build against it. The thrill of his immortal eyes on her quickened her pulse.

"Tomorrow. I got all the info from Dave, but you can't possibly think of going?"

Did she need to go for Claudio's sake? Maybe not, but the geisha's glower flashing behind her mind's eye demanded repentance. "It's my fault that he's dead."

"You don't know that for sure, Evie. We don't even know which one of us did it. There are so many in the city. Claudio could have been killed by someone new to the Sempiternal, someone too raw to control himself."

"Why would you think that?"

Evan's heavy breath relayed his reluctance, but he continued nonetheless. "The man was mangled beyond recognition, Evie. We don't need to get into specifics, do we?"

The temperature surrounding her body plummeted. She shivered and squeezed her waist. The one small tear that managed to run down her cheek was quickly caught up by Evan's warm palm as he came over to settle by her side.

"This isn't about Claudio, is it?" he asked, searching her eyes. "Evie, he wasn't Rob."

"You were jealous of him," she said through a whimper.

He shifted back in his seat. "You think I did it?"

A sob—unwillingness to admit suspicion that had weighted on her over the past few days in isolation—burst passed her lips. "I've been thinking about what you said when I was drunk, that you were jealous of Claudio. Then the next day you said you went out while I slept."

Evan's head drifted back and forth, his incredulous eyes remained locked with hers. "I do not kill—not unless I am forced to." The warmth of his hands rushed over her face

299

as he caressed her cheeks. A relay of convulsions set off in her core, and the high priestess writhed in the fathoms of her subconscious. Evie latched onto Evan's wrists to steady herself against the converging vertigo. His grip tightened, framing her face. "You must believe me, Evie. I did not kill Claudio."

"Someone I know did. You can't tell me it was just a coincidence." She cracked the tiniest self-defeating smile. "Please let me go, Evan. I need to say goodbye."

Her heart pounded in her chest, reverberating between her ears and drowning out the harmonies playing in the background.

Evan's grip softened.

"Fine... We can go to the wake this evening."

THIRTY-ONE

The line of mourners stretched out to the entrance of the funeral home and set Evie's nerves into overdrive. She wrapped around Evan's arm, hand clasped with his.

"You don't need to do this." He pressed his lips into her hair.

She squeezed tighter.

Incense, dust, and floral arrangements suffocated. Her stomach knotted with tension and nausea. She burrowed into Evan's suit jacket and inhaled. His spiced aroma eased her anxieties, minimally.

As they proceeded into the funeral home, one or two faces from her office passed by—a pencil skirt here, a shirt and tie there—faces she knew but could not name. They gave her a flash of recognition, a quiet glance exchanged, but no one spoke a word to her as they passed by.

Evan stopped in front of the guest book set atop a large red oak podium, and signed his name. Evie's pulse quickened. The old world beauty of his script reminded her that he was more than a shoulder to cry on. Observing him in this morbid and real world setting made her crave his bite embedded deep under her skin. She needed his immortal hunger to numb the tempest thrashing inside.

Just a pinch.

Claudio's whispers echoed through her subconscious, and she took in a deep breath. Evie held the tears in and forced her digressive wants out through her next exhale.

They continued down the receiving line toward the viewing room. Over the sobs of mourners, acoustic guitar strumming drifted through the funeral home. Evie stretched her neck out from the line. A man, likely a family member, sat playing amongst a spray of carnations, roses, and lilies. Not nearly as beautiful as Claudio played, she thought.

To the side of the musician, high gloss oak veneer and brass handles shown under a mass of arrangements. Evie identified the closed coffin.

Her chest tightened, vision blurred. Her feet sank into the plush red carpeting. She stumbled against Evan.

"Evie, what's wrong?"

He held her up, minimized their spectacle as best he could, though whispers fluttered around them.

She pinched her eyes shut and grasped at him. Images from Rob's funeral replayed through her mind. The memories made her sick. Faceless figures offering condolences that meant absolute shit to her as she buried him in the mud. Evan's supportive hold was nowhere to be found that day, but his physical strength pulled her up now.

What makes you think I'll ever forgive you? Rob's voice drifted through her mind. The geisha held his severed head dripping carmine. Her subconscious was screaming, but Evie couldn't make out the cries.

"You're right. This was a bad idea. Take me home, Evan." Her whimpering enraged her migraine more, and she clawed at his lapel.

"Good, let's go." He directed her out of line.

As they turned to leave, the hairs on the back of Evie's neck stood on end. A charge in the air pulled her eyes back toward the viewing room. She glanced over at a petite figure standing by Leda's side to the left of the coffin. Had it been any other figure, Evie would have fallen in step with Evan, but

302

no. She paused and pushed back from him, mesmerized by Sister Lima's glare.

"No, wait..."

"What's the matter?" Evan asked and scanned the crowd. He followed her sights to the priestess consoling Leda. He growled low. His hold on her elbow intensified. "Who is that?"

"She's a distant relative or something. I met her at Leda's place."

"Is that so?" Possessiveness radiated off Evan's body. His jawline flexed as he rolled his sleeve up his forearm, exposing his right wrist. He nudged her forward with his left palm at her tailbone. "C'mon, let's offer our condolences to the bereaved."

***

Following down the line, Evie clung to Evan. In front of the coffin, she dropped down to her knees—not in prayer. She couldn't recite a damned Hail Mary or Our Father if her life depended on it.

In the shadows of her mind, her inner voice was poised, ready to square off with the geisha and reclaim Evie's body.

"Please forgive me." She whispered her prayer into her folded hands.

The deathly concubine drifted through her subconscious, mute as always, her judgmental glare unrelenting. Evan's hand squeezed her shoulder, and the geisha ebbed into the shadows.

The time is coming, stupid girl.

A small cry worked past her lips, and Evie stood to face the grieving Veiga family.

"I'm so sorry for your loss," she said to women whom she recognized as Leda's mother and aunt. The mother wailed, barely aware of the line of mourners as she was burdened by the loss no mother should ever know. The poor woman shook, and then doubled over in her seat.

"*Obrigado.*" The aunt thanked Evie with a warm and soft, wrinkled set of hands before tending to Claudio's grief-stricken mother. Evan offered his condolences in their native Creole tongue. The elderly aunt smiled appreciatively.

Next in line, Leda sobbed and pulled Evie into a hug. "Thank you for coming."

Evie's arms found their way around Leda, but she knew such physical support made no amends for the culpability choking her.

"I'm so sorry this happened, Leda. I never wanted to put Claudio in danger."

Leda sniffled and softly pushed away from their embrace. She dabbed her runny nose with an already snot-saturated tissue and arched one eyebrow. "What are you talking about? You had nothing to do with this. Claudio was found overdosed somewhere near the beach."

"But I thought he...?"

"He OD'd." Leda's volume elevated, the inflection in her tone more insistent than Evie expected.

Evie's heart beat faster, her cheeks burned, and her empty stomach flipped. Before the anxiety could knock her down, Evan wrapped his arm around her waist.

"I thought I told you, Evie. His autopsy report indicated lethal blood morphine levels. I'm so sorry for your loss, Leda." Both girls looked up to the genuine sympathy relayed in his softened gaze.

Leda's lip quivered as she struggled not to hyperventilate and brought the snot rag back to her nose, tears pooled. "Tha... thank you, Mr. Carver." She cracked under the pressure of the sobs breaking her vocals. She buckled forward, and was then comforted by another set of hands.

"Thank you for coming, Evie." Sister Lima's sharp eyes hooked onto her like the geisha's serpent. "As you can imagine, this is a difficult time for Leda, for all of us in the family. Your presence is most appreciated."

Evie stared, jaw agape at the priestess, mind still reeling over Claudio's reported—and bogus—cause of death.

Evan extended his right hand. "Yes, well we were both very distressed by this senseless tragedy." His tone had stiffened along with his spine.

The priestess' gaze shifted up to meet his set jaw. "*Senhor Carver, Modi bu sta*? I am Sister Amalia Lima."

"I'm just fine, Amalia. Thank you for asking. Tell me, how does your lady fair?"

Evie stood like a Baroque statue, emotion amplified across the features carved into her marble complexion. The subconscious strife twisting inside her paused to direct all attention toward Evan.

"My lady is quite well and will be pleased to know you've asked," Sister Lima said. "She will be most interested to learn of—" Her words cut short as she recoiled from Evan's handshake.

Evie studied the priestess' concern, and then turned to Evan, still holding his hand out. His resolve worn firmly across his pursed lips. She volleyed her sights back to Sister Lima, who stared down at Evan's palm.

Not his palm.

Evie realized she was transfixed by the small collection of silvery-blue stars therein.

A chill ran through her. Evie would have taken a step backward had Evan not held her firmly at his side. She checked, but Leda was swept away in her own grief and the progressing wave of mourners to take notice of their discourse.

One moment beyond what Evie thought her weakening knees would last, Sister Lima's smirk faded. She bowed subtly and placed her hands back around Leda. "Of course. Yes, thank you for supporting Leda and her family at this time. *Obrigado*."

The priestess admitted defeat—to what, Evie had no clue—but Evan stood tall, jaw ticking. Evie scarcely recognized the austerity in his eyes.

"You'll give my regards to Maradonna, and with all due respect remind her of her jurisdiction," Evan said to Sister Lima, who nodded and averted her subordinate gaze away from the couple.

Mystified by whatever existed between the two, Evie wanted to interject, but was too dumb to muster a word.

"Bye, Evie," Leda extended a final limp handshake.

Evie teared up accepting it. "I'll be in touch," she said.

With the tender influence she'd come to recognize from him, Evan nudged her along through the procession.

"Can we go home now?" he asked. She answered silently with a nod.

***

"What the hell just happened back there?"

Their steps quickened. The sharp clacking of their dress shoes sounded through the abnormally quiet side streets of South Boston.

"I was stupid to think this time would be any different," Evan said under his breath and shook his head. Agitation lined his brow.

She craned her neck out. "I'm sorry, what? Evan, stop mumbling."

He yanked down his sleeve, concealing his wrist once more as he set an aggressive pace to the nearest T-station. She scurried after him as best she could, but Evan's long strides made it difficult to catch her breath much less press him for details. He came to a halt across the street from a Red Line stop.

"Shit, I knew he'd have her watching," he said, barely audible.

Evie came huffing and puffing to his side, her heart pounding inside her cardigan. "Evan what the fuck is going on?"

He sighed and twisted his lips into a sort of apologetic smirk. "Lucca has happened—as always. I'm pretty sure I was right, and Claudio helped lead him to you."

Her eyes widened. Her head moved back and forth, but she wasn't in her body. Evie was hurtling head first back into her subconscious, lost.

"No, Claudio was normal—mortal, just like me."

Evan took her hand and lifted it to his lips. "There's no such thing as normal."

She shivered.

No, never again.

THIRTY-TWO

Evan locked the door behind them and tossed his suit jacket across the bed before joining her on the futon.

"Evie, what's wrong? You've been very quiet since the wake."

She was almost unwilling to look him in the eyes—almost. Evie watched through her periphery. A new line of worry had formed across his forehead. Defensiveness was detected in his tone, the beast caged and cornered.

"What are you?" she asked.

"What do you mean?"

"What was with Sister Lima's reaction to you? Who is Maradonna? And why does Leda think Claudio overdosed?"

He sighed, lips thinned into a firm line. "Sempiternal do what we must to remain invisible to the mortal eye, Evie. Our world is very complex. We've already discussed this. It's my—"

"Is Leda going to die next?"

"What? No. You just need to stay away from her. She's obviously involved with immortality." Evan pinched the bridge of his nose with his fingertips. "You know what, I'm calling Don—you're not going back to that office. In fact, I don't think I like Leda working there."

"You are not getting her fired for this shit."

"Evie, she shouldn't be working in that office if she's mixed up with another house."

"Listen to you—in my office—the one you insisted was perfectly human? One of my co-workers has a very interesting tattoo, by the way. Pretty little stars behind her ear." He opened his mouth, but no, she wasn't ready to let him make his case. "Why did you lie to me? Why couldn't you just tell me it was tied to your house? To your world?"

"It's complicated."

This is bullshit. Lucca was right.

The twisting in her core gave her pause. She closed her eyes, focused on a deep, clarifying breath, and then looked back to Evan. Her chest tightened, cold and numb.

"I don't know you at all, do I?" Her voice was little more than a whisper.

"Of course you do." He took her hands in his. "Evie, everything I've done has been for you. You must believe that, right?"

She retracted from his grasp, her arms self-comforting around her waist. He tried to reach out again for her, but she recoiled further. It was as though for the first time, he posed a greater threat than Lucca ever could.

Hurt etched across his brow.

From the shadows of her mind, the geisha came, calling to her in Rob's voice. *He means to keep you to himself.* Her head ached with an instant hangover banging against the back of her eyeballs. She winced and curled into a ball. Tears rimmed her eyes. The high priestess pulled Evie inward—to the geisha—away from Evan's hidden agenda.

Make the pain go away.

"Evie...?" Evan called out to her, but she was already fading. "Evie, no. Don't do this. You wanted to go to that wake—to say good bye. You said you needed it. Please don't drift away from me again." He grabbed at her shoulders with more urgency. "We were so close to—"

The hum of his cellphone vibrating in his jacket pocket atop the bed softened his grip. The two held each other's stare as the buzzing continued.

"Answer your phone, Evan," she said in a thin voice. "Just let him kill me—change me—whatever. I don't want anyone else to suffer because of me. I'm not worth it."

Hurt, anger, and defeat flashed across Evan's face, only to be replaced by stern conviction. "This conversation isn't over."

***

He took his call out on the balcony, leaving her on the futon. Over her shoulder, Evie heard him talking to whom she presumed to be Mr. Slithery—no doubt, another member of the immortal houses fucking up her life.

"Did you realize who she was?" She heard him snap at the caller. "She's sending emissaries, now...? What the hell are you up to, exactly?"

As Evan argued, Evie stared into the blank space somewhere beyond her coffee table. She realized she'd need to shake her fears of Lucca's unknown, stop the killings, because surely they would only continue. More importantly, she needed to decode Evan's motives.

Before her thoughts could provoke judgement from her inner voice, Evan was back in from the balcony, still arguing with the caller.

"If you didn't want me doing my job, then you shouldn't have done this to me in the first place."

He ended his call with a roar and threw himself onto the small desk chair. The force of his impact sent the chair, and himself in it, skidding sideways into the computer desk. He didn't bother to brace for impact as his ribs slammed against the edge with a *thud* that likely hurt the desk more than him. Evan tossed his cellphone on top of it and sat slouched in his seat. His legs stretched wide and fingers pinched around a roach he retrieved from the nearby ashtray. He sparked up the remnant of the joint and glimpsed over in her direction. His head dipped down. He looked up at her through a cloud of smoke.

Wet and scorching pangs shot down to her seat when he caught her staring.

"Change me," she said with more gumption in the pit of her core than transmitted through her tone.

He declined with a faint headshake. Though, the subtle catch in his breath and the glimmer dancing across his irises gave away the excitement in her proposal, regardless of his inevitable answer. "Not a chance," he said, wheezing through another hit.

"Why?"

He placed the diminishing joint back in the ashtray and laced his fingers across his sternum. "Evie, even if I was willing to risk it—which I'm not—I can't. I shouldn't have even..."

Each time his voice trailed off along with his thoughts, she took notice. His secrecy pissed her off, and their constant bickering did little to prepare her for whatever the future had planned for her—death or otherwise. So she persisted.

"Then tell me about the Sempiternal." Her confidence carried more clearly now, but the sardonic gaze of the caged beast continued to hold her at bay.

"Like what?"

"Where do they come from?"

Silence gave way to low growls rumbling from Evan's vicinity.

"I told you before, you'd have to go back to the beginning of time… and then some." He continued to kill the joint.

"But there has to be a beginning. What do you believe?"

Evan glared, smoke curling from his nostrils like a dragon. "It doesn't matter. It's all bullshit, anyway."

"Humor me. We have nothing better to do unless you want to feed off me."

He huffed and poked out what was left of the roach. The tiniest smirk twisted the corner of his mouth creating the illusion he was willing to amuse her fancies. "Are you familiar with the old fables about the sun and the moon?" Embarrassment and ignorance shook her head slowly. "No, well there were several pagan cultures around the world who believed the sun and the moon were lovers… of sorts."

"You mean like the sun dying for the moon, or breathing… or some poetic shit like that, right?"

He bowed his head. "Everything comes from somewhere, Evie. The Sempiternal believe whatever life force it was that represented the sun, light, and all things pure and true created the mortal world for his consort: the moon, darkness, and those lesser virtues that are commonly recognized as the original, mortal sins."

"Are you trying to say God created Earth for his lover?"

"That's a very narrow view, but I guess that's one way of looking at it, yes—for her twisted amusement." Evan adjusted in his seat. "Regardless, he was said to be vexed by her darkness and attempted to purge her sins from her being. As a result, he created a darker essence who claimed her soul." Shadows twirled through the blackened corners of Evie's mind as Evan continued. "In an effort to protect her from the… evil spirit, I guess you could call it… the sun sent the moon into the mortal world, and she hated him for it. The moon craved her soul back more than his love, so it's believed she created the Sempiternal in spite of her light's efforts to cure her from darkness. She festered here on Earth and bred her immortal abominations, tainting what he'd gifted her."

"So she created vampires to get back at God?"

He lifted one shoulder. "That's what the Sempiternal believe. It's said that the essence of the sun and the moon still live and breathe somewhere on Earth, destined to cross paths from one life to the next, but never transcending to the immortal plane together because she has never been able to recover from her sin."

"That's a fucked up story, Evan."

"I told you it was bullshit."

"What about the houses?"

He cleared his throat. "They were all originally created to worship her, track her down from one life to the next. Over the years our goals have shifted, though. Now, we just keep the peace with humans. Maybe some of us are finally willing to admit the story is nothing more than legend, a bogus excuse to give origin to that which cannot be explained. We exist. It shouldn't matter how or why."

"Do you worship the sun and moon like gods or something?"

Evan fought a smile. "Vampires don't like sunlight, remember?"

"I thought you said that's because it was easier to hunt at night?" she asked, perplexed.

"That's true. I'm teasing you, Evie. It's just a story. I guess some do hold a certain level of reverence for the moon and darkness because of it though."

Reverence, Evie thought, was the perfect word to describe Sister Lima's awe. Chills spidered their way across her skin. "Is Lucca supposed to be the sun?"

Evan's amusement soured. His lip curled up to reveal his pearlescent threat. "What about Lucca makes you draw a parallel with purity and virtuosity?"

Bitterness churned in her stomach, burning with the acid creeping up her throat. "Fine, the story doesn't mean anything. It doesn't change the fact that you won't change me, but Lucca will. Is he a believer, and you're not?"

"Lucca's deranged." Evan lunged forward in his seat.

"Then bite me—change me." Her pulse raced with a thorough mixture of dread, adrenaline, and feening need.

His body appeared relaxed in his seat, but she could see through his designer button down shirt to the muscles strained to hold himself down.

Evan gritted his teeth. "Lucca won't allow it."

He means to keep us for himself.

"So that's what this is all about? Stupid, fucking jealousy?"

Buzzing filled the void, breaking through the hydroponic laced air. She watched the beast pace back and forth behind his guarded gaze.

Evan reached for his cell phone. "You have no idea what you're talking about," he said and escaped out to the balcony again.

***

A curious and resentful eye checked over her shoulder to Evan bickering with his caller.

"Who do I trust?" She looked down to her feet, careful not to let her conversation clash with his.

He can give us the release.

"What does 'he' mean? Who?"

Remember to feel me.

The wound on her collarbone tingled. Evie lifted a gentle touch to the outer layer of her cardigan, the poly-blend fabric was cool against the warm wound.

"He won't change me."

We have a choice.

"No." She traced her hand along her neck up to the back of her ear, feeling the faint bump of her healing stars.

This is all our choice, not theirs. Now they're the ones being selfish.

Her inner voice pushed her gaze back over her shoulder and watched Evan cautiously.

If you want him, you must make him give us what we want.

"How?"

Before her internal dialogue could continue, Evan glanced over. His eyes connected with hers. With the cellphone still held to his ear, he came and sat back by her side. The sorrow in his eyes softened to pure apology. "No sir… Yes sir… No, of course I don't want that… Yes, I understand," he said and ended his call. He placed the phone on the table in front them and reached out for her. "Well, that's that. You won't be going back to DC any time soon."

"Change me." She made her demand quietly yet stern.

Evan shifted his head side to side. "You know I won't."

"Not ever?"

"Evie, don't push this." She turned away with wet eyes and pulled her hands from his. "Evie, please don't shut me out again—not over this."

It tortured, burning in her chest to deny whatever solace Evan's arms did offer, but she couldn't trust him. Not until she knew what she wanted or needed from him—not until she knew how much of Lucca's warning was true.

"You want to deny me?" She swallowed her desires and mustered her resolve, staring him dead on. "Two can play this game, Evan."

Fear washed over his features. "What's that supposed to mean?"

She set her jaw. "You have two options. You can either stay with me, bleed me, and be what I need right here in this moment… or you can let me face fate on my own."

His eyes widened. "Evie…"

"Those are my conditions, Evan. You can't force your lifestyle on me—or away from me. I need to decide on my own."

"But, Evie, I—"

Her phone chimed on the coffee table. She fingered the touch screen.

STOP IGNORING ME. WE NEED TO TALK!

"It's just Nate." Despite the menace in his caps lock, Evie found his text inconsequential to the subject at hand and pushed the phone aside. She was far too preoccupied with Evan, awaiting his response.

"Evie, I—" Her cell rang out now, Nate's number popped up on the caller ID. Evan glowered at the phone and snatched it up with a growl. "Back the fuck off, Nate!"

Evie's body thrummed with excitement as the beast snarled into the phone. She inched to the edge of her seat, mouth wetted with anticipation.

"I don't give a shit what you have to say about it. Evie's my concern, not yours." When Evan slammed the phone down, the beast fixed her in his sights.

Yours?

"Dammit!" Evan lunged forward and knocked her back into the futon. He ripped into her blouse, quick to lock his jaw into the gaping wound throbbing at the fold of her breast. She gladly fell to him.

THIRTY-THREE

In the weeks following his outburst, fall descended upon Boston. Trees stripped down to their skeletal branches. Evan spent his days tending to the business of his uncle's house, and his night to Evie's whims.

"Tell me again," she said, lying opposite him in blood-stained sheets.

He smiled and focused on the path of his fingertips across her hip. "What's that? Happy birthday?"

"No," she giggled. "Tell me you love me."

He chuckled. "More than all the world." His tips sauntered their way to his preferred points of feeding; under the tender fold of her breast then up at the base of her neck just behind her right ear.

A smile spread across her face. "I don't understand. You said sex wasn't important to an immortal—that consumption was. But since you attacked me, you've been quite content acquainting yourself with every orifice in my body. We barely leave my bed, and yet I'm the one begging you to feed?"

Evan bowed his head in a bashful smile, the beautiful glimpse of the sun that brought tears to her eyes. If she could sustain that expression across his face for the rest of her life, she decided she would. He bit at his bottom lip and grunted softly.

"I also told you once that I only need to sustain myself every couple of weeks. You're asking me every other hour to bite you. The act of bleeding is daunting on the body, Evie. Every time I do it, you beg me to bleed you to the point you're wilting like the leaves outside. You grow paler than usual and your lips turn ashen. That's not good. You need time to recover."

"But I love those fangs." She dragged her fingertip across his grin, scraping against the tip of his canine. She wanted to add that being holed up in her apartment with him had quieted her inner voice to a dull murmur, but she didn't. She wanted to add that the alternative, the burning ache in her gut, was unbearable. Just thinking about it roiled her stomach, but that wouldn't help.

Don't forget the high is magnificent.

She hummed contently, and Evan laughed under his breath.

"What I'm saying, Evie, is that I can only consume so much of you before it borders on deathly. You just need to accept that."

"No, I think you just said that you're full of me." She smirked.

"In the best way possible." He rolled on top of her, pinning her arms up above her head, their hands clasped tightly together. "*Mon erreur fatale.*" He rested his forehead against hers, his eyes closed.

"Mo—what?"

"You are my fatal flaw, Evie. For all the blood in the world, I'm hopelessly addicted to you alone."

His comment would stow itself away in the dark corners of her mind. Her inner voice would hold onto it, inspecting it for the truth. Until her inner voice was able to decipher Evan's ramblings, she'd bask in his glow.

Evan leaned over and grabbed a joint burning down on its own in the ashtray atop her nightstand. He took a hit and held it to her. "Want some?"

She smiled and shook her head. "It's funny. I haven't felt the need since you've been bleeding me."

His brow knit. "Weed's a healthier addiction, don't you think?" He sat up and wrapped the bed sheets over his bare hips.

"I thought you'd be happy to know you satisfy my hunger. You make me feel safe and content... numb." She traced her nails along his back and sat up to run her lips across his broken wing.

He exhaled his next toke. "But it's not enough, is it?" He shifted to face her. "Taking things day by day, like we have—it's been amazing—but this is just the calm before the storm."

She felt her eyes light up. "What are you saying?"

He bowed his head. "I'm treading into some uncharted waters here."

Uneasiness stirred in her belly. She frowned and plucked the pot from his fingers. "What's that supposed to mean?"

"Lucca," he said. Tremors shook her. Warm shivers tickled down her spine. "You've been dreaming about him, Evie. You call out to him in your sleep. You're not truly satisfied are you?"

I will always want more.

Evie sunk into herself and shielded her guilty gaze from Evan. All the waking bliss in the world hadn't totally quashed her desires for eternity—or Lucca's promise to deliver her to his immortal existence. It festered in the center of her being.

"That's what I thought." He took the joint and snuffed it out in the ashtray before bracing her tattoo against his. The telltale electric current ran through her and she gazed, awed by the sensation. "Happy birthday, Evie. Get some sleep… I love you."

***

At night, in the dark of her dreams, Evie rolled through the shadows. She nestled up to Evan's erratic heartbeat, but it wasn't his scent. There was no sweet spice tingling her senses. She detected orange blossoms.

She sat up in bed and met the black shadow lounging across the futon—watching her. Reconciling her visions, she knew it was Lucca. Unlike months ago when she didn't know enough to direct her dreams, now she found his signs. His eyes glistened in the black, the golden flecks dancing off their dark pools. He flashed his wicked side smirk at her.

"I hope you're enjoying yourself." Her body quivered like a tuning fork to his low, melodic tone. She found herself inching toward the end of the bed.

"What are you doing here?" she asked.

"In your dream? Come now Evie, we are destined. Even you know it. Otherwise, why would I be here?"

Each time the reverie occurred, she was taken aback by the lucid realization that she was in fact dreaming. She checked all around her. There was no light, no sign of Evan. Evie was shrouded in Lucca's nothingness.

"This is a dream," she said in half wonderment and disbelief.

"You're beginning to see how wonderful this life is, aren't you? But Evan will never give you what you want. He's too addicted to your flesh. He'll never give you the release— and you will crave it. I know you will. You always do. I can give that to you, Evie. That is why we are destined."

"Where are you?"

He lifted his hand through the shadows. "I'm right here."

"Are you finally going to end this?"

His silhouette lifted off the futon. The invisible chain linking them together pulled tight. Her body jerked forward and she fought her restraints. Golden lights danced through the darkness toward her. Her pulse raced.

"Aren't you enjoying their games? Your games?" he asked in his low thrum that vibrated through Evie's entire being. "That is what they are, Evie—games. They mean nothing. Evan knows."

"But…?"

"Haven't you asked him? I told you to do so."

His amorphous black cloud loomed over her, flowing around her—through her—in her. Her raspy mew rolled off her tongue. Lucca washed over her, his waves a blissful torture.

She reclined back, arching her scarred body up to him.

"This isn't real," she said.

"Isn't it?"

***

"Evie, wake up." Evan's voice was soft as he brushed his lips against her ear. "It's just a dream."

She rolled over to bright light beaming through the windows, haloing his image.

"What time is it?"

"It's almost five in the evening."

She sat up in bed, and sure enough, the orange glow filling her room was from the sun setting over the harbor.

"I slept fourteen hours? How the hell did I do that?"

"I told you feeding was taking a toll on your body. You needed rest."

She looked down, Evan was in his usual business attire. "How was work?"

He dropped his gaze. "Quiet," he said. "It's a bit disconcerting, actually."

Evie tilted her head and ran her hand along his lapel. "What's wrong?"

A veil dropped over his features. He looked away. "Evie, I'm not supposed—" Her cell buzzed on her nightstand. Evan groaned and cast a hard glare at it. "Nate's still texting you?"

Evie rolled her eyes and retrieved her phone. "It's Blythe," she said. "She'll be here in a few hours to pick me up for that costume party."

Evan stood in an opposing stance; back stiff and hands on his hips. "I thought we decided that wasn't a good idea."

She stared up at him, her lips pursed. "You decided, Evan, but I want to go."

"Do you want me to go with you?"

The sheets tumbled off her curves when she propped up on her knees. Evie reeled him in with his tie and licking the mischief from her lips. "No, this is my tradition with Blythe," she said. "As much as I know she can be a bitch, at least it seems like she's trying. I want to spend some time with her— just the girls. Believe it or not, I miss my best friend."

Evan pouted down at her bare flesh. He redirected the angst brooding along his features to the tips of his thumbs kneading into her hip bones. "But—"

"No buts." She shook her head, loving how his massaging hands released their tension on her. "It's my choice, Evan. Got it? I haven't left this apartment since Claudio's death, and Lucca hasn't made any attempts on my life." He glared at her. "I know you don't like it, but I'm going out tonight. That's final."

His scowl flipped to a playful smirk. "So that's it? Evie gets what Evie wants. Even if it means risking her life?"

She grinned. "I do that every night with you, and yet somehow I just won't die."

"You think you're cute, don't you?" Evie winked at him. He snickered and kneeled on the bed with her. "I could drink you into a state of immobility."

"Promises, promises, Evan." She pulled him on top of her.

***

So the junky returns, but for such a drug as Evan Carver, it's worth it.

Staring in the mirror, she was sickly pale, but the reflection beamed back nonetheless.

"This isn't a bad move, right?"

No, we need to get out for a while.

Her stomach knotted as she painted her face in shimmery hues of gold, red, orange and charcoal. She prepared for the costume party, going so far as to add some new highlights to her wavy locks. When she was done hiding the ghost, a fiery devil beamed back in a tight red vinyl corset and matching miniskirt with black crinoline lining. She pulled up some black fishnets and her black patent leather Dr. Martens. It was odd how easily she could still paint herself up, how easily she molded into a different person all together.

Let's play.

When Evie emerged from the bathroom, Evan gasped.

"Fucking hell, Evie! You can't go out looking like that."

She smirked and curtsied. "Have you decided what to do with your night? And, not that I mind, but put some clothes on before Blythe gets here, please."

Evan stood from the bed speckled with fresh droplets of her blood and their sweat. He tucked himself away in a pair of pinstripe dress pants. "I just got off the phone with my uncle. He wants to feed tonight. I've been trying to come up with some excuse not to join him."

Jealousy knocked the wind from her. The thought of him feeding off of anyone else was absolutely out of the question.

"Can't you just tell him you've been feeding outside of Bendis?"

"It's not that simple."

"Why not?"

Evan approached with a smile and hands planted on her hips.

"He doesn't know I've been here."

"Why not?"

"Let's just say he'd be extremely pissed off if he knew I was here with you."

The heat radiating off his body warmed through her vinyl outfit. A bitter taste overwhelmed the inside of her mouth, she scowled and dropped a listless gaze to the floor. "I don't like to idea of you biting someone else," she said.

He cocked and eyebrow. "And I can't stand the idea of someone else bleeding you—or changing you," he said with a cocked eyebrow. "So we're even."

"If you hate the idea, then why can't you change me yourself?"

The doorbell rang out, but they failed to acknowledge it.

"Evie, the Sempiternal have their restrictions. You think I like the fact that I can't? I hate it. The one thing in this world I wish I could do… and my hands are tied."

The doorbell struck again. Evie couldn't take her eyes off him though. The raw hunger in Evan's gaze was maddening. "You just don't understand. Lucca's made it very clear, this is bigger than just you and me. I can't risk it."

Her body tingled. "Evan…?"

"Just get the door," he said and stepped back from her.

Lost in his words, she drifted toward the call box. "Yeah?"

"It's Blythe," the familiar voice came through, distorted by the aged electronics. Evie pressed the button to unlock the front door, and then unlatched the deadbolt.

"C'mon up, Blythe," she said and turned back to Evan.

Even from across the room, the tension flexing his muscles was unmistakable.

"So all this time with you meant nothing? Why would you do this to me?" she asked, barely able to bring air into her lungs.

In a flash, he rushed her, grabbing her up with demanding hands. The surge of endorphins coursing through her veins was explosive. She clawed the back of his head, drawing him to her. They gnawed at each other's mouths with ravenous grunts and moans until Evan pulled away. He clutched her body against the wall, hands cradling her ass, her legs draped over his hips.

Evan pressed his forehead to hers, his breath heavy. "Lucca may be the only one who can change you, but I've marked you, Evie… and that means everything."

His possessiveness grated against her. Her defiant inner voice, though enthralled by his prowess, glowered within.

"Then do it. Change me." Her challenge was immediate and genuine.

He bit down on his lower lip, salivating with a subtle smirk very much like the wicked grin belonging to Lucca. The beast paced behind his pained stare.

Neither reacted to the creaking of the door. Evie shifted her eyes over to Blythe, and found herself indifferent to the distress weighing the petite brunette down by the sight of a shirtless and lust-filled Evan holding Evie in his arms.

Evan hadn't acknowledged Blythe at all, but continued to glare at Evie with a voracious mix of yearning and trepidation.

"No," he said after a long pause and lowered her to the ground.

Selfish.

Blythe harrumphed. "Are you ready, Evie? Or did I interrupt something with your boyfriend, here?" Her tone oozed with sarcasm. Even Evan tossed his usual courtesy to the curb and cast her a reproachful glare.

"You're not interrupting anything," Evie said with the cold hard stare of her inner voice fixed on him. "Evan's not my boyfriend, remember? Let's go."

Remorse jabbed at her chest, but the high priestess held firm. She followed Blythe downstairs.

No one owns us. We'll get what we want, one way or another.

"Evie," Evan called out and chased her to the third floor landing.

She glanced up the stairwell at him as Blythe led her downward. He stood floating like Icarus high above. The light from her apartment, like the warm glow from the setting sun framed his silhouette. Her daylight was fading.

"I'm sorry." She saw him mouth to her. Her pulse raced and her heart clenched tight as the distance between them grew, and then Evan was out of sight.

THIRTY-FOUR

"Okay, we can go now," Blythe said to the cab driver, who was waiting for the girls outside.

Evie sat next to Blythe in the backseat. As the taxi pulled out from in front of her three-story tower, Evie watched it fade into the distance, with Evan in it.

"Are you going to be all right?" Blythe asked, a hint of annoyance tabbed her tone.

Listening to, but not really hearing her, Evie looked Blythe up and down. Her angelic costume clashed with the bitchy scowl and folded arms she accessorized with.

"Fine," Evie said and peered to her left, to the streets blurring by.

She was dying to run back up to Evan and argue—ask more questions—but most of all apologize for calling, whatever it was they'd become, nothing. Surely, it was something. That didn't prevent her from resenting the way he claimed possession of her. It echoed Lucca's warnings. Each man accusing the other of some sick game of ownership made her blood boil.

They want us to themselves. They're being selfish. We own them.

Remorse burned off into hatred. It was directed toward both immortal monsters for manipulating her.

In all her angered thought, Evie paid no attention to the course they'd set into the heart of the city. The cab pulled down an alley, somewhere amidst the corporate cityscape. Dread seized her.

"We're downtown?" she said.

"Is something wrong with that?"

"Who's throwing this party?"

"Friends of the guy I've been seeing. Why?"

Blythe stared at her with a sour expression. Evie shook the demons back to their shadowy corners in her mind.

"No reason," said Evie. "Evan's not a big fan of downtown. He doesn't think it's safe."

Blythe scoffed back. "I thought he didn't matter to you?"

Evie's heart stopped. Evan means everything to me, she thought but kept her thoughts pressed behind her lips.

Blythe appraised her silence through squinty eyes. "Right, let's go." She tossed the cab driver the fee and headed down the alley.

Evie followed her under tarped scaffolding and into what appeared to be an abandoned building. Graffiti lined the walls of a hallway illuminated by the flicker of florescent lights. Her eyes watered. The rank odor of piss and filth singed her nostrils.

"Remember last spring when we drove down to the city to visit that psychic?"

Blythe huffed. "That dumb bitch, Hope. Yeah, why?"

"I couldn't believe you knew about that hole in the wall, but damn Blythe. This place is a fucking pit." Evie said, stepping over a hypodermic needle, here—a bag of trash, there—making small talk to stave off the chill creeping along her skin.

"The woman was a crack," Blythe said. "I should have known she was full of shit when she started throwing me all that drama about helping you."

Evie paused in her step. "Seriously Blythe, what has gotten into you?"

The brunette glanced over her shoulder to answer Evie with a sardonic smile. "The last few months have been transformative for all of us, Evie. Did you think you were the only one affected when you left town?"

Evie's jaw fell slack. "Blythe... I'm sorry. I didn't mean to—"

"Shit happens, Evie. Let's go."

I'm starting to like Miss Prissy.

"At least someone is," Evie said, mumbling to herself a safe distance from Blythe.

Ducking under a heavy plastic sheet, Evie took the moment alone with her friend to finally notice her. Still the beauty she'd always known Blythe to be, her hair fell in perfect chocolate ringlets cascading down her back and just above her round ass. She was dressed in all white velour and soft feathers.

"A sexy angel. Cute costume," Evie said and meant it as a genuine compliment.

"I'm sure my guy will find it amusing. He always says I'm not the angel I used to be, thanks to him." Blythe snickered. "I can't imagine Evan approved of your costume," Blythe said.

Evie checked her exposed flesh and blood red vinyl.

"He wasn't thrilled letting me leave dressed like this, no. That's kind of how we started arguing when you showed up."

"I'd hate to tell you, but that didn't look like arguing."

Blythe halted in front of an old service elevator and pressed the call button. As the mechanisms squealed like a pig being torched, she rocked back and forth on her white platform boots. With a shake of second thought, she turned a set of brown doe-eyes at Evie, revealing the girl she once knew.

"Answer one question for me." Blythe paused. "What's he like?"

"What do you mean?"

"Evan, what's he like in bed?"

"Blythe, really? Do we have to get into this?"

"I want to know."

Evie looked down to the dirt-grimed floor. The question was invasive and made her heart flutter. Her inner voice hummed deep in the darkest crevices of her body, where he knew her intimately.

Blythe stood silent, waiting.

Just fucking tell her.

Evie raised an apologetic gaze to Blythe. "He's... amazing. He's beautiful in every way."

Blythe eyes flared as the elevator door scraped open. "That's what I thought." She groaned and stepped inside. Evie followed.

It was difficult for her to read Blythe's reaction. The more she considered it, the more she resented her for asking.

Evan belongs to us.

Evie shook her head and pushed her possessive thoughts aside. Descending to a lower level in the abandoned building, she regretted her decision to try and mend fences with her old friend. She would have given anything to find Evan waiting on the other side of the doors.

***

Even before the elevator opened, Evie could hear the music. Dark trance, industrial rock and array of melodious debauchery sent her inner voice tingling with anticipation.

When she followed Blythe onto the landing, her senses were bombarded with deep bass, the musty stench of musk, smoke and sweat. All was black save for shades of crimson and chartreuse wafting through the condensed mist.

The underground costume party was electrifying. Her eyes went wide. The crowd thickened as they walked further down the darkened hallway. Evie's fingers itched to reach out and grab the bodies around her. Her hips swayed side to side as she stalked forward, aching to submit to the music. Assorted demons, naughty nurses, zombies, any and every dark fantasy was personified through vinyl, lace, and sequin.

Her body throbbed all over with want.

Blythe brought her across a dance floor in an otherwise dark and dank cave. Straining her eyes to acclimate to the gloom, Evie noticed alcoves lining the open space and decrepit columns offering little support to a high vaulted ceiling. The floor beneath her felt soft and gritty like dirt.

Evie's pulse quickened. With the exception of the bodies surrounding her in a sea of lust and costume, the club was in fact familiar, direct from a dream. Fear threatened to quell her inner voice's excitement, but was fought off.

"Here, want some?" Blythe had to yell over the music and offered Evie a glass of wine. She stared down at the blush drink.

"I really shouldn't," she said.

"C'mon Evie. Evan's not here. He doesn't have to know. What's one little drink?"

One little drink...

Evie hesitated, but inevitably accepted. What would one glass of wine hurt?

Unlike the cheap vodka, the zinfandel went down like a dream; sweet, fragrant, and natural. Even after one sip, Evie tingled all over. One glass turned into two, turned into three and four. The girls spent the next few hours reveling in the orgy on the dance floor. They pawed each other. Unknown hands groped them. Evie was elated from the sinful sensation of flesh consuming her.

A coarse, industrial guitar riff pierced through the air, followed by crashing cymbals and whispering lyrics. Evie twisted and twirled, closed her eyes and gave herself to the music. The lights, the dancing, the drinking—the apathy was exhilarating.

More…

Blythe's hands released her hips, but Evie barely noticed with all the other hands feeling her up. She turned to find Blythe, all the same.

"He's here." Blythe disappeared into the mass of bodies folded over each other in rhythmic celebration. Before Evie had a chance to follow, Blythe's angelic image was swallowed but, and she was alone in a sea of depravity.

She decided to leave the throngs of wanna-be lovers on the dance floor, and stepped up to a lounge area. From there, she'd secure a better vantage point to locate Blythe amongst the fray.

A curious hunger, like she'd never known before, gnawed in her core and permeated from the center of her subconscious. The innocent sin of her overindulgence was intoxicating.

I want more.

She wished Evan was with her to partake in her dissipation. She wanted a body. She wanted a bite—her own bite.

The music played on, and Evie swayed her hips in inebriated bliss.

THIRTY-FIVE

"Well, look who we have here."

Evie turned to find a petite, dark creature with wild curly hair streamed with gold ribbon and dramatic glittering make-up. She was exotic, adorned in brightly colored feathers and gold sequin. Her cat eyes glowed sinisterly, and her dark red lip liner created a grotesque sneer across her face. It contrasted the otherwise seductive costume revealing an ample bosom. At first it was her voice, then her wild eyes aflame with excitement, and Evie recognized her.

"Sister Lima?"

The priestess slithered closer, revealing greater detail to the glistening red liner dripping down the corner of her mouth. Evie's pulse quickened as the goddess pressed against her body, her chest swelling over the lip of her corset with each anxious breath. Sister Lima's eyes dipped to Evie's creamy cleavage glowing in the twilight of the club, and then beamed up at her.

"Have you discovered your fate then, Evie? What have you decided?" Her hiss coated Evie's skin like silk.

Surrounding them, bodies collided to the ruckus of raging trance techno. Hands groped. Tongues lapped. Shadows melded together in the orgy of chartreuse, gold, and ruby. Though none interrupted their discreet discourse.

Evie searched for Blythe, her absence was trivial. Blythe shouldn't have been there. She shouldn't have been there.

Evie ogled the priestess, and the woman glared back with wanting. The phantom memory of Sister Lima's touch tingled under Evie's red vinyl, stirring a curious anticipation inside her.

"I have no idea what you're talking about," Evie said with a weak breath over the music.

Her eyes encased in golden shadow sparkled, and Sister Lima's hands roamed Evie's contours. They coaxed their bodies together, grinding vinyl against sequence. Adrenaline raged through Evie's veins. She countered Sister Lima's hold with shaky hands and found the intimacy of the priestess' curvature under her fingertips to be distinctly arousing.

"You're insistent to keep them all to yourself." Sister Lima wagged her head side to side. "No, my lady won't have that."

"What are you talking about?"

"Have you found the light, or have you fallen?"

Evie attempted a step back, but the priestess' grip held her hips in motion. Thirst stirred inside, listing from her dreams. She looked around again. The shadows moved, wrapped around each other, writhing.

"If you tell me, I will lie to my lady." Sister Lima pulled Evie closer to whisper into her ear. "She need not know about you." Her breath rasped against Evie's tattoo and burned.

Anxiety cracked through the wine-infused temptation of her déjà vu with the priestess. She searched into the black mass of bodies for Evan, knowing he was nowhere to be found. She grew lightheaded. Each breath pitched her shoulders up. The undertow of her converging panic attack dragged her down.

"I don't know what you're talking about," she said to the priestess.

"Accept his gift, Evie. Fall. You'll see that what he has done... it has all been for you. Because he—"

The priestess' words cut short. Her fingertips taloned Evie's hips. The cold chill running through Evie's body reflected in the priestess' fiery green gems ensconced in gold dust.

"His gift..." Sister Lima said, her lips quivering. "It is dark... beautiful... and it is all for you." Like a timid animal, she cowered and slinked back into the orgy of partygoers surrounding them.

Evie held a hand out, confused and mute.

***

"Pious bitch."

His voice washed over her from behind, like a frigid winter tide.

Evie turned to face Lucca. He was breathtaking concealed by the cloak of the party's gloom. His devilish smirk shone under his dark eyes. Sharp canines glistened in the multicolored luminescence of the underground club. Unlike most partygoers, Lucca was not in costume. He was dressed head to toe in black, his beautiful skin protruding from his t-shirt.

He pulled her against his body and caged her with his arms.

"What is she?" Evie asked, mystified.

"I should think you already know." He snickered and rolled her over his hips, side to side. Her body a willing sacrifice to his wickedness, she moved in fluid motion to his whim. "She's a Sempiternal spy."

"Spy?"

Lucca smiled wide, licking his lips.

"Evan's kept you so pathetically oblivious, hasn't he? You are no longer amongst humans, Evie... Not any normal ones anyway."

She obsessed over his sinful features. Finding nothing but ill-intent in his depths, she forced her eyes away from him and scanned the crowd. The shadows gave way to more detail. Bodies hunched over each other—dancing—writhing—feeding. She was in the middle of an immortal den—a frenzy—bodies enraptured in the thrill of consumption. Blood pumped through Evie's body, shooting pangs of hunger, the need to get high. Her chest heaved, pressing against Lucca's body. She focused on his tongue tracing the edge of his lips, using it to keep her grounded.

This is it.

"What is this place?" she asked.

"This is a safe house. Surely, Evan's told you about them? He hates them." Boastful victory further stoked the excitement blazing in his fiery orbs.

Evie nodded, disbelief and awe etched along her brow. Yes, she was in Lucca's unregulated territories, unprotected and vulnerable. Even with her fate looming over her, suffocating her in his night, Evie envisioned the warm glow of Evan's skin haloed by the setting sun.

"You look..." Lucca eyed her up and down, salivating. "There's always something about the red. Evan was foolish to let you out of his sight like this. I wouldn't trust the heathens in this place."

His arousal pulsated against her lower abdomen. Their bodies, finely tuned, harmonious with each other. His hands pushed into her skin. She whimpered and leaned into his hold.

"Where's Blythe?" She forced the question, fighting the urge to fall into his nothingness. She was exactly where her body wanted to be, and still her heart fought to maintain control. It selflessly implored her to deflect attention from her burning flesh, itching and aching for his teeth to be secured under her skin. Damn Lucca for intensifying that scorching need with his brilliant, beaming gaze.

"She's exactly where she wants to be."

"Where?"

Lucca snickered and spun her around in rhythm to the trance. Such a sudden flurry of movement was disorienting. He thrust her backside against his body. Her breath caught for just a moment, then regulated while his hands acquainted themselves with her body, pulling playfully at the low-cut crest of her corset, flicking at the zipper holding her breasts within their vinyl casing. He groped her with unabashed lasciviousness. Her body was set to spontaneously combust. A moan drifted past her lips.

"Over there." He panted into her right ear and reminded her why she'd been flipped around into position in the first place. He directed her attention to a set of columns outlining a shallow alcove across the dance floor.

There at the lit edge, stood Blythe. The red lighting turned her angelic costume a twisted shade of scarlet. She glowered at Evie from across the room, making direct and purposeful eye contact.

Evie shrieked when she recognized the man behind her. His open palm slid across Blythe's belly. His image creeped over her shoulder, and he locked in on Evie. Khan smiled at her with foreboding deprivation. His sneer was invasive.

Evie cringed and clawed at Lucca's arms snaked around her own waist. Lucca howled with joy over the synthesizers and whirled her around, back into his chest.

"He won't hurt her, Evie. I assure you," he said.

"How do you know that?"

"Khan enjoys his pets. Especially when they've proven themselves loyal. And Blythe has certainly done just that. She's brought you to me. You can rest assured, she'll get exactly what she's been wanting."

"No, you can't," Evie said. "He'll kill her."

Lucca nodded. "Yes, I suspect at some point, he will. Not yet though. He's having far too much fun demeaning her. Besides, like I said, she wants it. She's felt the bite, and she's obsessed with it now. You'll see."

Anxiety drowned her senses. Her lungs burned for oxygen. Yes, she already knew.

Tears rained down her cheeks as Evie watched pure elation wash over Blythe. Khan bit down on the base of her neck. A trail of dark liquid, nearly black in the dim lighting, trickled down and stained the purity of her feathery costume.

Evie knew the feeling, the light-headed high, the bliss. It pained her to see her friend reduced to such a helpless state. Still, undeniable envy held her body in place.

"It's time, Evie," Lucca said.

Yes! Now!

Fight or flight, either reflex was preferable to falling. No, she wasn't ready—much to her inner voice's dismay. She was confused. She was horrified. She squirmed in his arms, and her anxiety grew.

"No, wait."

"I'm tired of waiting, Evie. I've claimed you. You're mine."

Goddamned possessiveness!

Hunger subsided. Fear was chased away. A defensive fire ignited in her bloodstream, ready to unleash a torrent of spite and anger at the next man to claim her as his own.

Evie ripped herself out of his arms and pulled away. Lucca swiped through the air and hooked her back in. He jeered at her struggle.

"There's the fire, Evie. Yes, there's my *Lilitu*."

Her eyes bugged out of her head and a final burst of endorphins exploded inside her. She wriggled in his hold.

"I don't know what kind of sick fucking game you're playing. You and Evan have this warped idea that you own me," she said, grunting as she fought him off.

"Evan knows the consequences of acting against the treaty. His virtues have always been his blessed downfall."

The anger bubbling over in her core spread throughout her body, and her heart raced uncontrollably.

"I'm sick of your goddamn riddles—both of you. I don't belong to anyone." Anxiety was stirring, she could feel it. Her burst of energy waned, and her vision blurred. She protested, but his grasp on her was too controlling.

Lucca exacerbated her panic attack by smothering her mouth with his, denying her much needed oxygen to her lungs. His orange zest, normally an aphrodisiac to her senses, nauseated.

Evie pushed, but found no purchase, no escape from his darkness. Lucca claws became more demanding. His pressure, like a vise around her ribcage, made it impossible to breathe. The night was closing in. Splotches of light flickered behind her closed eyelids. The surrounding cacophony of the party muffled, and Evie was lost.

THIRTY-SIX

Cold air, crisp and sharp revived her. Evie awoke to the sickening sensation of something repeatedly jabbing into her belly. She opened her eyes. The world was upside down. Her vision bobbed, and something hard continued to jam into her gut. Through her haze, the streets of Boston came into focus.

She blinked, swollen blood vessels thundered in her head. Evie pushed her hands down. The mass below her was firm, but somewhat squishy, like muscle. She blinked again and realized she was grabbing a hold of someone's back.

"Put me down." She growled and thrashed, flung over someone's shoulder. It wasn't Evan's. She knew the feel of his warm body like no other. And she guessed it wasn't Lucca either. His body was too similar to Evan's. The man who carried her was bigger, thicker, and brawnier.

"It's okay, Babe. I got you," Nate said patting her ass with a large bear paw.

Evie propped herself upright and looked around. They were in her neighborhood, not one block from her apartment and closing in fast.

"Nate, what the fuck? Put me down."

He huffed, but stopped short in his tracks and lowered her to the ground. She slid down his six foot four expanse and gawked up at him. In turn, Nate ran his eyes across her body for a damage report.

"What is going on?"

Nate's massive body weighed down under his regret. "That motherfucker just loves rubbing it in my face," he said, shaking his head to himself. "I caught the bastard with a right hook when I saw you struggling. You don't belong there, Babe. Not yet."

Evie tossed her head side to side. "What are you talking about?"

"That wasn't a party, Babe. That was a feeding. She shouldn't have brought you there, that stupid fucking cunt."

"Blythe? Nate, what the hell is going on?"

His expression soured. Both checked their surroundings. For a Friday midnight in Boston, plenty of people lined the streets. Some passers-by took notice to their discourse. They stared, some likely wondering if Evie needed help, but no one offered it.

"C'mon Babe. Let's go upstairs and talk," Nate said.

She pulled away when he extended his hand. "Fuck you, we can talk right here."

He growled.

Upon realizing what Nate was, her anger morphed to awe. Goose bumps ran wild across her flesh, and each breath was an immense task.

"You...? Okay, fine," she said. "Fine, let's go talk."

Nate extended a ceremonious arm out. When Evie turned around, she was startled to find they were already on her doorstep.

"Wait." She pulled away once more.

"What's wrong?"

"I don't—I'm kind of living with someone. I don't know if he's up there." She heard another rumble surface from Nate's puffed out chest.

"I know about Evan," he said.

"You do? How?"

343

"You told me, remember? It doesn't matter. Evan's not here, let's go."

"How do you know that?"

"I just do, Evie. Now move."

***

Nate led her up the three flights of stairs. She drifted, baffled, across the studio's threshold. Once inside, she flicked on the overhead lights and gazed at his immortal features, now all too obvious to her. His fangs were faintly visible through his ginger-dusted beard.

"Nate, what happened?"

Pain, regret, and wonderment washed over his face. Sempiternal or not, she found it odd she felt no desire for him. No burning hunger. No anger. Only pity filled her heart for the poor brute.

"It was that fucking asshole, Khan," he said. "The bastard was there the night you kicked me out—when I caught you about to bang Lucca. He saw the whole thing; you and Lucca—your foreplay, us fighting. He attacked me outside the house. The next thing I knew I was half-conscious in my apartment, choking on his fucking fist. The son of bitch forced his blood down my throat. When you came looking for me the next day, I said I wasn't feeling well, but I was literally dying. He was there with me, and so was Lucca. They watched me change. Lucca, that piece of shit, kept telling me some bullshit about learning my place, that you were his. That's why I wouldn't let you inside when you called me from out on my porch. All I wanted to do was die, but I couldn't let him get to you. Pushing you away hurt like hell that day, but it was worth the broken jaw from Lucca. This way of life has its moments of excitement, but overall it just feels like death—cold and dark."

Evie's heart raced.

"Why did he change you?" A very large part of her truly didn't want to know, but she asked regardless.

"Khan said something about getting back at Lucca for taking away another one of his toys—or some bullshit. I honestly can't remember. That bastard rambles about the dumbest shit. I don't understand him, so I've learned to tune him out. I guess he got pissed when Lucca killed that bitch, Mae. That's what he said anyway." Evie cringed remembering how gruesome it was watching Lucca tear into another immortal's throat. "Khan thought it would be funny if I survived the change. It hasn't made Lucca very happy dragging me along to find you, but I've been doing my best to play along."

"You've been the other party traveling with them?" Her eyes widened.

"Yeah, me and Blythe," he said. "Khan said he wanted some pussy too, so he sought her out. He knew when you and Evan found out he'd been bleeding her, you'd freak. He's a sick fuck. He gets off on other people's problems."

Evie trembled. Anxiety clutched her once more, but she needed to know the truth. She watched Nate and waited for him to continue.

"Anyway, Blythe's been more than happy to take it from Khan any way he wants to give it to her. She's been helping them track you. I tried so hard not to leave a trail, but I should've known he'd follow me. I swear, Babe, I didn't mean to. I just wanted to find you."

"Wait, I don't understand. You weren't helping Lucca?"

"Help him?" Nate scoffed. "Why the fuck would I help that motherfucker? All he's done for months is tell me what he's going to do when he finds you. Shit, from day one, Lucca's been so damn possessive of you. I can't stand it. We're always at each other's throats. Khan thinks it's hilarious to watch, of course." Nate paused, teeth grinding. "So no, I haven't been helping him. I thought maybe if I got to you first then I could..." His eyes rolled over her.

Get Nate the fuck out of here. Now!

***

Dread crackled through her chest and bled out to all extremities.

As the sorrow dissipated, resolve set in Nate's scruffy jawline, indicating he had no intentions of saving her from Lucca. Not unless it meant he had the chance to taste her first. She saw the look in his eyes—the beast—the junky feening for a hit. Evie took a step back, but there was little room to run in her barely four hundred square foot studio. Nate closed the distance between them, easily.

She screamed out in protest as Nate lunged onto her with threatening canines. The wind knocked out of her when he threw her onto the bed. His weight pinned her to the mattress. A loud rip pierced the air and mixed with her cries. Nate forced himself on her, tearing the crimson vinyl from her flesh.

"Get off me, Nate. Don't do this." Sharp teeth scraped along her collar bone where scar tissue had formed over Evan's first bite. In a panic, she thrashed, and he weighed down on her harder.

"It's me, Babe. It's okay."

Nate strained, fighting her resistance, but broke through the toughened flesh. Her shrieks tore through her throat and her body burned from his attack. A fresh spray of her blood painted her upper body and splattered across her face.

"Nate, stop!" His hands reached down between her legs. Whatever short burst of adrenaline she had was fading fast.

"It's okay, Babe. It's me. I'd never hurt you. Just let me do this."

Flashes of the Devil tarot card raced through her mind. The echo of the CEO's cackling in her dream pierced her brain. The geisha flashed and sneered over Nate's broad shoulders. Evie writhed beneath the man she'd taken for granted for far too long. Her body weakened, her lungs deflated.

Through tear-soaked eyes, Evie gazed up at the ceiling, envisioning Evan looking down on her. Not Lucca—not Evan—Nate was about to tear her to shreds. How much of her would be left to greet Evan when he came home?

Her body was on fire as he gnashed on the scar tissue. His status as a newly changed vampire was made apparent by his clumsiness. He struggled to latch on. All that meant was she was covered in her own essence. She wriggled under him, pushing out the last of her adrenalized efforts.

"Stop squirming." He grunted and nearly snapped her neck with a hard jolt. He pinned her to the mattress with both hands. An otherworldly passion raged in his eyes. Nate came down on her with a fresh layer of crimson staining his teeth.

An unseen force propelled him backward like he'd been sucked through a vortex.

Her lungs filled with air, muscles flooded with oxygen. Evie mustered the strength to lift herself back and recoiled into a tight ball in the far corner of her bed. Her shrill cries echoed through the small studio as Lucca held Nate by his throat, suspended in the air. Even with the extra five inches of height between them, Nate's feet tangled like a rag doll's.

"You stupid fuck." Lucca snarled and spit up at Nate's face. "How many times have I warned you?"

Nate flailed, but not because he was choking or gasping for air, but because he was taken off guard. Once he recovered from the surprise attack he swung wildly at Lucca, knocking him off balance. Both men stumbled to the ground.

It was terrifying watching the two immortals brawl right in front of her. Their movements were swift, sheer muscle moving like lightning. Evie cowered in fear, praying to remain apart from the fray.

Unlike the last time she witnessed their fighting, Nate was stronger now. He deflected Lucca's advances more easily and landed an upper cut to his solar plexus that propelled Lucca on top of the coffee table, crushing it under his weight. Broken milk crates scattered across the room. Lucca recovered, bouncing back up to his feet with feline grace. He pounced on Nate. The resounding crush of eternal bones shattering on impact thundered between Evie's ears as Lucca charged Nate, lodging his shoulder into his ribcage. Nate's body flew through the air and crash landed across the futon, which buckled under his mass and snapped in half. He stammered to his feet but was back on the attack.

Like a familiar dance, the two men grappled until finally Lucca prevailed, pinning Nate beneath him. The once gentle giant wheezed and growled—defeated.

"You could have killed her," Lucca said. "You're too young—too raw. I warned you. I told of how easy it could be—how difficult she would be to resist. I've faltered. So has

Evan Carver. I won't have you do the same. You would have bled her dry and taken her from me, again."

"Good." Nate spat a globulous wad of blood in Lucca's face. "Evie's more than a goddamned vessel."

Lucca came down on him with a hammering fist. The crack of Nate's jaw reverberated through the small studio.

"You don't know anything about her, or the fate we share."

Anxiety be damned, Evie's mind seized with confusion. Her vision blurred. She observed Nate and Lucca's discourse, fear subsided and trepidation waned, but doubt consumed. Evie crept closer to the foot of the bed.

Nate chuckled in Lucca's choke hold.

"I know you're the worst part of her," he said. "You better kill me asshole, because if I get off this floor I'm gonna rip your fucking heart out."

"Nate!" Evie's voice cracked. "Please I can't go through this again—not like Rob—not like Claudio."

"Claudio?" Lucca said as Nate thrashed beneath him.

"I killed that dumbass musician," Nate said. Both, Evie and Lucca stared down at him in their own versions of bewilderment, hers plain and Lucca's hidden behind a pensive brow. "I followed him for a week after I saw you at the bar. I saw him on the beach with you. I saw you hanging all over him..." Nate paused to force his words past Lucca's clamp on this throat. "None of you assholes know Evie, like I do. None of you deserve her. That's why I killed Claudio. I'll kill that Carver bastard too, once I'm done with you."

Disbelief, shock, and horror swirled through the wild tempest inside her. The blackness crept up in the form of the vengeful geisha, but her retribution was stifled quickly. Evie recognized the regret in Nate's eyes, drowning in his own salty tears.

"I'm done," he said, succumbing to Lucca's vise grip. "Make sure I'm dead, motherfucker. Because if not, I'm coming after every single one of you."

Lucca tightened his claw around Nate's neck. "You have no appreciation for the gift you've been given, you ungrateful fuck. She is so much more than you could ever be. Evie was meant for this life." He looked up at her with the Devil's cat-eyes. "Death is a blessing for him."

She couldn't stop shaking. She didn't bother fighting the tears. They cascaded freely down her cheeks, doing their part to dilute the blood covering her face. She wanted to protest, to save Nate, but remained motionless due to the heavy cloud of doubt fogging her mind and the determination glistening off the golden-flecked surface of Lucca's depthless eyes.

"Goddammit, Nate," she said, huffing through each breath. Evie dropped her gaze to the floor, unable to sanction the death sentence.

Without a moment of hesitation, Lucca descended on Nate's shoulder, tearing through the base of his neck with his teeth. Nate howled, but only for a moment before his cries were muffled by a bloody gurgle. The sound of Lucca snorting his way through Nate's bone and flesh turned her stomach, but Evie managed to hold the vomit down. Her inner voice vibrated uncontrollably watching Lucca in his most primal state.

Lucca's gore-caked face lifted and contorted with effort. His hands dug into Nate's neck, searching, grabbing. Lucca grunted as he worked on Nate's corpse. With an inhuman strength, his biceps flexed, and Lucca tore Nate's spinal cord through his body. Entrails splattered across the tiny square footage of Evie's studio. The wet suctioning rip rang out and would surely echo in her nightmares for years to come.

Nate was gone.

With silence engulfing the studio, faint thumping and mumbling filtered through the walls. Surely her first and second floor neighbors heard their skirmish. It was just a matter of time before the high-pitched squeal of police sirens followed.

Panting heavily and elated, Lucca stood with his wicked and prideful grin smeared with Nate's slaughter. Convulsions held Evie immobile, only to stare terrified at the beautiful immortal beast. Her teeth chattered as he stalked closer.

Finding her nerve, Evie slinked her way back to the head of the bed and was stopped short by the wall. She jumped sideways to her feet, stumbled off the nightstand, and was pinned near the bathroom.

"Now, Evie. Even with your damned fisherman's blood on me. No more games. I've waited long enough."

THIRTY-SEVEN

"Don't you care for me anymore, Evie? Don't you want me?"

His whispers pulled at her core, tiny strings attached at the nerve endings causing a relay of disorienting vibrations throughout her body. Gazing down at Nate's lifeless body through a film of tears, she hated her own arousal.

"Of course I do." Shame coated her admission, and she locked glares with him. Lucca's features hardened, jaw clenched.

"Then why?" He hissed and approached her. She caught her breath, beyond conflicted and unsure of how to answer. "Have I ever hurt you?"

"No," she said in a whisper.

"Have I ever given you reason to fear that I would hurt you?"

She shook her head back and forth. "You've hurt people," she said.

"Not you."

"You've killed people."

"Not you," he said. "Have I done anything other than protect you, Evie?" Lucca spoke with such love—if such a word could be used—and intent. Heat radiated off him and threatened to set her sweat-soaked, energy-drained body on fire.

Hasn't he protected us?

Caught between her own Scylla and Charybdis, Evie fought the enticing familiarity of his body barring hers to the wall. Vertigo ensued, and the room spun.

Each breath became a conscious effort. Yes, he'd stopped Nate, not once but twice from attacking her. He'd killed the college boys when they drugged her back in Fallhaven. He did protect her, didn't he?

Onus consumed as she realized that while he was cold and callous, Lucca was no threat to her.

"Well, Evie? Have I?" He came within inches from her. She looked into the depths of his eyes. Their menacing fire had cooled, and the dark pools with wondrous gold rims reeled her in, unrelenting in their mesmerizing gaze.

"No," she said, heavy with defeat.

Lucca snickered. "Then tell me why?"

"I thought... I thought you wanted to hurt me." She whimpered, unable to shift her eyes from his.

"How?"

His hands hovered beside her body, teasing her with their touch. She rocked to and fro, teetering on the edge of her nerve. She wanted so badly to let go and fall into him.

"I don't know." Each word bled out like the tears wetting her face.

The anxiety twisting inside continued to dizzy her. Beyond all measure, she wanted to make things right. She needed to find her way to him. Each time her mind allowed itself to step closer to Lucca, her heart pushed her away. As her eyes moved over Lucca and then across the home Evan created for her, the invisible choke collar around her neck tightened to near suffocation.

Choose, stupid girl. Choose now!

"I don't know how." She buried her face into his chest. Amidst the filth of Nate's remains, he hushed her, nestling his lips into her hair, smearing Nate's blood into her dyed locks.

"Come down with me, Evie." He cooed lovingly into her ear. "Fall out of your grace with me."

This was what she had begged Evan for—to infect her, but he wouldn't do it—said he couldn't. Only Lucca had that right.

A new consciousness emerged, and her tears subsided. Evie looked up. His smile was still shrouded with malice, but no longer fearful to her. She licked her lips with her own anticipation.

"There is no choice," she said through him, not at him.

"There's never been a choice, Evie. Only foolish hope and fruitless promises."

She grimaced, like his words had bite and gnashed down to her bones, plucking the undeniable truth from therein.

Her next word, a soft prayer, drifted past her lips. "Yes."

Lucca inhaled her remark, savoring its meaning with eyes closed. A noticeable weight lifted from his shoulders. Eyes opened, wild with hunger as fractured light flickered off his fanged smile. He leaned in.

Her need, too immediate to deny. The dark Sempiternal in front of her was the root of her carvings, capable of delivering the high she feened for. He would take her down into his depths, the way Evan refused. Her choice was nothing more than a thin veil of false truths.

He wrapped his hand around the back of her head, pressing his lips to her forehead.

"Shh." He hushed like a child.

Evie convulsed from the emotional maelstrom ripping her apart. With white-knuckled fists, she dug into Lucca's sides, wishing and praying to summon the will to tear his gorgeous flesh from his immortal bones.

"Do you want me to take the pain away, Evie?" Lucca's voice was softer and more soothing than any of the haunting acoustics that normally filled her apartment. "I can make the hurting stop. Just say the word, Evie, and it will cease."

Through her sobbing, his words rang out like church bells. She needed to get high and feel him secured under her skin. She needed the light-headed bliss of emptying her body into someone else, intravenously baptizing her and washing away her original sin.

"Yes." She breathed into his chest. "Please."

Lucca held her face in his hands. The golden flecks dancing across his irises sparkled. His devilish grin parted to give way to glistening canines.

"I want to please you, Evie."

He lowered his mouth to hers. She flinched at first, but found the need for his darkness too sweet. Evie was relieved Nate's essence did not linger on his lips. She sucked in Lucca's zest, starved for more.

"No more denying us, is that understood?" His tone was that of a reprimanding parent as he pulled back from her.

Nevermore.

Evie nudged her head up and down in his firm hold. His thumbs rubbed against the tear-slicked skin along her cheekbones.

A small pinch in her chest gave her pause. She let a small tear fall specifically for Evan. Conquered by apathy, her want for Lucca was too great and always would be.

She closed her eyes and tilted her head to the right. As she offered her neck to Lucca, her body tingled, and her inner voice soared on the inside.

Lucca purred in his low melodic tone, a soft coo, while his hand skated along the length of her exposed jugular. A gentle wisp of warm air caressed her neck. He breathed down on her. She was ready for him. Mind blank, her emotions dissipated until all thoughts of Nate's broken body vanished, Rob's shredded corpse was laid to rest, and Claudio's smile escaped her memory.

His purring hardened to a growl. Lucca's fingertips dug into her skin.

"What is this?"

"What is what?"

"You let him mark you?" Rage emerged from the depths of his eyes, like molten lava.

She tried to pull free from his grasp, but Lucca held her firmly by the shoulders. The force of his grip nearly crushing the fragile structure of her collarbone.

"What does that mean? What did I do?"

Evie thought for sure she'd seen the same blinding heat that must have been unleashed on her ancestor, Evelyn, just before Lucca bled her dry, or on Rob just before he was torn limb from limb.

"Evie!" A voice called out from behind Lucca. Both shifted their sights toward the door where Evan stood enraged by their spectacle.

An inhuman and feral growl rumbled through Lucca's body and reverberated through Evie's bones. She was amazed he possessed the capacity to contain such a horrid sound inside his body.

With a low bellow, Lucca unleashed that building tension. Evie was barely conscious in his arms.

"You think this will stop me?" Lucca snarled over his shoulder to Evan. "You want a purge, Carver? I'll give you a goddamned blood bath with Evie leading the charge."

He propelled her backward in order to attack Evan, who stood eagerly awaiting his advance. She slammed against the wall, her head lodged therein and pulled crumbling sheet rock down to the ground with her broken body.

The lights in her eyes flashed, and everything went dark.

***

Blood pulsated behind eye sockets as she floated through the black. Evie lost control and found herself suspended in the cold nothingness. Warmth emanated from the throbbing behind her vacant eyes. A fluid sensation told her she was reaching back to find her head, but she had no hands—no feeling.

Her chest heaved up and down, but there was no chest to be found—no body. In any other dream she may have detected a range of emotions from desire to fear. But not now, Evie was euphoric and dazed—a pulsing beam of energy and nothing more. She attempted to cry out, but with a voiceless sound, was held prisoner to silence.

A muffled fracas enveloped her. With what she presumed would be her ears, she strained to hear the disruption. Growling, howling, crunching and thrashing. Everything remained black.

Floating through thick dark nothingness, she drifted within the darkest depths of the ocean. She searched for the source of the sound, but it wasn't sound that she found so much as waves pushing up against her. Vibrations washed over her energy. Her amorphous shape thrummed to the sensation of the black rolling over her.

She moved her mouth. She knew it was moving because she willed it so, but there was no feeling, no mouth, no sound. She gasped, a burning sensation filled where her lungs would be, but there were no lungs. She thought for sure she'd choke on the thick black nothingness surrounding her, but she didn't.

The growling intensified.

A tiny pinpoint of light pierced the black. That tiny hole widened her vacant eyes in amazement, and she was compelled to float toward it. The closer she came to the light, the wider it bled across the darkness, a white hot prism bisecting the horizon, like flying into the sunrise from the dead of night. A brilliant beam of color burst above, slicing the dark horizon. As she neared it, her energy increased, she pulsated with heat, and the growling grew more distinct. It was like watching the light of her day and the dark of her night converge. And it was wondrous to behold.

Evie made out the sounds of animals, dogs, wolves, similar beasts scuffling. She floated closer. But it wasn't a scuffle—that was too innocent a description to the hate she felt reverberating through the gloom. The beasts fought ferally. A thrilling sensation brewed from within her core.

The sharp sounds of the beasts' low bellows and barking pierced her non-existent ears. Still she floated closer, too curious. Shadows moved through the black, silhouetted against the sparkling prism. Gigantic beasts brawled, tearing into each other, shredding each other. One paw lashed out. The beast fell, but then pulled back up on its haunches and lunged for the other, clamping down with its wide jaw. The terrifying shadows danced hazardously through the black. It was exhilarating to watch their parry. Evie shimmered raw energy amidst the darkness.

The shadowy creatures puffed their chests defensively until the fallen beast skulked away, licking its wounds. In her humming ball of energy, Evie never felt so energized, so elated in all her life.

The beasts parted. The prism dulled. Thrill waned and panic set it. She felt herself being pulled back down into the nothingness. The spark of daylight vanished through the vortex of black, her verve ready to implode.

She strained to reach out to the prism, but it diminished to the tiny pinhole before all but disappearing into nothing. Her non-existent ear drums burst, and her stomach flipped from her free fall. The nothingness closed in. Her energy faded.

"My light!" She fought to make sound, but the nothingness was too great. She fell.

***

"Evie, please. Wake up!"

Her eyelids fluttered.

Lights and shadows flickered and blurred. She was disoriented, like being drunk, like being drugged, out of control. Her inner voice jilted her alert. Her heart pounded in her chest, almost as intense as the throbbing pain from the back of her head.

"Thank fucking Christ." Evan pulled her into his chest.

She was muzzled, suffocated by his mixture of sweat and blood mixed into his cotton shirt. Her weak and trembling hands lifted up and caressed his sides. His shirt was tattered in her grip. His skin felt clammy to her touch. Desperate for air, Evie pushed away from him.

"Where's Lucca?" Her voice croaked as she asked, defeated and barely audible.

Evan glowered. "He's gone. What happened?"

She was tempted to ask him the same, but her mind was still shrouded in a thick fog. She looked around the small studio. Nate's corpse remained at their feet. Evan had her cradled on the small space of flooring between the bed and the bathroom that wasn't stained by blood. The rest of the apartment was in a state of disarray, like a hurricane had come through and reduced the room to rubble.

The pain to focus was tremendous, but Evie blinked, forced her efforts. She gazed up to Evan's angst-colored face. Faint traces of bruises and gashes telltale of a fight couldn't hide his immortal beauty.

"Did Lucca do that?" Her hand glided across the abrasions. He pulled her hand away and sat her at the edge of the bed. The sensation of being lifted up by him was painful, the room spun, and pins and needles spidered across her body. Light-headed, she still couldn't drag her eyes from his wounds.

"Don't worry about my face, Evie. I'll be healed soon enough." He appraised her current condition, Evan fell back and gasped at her collarbone. "Did Lucca do this?"

The ache at the back of her skull screamed for her attention.

Evie had full control of her faculties, but she wasn't hearing Evan. The faint tremble in his voice wouldn't register. She gazed, distracted by the chaos of the room, before glancing down to herself.

Her collarbone was caked over in coagulated blood from where Nate had gnashed into the bone. Upon inspection, the reality of her current condition smacked her across the face. Heat blossomed from her cheek bones and ran a course through her body.

"No… Nate," she said in a soft whisper melting into a pout, and glanced to his remains.

"Evie, I'm not going to get angry or upset. I'm just glad you're all right, but please tell me what happened."

He took a split second to peek over his shoulder at Nate, but the intensity burning in his dark gaze fixed on her. She shuddered, but detected no trace of the beast inside.

"He didn't mean it."

"Who didn't mean what? What the hell happened here?" Evan was insistent. His strong grasp planted firmly on her shoulders, the difficulty to restrain his emotions apparent in his tense grip. "Jesus, Evie, look at you. He attacked you."

She followed his search down her body, her eyes heavy with weariness. Her costume dangled off her frame in peeled back layers of red vinyl skin, revealing a delicate black lace bra barely covering the lower cup of her breasts. Past the shredded layers of vinyl and black crinoline below her waist, her fishnets threaded from the crotch to the top of her Doc Martens. Purplish splotches of skin shone through the mangled outfit.

"He was too young. Lucca said..." Evie mumbled into her chest, though her introspective comment piqued Evan's interest. He bent over, into to her line of sight. His beautifully pained expression glossed over in a fresh coat of tears.

"Nate was too young?" he asked. "Evie, are you trying to say Nate was...?"

The corner of her lips curled upward to a mocking grin. "You were right all along," she said. "It wasn't Claudio. It was Nate who led Lucca here."

Evan's mouth gaped open.

"Lucca said that he'd warned him," she said. Her expression soured recalling their discourse. The acid churned, gurgling up her throat, but stayed down. "He said Nate wouldn't be able to control himself around me. Lucca said he'd made the same mistake in the past. He said..."

361

As the shiver flushed her body, Evie held Evan's stare.

"What?" He was panicked. Tears beaded on his lashes, his lower lip quivered. "Evie, what else did Lucca say?"

She held in her breath, conjuring the will to confront her past yet again. A drawn out exhale sputtered past her lips. "He said you made the same mistake too."

Evan matched her silent stare for what felt like eternity, but which was merely a few breaths if she would've counted. Any color in his cheeks vanished. His eyes pinched shut, lips now sealed tight as a tomb, muscles pulsing along the jawline. Evan knelt before her like an alabaster statue, mute, and wearing the sorrowful expression Evie had committed to memory months ago.

"You knew me." Her accusation-lined hissed chipped away at his stone facade, but he didn't answer. "Answer me."

No, he shook his head back and forth.

"Dammit, Evan, answer me!" Her pulse raced. The angst rushing over her numbed any physical ailments. She glared at him. Evan refused to open his eyes to meet her head on.

"He's doing this on purpose," he said. "He's turning you against me."

Evie dropped to her knees and grabbed onto Evan's wrists, demanding his attention.

"You're turning me against him, Evan," she said. "We have a past, don't we? Lucca said you want me all to yourself. He told me you just want me to live, die, and be reborn again to feed your addiction. He—"

"No." Evan growled. "He's manipulating you. It's what he does. You're not seeing the truth clearly. I love you, Evie. I only want to save you."

"Why? If you know he's the only one who can change me, then why would you keep me from him?" Her annoyance full to the brim. "Did you really think this little intervention you've been staging over the past few months would work? I asked you to help me—buy time so I could understand. You knew all along what was going to happen."

"This type of existence is cursed, Evie. It's lifetimes of death and spite… and it's never ending. I thought I found a way out for us." Mirroring her spiritless gaze from earlier, Evan engaged with her stare. "I was wrong."

Even as her heartbeat pounded in her chest, Evie paused. Her anger was misplaced, wrongfully projected onto Evan. He was third party to the conflict raging inside of her. When she realized that, Evie sat back on her feet. "None of that makes any sense, Evan."

He reached out for her. "I thought maybe if I intervened early enough that I could save you from him."

She held herself back from bursting forward into his reassuring arms. She wanted to overwhelm her senses and fade away into his embrace, but she didn't. "You owe me answers."

"I know," he said. "But not yet."

"This isn't just about Lucca, you know. You're trying to save me from you too, Evan. It's impossible. I need him—I need you—in my blood."

Evan's chest puffed excitedly, like she'd thrown his own words—his own truth—back in his face. "This has grown bigger than us, Evie. We need to go to Bendis and speak with my uncle."

She froze, her eyes widened. The impression of the devil card skittered across her mind, his leathery tail flailing about. Evie raised a hand to clamp around her throat. "Why?"

"Lucca poses a real threat to the security of the Houses and all the Sempiternal they serve to protect."

Her mind clouded over. "I don't understand."

Evan answered her unspoken plea with a gentle yank, calling her into his arms. She folded into him. The world around them—the mortal world she thought she knew—deteriorated.

"We'll get through this." He burrowed into the crook of her neck. "One moment at a time."

Epilogue

Oh God, they're here, she thought.

Hearing the knock at the door, Evan shifted and rose from the floor. With a softened strength, he pulled Evie to her feet.

"What are we supposed to tell the cops?" she asked, panic-stricken.

"No one's called the police, Evie." Evan sifted through the blood-spattered bed to yank the fitted sheet off the mattress. She stood in awe at his calm demeanor. He wrapped her in the—clean enough—bed linen, thereby covering the threads of her costume still hanging from her body. Only a hint of worry lined his brow, but it served to heighten her trepidation.

"Who is it, then?"

His lips pressed into a firm line. "The cleaning crew."

Her eyes widened beyond their capacity. "The what?"

"You were unconscious for a while. I had to put a call in to Bendis for this mess. It's okay, they won't hurt you." The apologetic pinch at the corner of his eyes, his forced grin, it all set her back a step.

Her lips parted, but she had no words. She dropped her gaze down to Nate's remains and resisted the urge to hurl. The rank stench of rotting Sempiternal was precisely the same nauseating odor she remembered from Rob's human corpse.

Evan motioned toward her, to comfort her, but she tossed up a hand. "No!"

She shook her head with vehemence and ran for the bathroom to hurl properly in the toilet. After voiding her belly of its minimal contents, Evie stared at her disheveled reflection. The specter returned her gaze with a knowing grin.

You're entering my world now, stupid girl.

She gawked at the red and irritated crystal gaze staring back. No, nothing would be the same for her.

The sound of familiar voices in the living room perked her ears. Evie gargled some mouth wash and sucked in a deep breath for courage's sake before turning back into the living room.

In what used to be her studio, Evan stood with his hands on his hips by a pool of blood that covered the small space like an asymmetrical area rug. His hardened stare was fixed on the beaten leftovers of Nate's body. By his side, she recognized Roque and Yeung Jae, who'd come to "clean up" as Evan put it.

Roque's girth barely fit in the apartment. He looked up, jutted his chin in the air, but did not react to her otherwise. It was Yeung Jae who peered around his beefy mass and smiled.

"Hey Evie, long time no see. Happy belated-birthday. How's that tat doing?"

She stood perplexed and still wrapped in the sheet, horrified he could speak to her in such a casual tone. Someone had died for Christ's sake.

"Let's just get this done and over with." Evan said and approached her. She clung to the thin fitted sheet like a magical cloak for protection, but his touch didn't hurt—not that she expected it would. His palm against her cheek soothed, but its warmth couldn't penetrate deep enough to settle the anxiety rumbling at her center. "Let's go out to the balcony and get some fresh air while they work," he said and led her on.

"What are they going to do?"

Her feet dragged as she followed. She looked down to Nate, and then over to Yeung Jae, who glanced back. His smile disappeared. His almond eyes dipped to the gory mess, and then ran over her body. He mimicked Evan's distress, in the sense that pain shrouded his once gleeful face.

She stepped in line with Evan, around the mess. A hint of shame crept up on her when she considered Roque and Yeung Jae likely knew what happened here.

Evan waited in the open doorway to the balcony, his hand outstretched to her. What lay hidden in his matte stare continued to twist in her chest. She took one more peek at Yeung Jae. Even amongst all the multi-colored ink that adorned his body, she identified the tiny blue-silver cluster of stars nearly identical to hers behind his left ear. Is this what it meant to be a "friend" of Bendis, she wondered.

"Get the bag and start shoveling," Roque said and whacked Yeung Jae across the chest.

"Why do I have to do it?" he countered and pointed at Nate's remains. "The dude was huge. I can't lift that."

"You want to play with the big boys, you gotta clean up the mess." Roque's quip disturbed Evie. His lack of care for the dead chilled her to the bone. He raised his attention to Evan. "We got this, man. Go ahead. Take care of her."

Evan nodded. "Just clean this up, so we can get ready to leave."

"You got it, boss."

Curious as to what he meant, she turned to Evan. It was as though he'd transformed right before her eyes. When they were alone, he was quiet, dark, and beautifully pained. She wanted to be wrapped in his comfort then. In front of his uncle's employees, however, he was confident and authoritative—hardened—a complete mystery to her.

Out on the balcony Evan stood looking down at her, like he was truly judging her for the first time since they'd met.

"Evan...?"

He called her forward with his hand held out, and she was pulled in by his gravity. He cradled her face in his hands and closed his eyes, releasing her from the judgmental glare threatening to do her in. By his touch—in his grasp—she trembled. Evie clung to his biceps as a means to stay grounded.

"This is a real fuck up, Evie. I'm really not sure what to do from here," he said in a thin voice.

"Are you giving up on me?" His silence encouraged tears along her lashes. "Evan...?"

"I... need to remember my place, Evie."

He stepped back, sniffling as he turned his back to her. Evan dug in his pockets and pulled out all the fixings for a quick pinner.

His rejection, like acid, was cool at first, benign even. Then it burned and festered in her core, churning with her omnipresent angst.

She checked through the window at Roque, who was busy pulling various plastic coverings and cleaning materials from a large rack sack. He lined them across the computer desk. Yeung Jae was busy tripping all over the crime scene, burdened with the task of spreading out a large black object that resembled a body bag. He looked up and winked at Evie, though she couldn't find the joy behind his mischievous smile.

"What's going on in there?" she asked Evan under her breath as he sparked up the joint.

"They're going to make it look like Nate was never here."

Never here?

She snapped her head back at Evan. The reticence in his words insulted her. "Is that because of what he did to me?"

"No." He took a long toke and exaggerated his exhale. "That's because his body needs to be disposed of in a way humans won't find him. We, the Sempiternal, would make fascinating case studies. Don't you think?" He flicked the dead ash off the head of the joint and inspected the tip.

Peering over her shoulder to the apartment, Evie pondered what that could entail. She imagined tiny blenders chopping him to bits then transporting the remains in that large black bag. Chunks of her chewed up stomach lurched up her throat.

"They'll bring him to Bendis and incinerate the body," Evan said and took another hit. "That's all."

"That's all? God, Evan, who the hell are you?" she asked at the edge of her breath, increasingly terrified by the callous immortal monster in front of her.

The impact of her words registered across his face, but Evan held his gaze from hers. "I'm a fool."

When his pained eyes lifted to hers, the anger searing her bloodstream overwhelmed the heartache flooding her chest.

He held out his hand, offering the joint. "Here, it's kush, one of your favorites. It'll help you relax."

She stared blankly at the weed. Disgusted, she scowled back up at him.

"Fuck your kush, Evan… and fuck you too."

ABOUT THE AUTHOR

Choose your poison: Paranormal Fantasy • Romantic Horror • Dark Fantasy With A Twist

J.C. Stockli is inspired by music, the past, and possibilities. Happily Ever Afters are only achieved through the cost of some blood, guts, or a soul or two… if at all.

Also an established full-time professional with her MBA, over the years she's moonlighted as a magician's assistant, a roadie for a heavy metal band, a dance fitness instructor. She's even dressed up as a promotional character at public events. She's a current member of RWA's Futuristic, Fantasy & Paranormal (FF&P) and New England (NECRWA) chapters, loves to dabble in cover design, and feels passionately about the power of authors supporting other authors.

She lives along the Massachusetts coast with her husband and two children. You'll likely find them dancing around the house, tearing up the dirt, or out on the water soaking in the sun and breathing in the sea salt air.

Blog: www.jcstockli.com
Twitter: @JCStockli (www.twitter.com/JCStockli)
Facebook: www.facebook.com/JCStockli
Pinterest: www.pinerest.com/JCStockli
Instagram: www.instagram.com/JCStockli
Goodreads: www.goodreads.com/JCStockli

Acknowledgements

Thank you, readers, for embracing Evie and her struggles. The positive energy I've felt since launching The Nothingness in January 2015 has been nothing short of humbling and inspiring.

To the early adopters, bless you. Shayanna, you rock! Ben, thanks for putting up with my nonsense.

To the fellow authors who've shown their support, your encouragement fuels my fire.

Lastly to my family, as always you are what drives me. You are the foundation to all of my dreams and goals. I love you forever and always.

COMING IN 2016
The

DESECRATION

Addictions Of The Eternal: Book Three

Treaties are broken. Houses conspire. When selfishness knows no boundaries, the structured society of the Sempiternal may pay the price for Evie's fate. While Evan is left with no choice but to tend to immortal politics, Lucca is eager to exploit his absence. All the while, Evie's hunger gnaws from the inside out, feening for blood. In the unregulated safe houses buried beneath the mortal eye, she'll seek out what she needs to numb the pain.

Caught in her own undertow of lust, elated by overindulgence, Evie falls deeper into Lucca's nothingness. How far can she descend before risking the only redemption Evan is capable of offering?

THE DESECRATION is the third installment of the ADDICTIONS OF THE ETERNAL series.

CREDITS

Cover Art © 2015 J. Coulombe

Cover Man © 2014 iStock/nensuria

Cover Tattoo © 2014 iStock/Polat_lights

Cover Boston skyline © 2015 J. Carpenter

Editing by A. Holmes & B.R. Martsen